T0160722

COMIC COLLECTION

- VOLUME ONE -

WORLD OF WARCRAFT

COMIC COLLECTION

- VOLUME ONE -

SCRIPTS BY
Raphael Ahad | Robert Brooks | Matt Burns |
Christie Golden | Micky Neilson | Andrew Robinson

ART BY
Antonio Bifulco | Linda Cavallini | Sebastian Cheng |
Alex Horley | David Kegg | Ludo Lullabi | Miki Montilló |
Nesskain | Suqling | Emanuele Tenderini

LETTERING BY
Comicraft | Clem Robins

FRONT COVER ART BY
Nesskain

BACK COVER ART BY
Antonio Bifulco

BLIZZARD ENTERTAINMENT

WORLD OF WARCRAFT: COMIC COLLECTION

Senior Vice President, Story & Franchise Development - LYDIA BOTTEGONI
Senior Director, Creative Development - DAVID SEEHOLZER
Vice President, Global Consumer Products - MATT BEECHER
Director, Consumer Products - BYRON PARNELL
Lead Editor - PAUL MORRISSEY
Editor - ALLISON IRONS
Production - BRIANNE MESSINA, DEREK ROSENBERG, ALIX NICHOLAEFF

WORLD OF WARCRAFT: WARLORDS OF DRAENOR #1-3

Art Director - DOUG ALEXANDER
Editors - CATE GARY, MICKEY NEILSON
Graphic Designer – MARCO SIPRIASO
Creative Consultation - CHRIS METZEN, ALEX AFRASIABI, DAVE KOSAK
Lore Consultation - SEAN COPELAND, JUSTIN PARKER, EVELYN FREDERICKSEN
Production – MICHAEL BYBEE
Director, Story Development - JAMES WAUGH

WORLD OF WARCRAFT: LEGION #1-4

Art Editor – LOGAN LUBERA
Editors – CATE GARY, ROBERT SIMPSON
Graphic Designer – JOHN J. HILL
Creative Consultation – CHRIS METZEN, ALEX AFRASIABI, CHRIS ROBINSON
Lore Consultation – SEAN COPELAND, JUSTIN PARKER, EVELYN FREDERICKSEN
Production – RACHEL DE JONG, MICHAEL BYBEE, JEFFREY WONG
Director, Consumer Products – BYRON PARNELL
Director, Story Development – JAMES WAUGH

WORLD OF WARCRAFT: BATTLE FOR AZEROTH #1-4

Editors – CATE GARY, ALLISON IRONS, ROBERT SIMPSON
Graphic Designer – JOHN J. HILL
Creative Consultation – ALEX AFRASIABI, STEVE DANUSER, GLENN RANE, CHRIS ROBINSON
Lore Consultation – SEAN COPELAND, CHRISTI KUGLER, JUSTIN PARKER
Production – BRIANNE MESSINA, PABLO A. LLOREDA, DEREK ROSENBERG, RYAN THOMPSON
Director, Consumer Products – BYRON PARNELL
Director, Creative Development – RALPH SANCHEZ
Special Thanks – FELICE HUANG

This volume collects WORLD OF WARCRAFT: LORDS OF DRAENOR #1-3, WORLD OF WARCRAFT: LEGION #1-4, and
WORLD OF WARCRAFT: BATTLE FOR AZEROTH #1-4, first published digitally by Blizzard Entertainment in 2014-2015,
2016, and 2018 respectively.

First edition: March 2020
ISBN: 978-1-950366-13-2

Library of Congress Cataloging-in-Publication Data available.

Printed in China.
1 0 9 8 7 6 5 4 3 2

Table of contents

WORLD OF WARCRAFT: WARLORDS OF DRAENOR

WORLD OF WARCRAFT: LEGION

WORLD OF WARCRAFT: BATTLE FOR AZEROTH

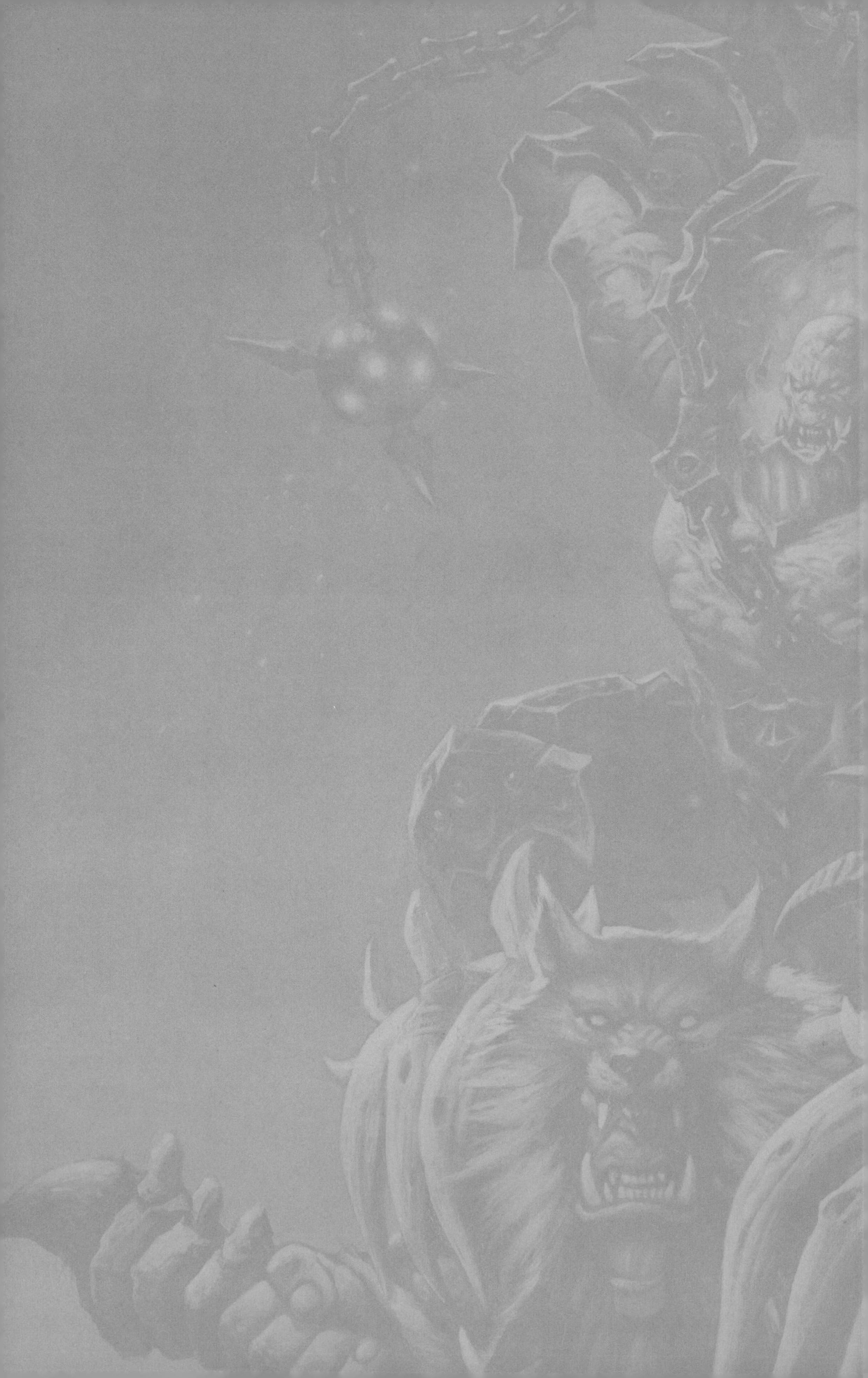

GUL'DAN AND THE STRANGER

SCRIPT BY **MICKY NEILSON** | ART BY **ALEX HORLEY** |
LETTERING BY **CLEM ROBINS**

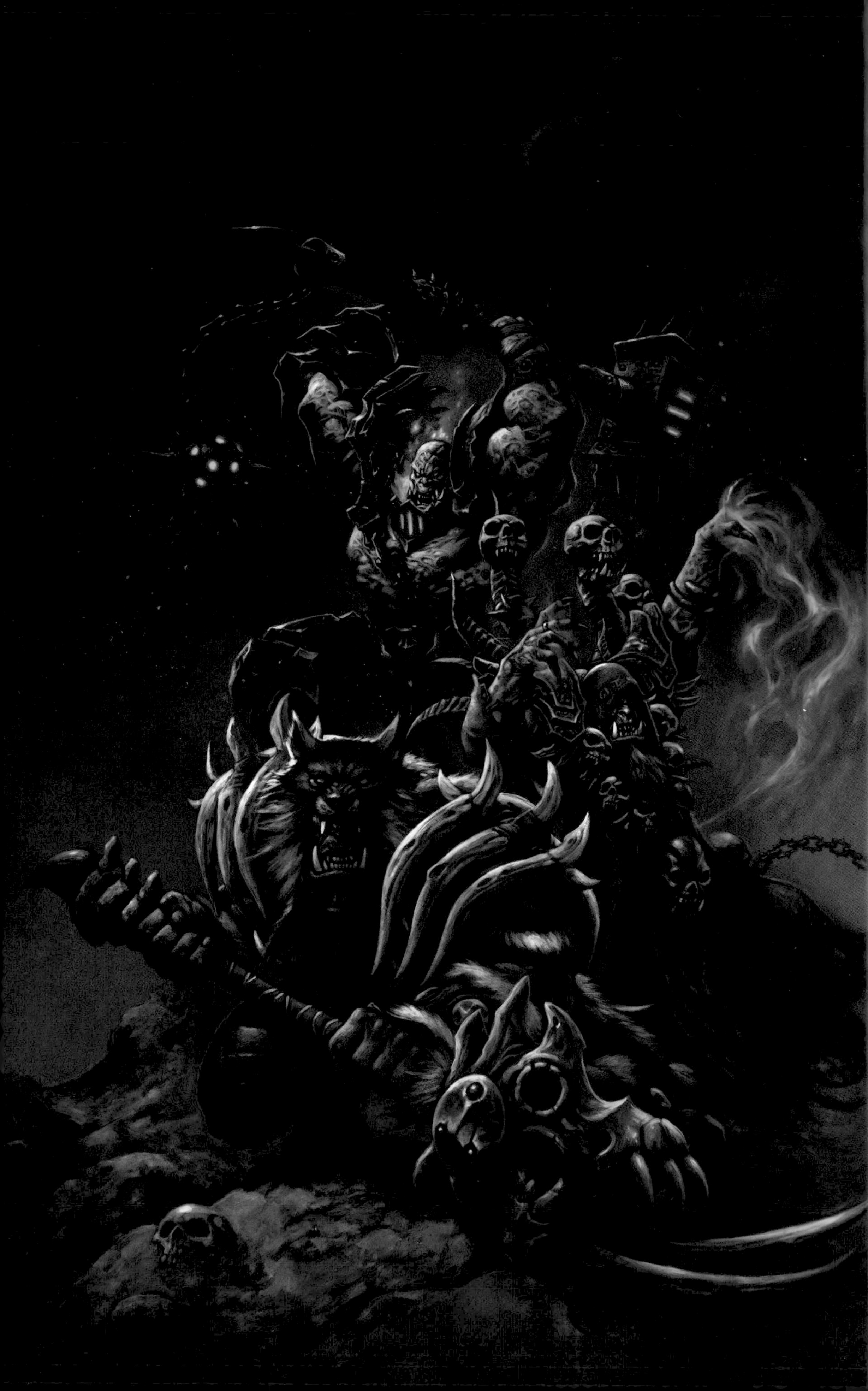

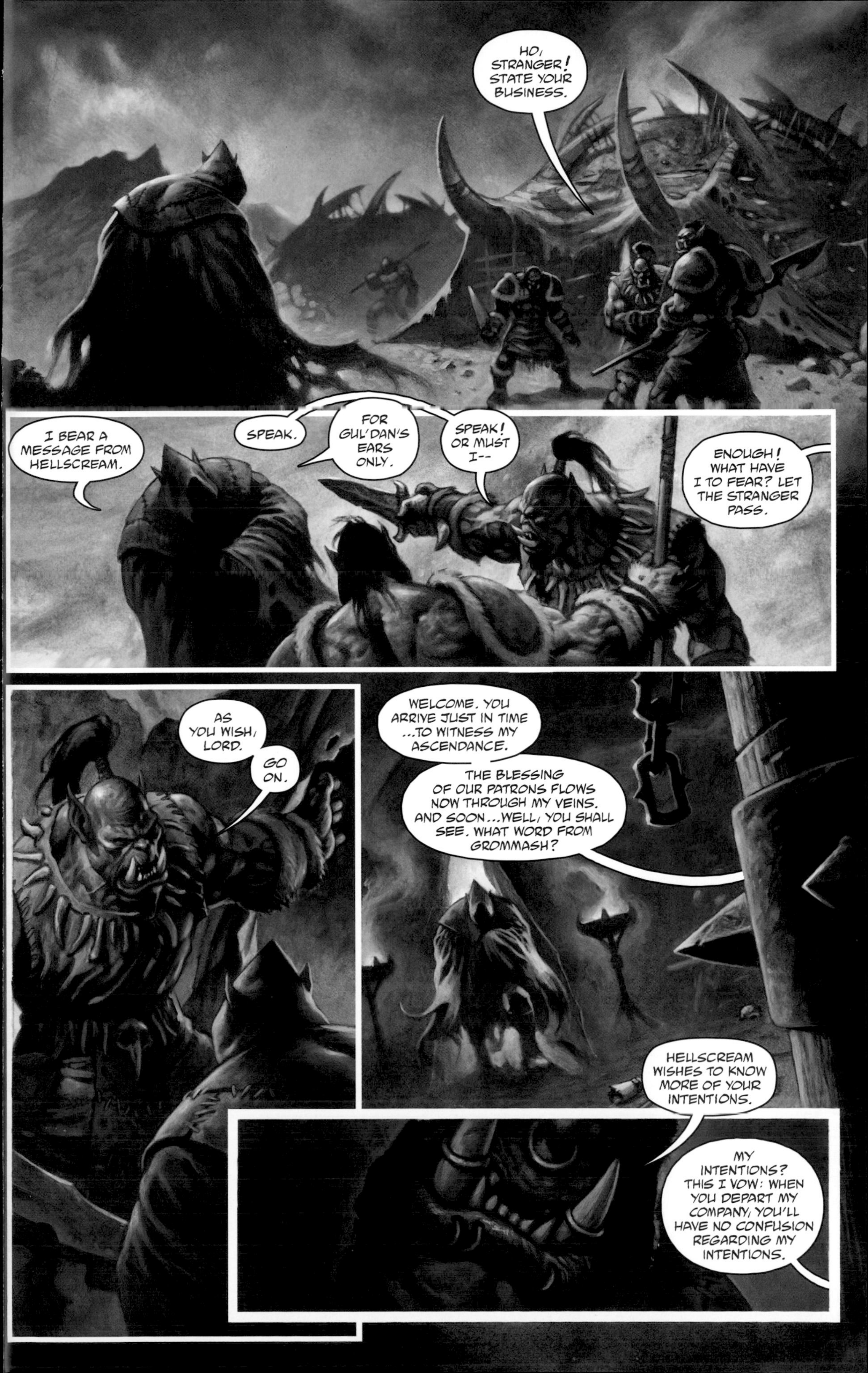
HO, STRANGER! STATE YOUR BUSINESS.
I BEAR A MESSAGE FROM HELLSCREAM.
SPEAK.
FOR GUL'DAN'S EARS ONLY.
SPEAK! OR MUST I--
ENOUGH! WHAT HAVE I TO FEAR? LET THE STRANGER PASS.
AS YOU WISH, LORD.
GO ON.
WELCOME. YOU ARRIVE JUST IN TIME ...TO WITNESS MY ASCENDANCE.
THE BLESSING OF OUR PATRONS FLOWS NOW THROUGH MY VEINS. AND SOON...WELL, YOU SHALL SEE. WHAT WORD FROM GROMMASH?
HELLSCREAM WISHES TO KNOW MORE OF YOUR INTENTIONS.
MY INTENTIONS? THIS I VOW: WHEN YOU DEPART MY COMPANY, YOU'LL HAVE NO CONFUSION REGARDING MY INTENTIONS.

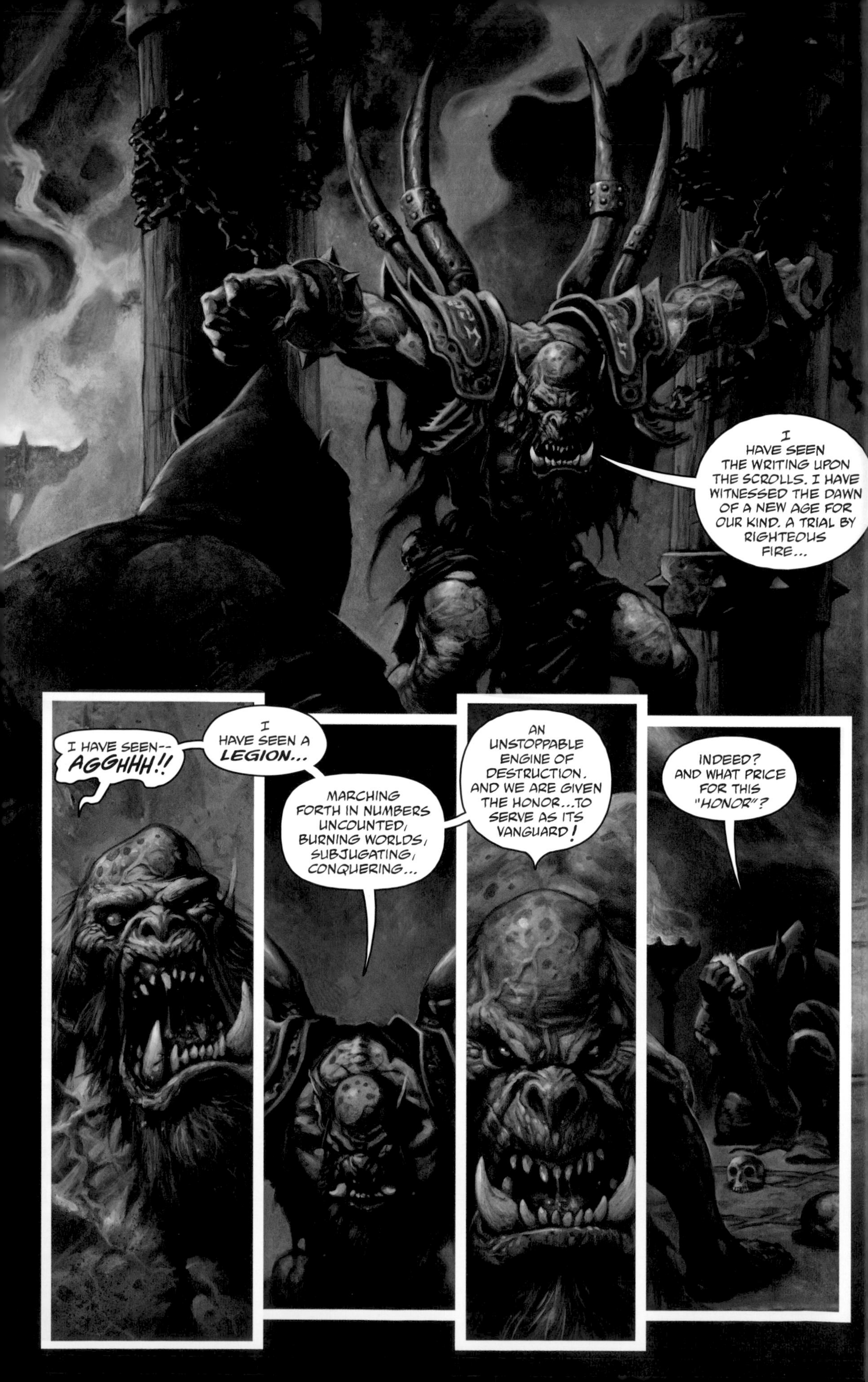

I HAVE SEEN THE WRITING UPON THE SCROLLS. I HAVE WITNESSED THE DAWN OF A NEW AGE FOR OUR KIND. A TRIAL BY RIGHTEOUS FIRE...
I HAVE SEEN-- AGGHHH!!
I HAVE SEEN A LEGION...
MARCHING FORTH IN NUMBERS UNCOUNTED, BURNING WORLDS, SUBJUGATING, CONQUERING...
AN UNSTOPPABLE ENGINE OF DESTRUCTION. AND WE ARE GIVEN THE HONOR...TO SERVE AS ITS VANGUARD!
INDEED? AND WHAT PRICE FOR THIS "HONOR"?

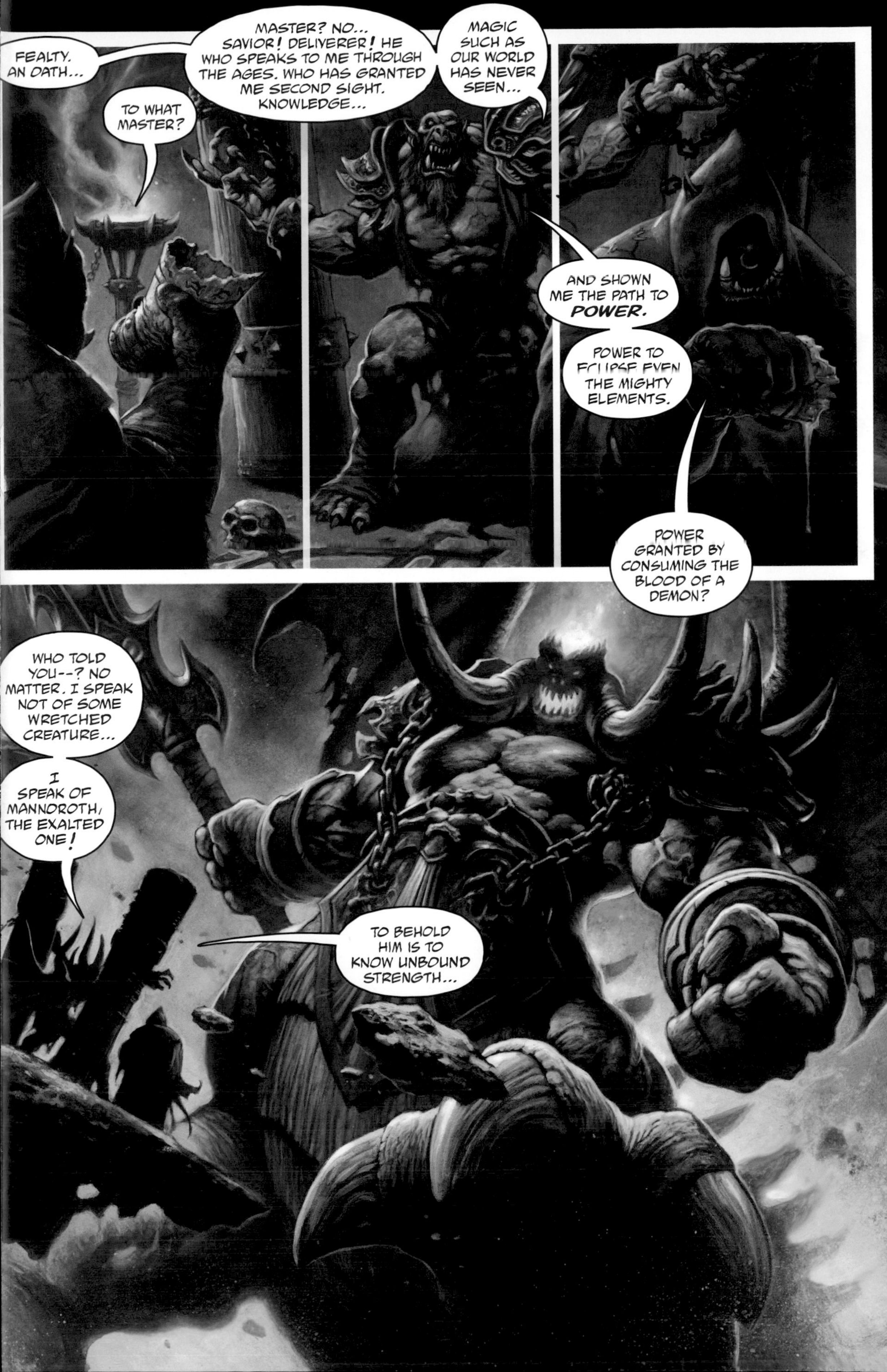
FEALTY. AN OATH...
TO WHAT MASTER?
MASTER? NO... SAVIOR! DELIVERER! HE WHO SPEAKS TO ME THROUGH THE AGES. WHO HAS GRANTED ME SECOND SIGHT. KNOWLEDGE...
MAGIC SUCH AS OUR WORLD HAS NEVER SEEN...
AND SHOWN ME THE PATH TO POWER.
POWER TO ECLIPSE EVEN THE MIGHTY ELEMENTS.
POWER GRANTED BY CONSUMING THE BLOOD OF A DEMON?
WHO TOLD YOU--? NO MATTER. I SPEAK NOT OF SOME WRETCHED CREATURE...
I SPEAK OF MANNOROTH, THE EXALTED ONE!
TO BEHOLD HIM IS TO KNOW UNBOUND STRENGTH...

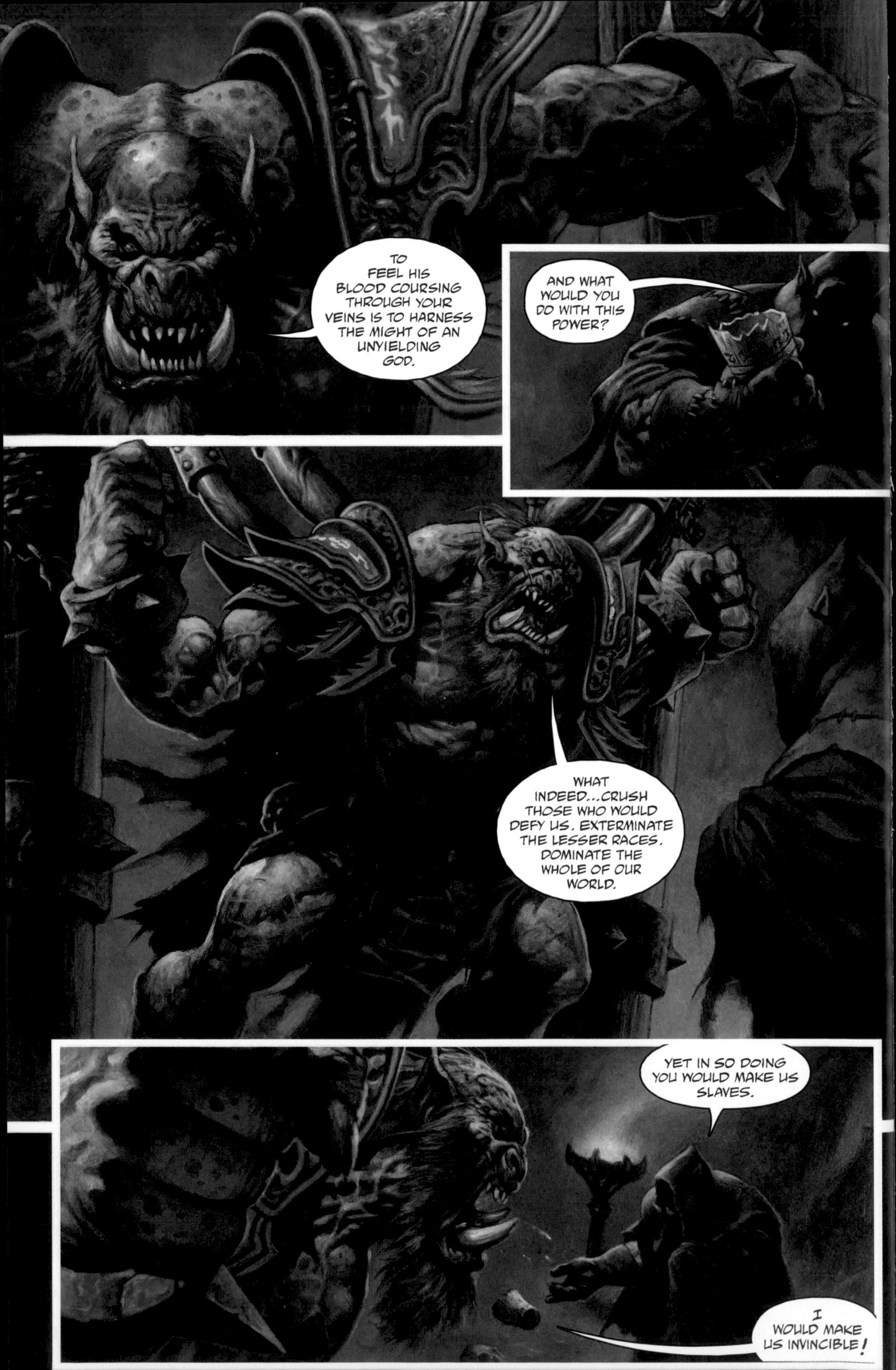
TO FEEL HIS BLOOD COURSING THROUGH YOUR VEINS IS TO HARNESS THE MIGHT OF AN UNYIELDING GOD.
AND WHAT WOULD YOU DO WITH THIS POWER?
WHAT INDEED...CRUSH THOSE WHO WOULD DEFY US. EXTERMINATE THE LESSER RACES. DOMINATE THE WHOLE OF OUR WORLD.
YET IN SO DOING YOU WOULD MAKE US SLAVES.
I WOULD MAKE US INVINCIBLE!

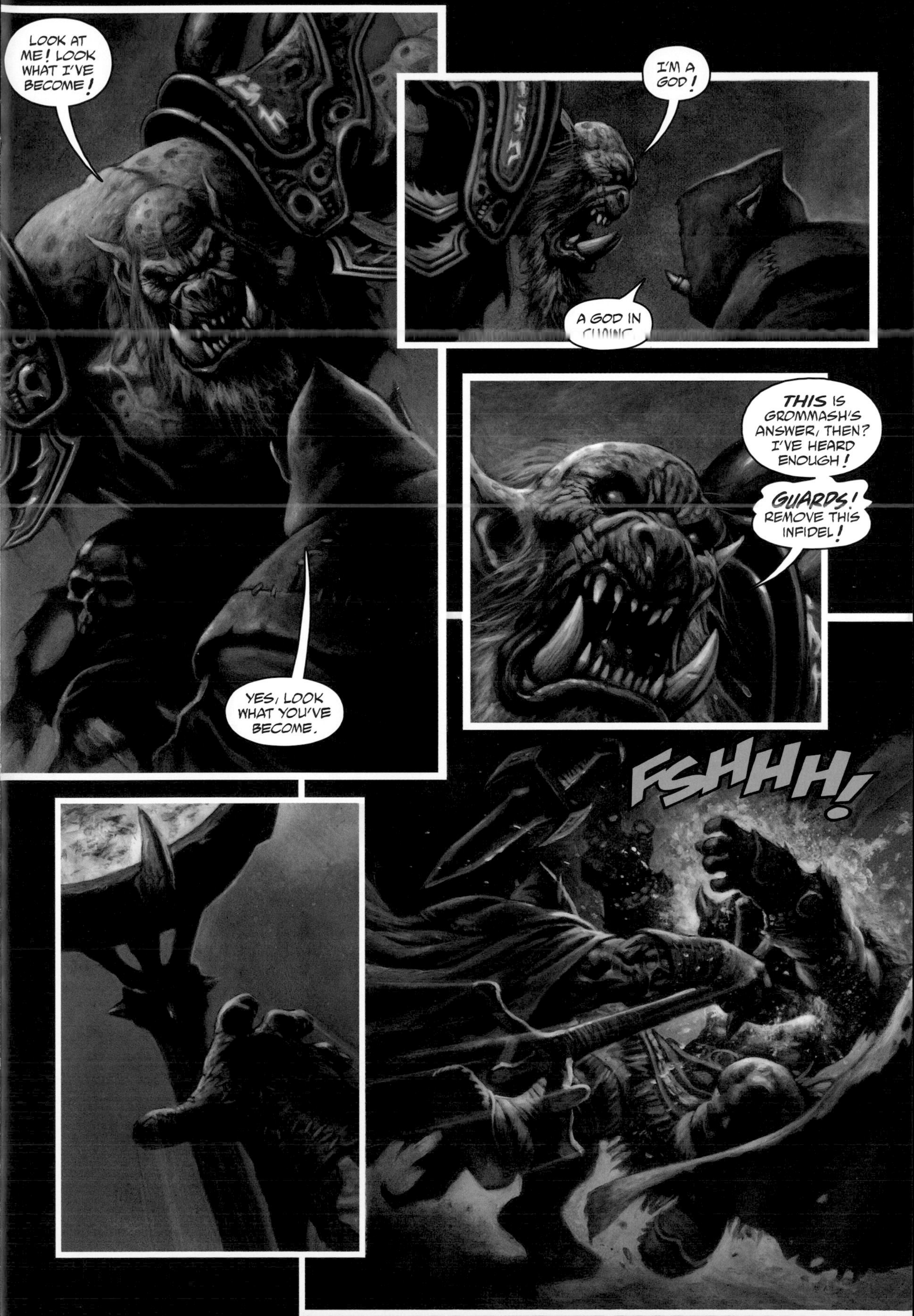
LOOK AT ME! LOOK WHAT I'VE BECOME!
YES, LOOK WHAT YOU'VE BECOME.
I'M A GOD!
A GOD IN
THIS IS GROMMASH'S ANSWER, THEN? I'VE HEARD ENOUGH!
GUARDS! REMOVE THIS INFIDEL!
FSHHH!

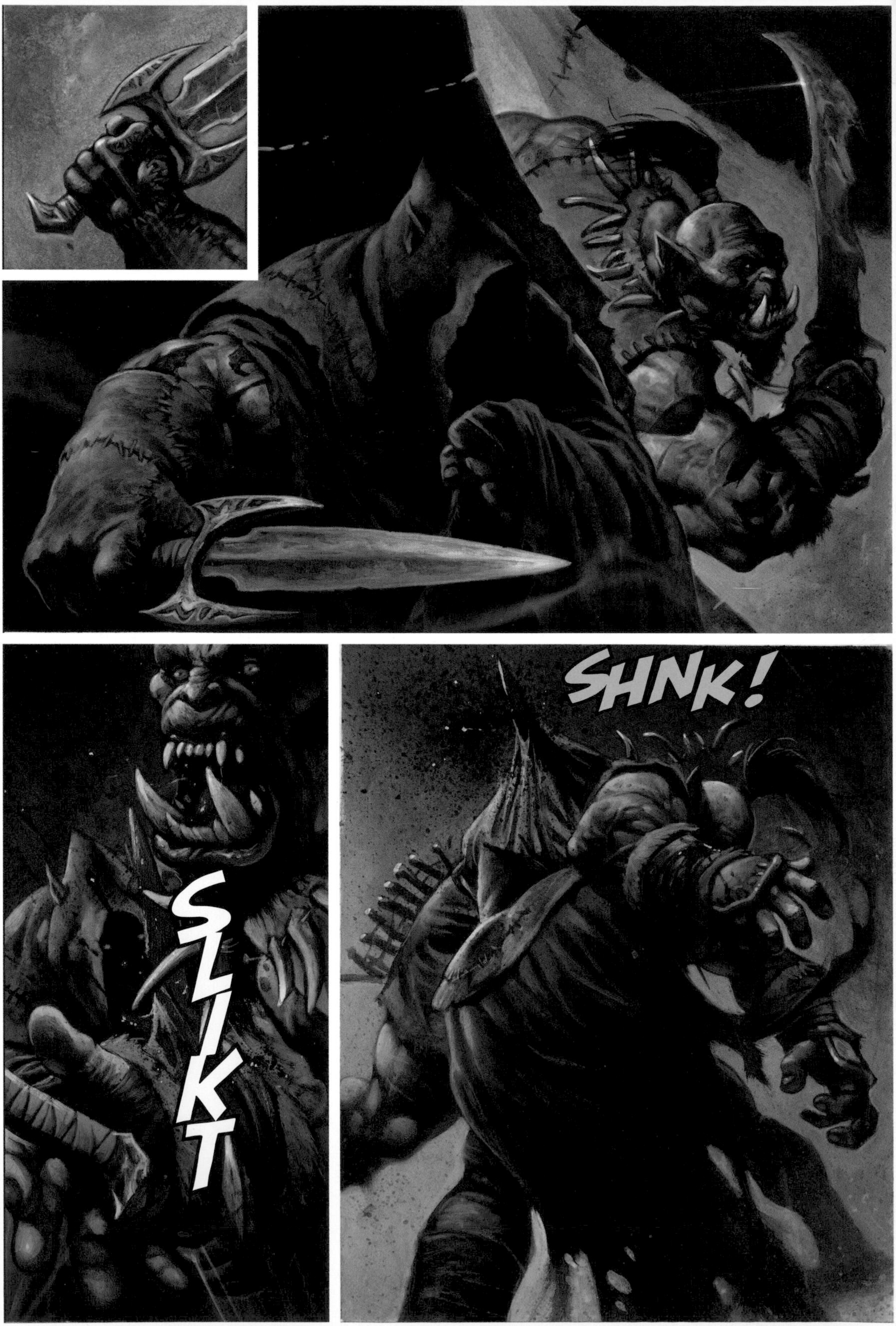
SLIKT
SHNK!

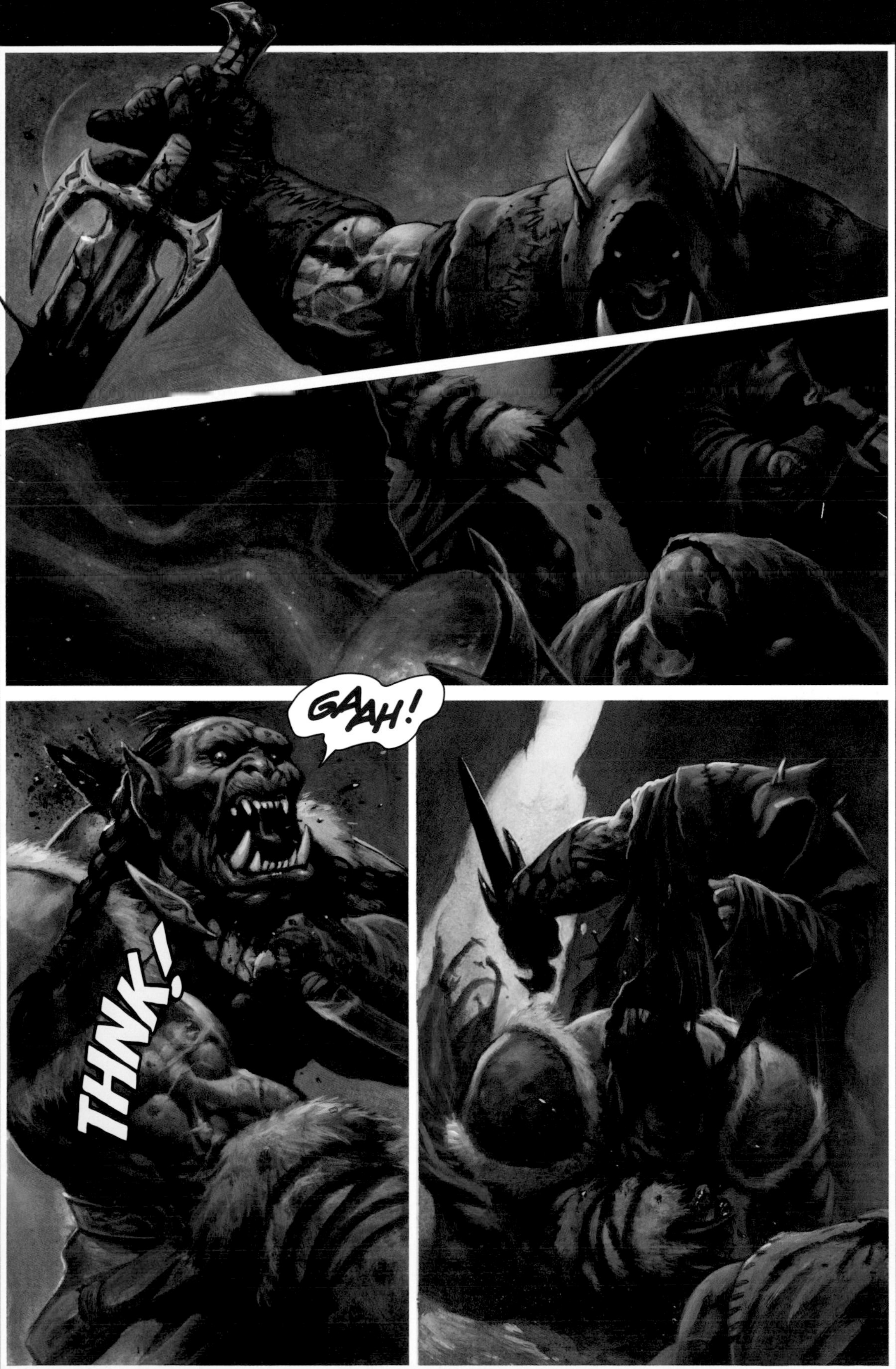
GAAH!
THNK!

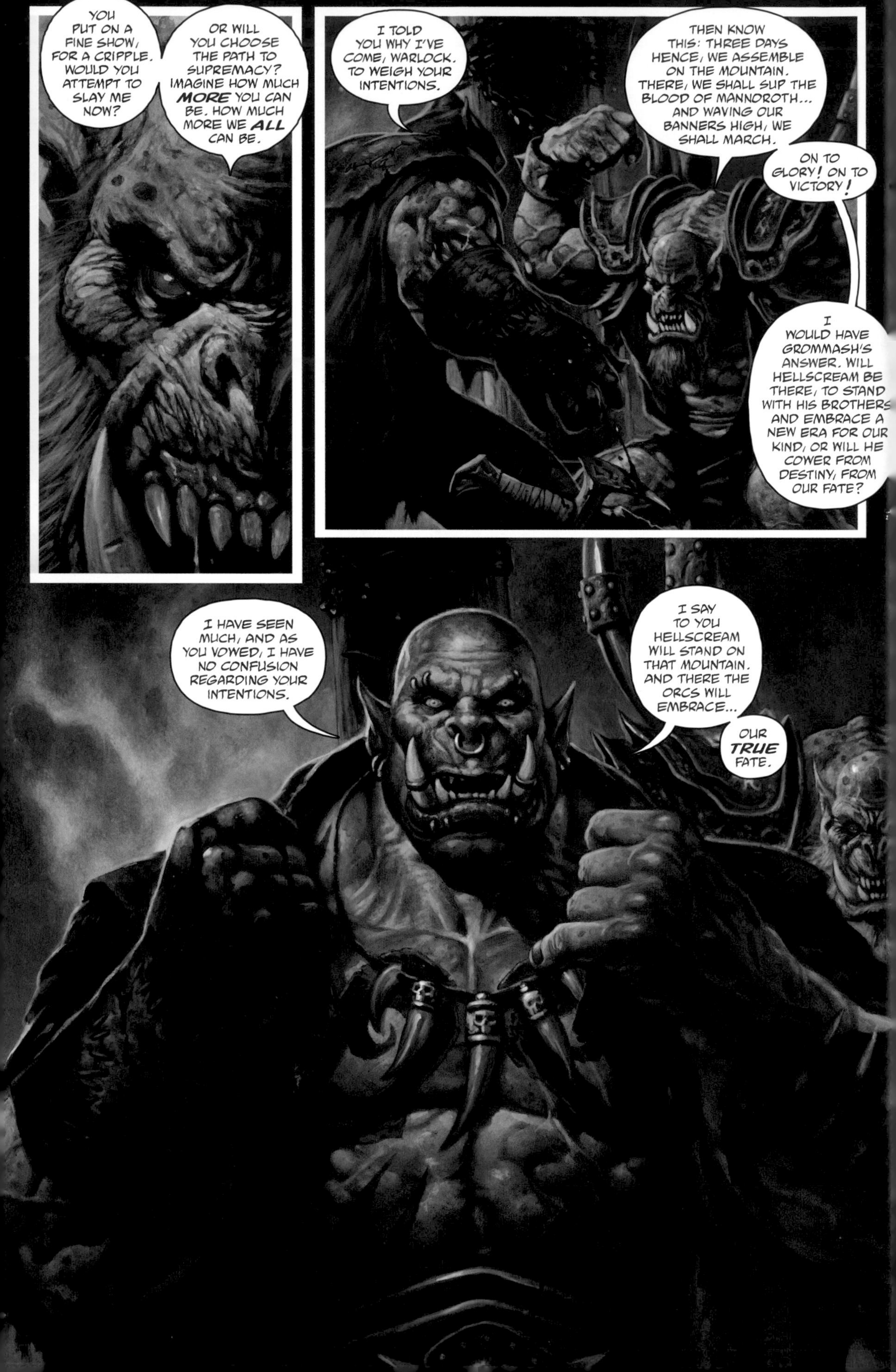

YOU PUT ON A FINE SHOW, FOR A CRIPPLE. WOULD YOU ATTEMPT TO SLAY ME NOW?
OR WILL YOU CHOOSE THE PATH TO SUPREMACY? IMAGINE HOW MUCH MORE YOU CAN BE. HOW MUCH MORE WE ALL CAN BE.
I TOLD YOU WHY I'VE COME, WARLOCK. TO WEIGH YOUR INTENTIONS.
THEN KNOW THIS: THREE DAYS HENCE, WE ASSEMBLE ON THE MOUNTAIN. THERE, WE SHALL SUP THE BLOOD OF MANNOROTH... AND WAVING OUR BANNERS HIGH, WE SHALL MARCH.
ON TO GLORY! ON TO VICTORY!
I WOULD HAVE GROMMASH'S ANSWER. WILL HELLSCREAM BE THERE, TO STAND WITH HIS BROTHERS AND EMBRACE A NEW ERA FOR OUR KIND, OR WILL HE COWER FROM DESTINY, FROM OUR FATE?
I HAVE SEEN MUCH, AND AS YOU VOWED, I HAVE NO CONFUSION REGARDING YOUR INTENTIONS.
I SAY TO YOU HELLSCREAM WILL STAND ON THAT MOUNTAIN. AND THERE THE ORCS WILL EMBRACE...
OUR TRUE FATE.

WORLD OF WARCRAFT
WARLORDS of DRAENOR

BLACKHAND

SCRIPT BY **ROBERT BROOKS** | ART BY **ALEX HORLEY** |
LETTERING BY **CLEM ROBINS**

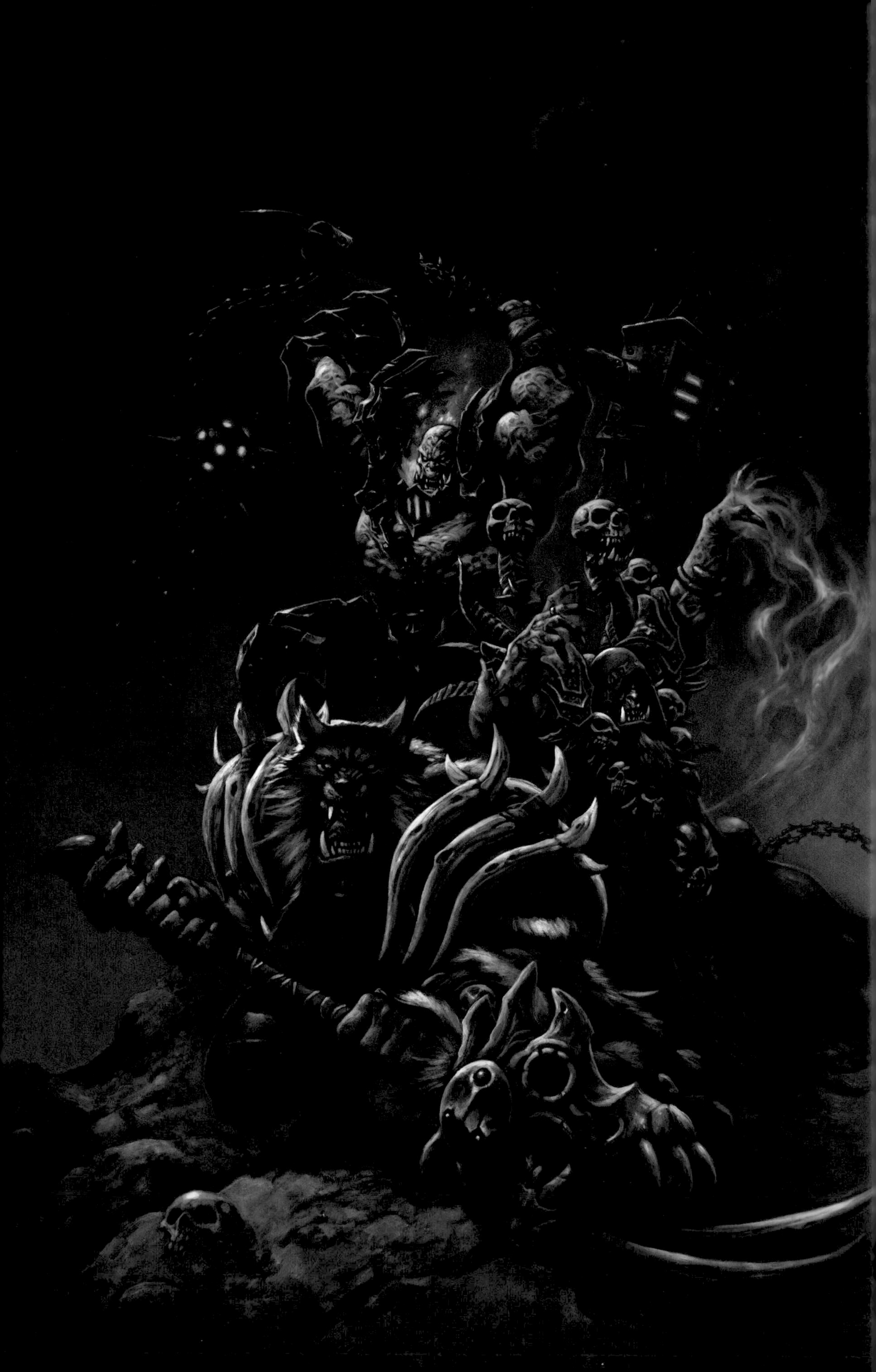

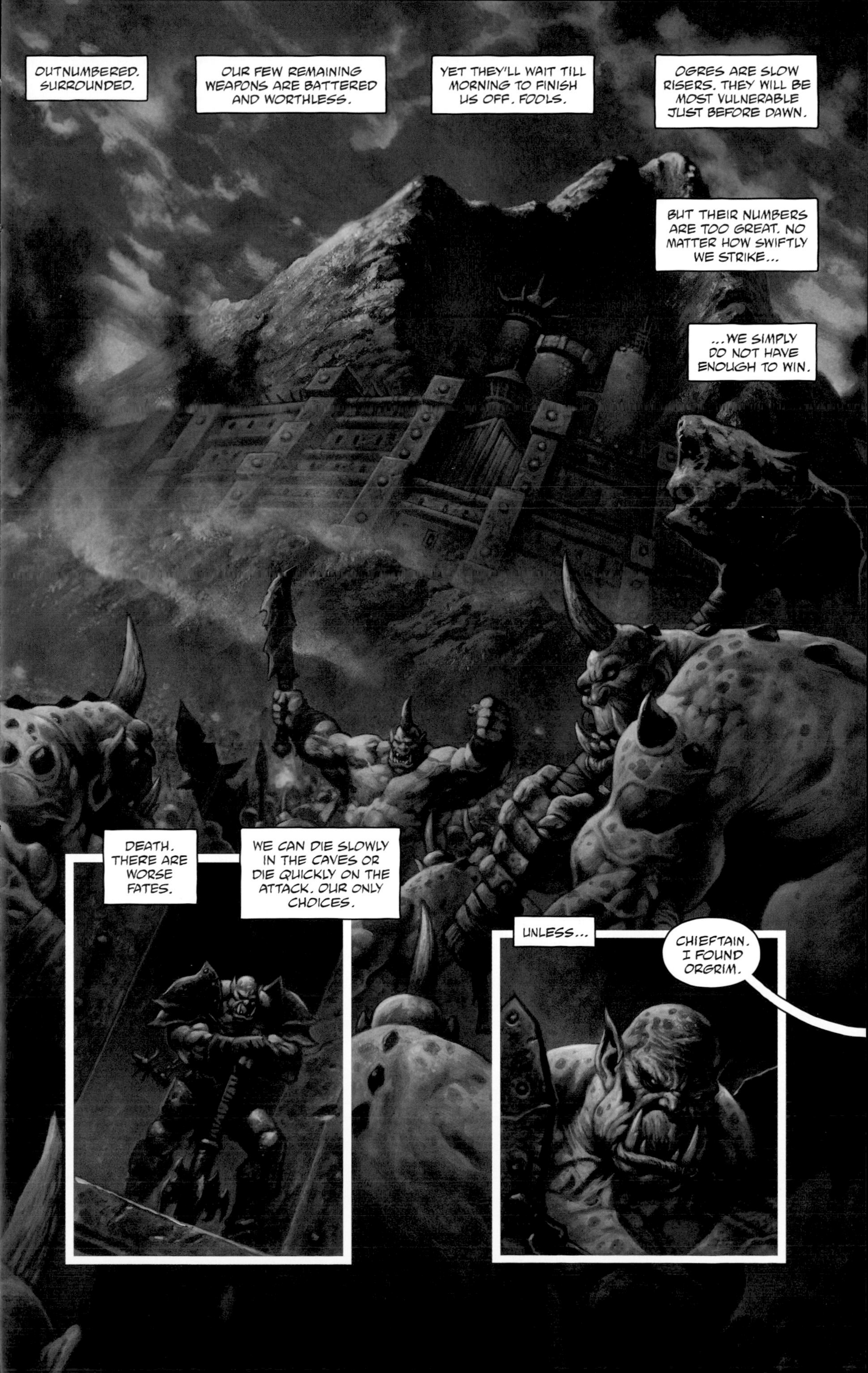
OUTNUMBERED. SURROUNDED.
OUR FEW REMAINING WEAPONS ARE BATTERED AND WORTHLESS.
YET THEY'LL WAIT TILL MORNING TO FINISH US OFF. FOOLS.
OGRES ARE SLOW RISERS. THEY WILL BE MOST VULNERABLE JUST BEFORE DAWN.
BUT THEIR NUMBERS ARE TOO GREAT. NO MATTER HOW SWIFTLY WE STRIKE...
...WE SIMPLY DO NOT HAVE ENOUGH TO WIN.
DEATH. THERE ARE WORSE FATES.
WE CAN DIE SLOWLY IN THE CAVES OR DIE QUICKLY ON THE ATTACK. OUR ONLY CHOICES.
UNLESS...
CHIEFTAIN. I FOUND ORGRIM.

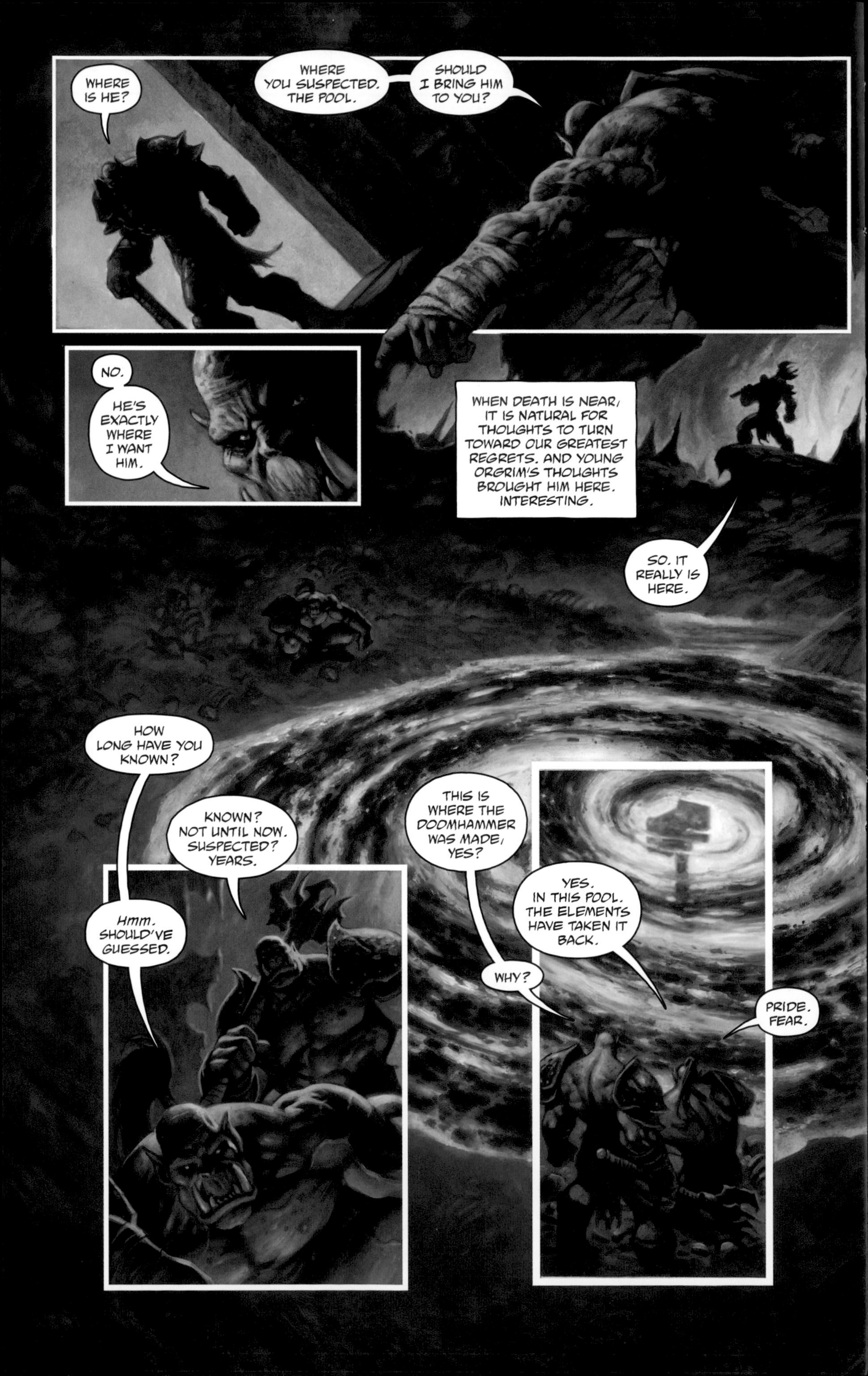
WHERE IS HE?
WHERE YOU SUSPECTED. THE POOL.
SHOULD I BRING HIM TO YOU?
NO.
HE'S EXACTLY WHERE I WANT HIM.
WHEN DEATH IS NEAR, IT IS NATURAL FOR THOUGHTS TO TURN TOWARD OUR GREATEST REGRETS. AND YOUNG ORGRIM'S THOUGHTS BROUGHT HIM HERE. INTERESTING.
SO. IT REALLY IS HERE.
HOW LONG HAVE YOU KNOWN?
KNOWN? NOT UNTIL NOW. SUSPECTED? YEARS.
Hmm. SHOULD'VE GUESSED.
THIS IS WHERE THE DOOMHAMMER WAS MADE, YES?
YES. IN THIS POOL. THE ELEMENTS HAVE TAKEN IT BACK.
WHY?
PRIDE. FEAR.

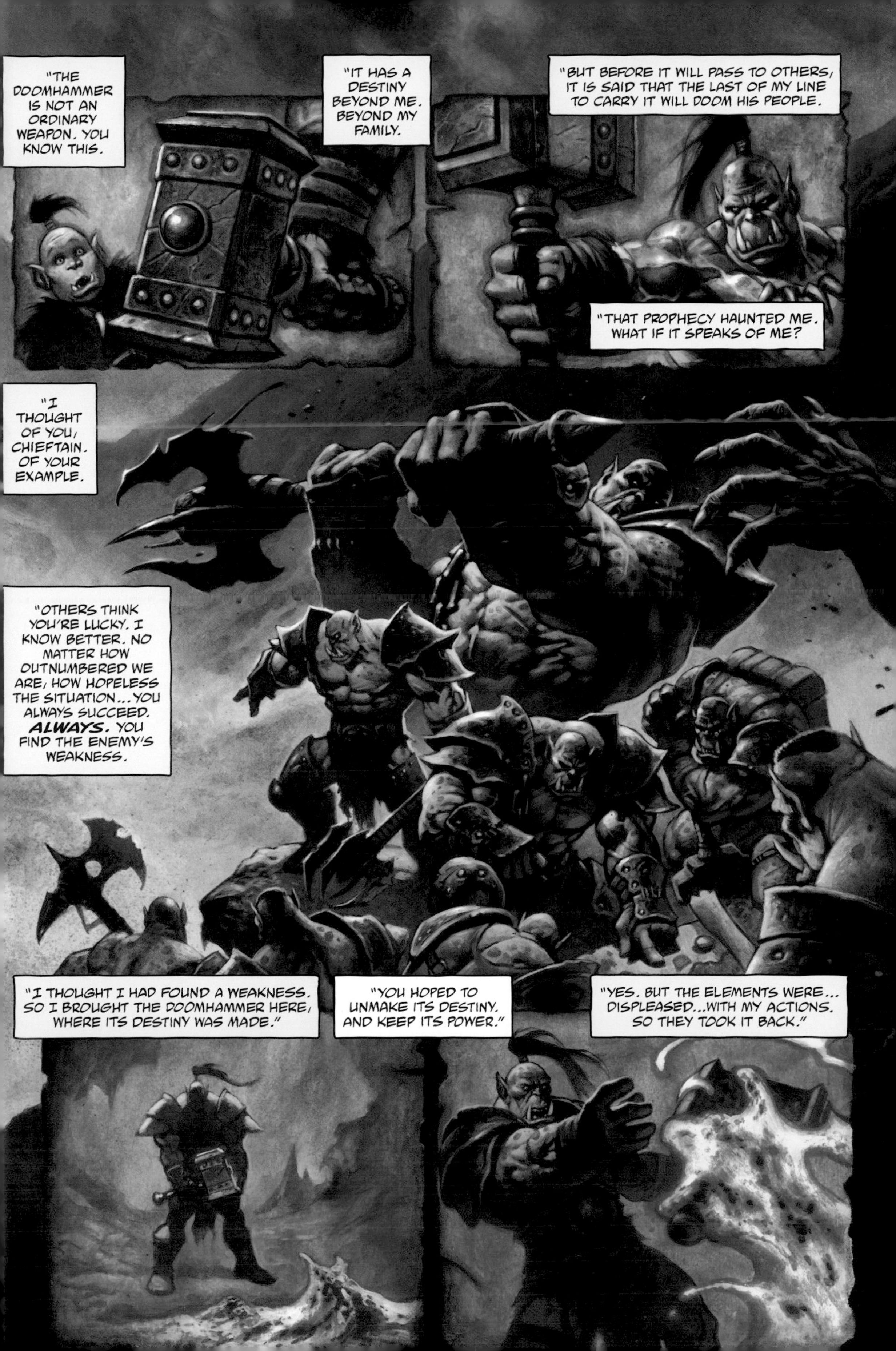
"THE DOOMHAMMER IS NOT AN ORDINARY WEAPON. YOU KNOW THIS.
"IT HAS A DESTINY BEYOND ME. BEYOND MY FAMILY.
"BUT BEFORE IT WILL PASS TO OTHERS, IT IS SAID THAT THE LAST OF MY LINE TO CARRY IT WILL DOOM HIS PEOPLE.
"THAT PROPHECY HAUNTED ME. WHAT IF IT SPEAKS OF ME?
"I THOUGHT OF YOU, CHIEFTAIN. OF YOUR EXAMPLE.
"OTHERS THINK YOU'RE LUCKY. I KNOW BETTER. NO MATTER HOW OUTNUMBERED WE ARE, HOW HOPELESS THE SITUATION...YOU ALWAYS SUCCEED. ***ALWAYS.*** YOU FIND THE ENEMY'S WEAKNESS.
"I THOUGHT I HAD FOUND A WEAKNESS. SO I BROUGHT THE DOOMHAMMER HERE, WHERE ITS DESTINY WAS MADE."
"YOU HOPED TO UNMAKE ITS DESTINY. AND KEEP ITS POWER."
"YES. BUT THE ELEMENTS WERE... DISPLEASED...WITH MY ACTIONS. SO THEY TOOK IT BACK."

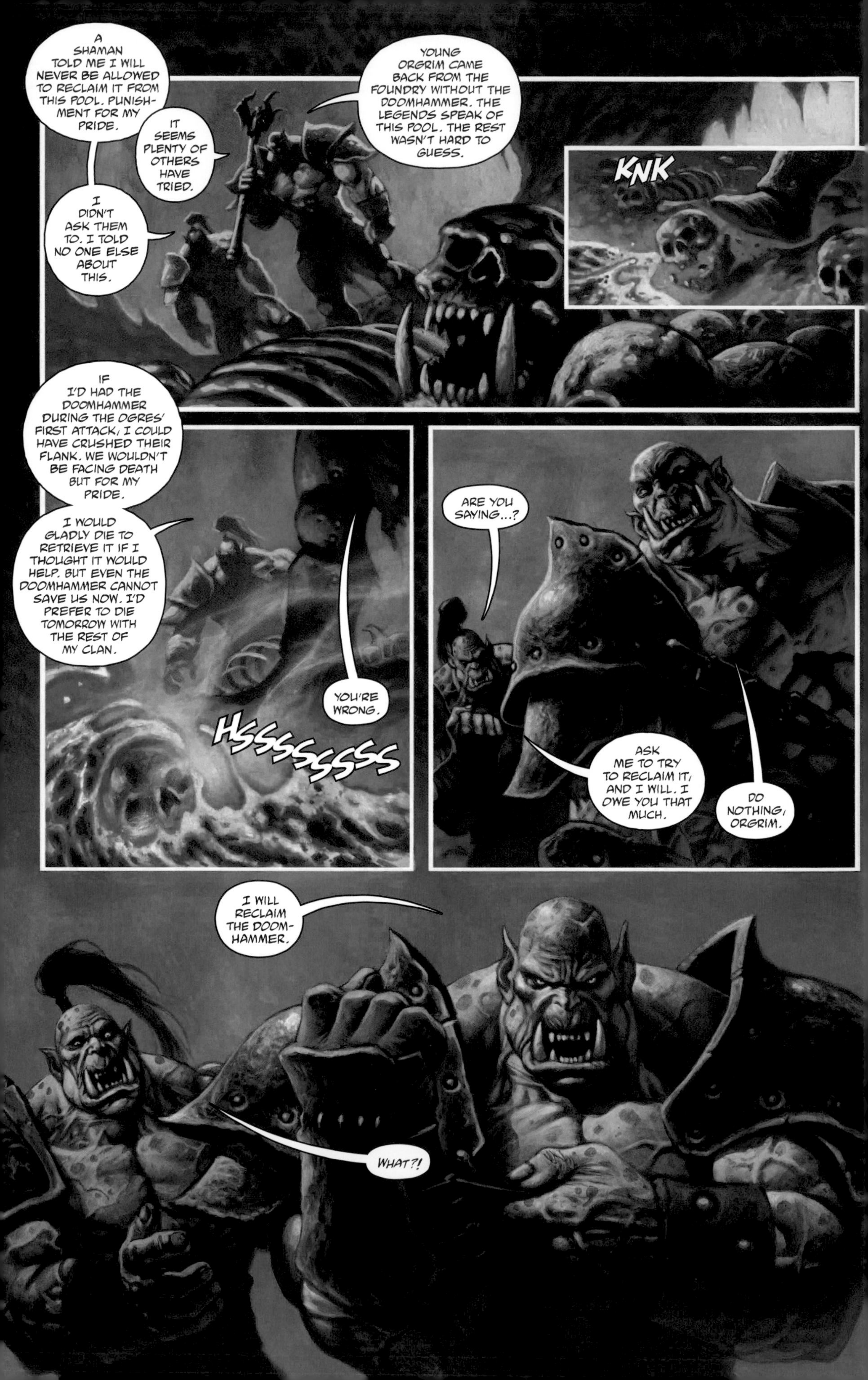
A SHAMAN TOLD ME I WILL NEVER BE ALLOWED TO RECLAIM IT FROM THIS POOL. PUNISHMENT FOR MY PRIDE.
YOUNG ORGRIM CAME BACK FROM THE FOUNDRY WITHOUT THE DOOMHAMMER. THE LEGENDS SPEAK OF THIS POOL. THE REST WASN'T HARD TO GUESS.
IT SEEMS PLENTY OF OTHERS HAVE TRIED.
I DIDN'T ASK THEM TO. I TOLD NO ONE ELSE ABOUT THIS.
KNK
IF I'D HAD THE DOOMHAMMER DURING THE OGRES' FIRST ATTACK, I COULD HAVE CRUSHED THEIR FLANK. WE WOULDN'T BE FACING DEATH BUT FOR MY PRIDE.
I WOULD GLADLY DIE TO RETRIEVE IT IF I THOUGHT IT WOULD HELP. BUT EVEN THE DOOMHAMMER CANNOT SAVE US NOW. I'D PREFER TO DIE TOMORROW WITH THE REST OF MY CLAN.
YOU'RE WRONG.
HSSSSSSSSS
ARE YOU SAYING...?
ASK ME TO TRY TO RECLAIM IT, AND I WILL. I OWE YOU THAT MUCH.
DO NOTHING, ORGRIM.
I WILL RECLAIM THE DOOMHAMMER.
WHAT?!

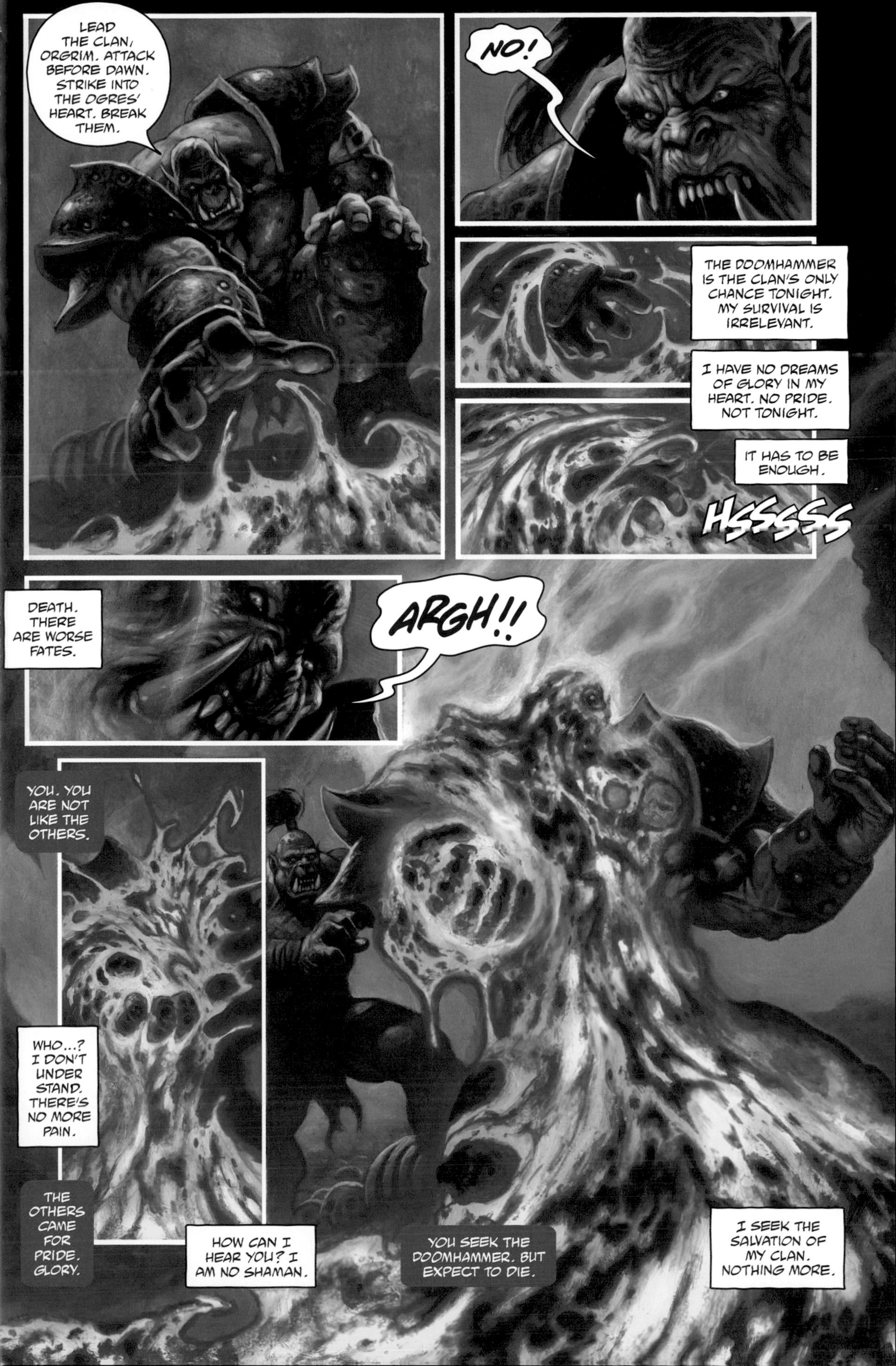
LEAD THE CLAN, ORGRIM. ATTACK BEFORE DAWN. STRIKE INTO THE OGRES' HEART. BREAK THEM.
NO!
THE DOOMHAMMER IS THE CLAN'S ONLY CHANCE TONIGHT. MY SURVIVAL IS IRRELEVANT.
I HAVE NO DREAMS OF GLORY IN MY HEART. NO PRIDE. NOT TONIGHT.
IT HAS TO BE ENOUGH.
HSSSSS
DEATH. THERE ARE WORSE FATES.
ARGH!!
YOU. YOU ARE NOT LIKE THE OTHERS.
WHO...? I DON'T UNDER STAND. THERE'S NO MORE PAIN.
THE OTHERS CAME FOR PRIDE. GLORY.
HOW CAN I HEAR YOU? I AM NO SHAMAN.
YOU SEEK THE DOOMHAMMER. BUT EXPECT TO DIE.
I SEEK THE SALVATION OF MY CLAN. NOTHING MORE.

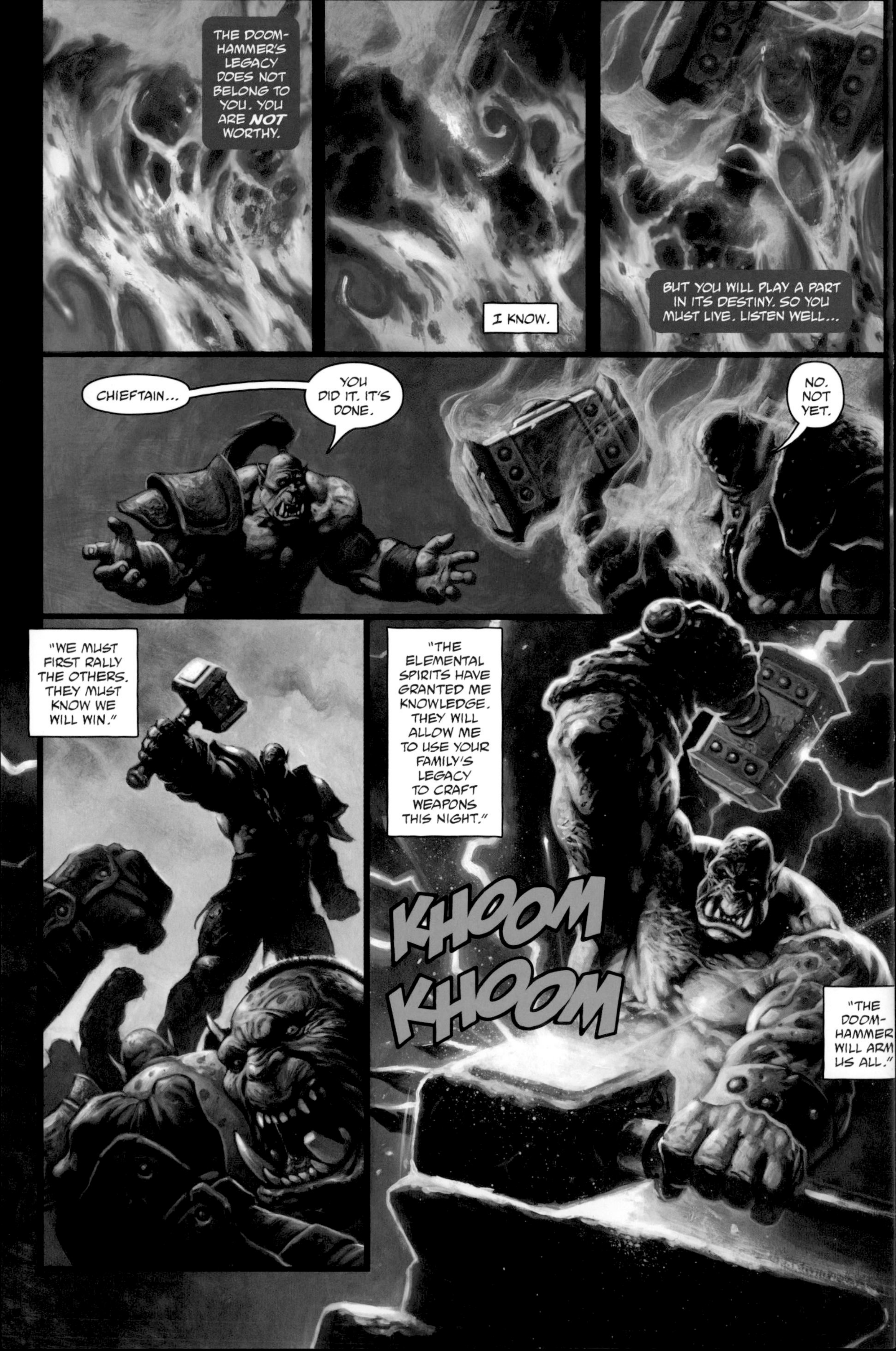
THE DOOM-HAMMER'S LEGACY DOES NOT BELONG TO YOU. YOU ARE NOT WORTHY.
I KNOW.
BUT YOU WILL PLAY A PART IN ITS DESTINY. SO YOU MUST LIVE. LISTEN WELL...
CHIEFTAIN...
YOU DID IT. IT'S DONE.
NO. NOT YET.
"WE MUST FIRST RALLY THE OTHERS. THEY MUST KNOW WE WILL WIN."
"THE ELEMENTAL SPIRITS HAVE GRANTED ME KNOWLEDGE. THEY WILL ALLOW ME TO USE YOUR FAMILY'S LEGACY TO CRAFT WEAPONS THIS NIGHT."
KHOOM
KHOOM
"THE DOOM-HAMMER WILL ARM US ALL."

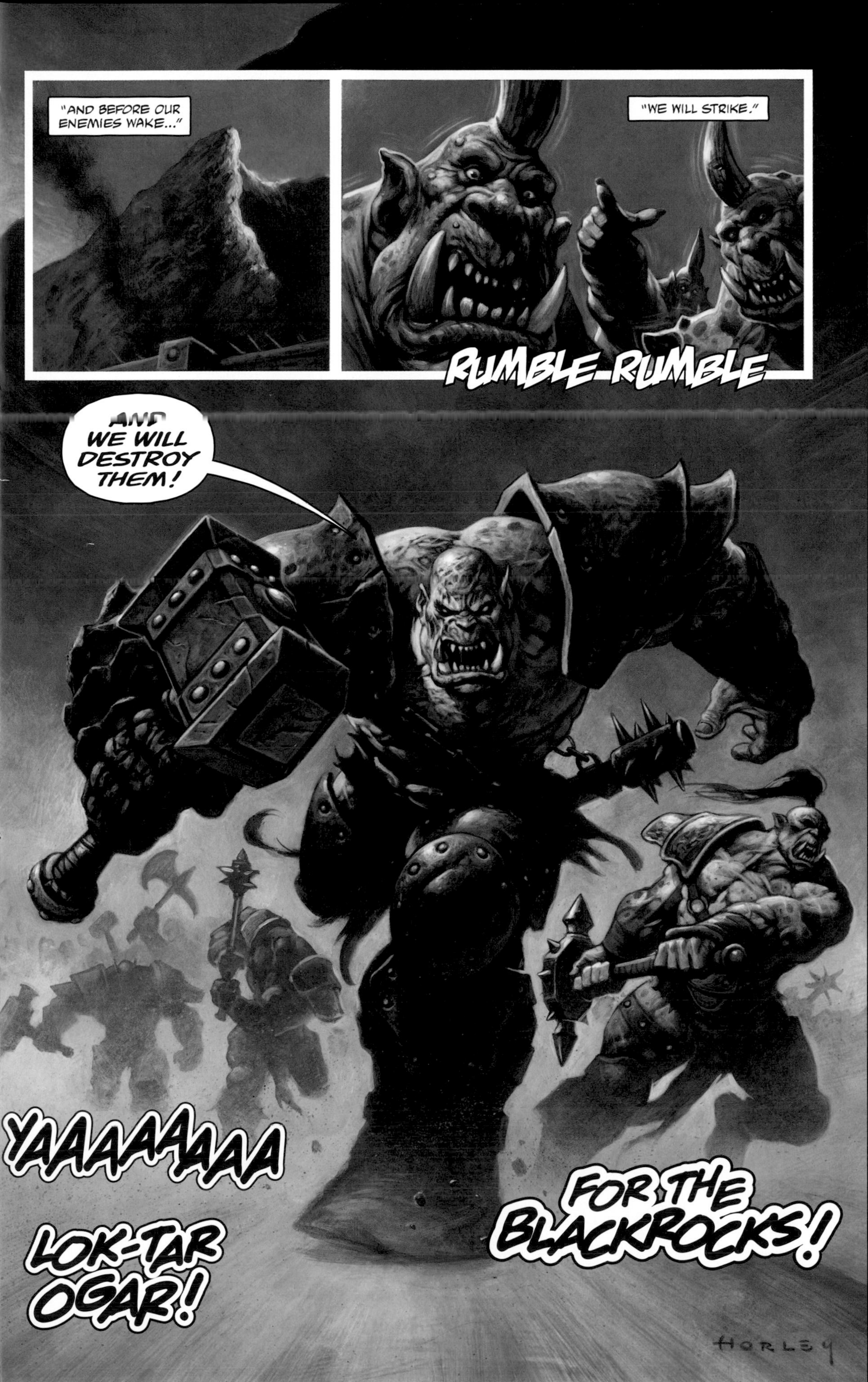

"AND BEFORE OUR ENEMIES WAKE..."
"WE WILL STRIKE."
RUMBLE RUMBLE
AND WE WILL DESTROY THEM!
YAAAAAAAA
LOK-TAR OGAR!
FOR THE BLACKROCKS!
HORLEY

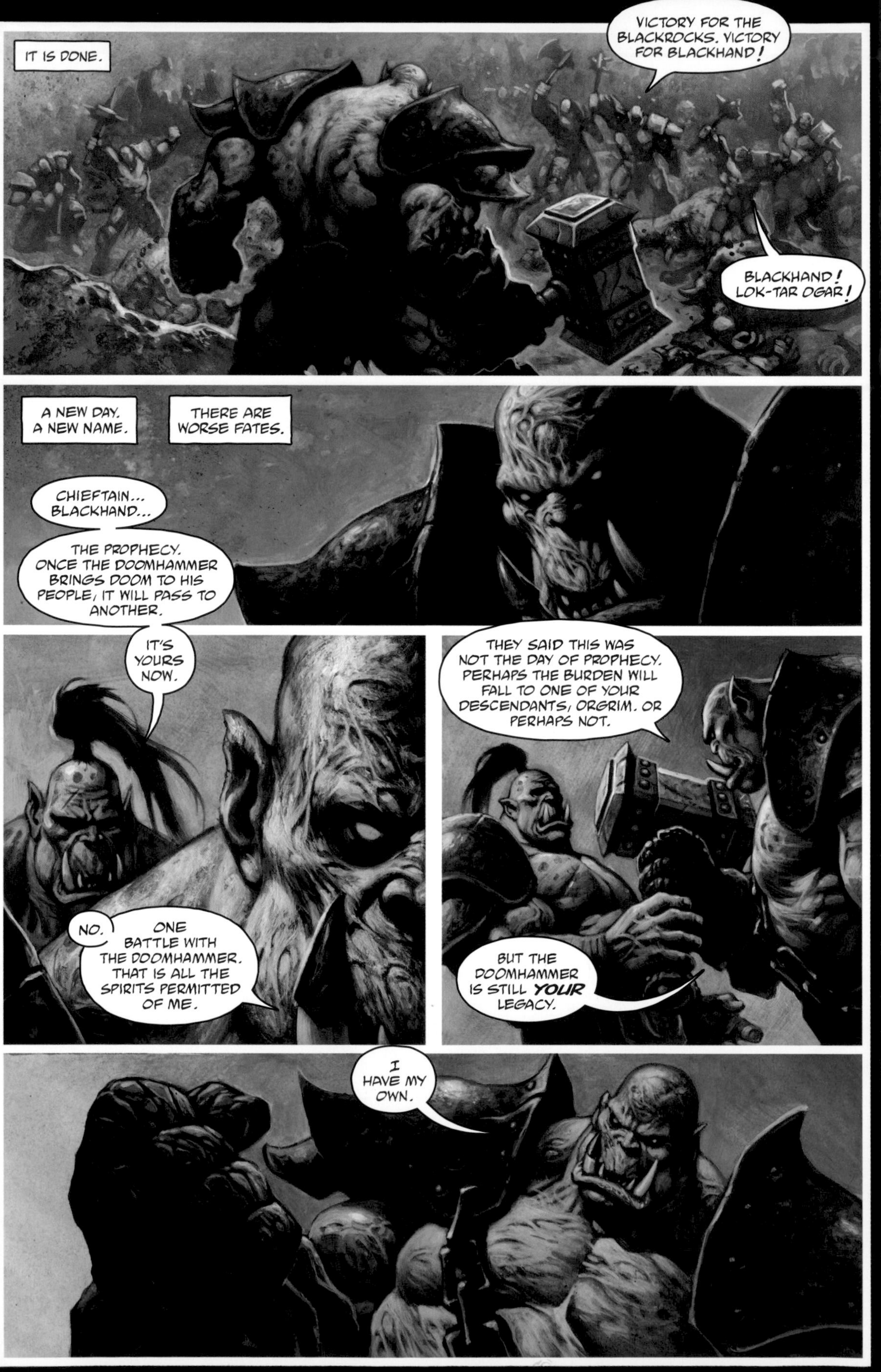
IT IS DONE.
VICTORY FOR THE BLACKROCKS. VICTORY FOR BLACKHAND!
BLACKHAND! LOK-TAR OGAR!
A NEW DAY. A NEW NAME.
THERE ARE WORSE FATES.
CHIEFTAIN... BLACKHAND...
THE PROPHECY. ONCE THE DOOMHAMMER BRINGS DOOM TO HIS PEOPLE, IT WILL PASS TO ANOTHER.
IT'S YOURS NOW.
NO.
ONE BATTLE WITH THE DOOMHAMMER. THAT IS ALL THE SPIRITS PERMITTED OF ME.
THEY SAID THIS WAS NOT THE DAY OF PROPHECY. PERHAPS THE BURDEN WILL FALL TO ONE OF YOUR DESCENDANTS, ORGRIM. OR PERHAPS NOT.
BUT THE DOOMHAMMER IS STILL ***YOUR*** LEGACY.
I HAVE MY OWN.

WORLD OF WARCRAFT

WARLORDS of DRAENOR

BLOOD AND THUNDER

STORY DEVELOPMENT BY **RAPHAEL AHAD & CYNTHIA HALL** |
SCRIPT BY **RAPHAEL AHAD** | ART BY **ALEX HORLEY** |
LETTERING BY **CLEM ROBINS**

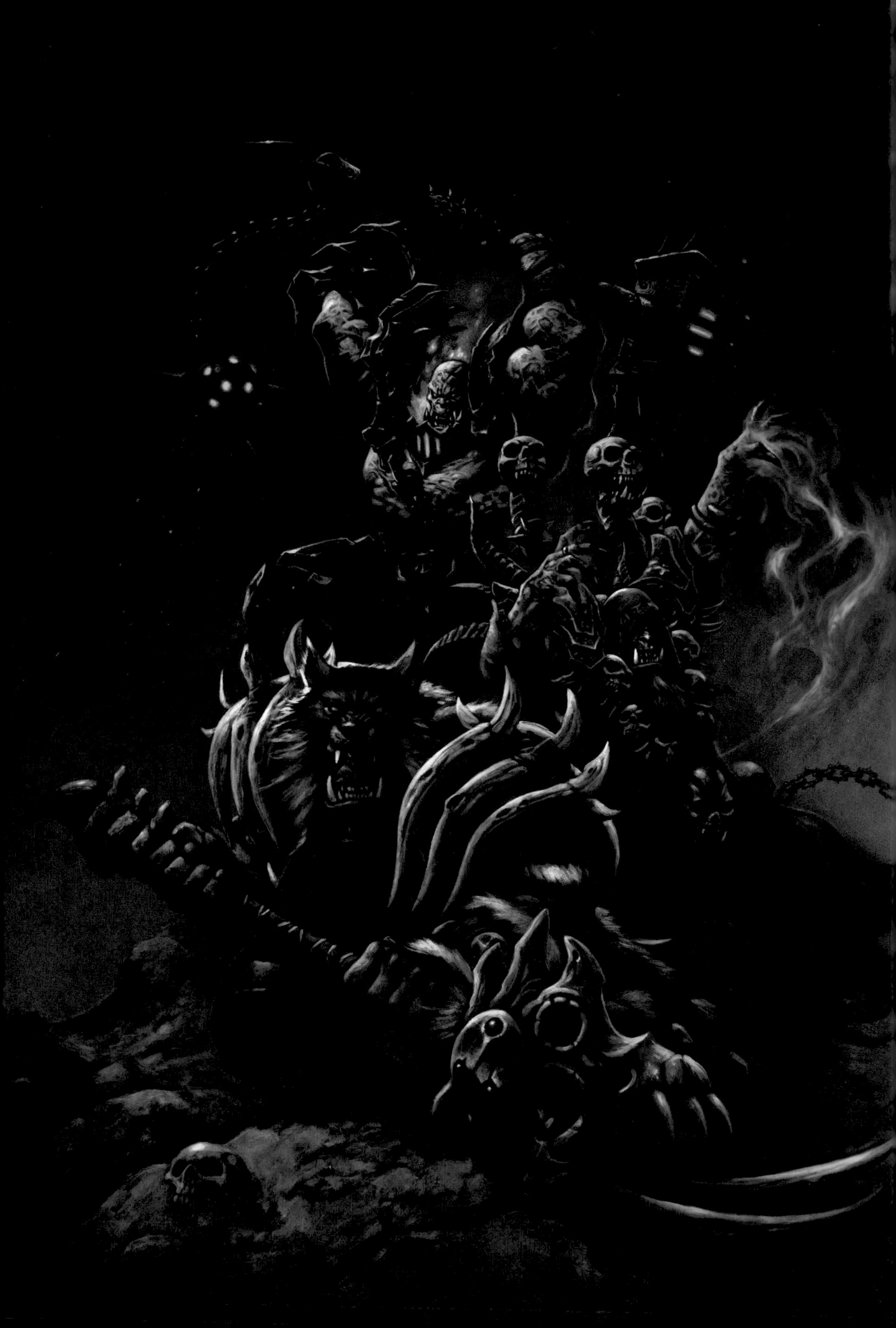

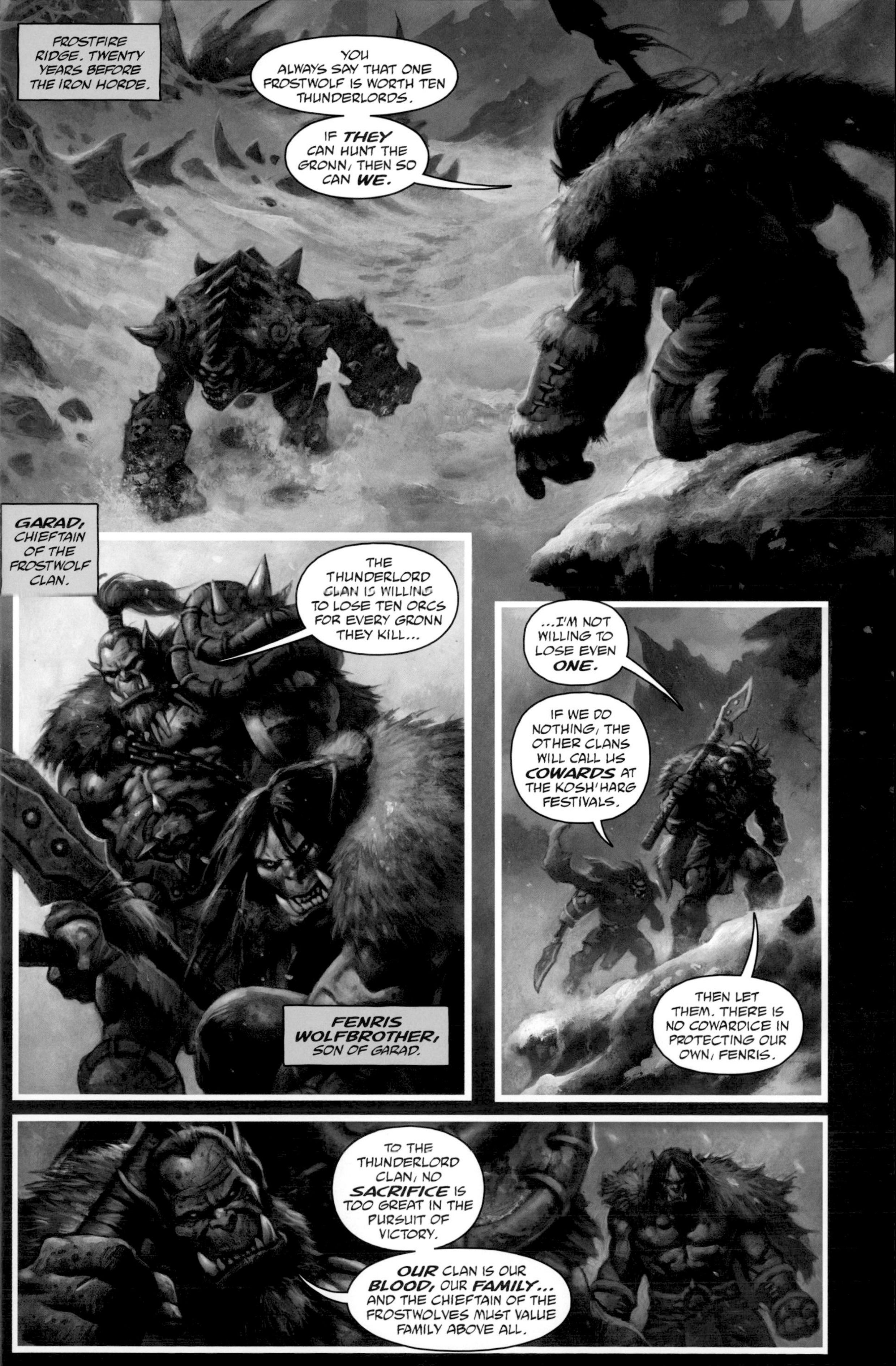
FROSTFIRE RIDGE. TWENTY YEARS BEFORE THE IRON HORDE.
YOU ALWAYS SAY THAT ONE FROSTWOLF IS WORTH TEN THUNDERLORDS.
IF THEY CAN HUNT THE GRONN, THEN SO CAN WE.
GARAD, CHIEFTAIN OF THE FROSTWOLF CLAN.
THE THUNDERLORD CLAN IS WILLING TO LOSE TEN ORCS FOR EVERY GRONN THEY KILL...
FENRIS WOLFBROTHER, SON OF GARAD.
...I'M NOT WILLING TO LOSE EVEN ONE.
IF WE DO NOTHING, THE OTHER CLANS WILL CALL US COWARDS AT THE KOSH'HARG FESTIVALS.
THEN LET THEM. THERE IS NO COWARDICE IN PROTECTING OUR OWN, FENRIS.
TO THE THUNDERLORD CLAN, NO SACRIFICE IS TOO GREAT IN THE PURSUIT OF VICTORY.
OUR CLAN IS OUR BLOOD, OUR FAMILY... AND THE CHIEFTAIN OF THE FROSTWOLVES MUST VALUE FAMILY ABOVE ALL.

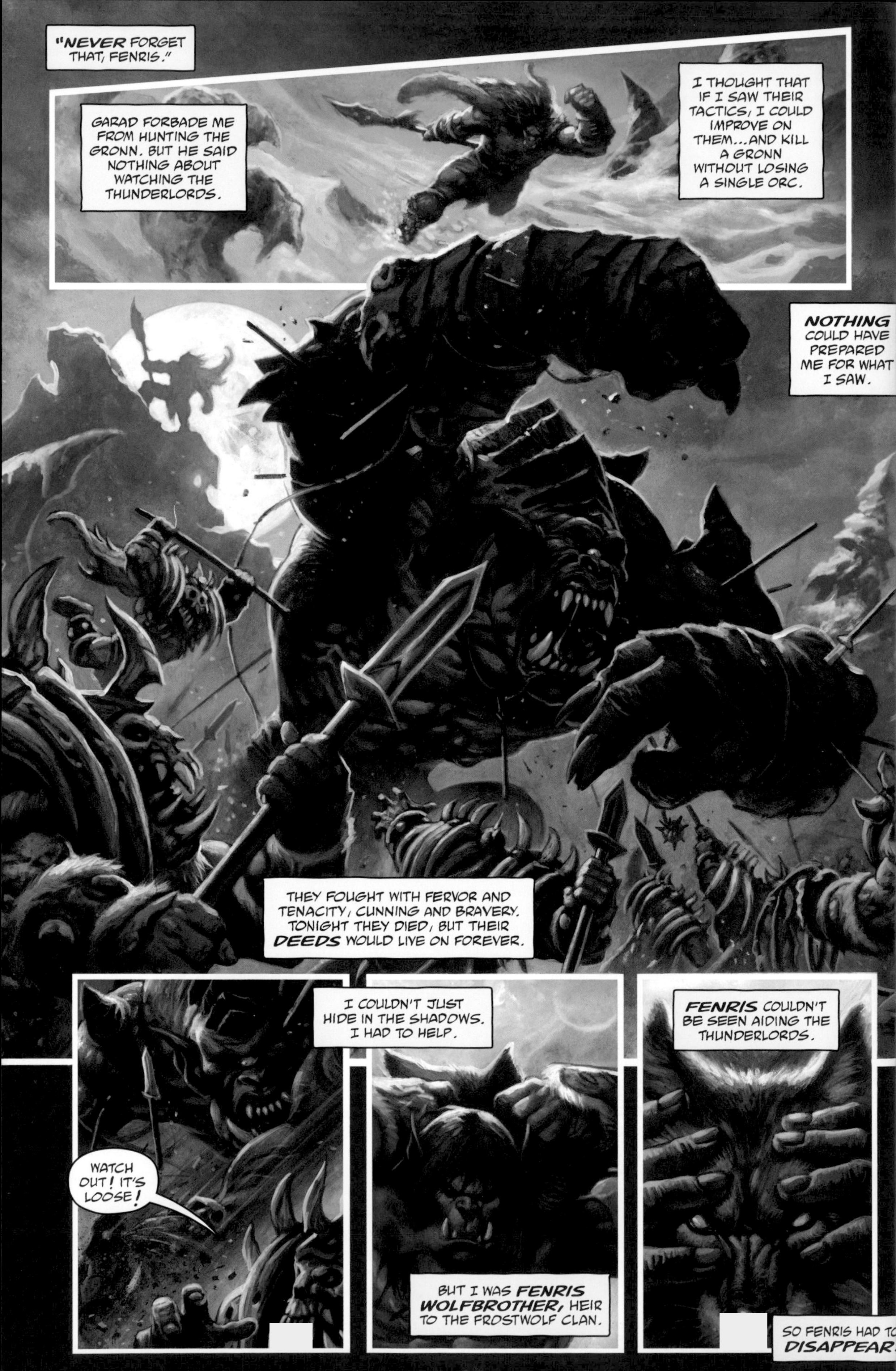
"NEVER FORGET THAT, FENRIS."
GARAD FORBADE ME FROM HUNTING THE GRONN. BUT HE SAID NOTHING ABOUT WATCHING THE THUNDERLORDS.
I THOUGHT THAT IF I SAW THEIR TACTICS, I COULD IMPROVE ON THEM...AND KILL A GRONN WITHOUT LOSING A SINGLE ORC.
NOTHING COULD HAVE PREPARED ME FOR WHAT I SAW.
THEY FOUGHT WITH FERVOR AND TENACITY, CUNNING AND BRAVERY. TONIGHT THEY DIED, BUT THEIR DEEDS WOULD LIVE ON FOREVER.
WATCH OUT! IT'S LOOSE!
I COULDN'T JUST HIDE IN THE SHADOWS. I HAD TO HELP.
BUT I WAS FENRIS WOLFBROTHER, HEIR TO THE FROSTWOLF CLAN.
FENRIS COULDN'T BE SEEN AIDING THE THUNDERLORDS.
SO FENRIS HAD TO DISAPPEAR.

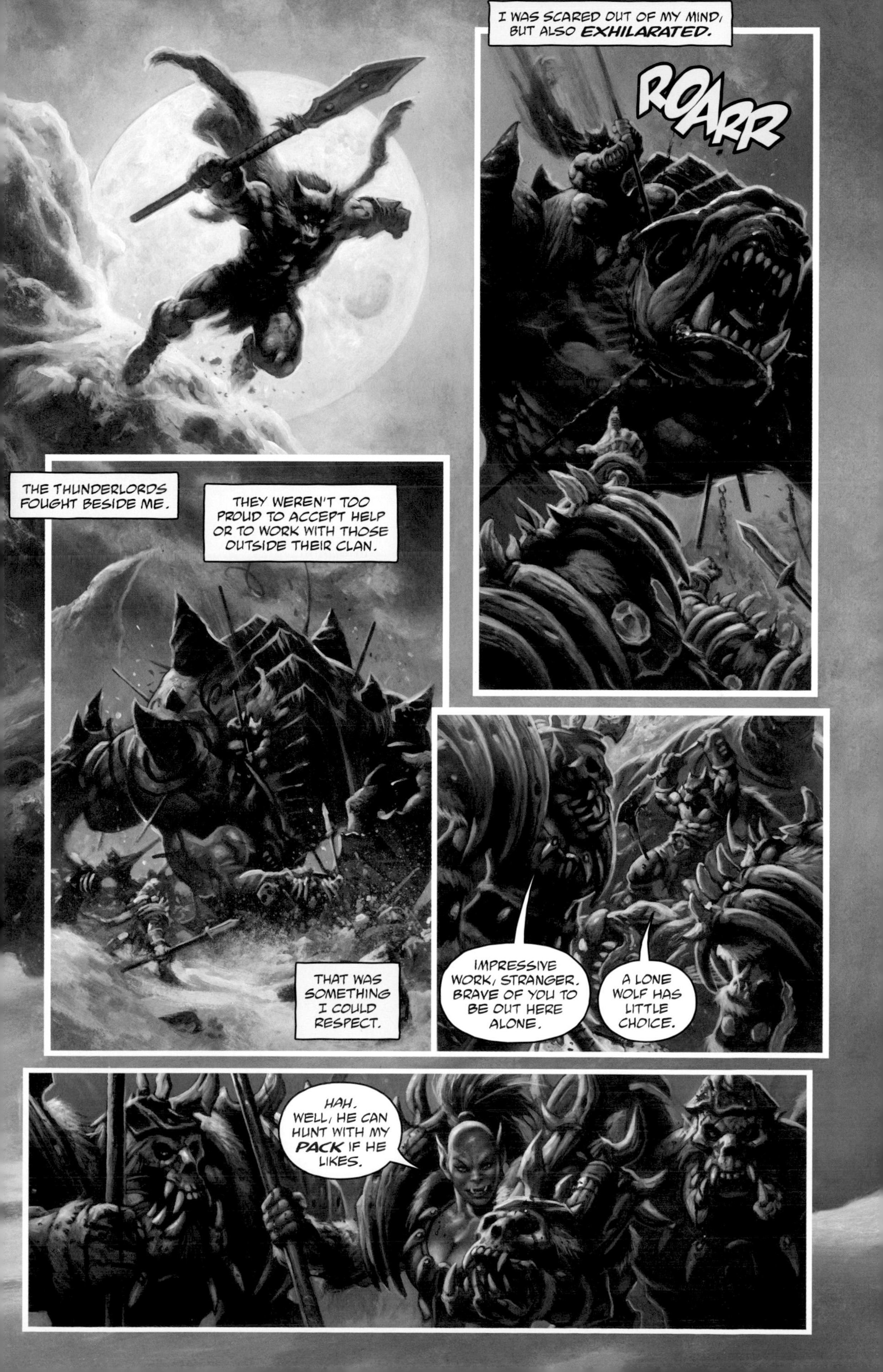

I WAS SCARED OUT OF MY MIND, BUT ALSO **EXHILARATED**.
ROARR
THE THUNDERLORDS FOUGHT BESIDE ME.
THEY WEREN'T TOO PROUD TO ACCEPT HELP OR TO WORK WITH THOSE OUTSIDE THEIR CLAN.
THAT WAS SOMETHING I COULD RESPECT.
IMPRESSIVE WORK, STRANGER. BRAVE OF YOU TO BE OUT HERE ALONE.
A LONE WOLF HAS LITTLE CHOICE.
HAH. WELL, HE CAN HUNT WITH MY **PACK** IF HE LIKES.

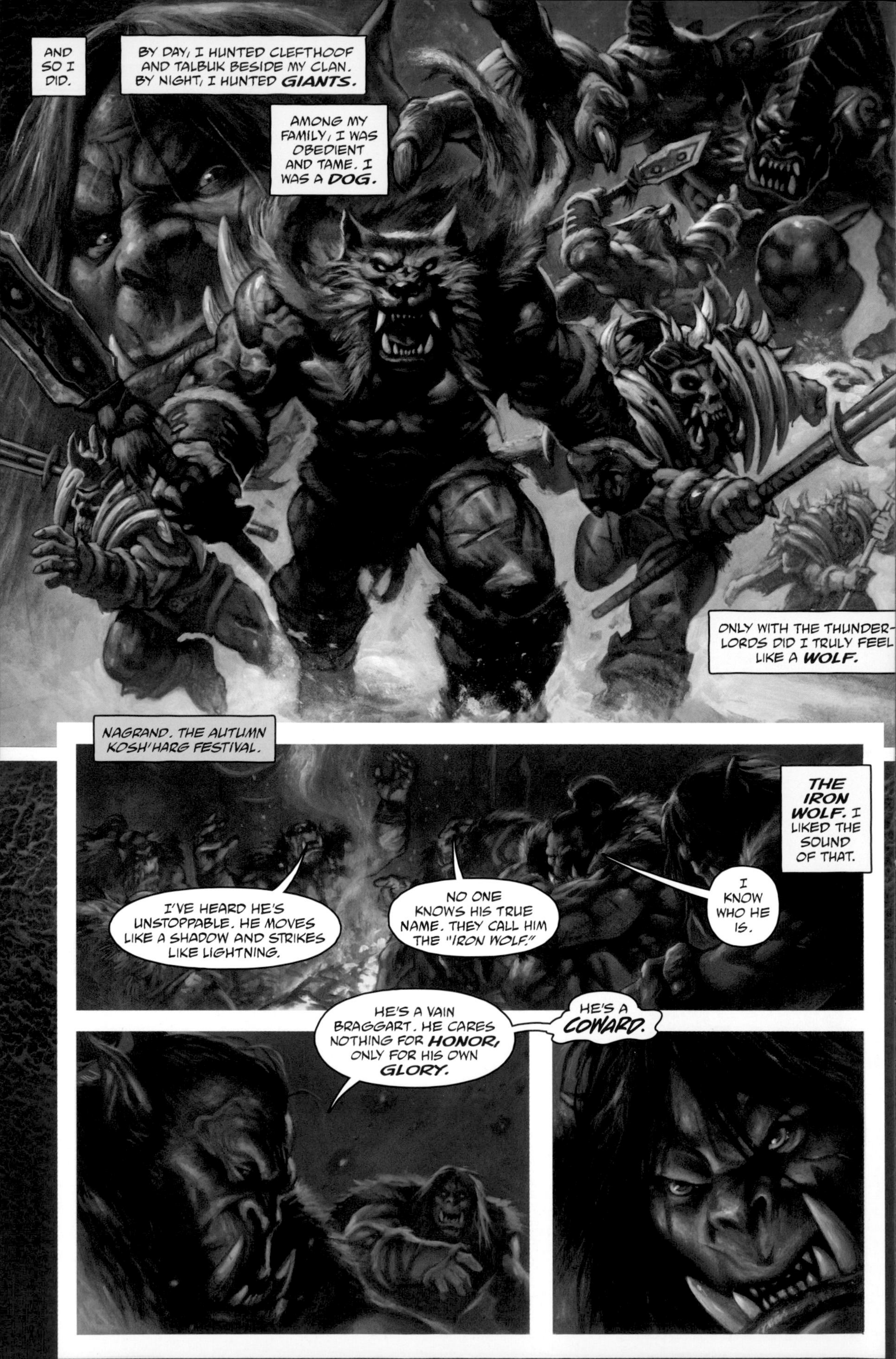

AND SO I DID.
BY DAY, I HUNTED CLEFTHOOF AND TALBUK BESIDE MY CLAN. BY NIGHT, I HUNTED GIANTS.
AMONG MY FAMILY, I WAS OBEDIENT AND TAME. I WAS A DOG.
ONLY WITH THE THUNDERLORDS DID I TRULY FEEL LIKE A WOLF.
NAGRAND. THE AUTUMN KOSH'HARG FESTIVAL.
I'VE HEARD HE'S UNSTOPPABLE. HE MOVES LIKE A SHADOW AND STRIKES LIKE LIGHTNING.
NO ONE KNOWS HIS TRUE NAME. THEY CALL HIM THE "IRON WOLF."
I KNOW WHO HE IS.
THE IRON WOLF. I LIKED THE SOUND OF THAT.
HE'S A VAIN BRAGGART. HE CARES NOTHING FOR HONOR, ONLY FOR HIS OWN GLORY.
HE'S A COWARD.

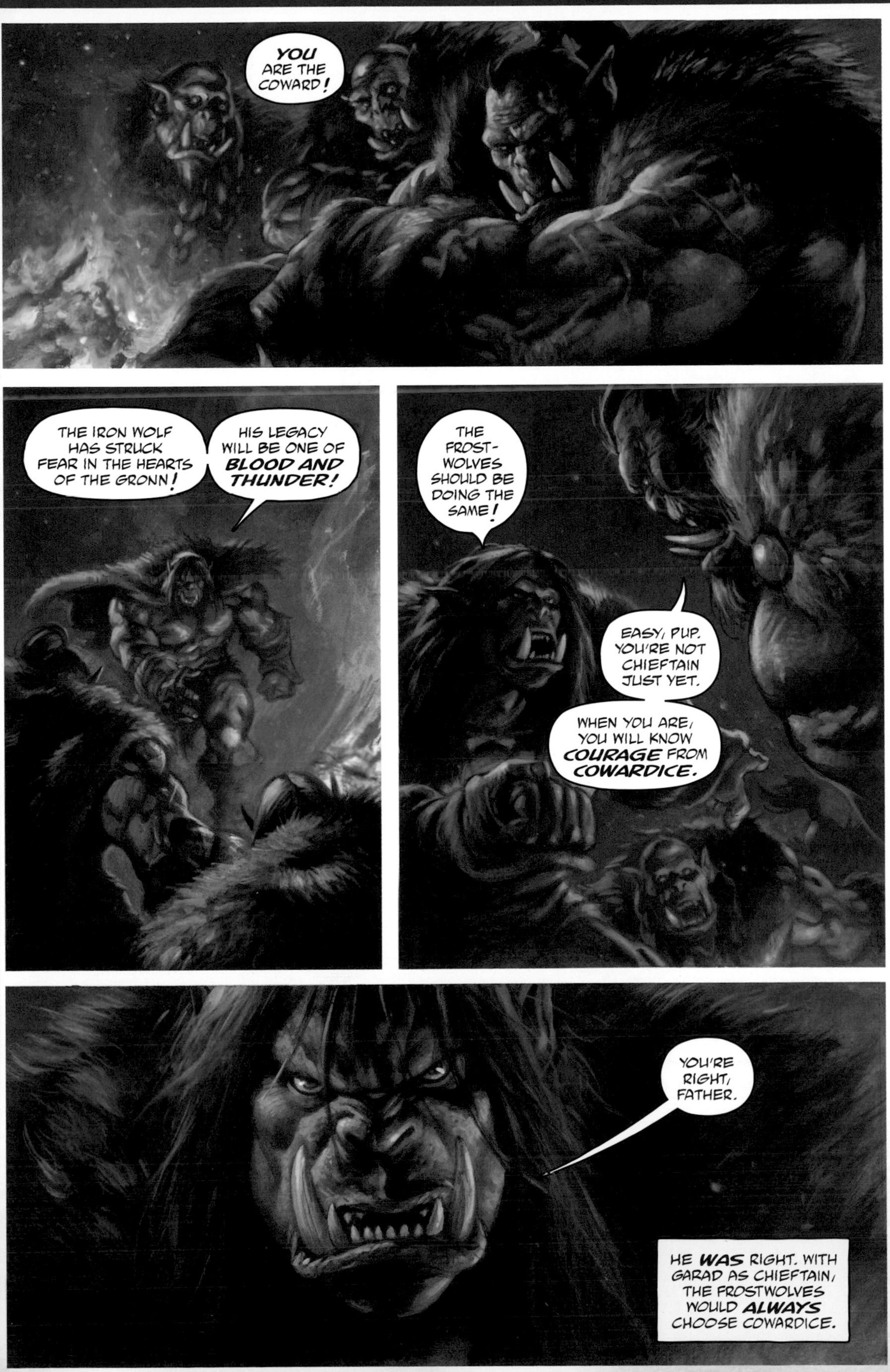
YOU ARE THE COWARD!
THE IRON WOLF HAS STRUCK FEAR IN THE HEARTS OF THE GRONN!
HIS LEGACY WILL BE ONE OF BLOOD AND THUNDER!
THE FROST-WOLVES SHOULD BE DOING THE SAME!
EASY, PUP. YOU'RE NOT CHIEFTAIN JUST YET.
WHEN YOU ARE, YOU WILL KNOW COURAGE FROM COWARDICE.
YOU'RE RIGHT, FATHER.
HE WAS RIGHT. WITH GARAD AS CHIEFTAIN, THE FROSTWOLVES WOULD ALWAYS CHOOSE COWARDICE.

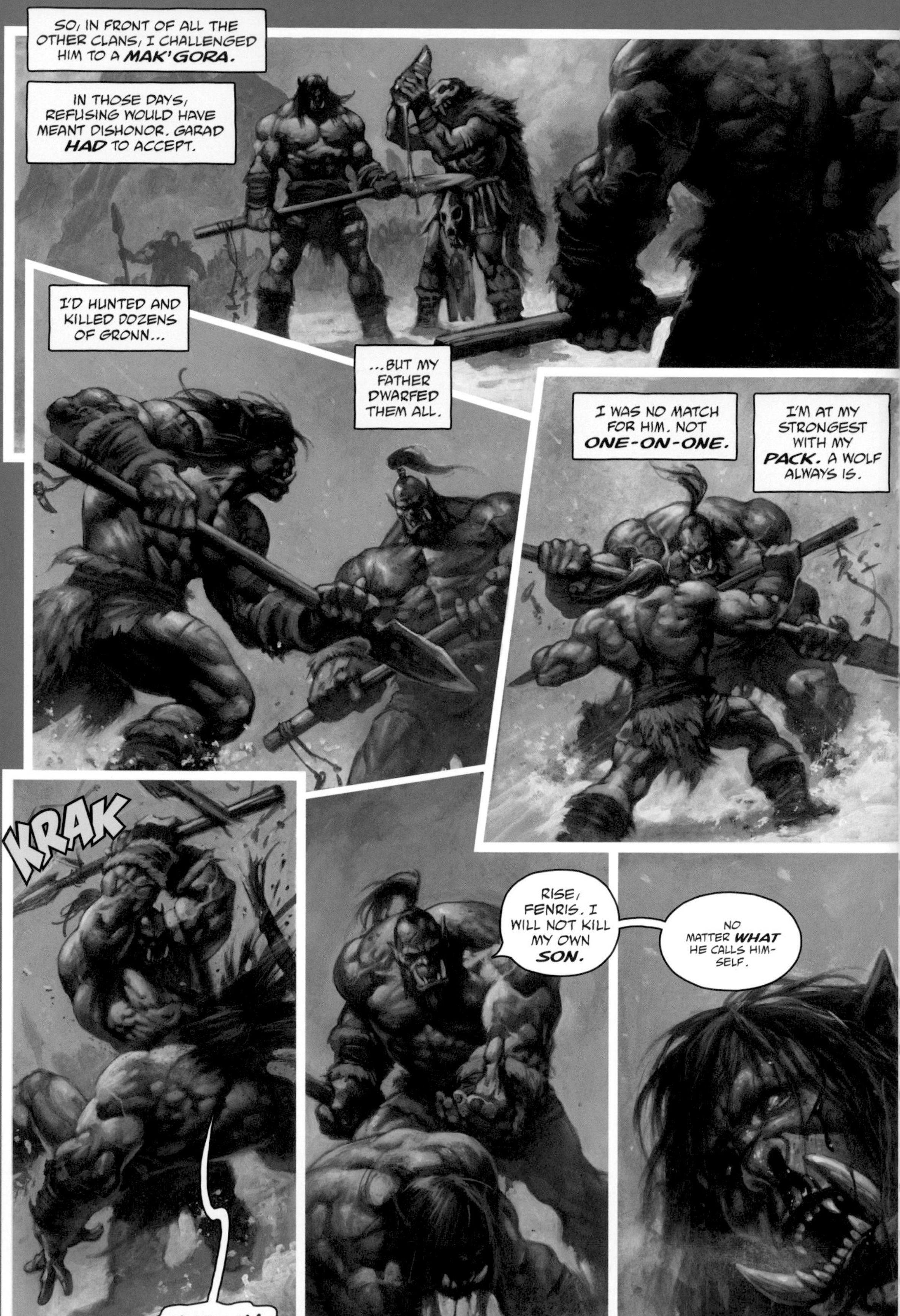
SO, IN FRONT OF ALL THE OTHER CLANS, I CHALLENGED HIM TO A MAK'GORA.
IN THOSE DAYS, REFUSING WOULD HAVE MEANT DISHONOR. GARAD HAD TO ACCEPT.
I'D HUNTED AND KILLED DOZENS OF GRONN...
...BUT MY FATHER DWARFED THEM ALL.
I WAS NO MATCH FOR HIM. NOT ONE-ON-ONE.
I'M AT MY STRONGEST WITH MY PACK. A WOLF ALWAYS IS.
KRAK
UNGGH!
RISE, FENRIS. I WILL NOT KILL MY OWN SON.
NO MATTER WHAT HE CALLS HIM-SELF.

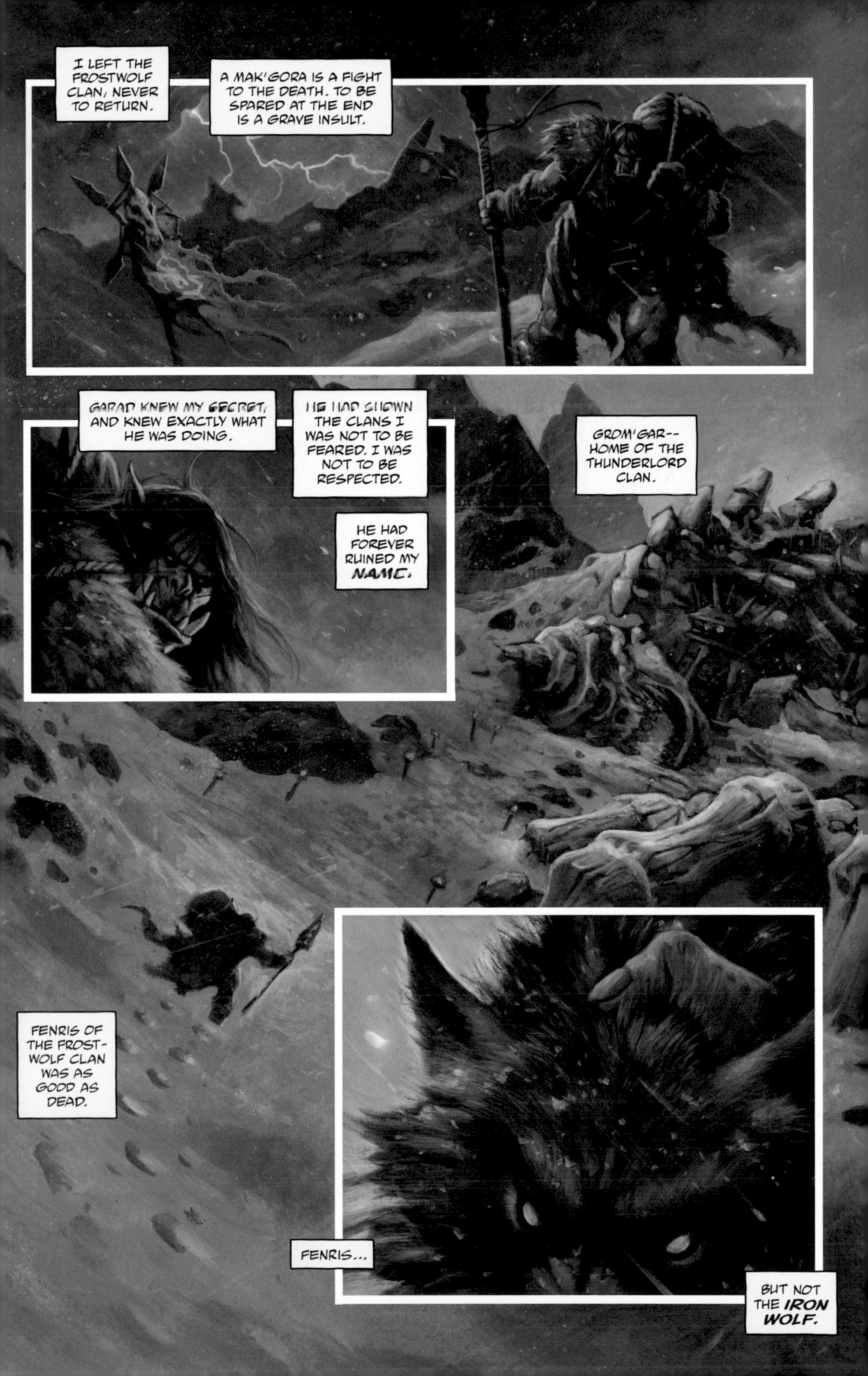
I LEFT THE FROSTWOLF CLAN, NEVER TO RETURN.
A MAK'GORA IS A FIGHT TO THE DEATH. TO BE SPARED AT THE END IS A GRAVE INSULT.
GARAD KNEW MY SECRET, AND KNEW EXACTLY WHAT HE WAS DOING.
HE HAD SHOWN THE CLANS I WAS NOT TO BE FEARED. I WAS NOT TO BE RESPECTED.
HE HAD FOREVER RUINED MY NAME.
GROM'GAR-- HOME OF THE THUNDERLORD CLAN.
FENRIS OF THE FROST-WOLF CLAN WAS AS GOOD AS DEAD.
FENRIS...
BUT NOT THE IRON WOLF.

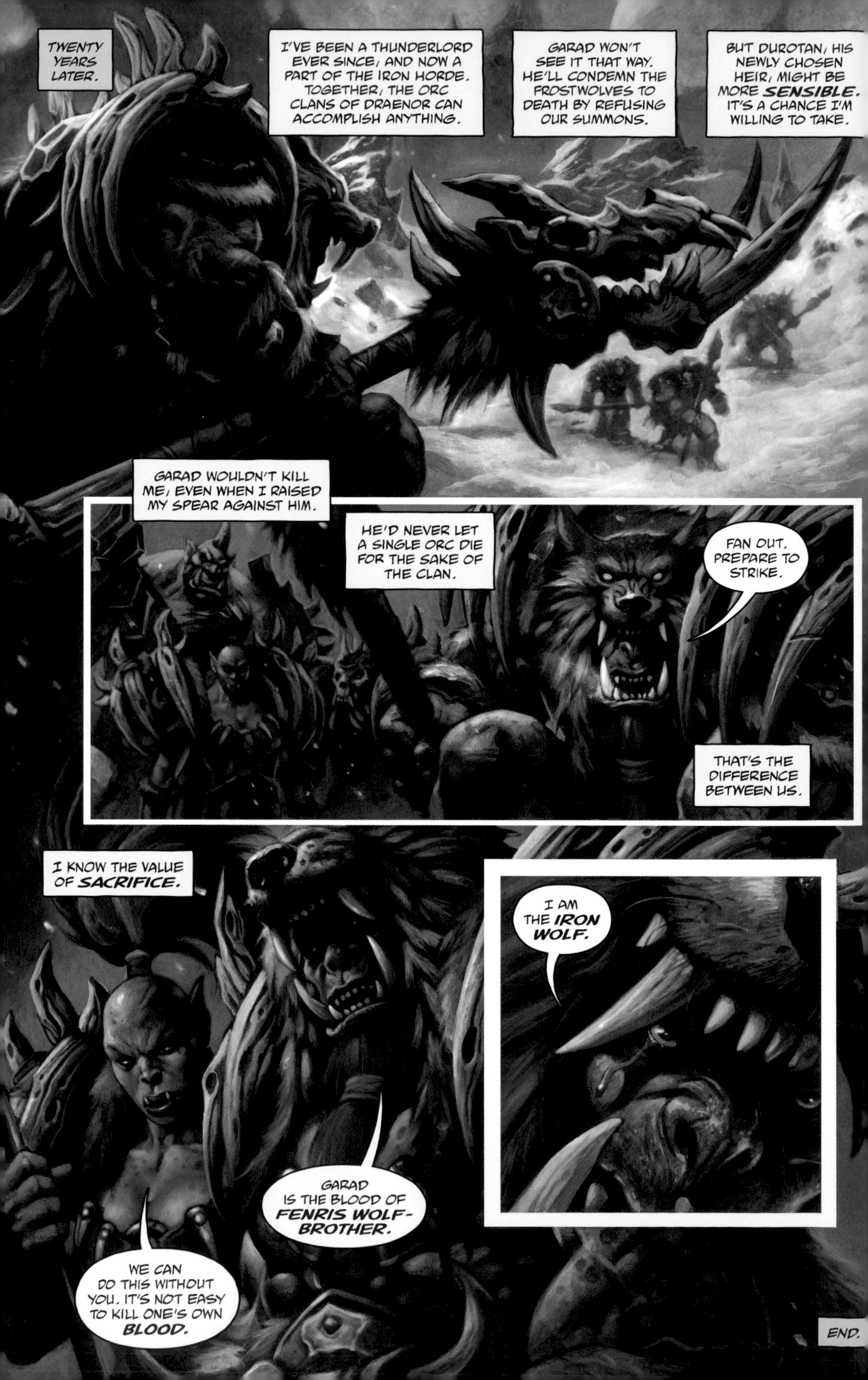
TWENTY YEARS LATER.
I'VE BEEN A THUNDERLORD EVER SINCE, AND NOW A PART OF THE IRON HORDE. TOGETHER, THE ORC CLANS OF DRAENOR CAN ACCOMPLISH ANYTHING.
GARAD WON'T SEE IT THAT WAY. HE'LL CONDEMN THE FROSTWOLVES TO DEATH BY REFUSING OUR SUMMONS.
BUT DUROTAN, HIS NEWLY CHOSEN HEIR, MIGHT BE MORE SENSIBLE. IT'S A CHANCE I'M WILLING TO TAKE.
GARAD WOULDN'T KILL ME, EVEN WHEN I RAISED MY SPEAR AGAINST HIM.
HE'D NEVER LET A SINGLE ORC DIE FOR THE SAKE OF THE CLAN.
FAN OUT. PREPARE TO STRIKE.
THAT'S THE DIFFERENCE BETWEEN US.
I KNOW THE VALUE OF SACRIFICE.
I AM THE IRON WOLF.
GARAD IS THE BLOOD OF FENRIS WOLF-BROTHER.
WE CAN DO THIS WITHOUT YOU. IT'S NOT EASY TO KILL ONE'S OWN BLOOD.
END.

World of WarCraft
LEGION

MAGNI
FAULT LINES

SCRIPT BY **MATT BURNS** | ART BY **LUDO LULLABI** |
LETTERING BY **COMICRAFT**

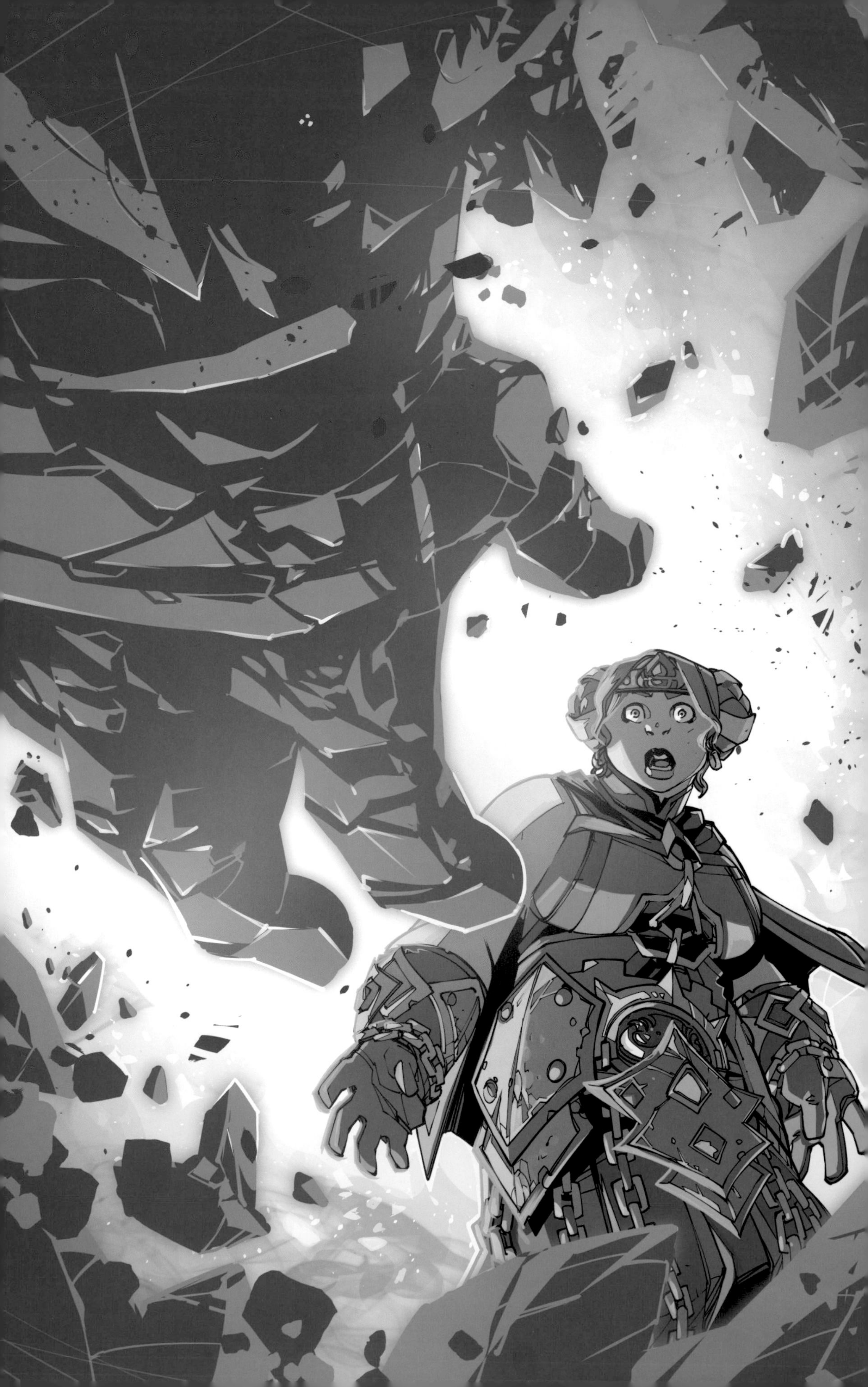

OLD IRONFORGE.

IT'S ME, FATHER. *MOIRA*, YOUR DAUGHTER.

BEEN FOUR YEARS SINCE YOU TURNED TO STONE.

MURADIN AND SOME OF THE PRIESTS HAVE REQUESTED THAT I TALK TO YOU. THEY SAY HEARING MY VOICE MIGHT WAKE YOU UP.

THE *BELOVED* DAUGHTER OF POOR KING MAGNI LAMENTING THE FATE OF HER *FAITHFUL* FATHER.

A FOOL'S ERRAND, IF YOU ASK ME. BUT A RULER MUST KEEP UP APPEARANCES.

MAYBE IT'D MAKE A DIFFERENCE IF I'D BEEN BORN A RIGHT AND PROPER HEIR. A *SON*.

IF YOU COULD SEE ME NOW, THE DAUGHTER YOU NEVER WANTED, SITTING ON YOUR THRONE...

...IT WOULD EAT YOU UP INSIDE, WOULDN'T IT?

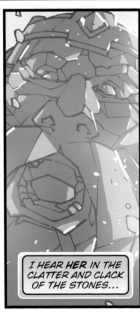

I HEAR *HER* IN THE CLATTER AND CLACK OF THE STONES...

39

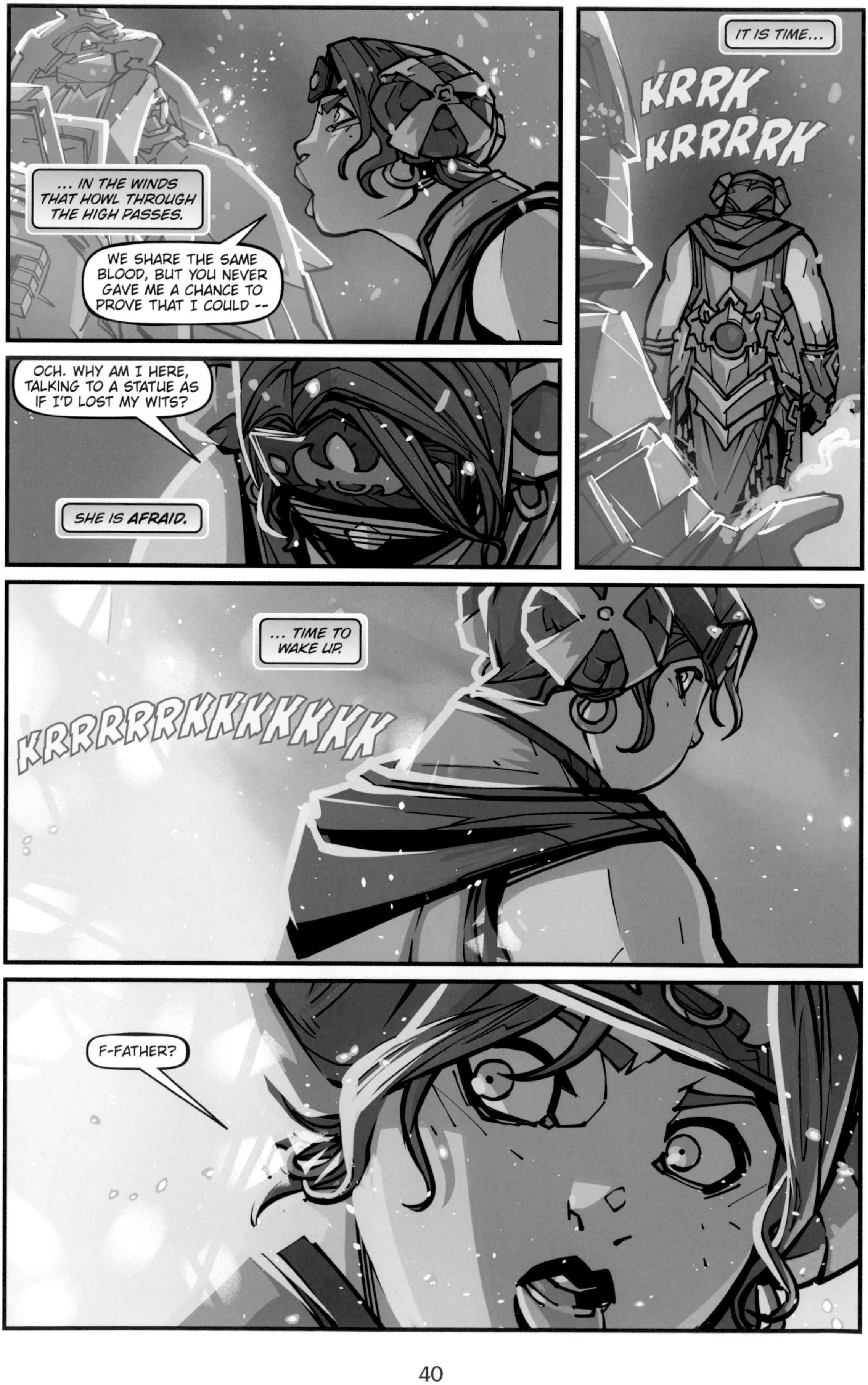

... IN THE WINDS THAT HOWL THROUGH THE HIGH PASSES.
WE SHARE THE SAME BLOOD, BUT YOU NEVER GAVE ME A CHANCE TO PROVE THAT I COULD --
OCH. WHY AM I HERE, TALKING TO A STATUE AS IF I'D LOST MY WITS?
SHE IS AFRAID.
IT IS TIME...
KRRK
KRRRRK
... TIME TO WAKE UP.
KRRRRRKKKKKKKK
F-FATHER?

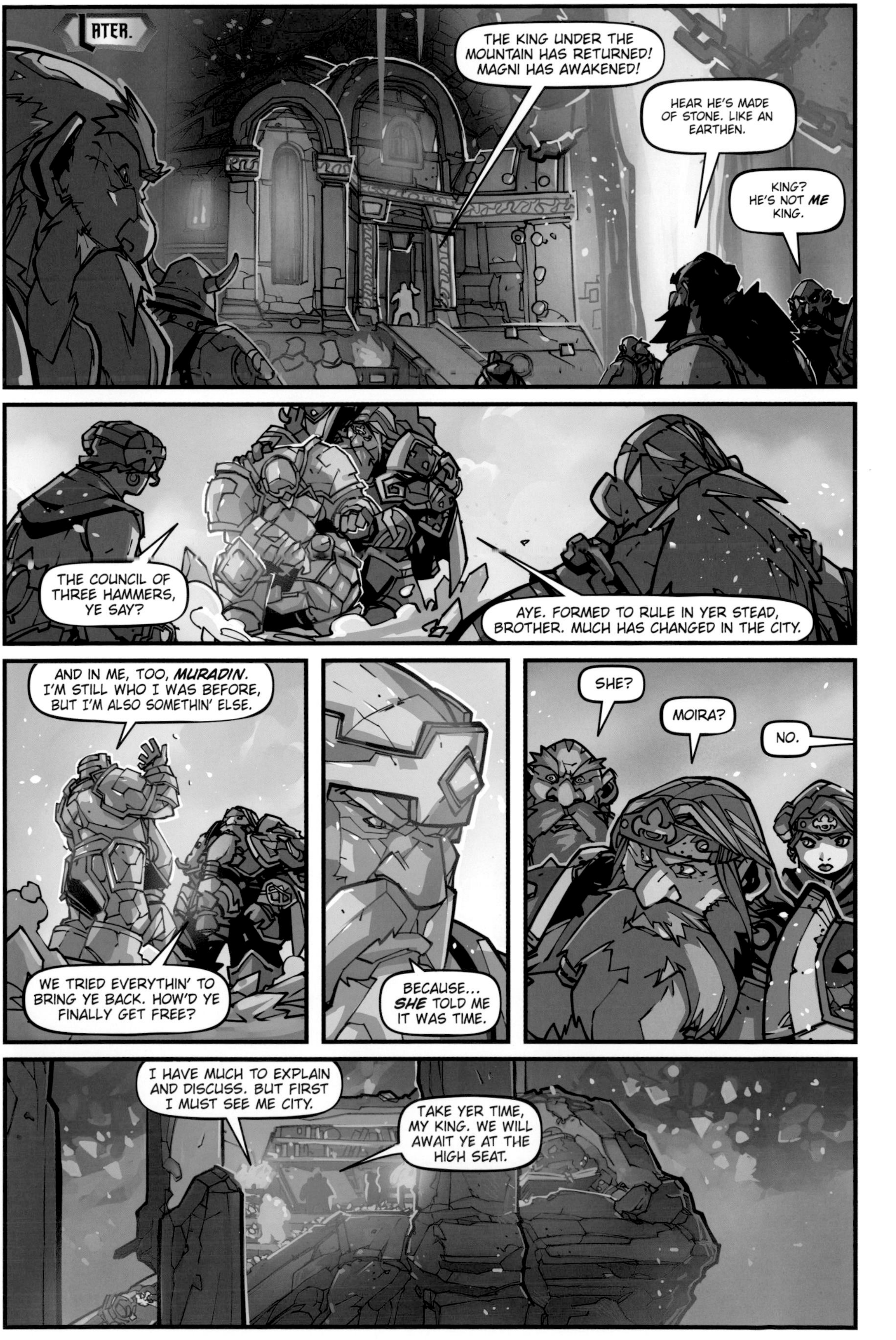
LATER.
THE KING UNDER THE MOUNTAIN HAS RETURNED! MAGNI HAS AWAKENED!
HEAR HE'S MADE OF STONE. LIKE AN EARTHEN.
KING? HE'S NOT ME KING.
THE COUNCIL OF THREE HAMMERS, YE SAY?
AYE. FORMED TO RULE IN YER STEAD, BROTHER. MUCH HAS CHANGED IN THE CITY.
AND IN ME, TOO, MURADIN. I'M STILL WHO I WAS BEFORE, BUT I'M ALSO SOMETHIN' ELSE.
WE TRIED EVERYTHIN' TO BRING YE BACK. HOW'D YE FINALLY GET FREE?
BECAUSE... SHE TOLD ME IT WAS TIME.
SHE?
MOIRA?
NO.
I HAVE MUCH TO EXPLAIN AND DISCUSS. BUT FIRST I MUST SEE ME CITY.
TAKE YER TIME, MY KING. WE WILL AWAIT YE AT THE HIGH SEAT.

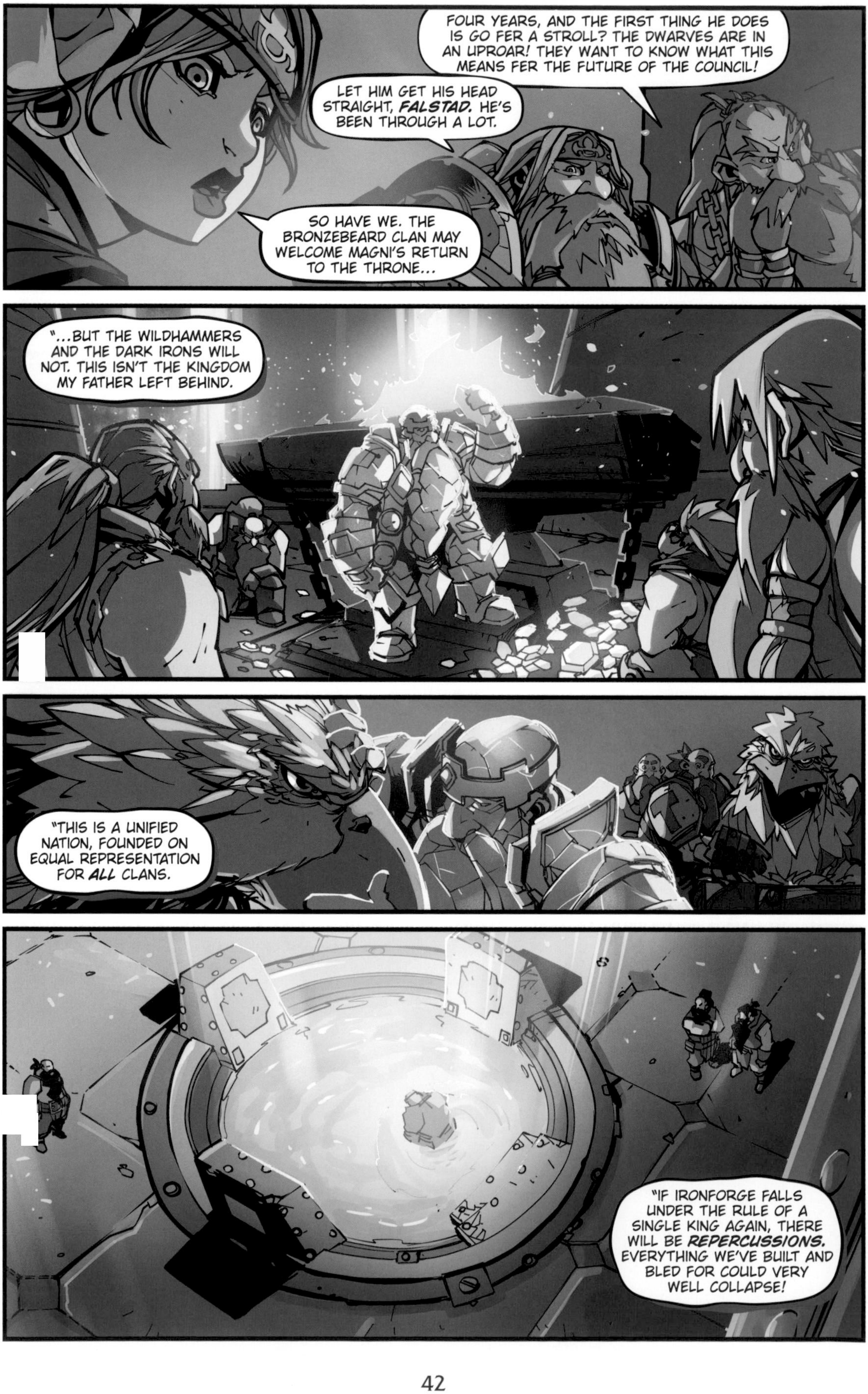
FOUR YEARS, AND THE FIRST THING HE DOES IS GO FER A STROLL? THE DWARVES ARE IN AN UPROAR! THEY WANT TO KNOW WHAT THIS MEANS FER THE FUTURE OF THE COUNCIL!
LET HIM GET HIS HEAD STRAIGHT, FALSTAD. HE'S BEEN THROUGH A LOT.
SO HAVE WE. THE BRONZEBEARD CLAN MAY WELCOME MAGNI'S RETURN TO THE THRONE...
"...BUT THE WILDHAMMERS AND THE DARK IRONS WILL NOT. THIS ISN'T THE KINGDOM MY FATHER LEFT BEHIND.
"THIS IS A UNIFIED NATION, FOUNDED ON EQUAL REPRESENTATION FOR ALL CLANS.
"IF IRONFORGE FALLS UNDER THE RULE OF A SINGLE KING AGAIN, THERE WILL BE REPERCUSSIONS. EVERYTHING WE'VE BUILT AND BLED FOR COULD VERY WELL COLLAPSE!

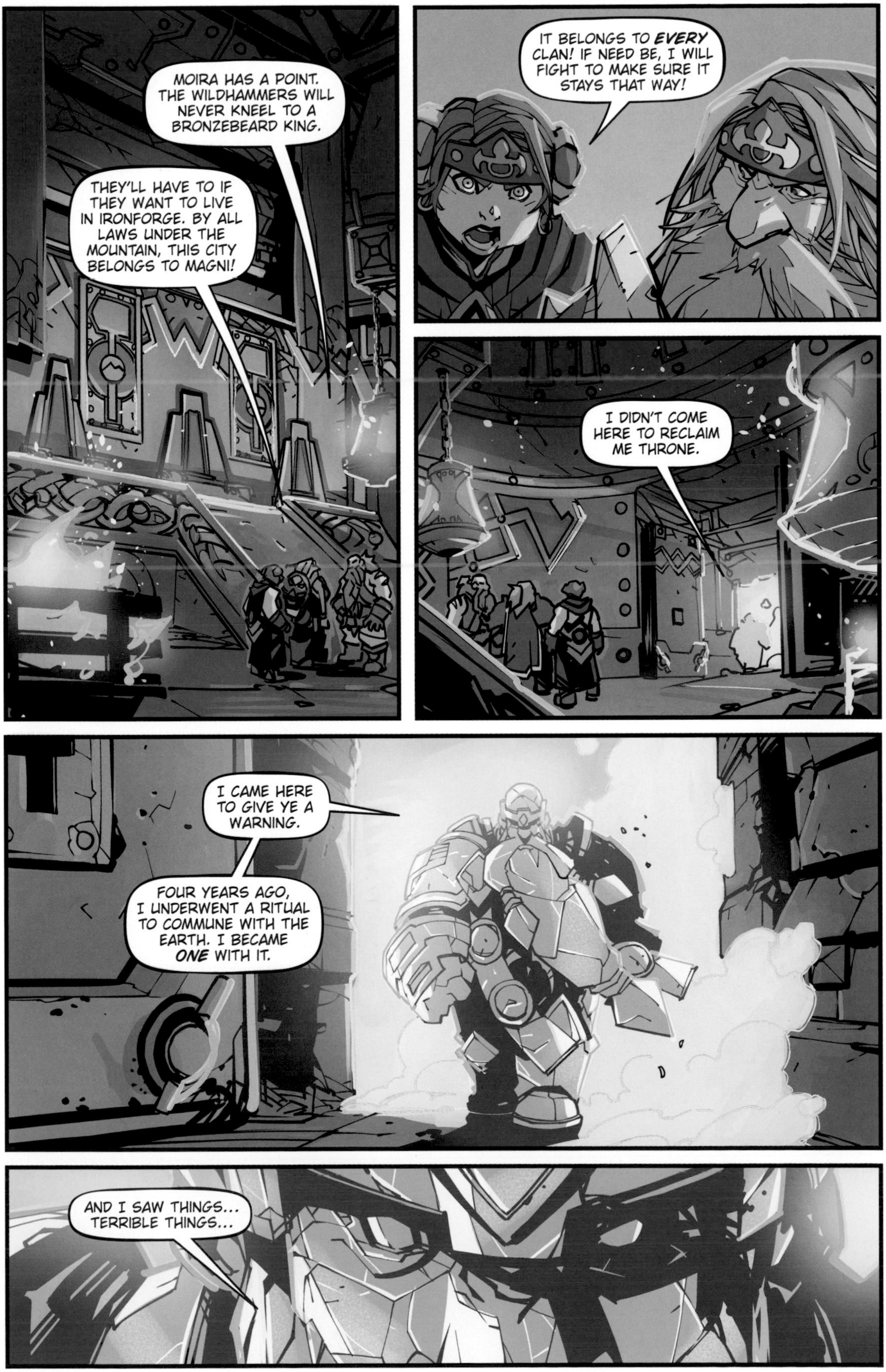
MOIRA HAS A POINT. THE WILDHAMMERS WILL NEVER KNEEL TO A BRONZEBEARD KING.
THEY'LL HAVE TO IF THEY WANT TO LIVE IN IRONFORGE. BY ALL LAWS UNDER THE MOUNTAIN, THIS CITY BELONGS TO MAGNI!
IT BELONGS TO EVERY CLAN! IF NEED BE, I WILL FIGHT TO MAKE SURE IT STAYS THAT WAY!
I DIDN'T COME HERE TO RECLAIM ME THRONE.
I CAME HERE TO GIVE YE A WARNING.
FOUR YEARS AGO, I UNDERWENT A RITUAL TO COMMUNE WITH THE EARTH. I BECAME ONE WITH IT.
AND I SAW THINGS... TERRIBLE THINGS...

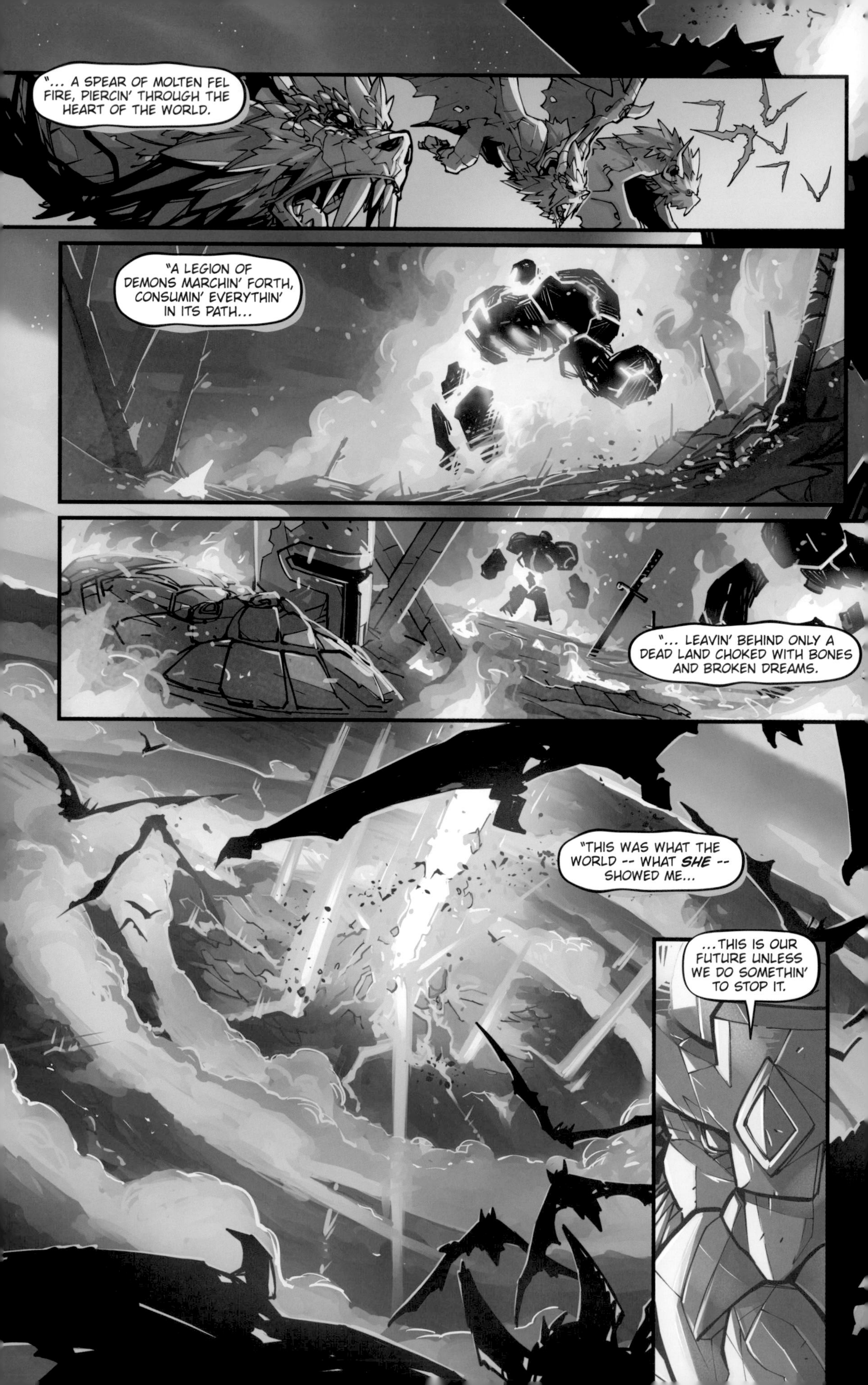
"... A SPEAR OF MOLTEN FEL FIRE, PIERCIN' THROUGH THE HEART OF THE WORLD.
"A LEGION OF DEMONS MARCHIN' FORTH, CONSUMIN' EVERYTHIN' IN ITS PATH...
"... LEAVIN' BEHIND ONLY A DEAD LAND CHOKED WITH BONES AND BROKEN DREAMS.
"THIS WAS WHAT THE WORLD -- WHAT *SHE* -- SHOWED ME...
...THIS IS OUR FUTURE UNLESS WE DO SOMETHIN' TO STOP IT.

A DEMON INVASION. BUT WHEN WILL IT HAPPEN?

I WAS ONCE A *KING*, BUT NO LONGER. I HAVE BECOME A *SERVANT* OF SOMETHIN' GREATER. YE THREE MUST PREPARE THE DWARVES FER WHAT'S TO COME.

I FEAR IT WILL BE SOON. THAT WAS WHY THE WORLD AWAKENED ME.

AND I MUST SET OUT TO WARN THE REST OF THE ALLIANCE.

YE'RE LEAVIN' ALREADY? THERE'S SO MUCH MORE I'D LIKE TO ASK YE.

TIME IS NOT ON OUR SIDE, BROTHER. EVEN NOW I SENSE *HER* TERROR RUMBLIN' UP FROM THE DEEP PLACES.

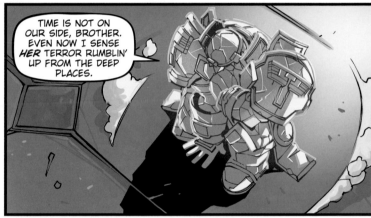

BUT THERE IS ONE LAST THING TO DO BEFORE I LEAVE.

THANK YE FER SEEIN' ME OFF, LASS. DIDN'T THINK YE WOULD AGREE TO IT.

YOU ARE MY FATHER. AND A RULER--

MUST KEEP UP APPEARANCES. THAT WAS WHY YE VISITED ME IN OLD IRONFORGE, AYE?

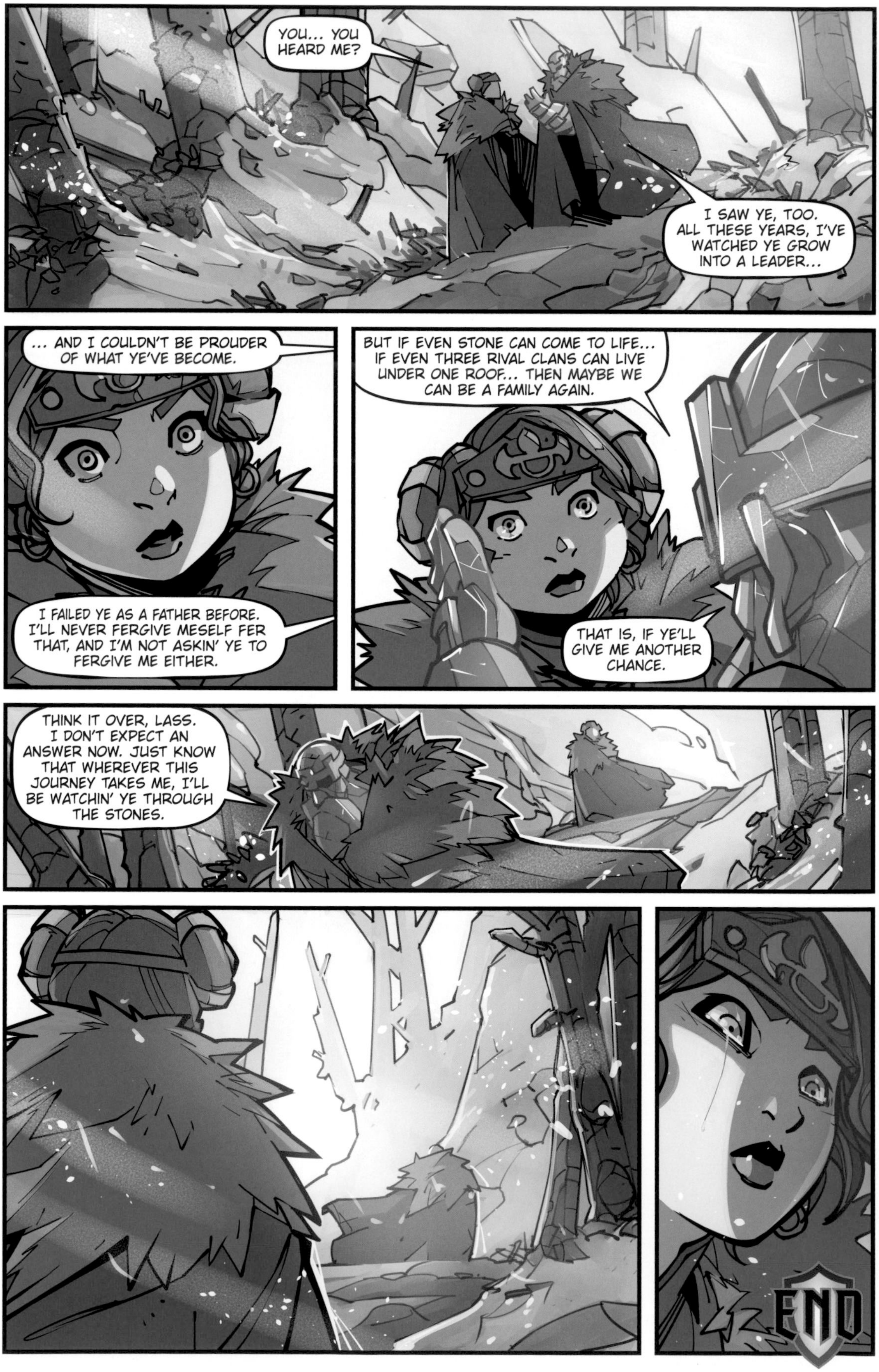
YOU... YOU HEARD ME?
I SAW YE, TOO. ALL THESE YEARS, I'VE WATCHED YE GROW INTO A LEADER...
... AND I COULDN'T BE PROUDER OF WHAT YE'VE BECOME.
I FAILED YE AS A FATHER BEFORE. I'LL NEVER FERGIVE MESELF FER THAT, AND I'M NOT ASKIN' YE TO FERGIVE ME EITHER.
BUT IF EVEN STONE CAN COME TO LIFE... IF EVEN THREE RIVAL CLANS CAN LIVE UNDER ONE ROOF... THEN MAYBE WE CAN BE A FAMILY AGAIN.
THAT IS, IF YE'LL GIVE ME ANOTHER CHANCE.
THINK IT OVER, LASS. I DON'T EXPECT AN ANSWER NOW. JUST KNOW THAT WHEREVER THIS JOURNEY TAKES ME, I'LL BE WATCHIN' YE THROUGH THE STONES.
END

WORLD OF WARCRAFT LEGION

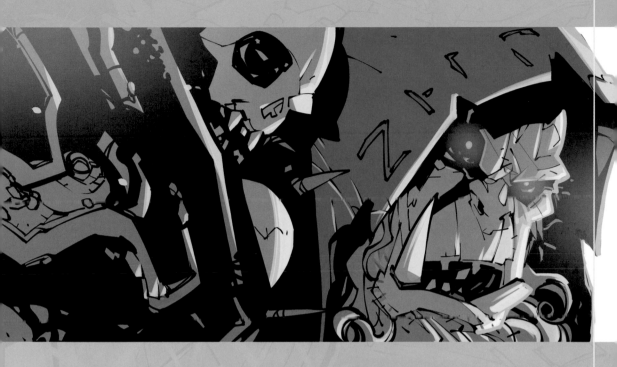

NIGHTBORNE

TWILIGHT OF SURAMAR

SCRIPT BY **MATT BURNS** | ART BY **LUDO LULLABI** |
LETTERING BY **COMICRAFT**

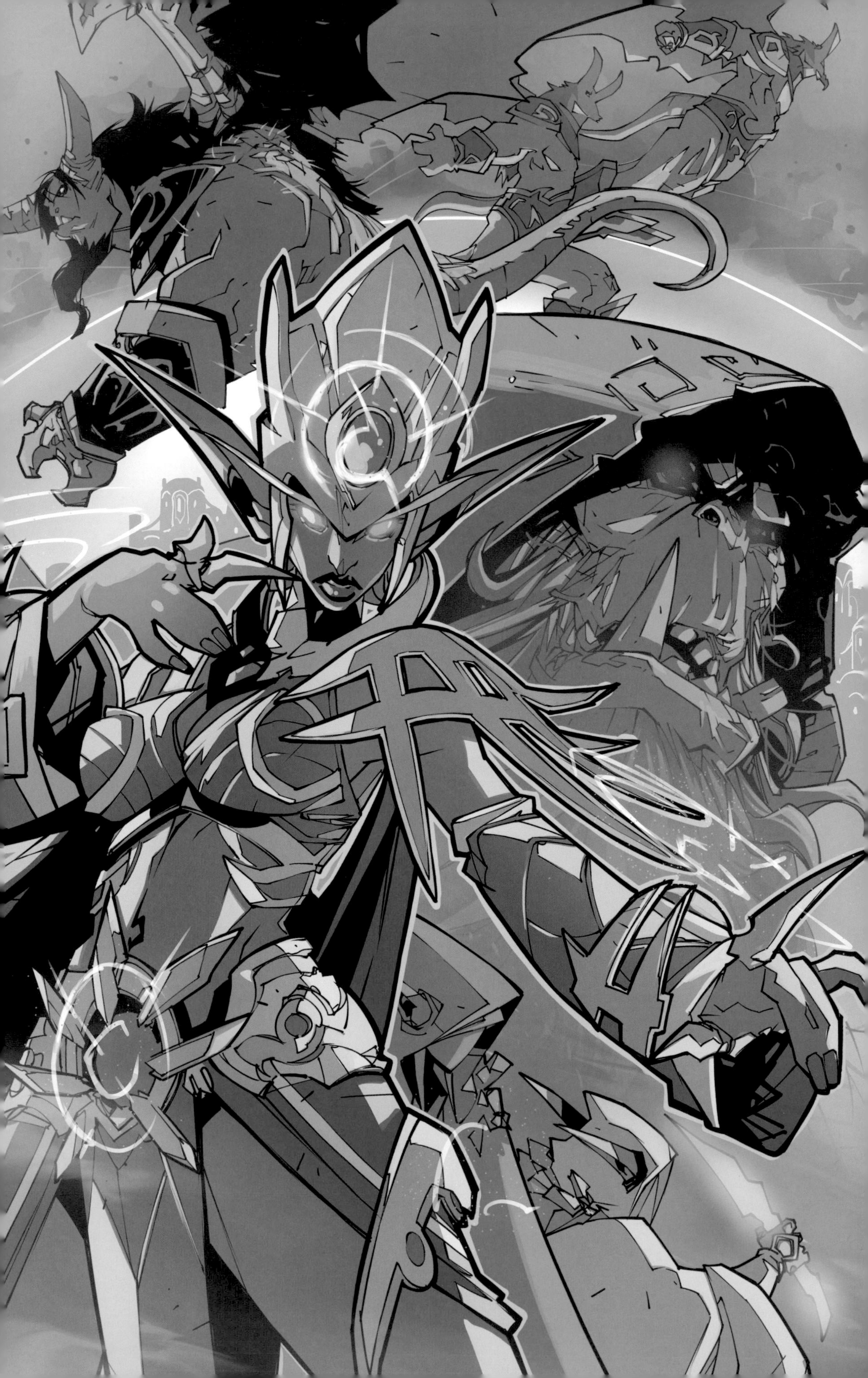

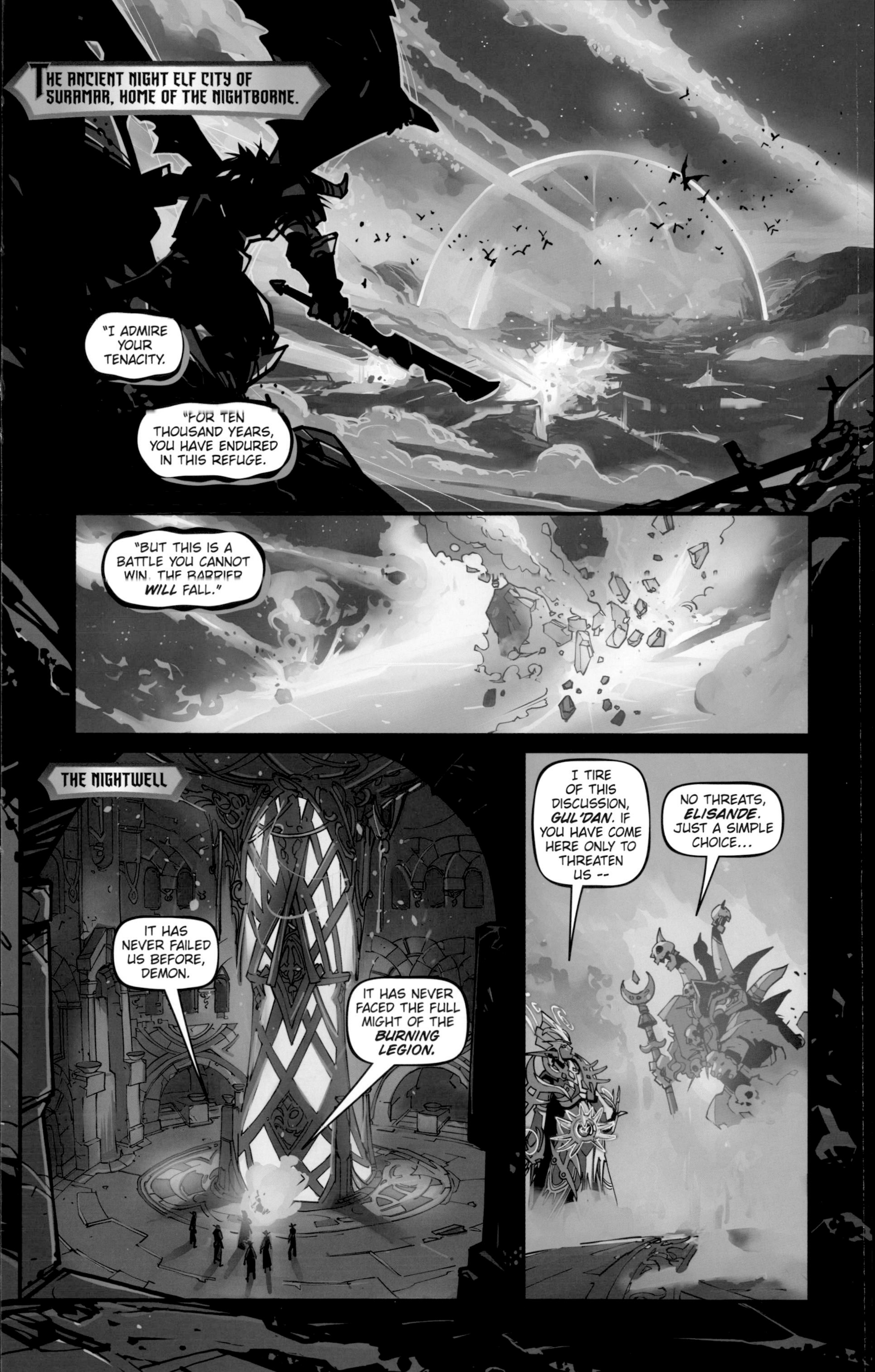
THE ANCIENT NIGHT ELF CITY OF SURAMAR, HOME OF THE NIGHTBORNE.
"I ADMIRE YOUR TENACITY.
"FOR TEN THOUSAND YEARS, YOU HAVE ENDURED IN THIS REFUGE.
"BUT THIS IS A BATTLE YOU CANNOT WIN. THE BARRIER WILL FALL."
THE NIGHTWELL
IT HAS NEVER FAILED US BEFORE, DEMON.
IT HAS NEVER FACED THE FULL MIGHT OF THE BURNING LEGION.
I TIRE OF THIS DISCUSSION, GUL'DAN. IF YOU HAVE COME HERE ONLY TO THREATEN US --
NO THREATS, ELISANDE. JUST A SIMPLE CHOICE...

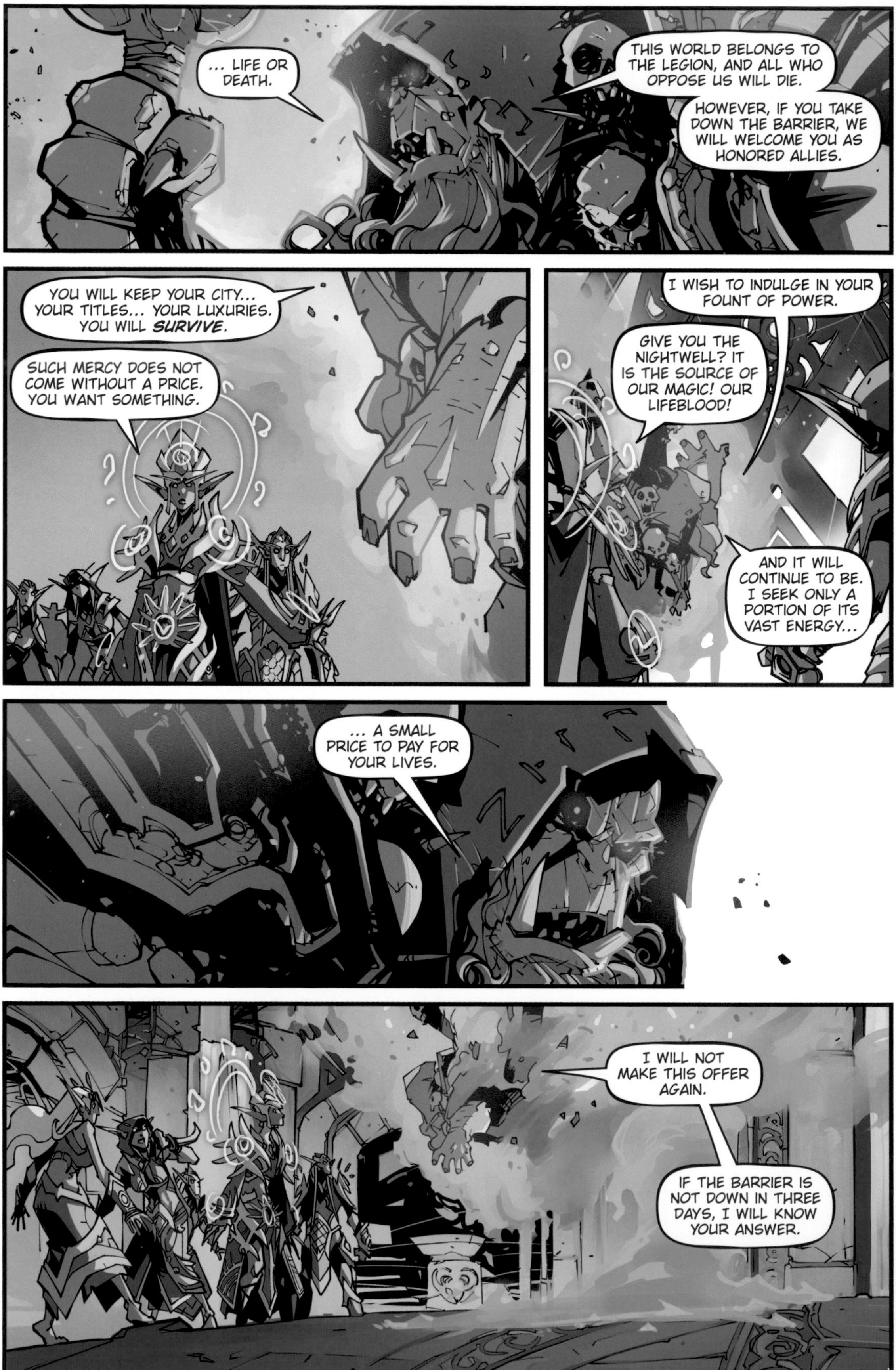
... LIFE OR DEATH.
THIS WORLD BELONGS TO THE LEGION, AND ALL WHO OPPOSE US WILL DIE.
HOWEVER, IF YOU TAKE DOWN THE BARRIER, WE WILL WELCOME YOU AS HONORED ALLIES.
YOU WILL KEEP YOUR CITY... YOUR TITLES... YOUR LUXURIES. YOU WILL *SURVIVE*.
SUCH MERCY DOES NOT COME WITHOUT A PRICE. YOU WANT SOMETHING.
I WISH TO INDULGE IN YOUR FOUNT OF POWER.
GIVE YOU THE NIGHTWELL? IT IS THE SOURCE OF OUR MAGIC! OUR LIFEBLOOD!
AND IT WILL CONTINUE TO BE. I SEEK ONLY A PORTION OF ITS VAST ENERGY...
... A SMALL PRICE TO PAY FOR YOUR LIVES.
I WILL NOT MAKE THIS OFFER AGAIN.
IF THE BARRIER IS NOT DOWN IN THREE DAYS, I WILL KNOW YOUR ANSWER.

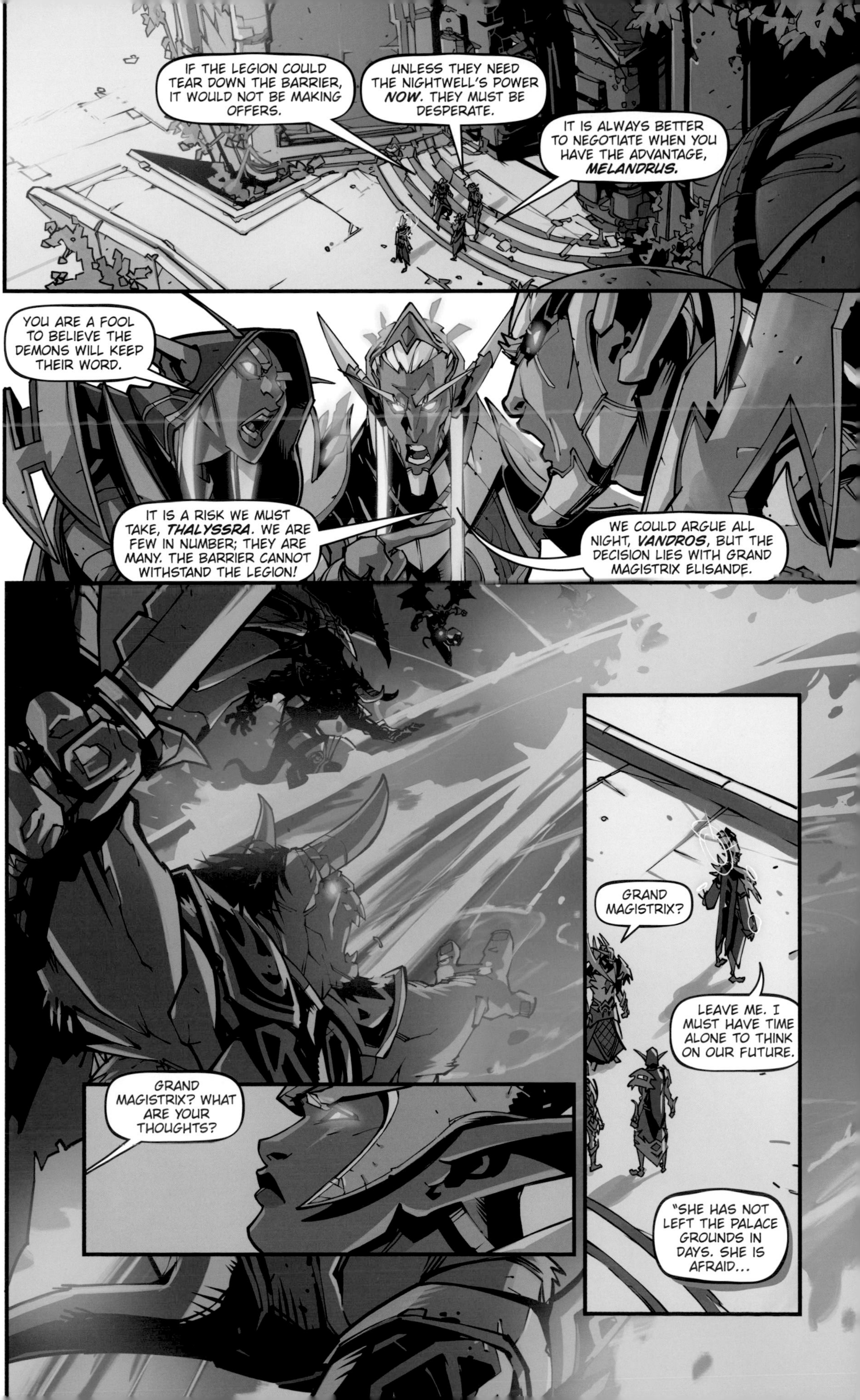
IF THE LEGION COULD TEAR DOWN THE BARRIER, IT WOULD NOT BE MAKING OFFERS.
UNLESS THEY NEED THE NIGHTWELL'S POWER *NOW*. THEY MUST BE DESPERATE.
IT IS ALWAYS BETTER TO NEGOTIATE WHEN YOU HAVE THE ADVANTAGE, ***MELANDRUS.***
YOU ARE A FOOL TO BELIEVE THE DEMONS WILL KEEP THEIR WORD.
IT IS A RISK WE MUST TAKE, ***THALYSSRA***. WE ARE FEW IN NUMBER; THEY ARE MANY. THE BARRIER CANNOT WITHSTAND THE LEGION!
WE COULD ARGUE ALL NIGHT, ***VANDROS***, BUT THE DECISION LIES WITH GRAND MAGISTRIX ELISANDE.
GRAND MAGISTRIX? WHAT ARE YOUR THOUGHTS?
GRAND MAGISTRIX?
LEAVE ME. I MUST HAVE TIME ALONE TO THINK ON OUR FUTURE.
"SHE HAS NOT LEFT THE PALACE GROUNDS IN DAYS. SHE IS AFRAID...

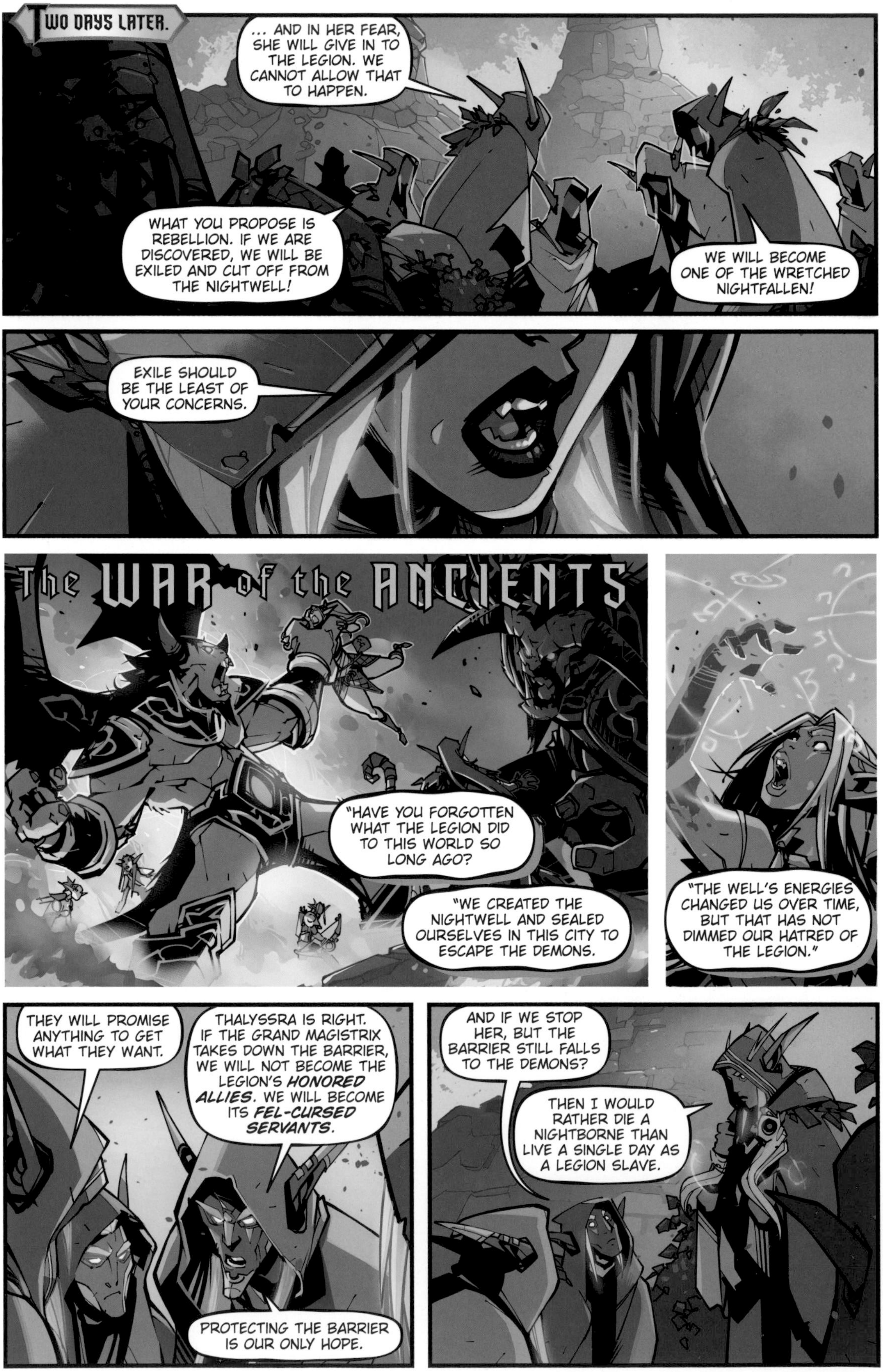
TWO DAYS LATER.
... AND IN HER FEAR, SHE WILL GIVE IN TO THE LEGION. WE CANNOT ALLOW THAT TO HAPPEN.
WHAT YOU PROPOSE IS REBELLION. IF WE ARE DISCOVERED, WE WILL BE EXILED AND CUT OFF FROM THE NIGHTWELL!
WE WILL BECOME ONE OF THE WRETCHED NIGHTFALLEN!
EXILE SHOULD BE THE LEAST OF YOUR CONCERNS.
The WAR of the ANCIENTS
"HAVE YOU FORGOTTEN WHAT THE LEGION DID TO THIS WORLD SO LONG AGO?
"WE CREATED THE NIGHTWELL AND SEALED OURSELVES IN THIS CITY TO ESCAPE THE DEMONS.
"THE WELL'S ENERGIES CHANGED US OVER TIME, BUT THAT HAS NOT DIMMED OUR HATRED OF THE LEGION."
THEY WILL PROMISE ANYTHING TO GET WHAT THEY WANT.
THALYSSRA IS RIGHT. IF THE GRAND MAGISTRIX TAKES DOWN THE BARRIER, WE WILL NOT BECOME THE LEGION'S ***HONORED ALLIES***. WE WILL BECOME ITS ***FEL-CURSED SERVANTS***.
PROTECTING THE BARRIER IS OUR ONLY HOPE.
AND IF WE STOP HER, BUT THE BARRIER STILL FALLS TO THE DEMONS?
THEN I WOULD RATHER DIE A NIGHTBORNE THAN LIVE A SINGLE DAY AS A LEGION SLAVE.

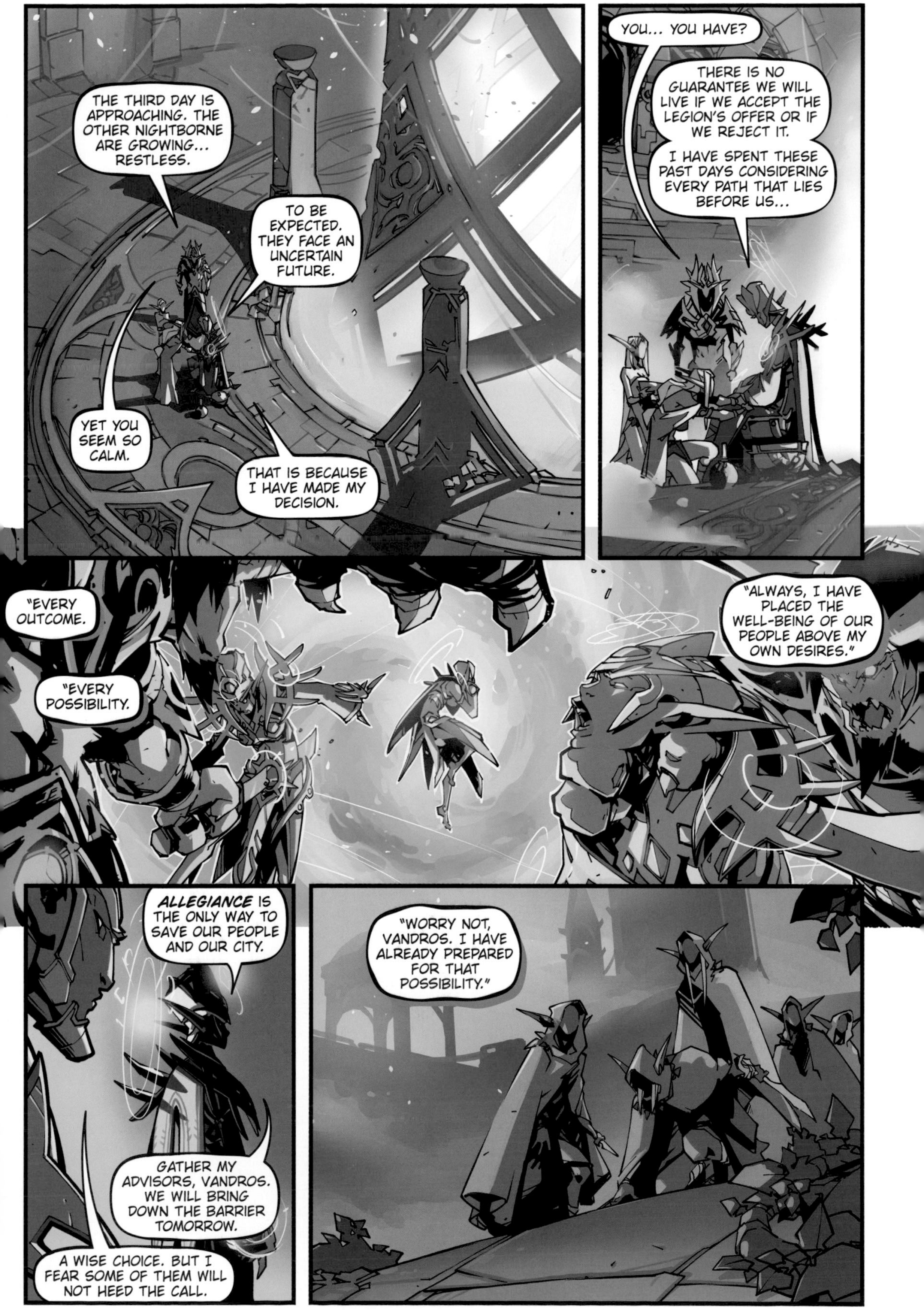
THE THIRD DAY IS APPROACHING. THE OTHER NIGHTBORNE ARE GROWING... RESTLESS.
TO BE EXPECTED. THEY FACE AN UNCERTAIN FUTURE.
YET YOU SEEM SO CALM.
THAT IS BECAUSE I HAVE MADE MY DECISION.
YOU... YOU HAVE?
THERE IS NO GUARANTEE WE WILL LIVE IF WE ACCEPT THE LEGION'S OFFER OR IF WE REJECT IT.
I HAVE SPENT THESE PAST DAYS CONSIDERING EVERY PATH THAT LIES BEFORE US...
"EVERY OUTCOME.
"EVERY POSSIBILITY.
"ALWAYS, I HAVE PLACED THE WELL-BEING OF OUR PEOPLE ABOVE MY OWN DESIRES."
ALLEGIANCE IS THE ONLY WAY TO SAVE OUR PEOPLE AND OUR CITY.
GATHER MY ADVISORS, VANDROS. WE WILL BRING DOWN THE BARRIER TOMORROW.
A WISE CHOICE. BUT I FEAR SOME OF THEM WILL NOT HEED THE CALL.
"WORRY NOT, VANDROS. I HAVE ALREADY PREPARED FOR THAT POSSIBILITY."

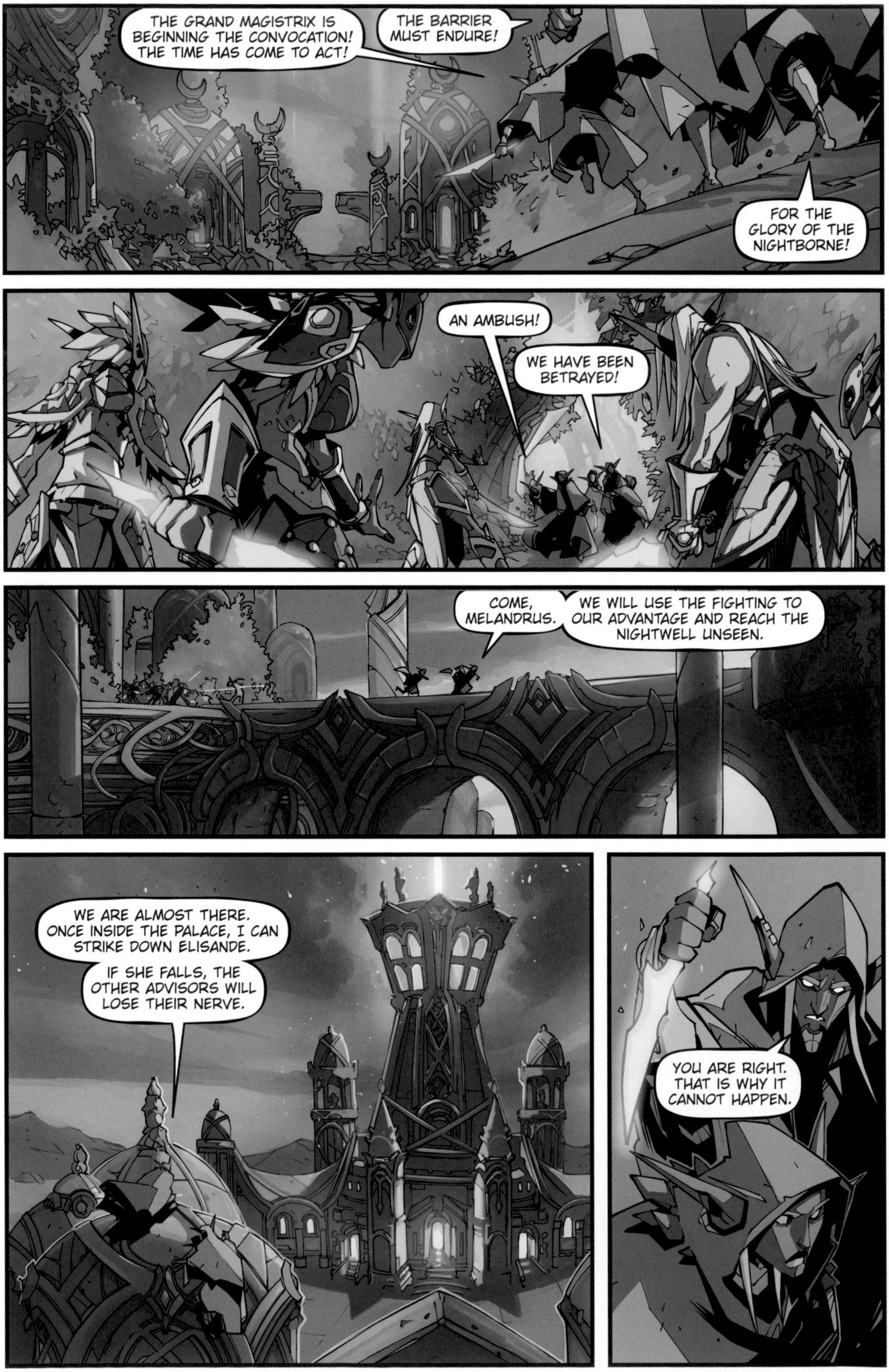
THE GRAND MAGISTRIX IS BEGINNING THE CONVOCATION! THE TIME HAS COME TO ACT!
THE BARRIER MUST ENDURE!
FOR THE GLORY OF THE NIGHTBORNE!
AN AMBUSH!
WE HAVE BEEN BETRAYED!
COME, MELANDRUS.
WE WILL USE THE FIGHTING TO OUR ADVANTAGE AND REACH THE NIGHTWELL UNSEEN.
WE ARE ALMOST THERE. ONCE INSIDE THE PALACE, I CAN STRIKE DOWN ELISANDE.
IF SHE FALLS, THE OTHER ADVISORS WILL LOSE THEIR NERVE.
YOU ARE RIGHT. THAT IS WHY IT CANNOT HAPPEN.

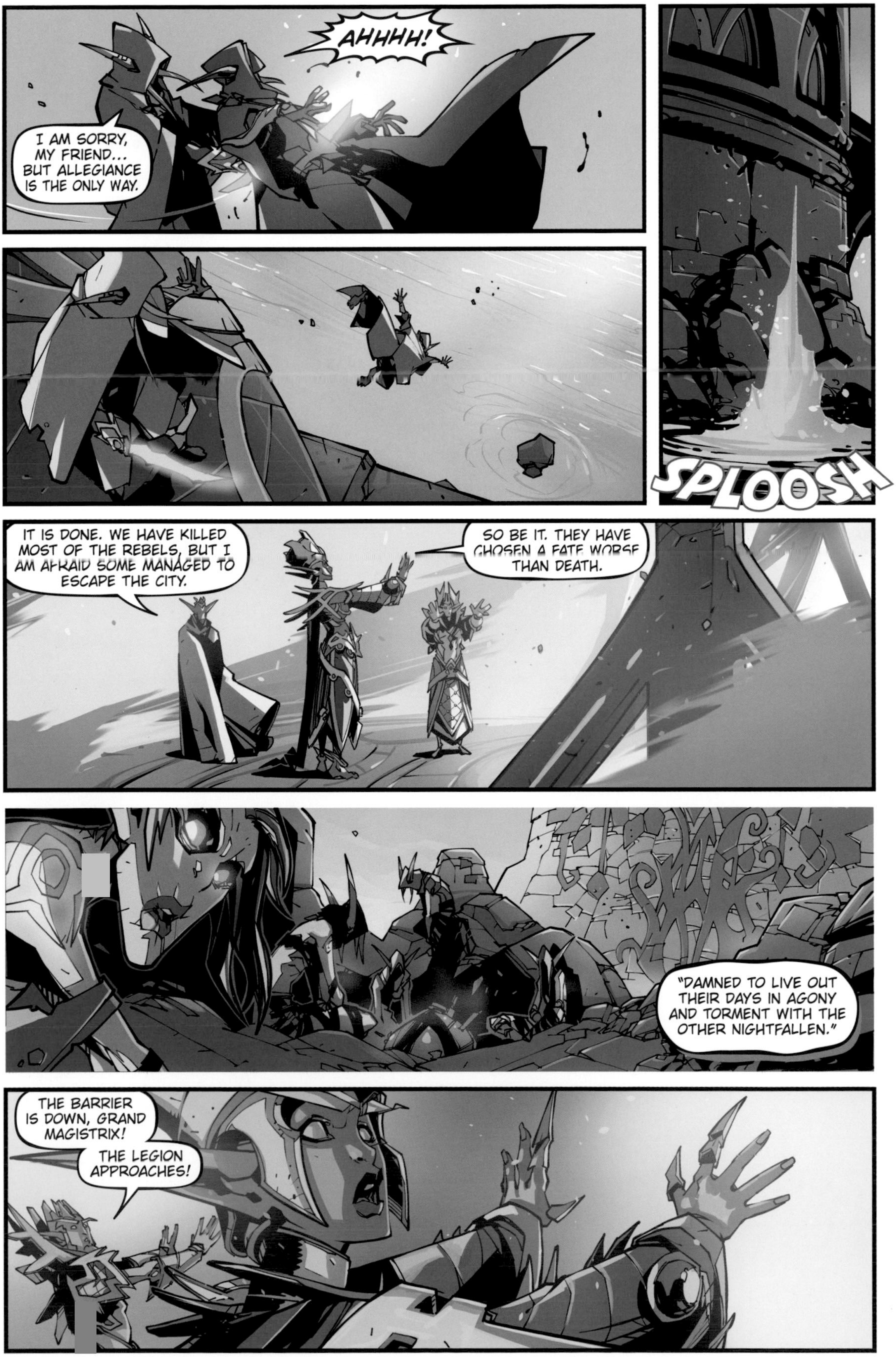
AHHHH!
I AM SORRY, MY FRIEND... BUT ALLEGIANCE IS THE ONLY WAY.
SPLOOSH
IT IS DONE. WE HAVE KILLED MOST OF THE REBELS, BUT I AM AFRAID SOME MANAGED TO ESCAPE THE CITY.
SO BE IT. THEY HAVE CHOSEN A FATE WORSE THAN DEATH.
"DAMNED TO LIVE OUT THEIR DAYS IN AGONY AND TORMENT WITH THE OTHER NIGHTFALLEN."
THE BARRIER IS DOWN, GRAND MAGISTRIX!
THE LEGION APPROACHES!

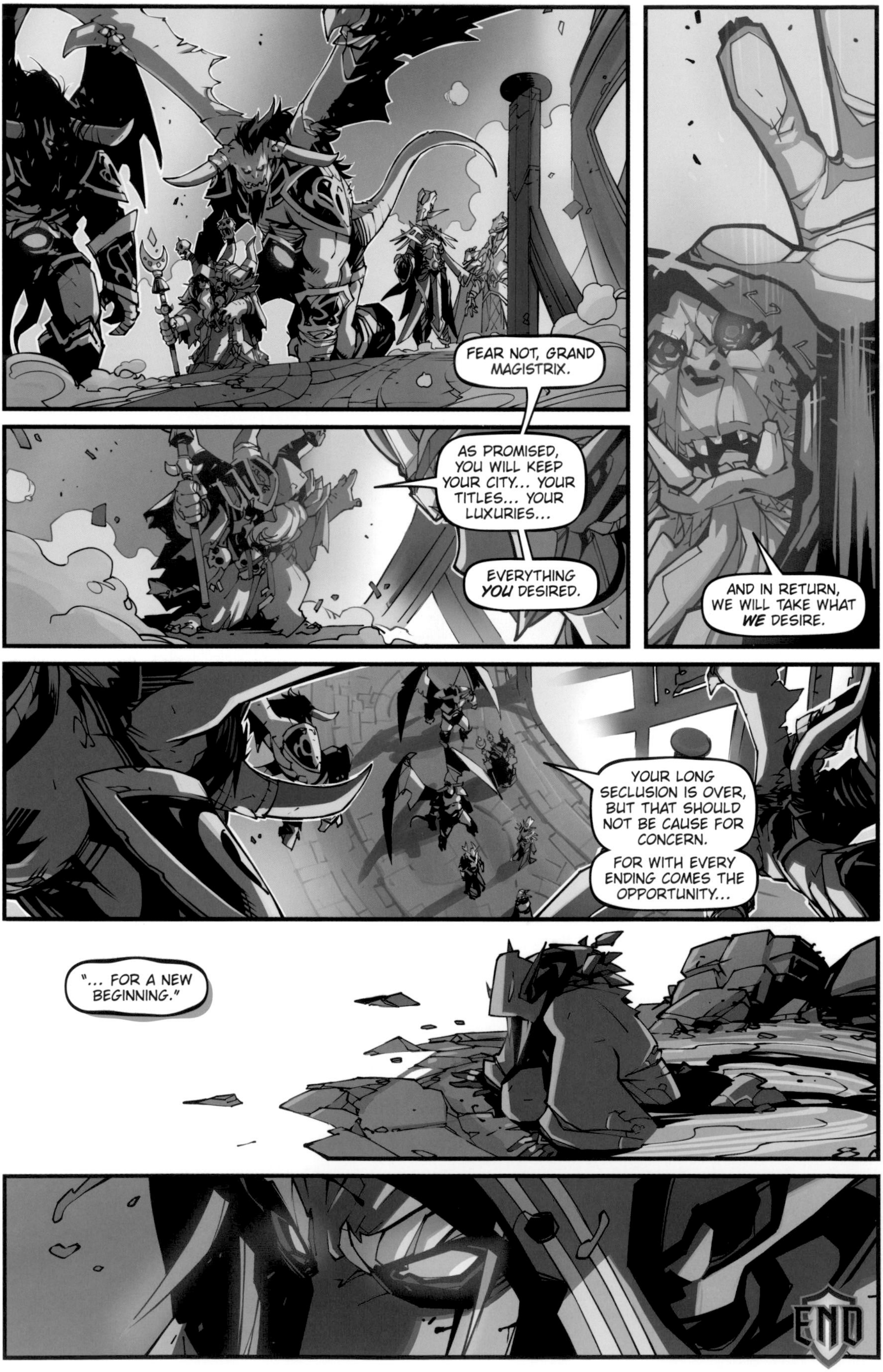
FEAR NOT, GRAND MAGISTRIX.
AS PROMISED, YOU WILL KEEP YOUR CITY... YOUR TITLES... YOUR LUXURIES...
EVERYTHING *YOU* DESIRED.
AND IN RETURN, WE WILL TAKE WHAT *WE* DESIRE.
YOUR LONG SECLUSION IS OVER, BUT THAT SHOULD NOT BE CAUSE FOR CONCERN.
FOR WITH EVERY ENDING COMES THE OPPORTUNITY...
"... FOR A NEW BEGINNING."
END

HIGHMOUNTAIN
A MOUNTAIN DIVIDED

SCRIPT BY **ROBERT BROOKS** | ART BY **DAVID KEGG** |
LETTERING BY **COMICRAFT**

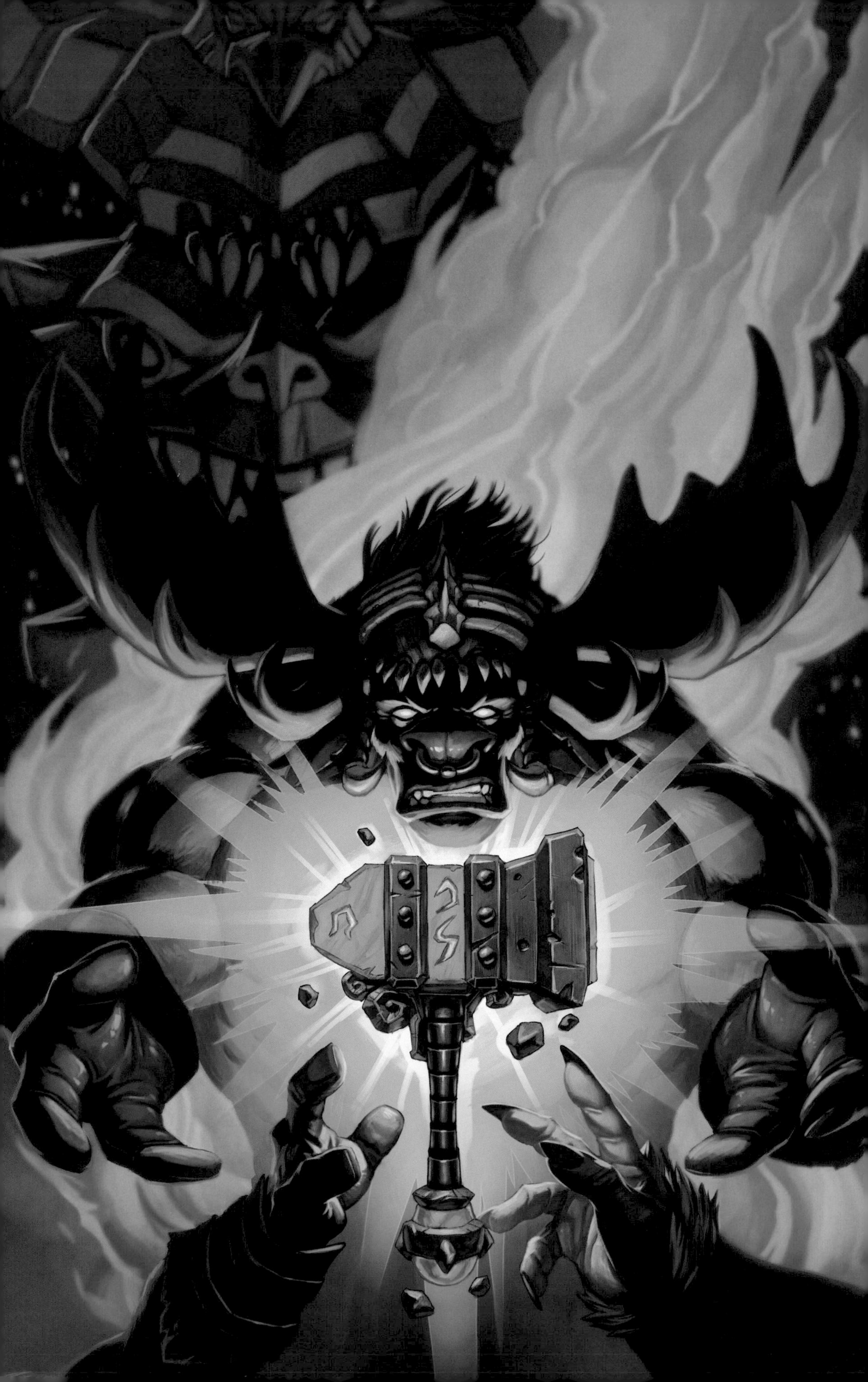

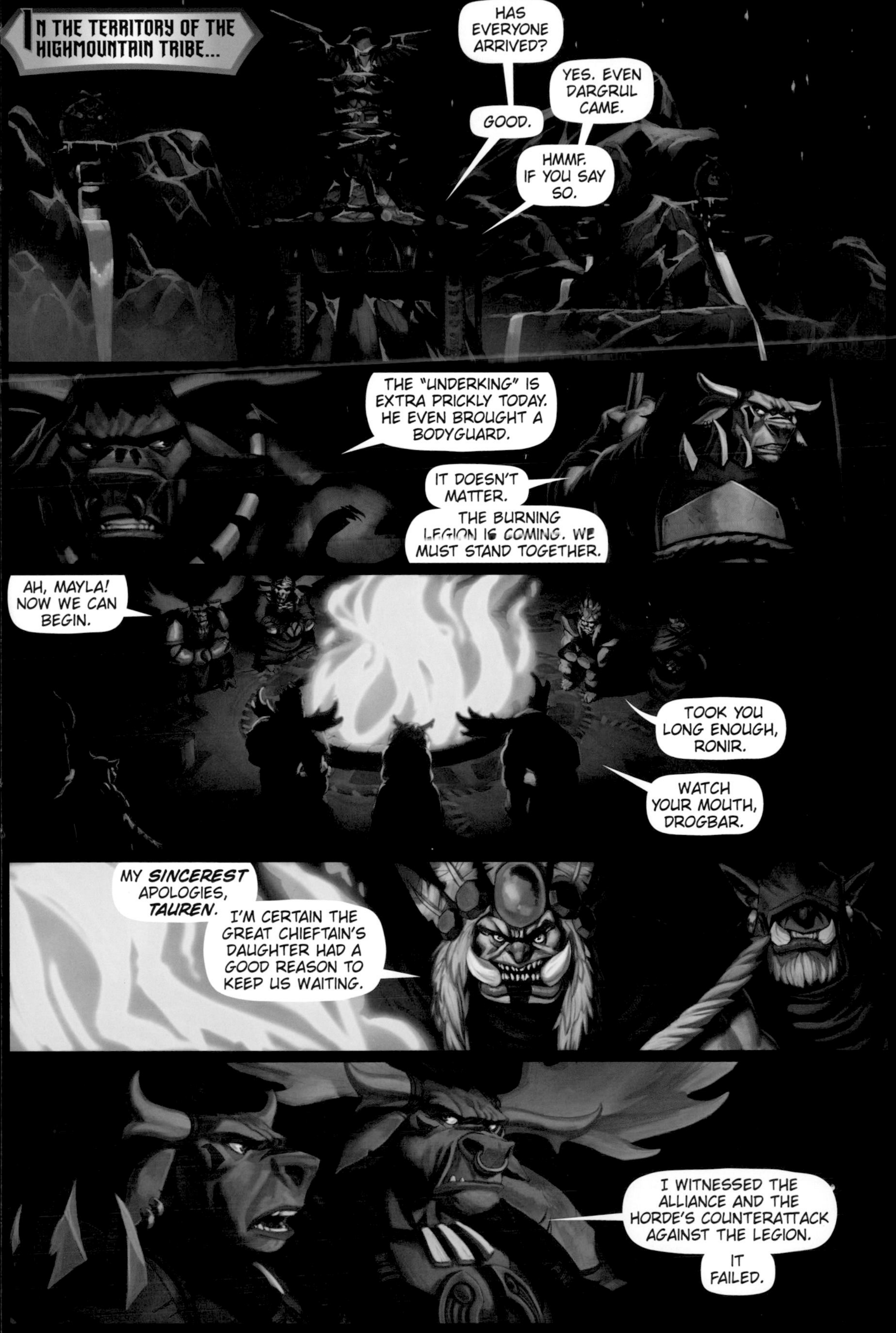
IN THE TERRITORY OF THE HIGHMOUNTAIN TRIBE...
HAS EVERYONE ARRIVED?
YES. EVEN DARGRUL CAME.
GOOD.
HMMF. IF YOU SAY SO.
THE "UNDERKING" IS EXTRA PRICKLY TODAY. HE EVEN BROUGHT A BODYGUARD.
IT DOESN'T MATTER.
THE BURNING LEGION IS COMING. WE MUST STAND TOGETHER.
AH, MAYLA! NOW WE CAN BEGIN.
TOOK YOU LONG ENOUGH, RONIR.
WATCH YOUR MOUTH, DROGBAR.
MY SINCEREST APOLOGIES, TAUREN.
I'M CERTAIN THE GREAT CHIEFTAIN'S DAUGHTER HAD A GOOD REASON TO KEEP US WAITING.
I WITNESSED THE ALLIANCE AND THE HORDE'S COUNTERATTACK AGAINST THE LEGION.
IT FAILED.

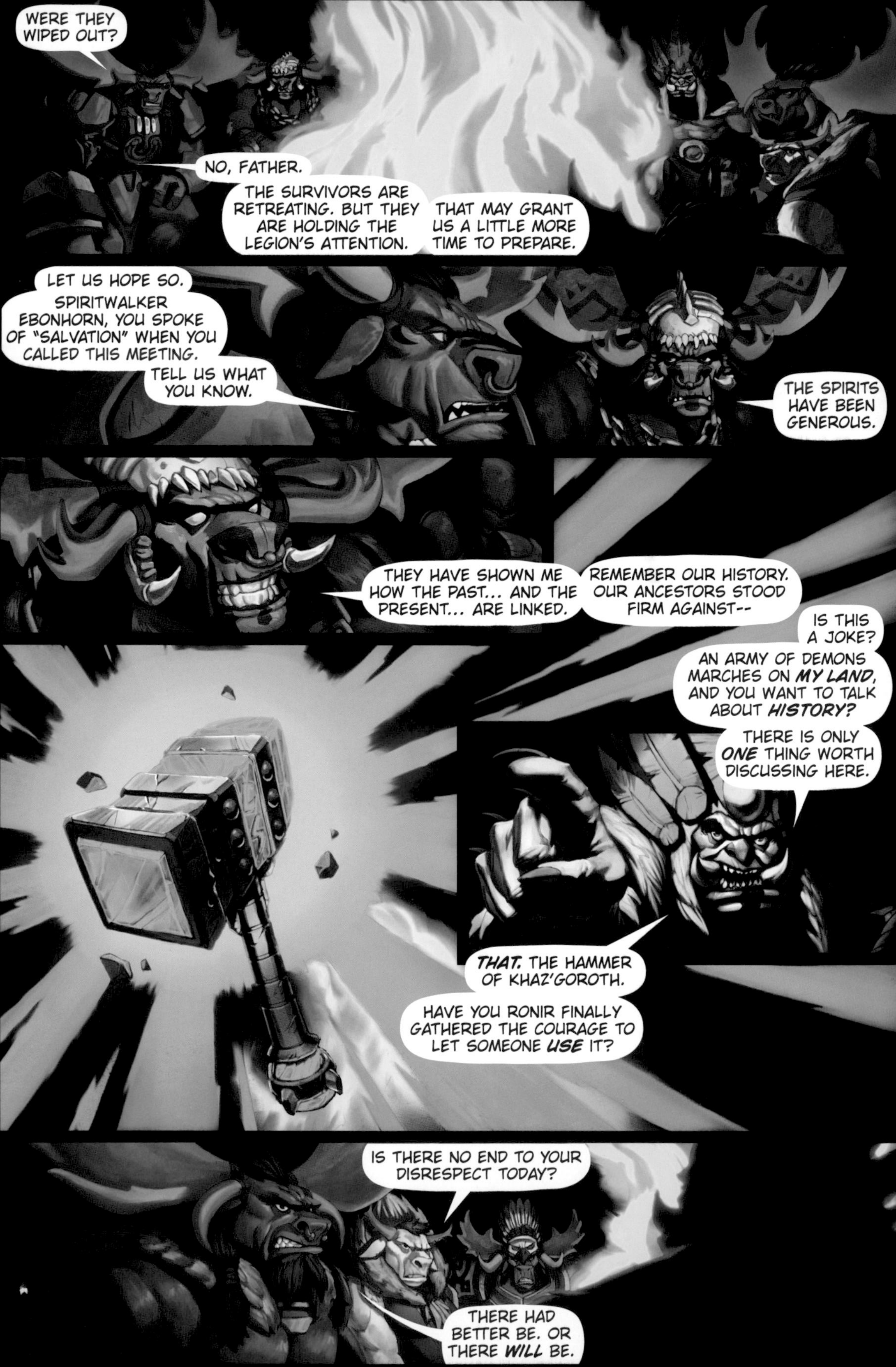
WERE THEY WIPED OUT?
NO, FATHER.
THE SURVIVORS ARE RETREATING. BUT THEY ARE HOLDING THE LEGION'S ATTENTION.
THAT MAY GRANT US A LITTLE MORE TIME TO PREPARE.
LET US HOPE SO.
SPIRITWALKER EBONHORN, YOU SPOKE OF "SALVATION" WHEN YOU CALLED THIS MEETING.
TELL US WHAT YOU KNOW.
THE SPIRITS HAVE BEEN GENEROUS.
THEY HAVE SHOWN ME HOW THE PAST... AND THE PRESENT... ARE LINKED.
REMEMBER OUR HISTORY. OUR ANCESTORS STOOD FIRM AGAINST--
IS THIS A JOKE?
AN ARMY OF DEMONS MARCHES ON *MY LAND*, AND YOU WANT TO TALK ABOUT *HISTORY?*
THERE IS ONLY *ONE* THING WORTH DISCUSSING HERE.
THAT. THE HAMMER OF KHAZ'GOROTH.
HAVE YOU RONIR FINALLY GATHERED THE COURAGE TO LET SOMEONE *USE* IT?
IS THERE NO END TO YOUR DISRESPECT TODAY?
THERE HAD BETTER BE. OR THERE *WILL* BE.

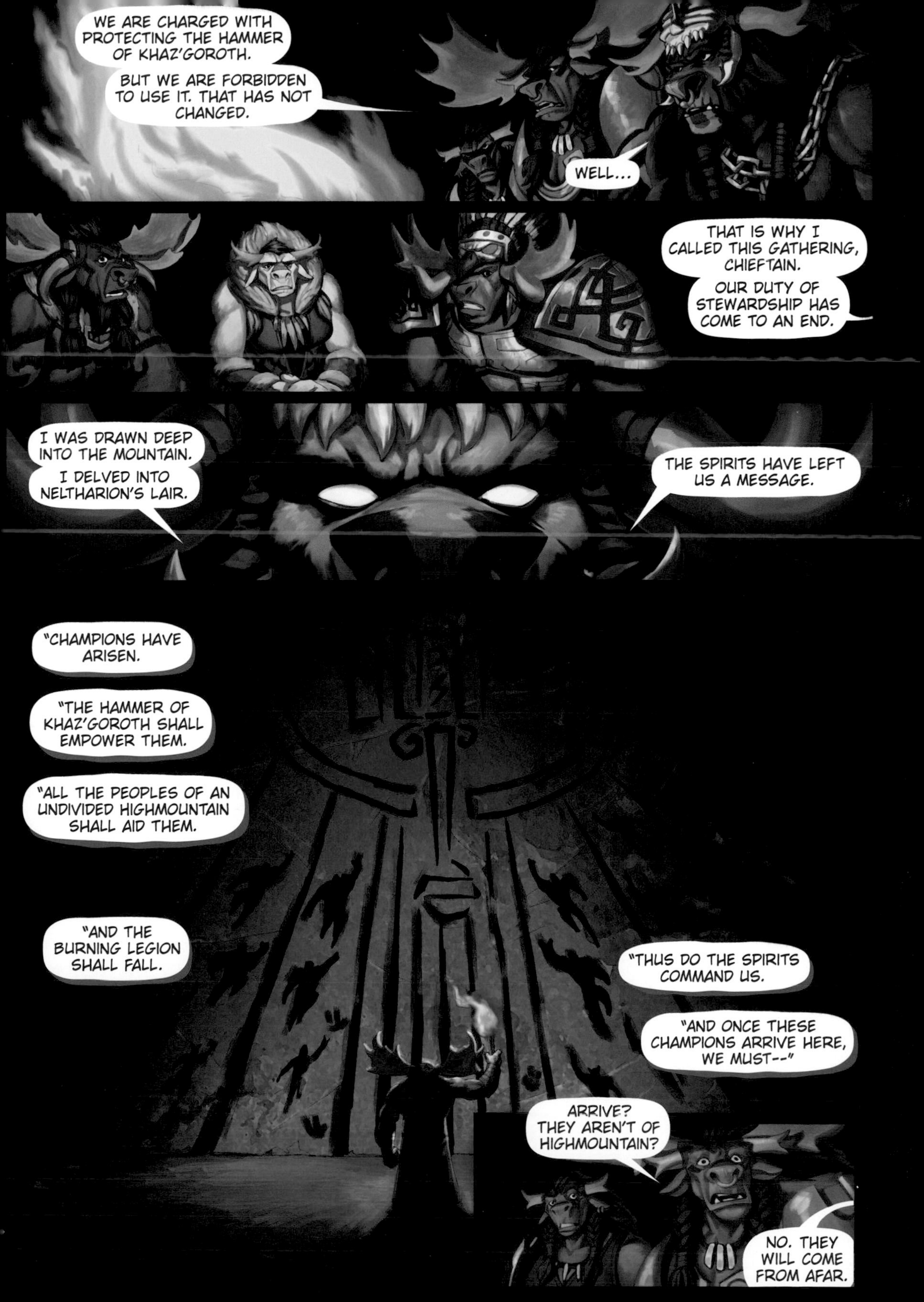
WE ARE CHARGED WITH PROTECTING THE HAMMER OF KHAZ'GOROTH.
BUT WE ARE FORBIDDEN TO USE IT. THAT HAS NOT CHANGED.
WELL...
THAT IS WHY I CALLED THIS GATHERING, CHIEFTAIN.
OUR DUTY OF STEWARDSHIP HAS COME TO AN END.
I WAS DRAWN DEEP INTO THE MOUNTAIN.
I DELVED INTO NELTHARION'S LAIR.
THE SPIRITS HAVE LEFT US A MESSAGE.
"CHAMPIONS HAVE ARISEN.
"THE HAMMER OF KHAZ'GOROTH SHALL EMPOWER THEM.
"ALL THE PEOPLES OF AN UNDIVIDED HIGHMOUNTAIN SHALL AID THEM.
"AND THE BURNING LEGION SHALL FALL.
"THUS DO THE SPIRITS COMMAND US.
"AND ONCE THESE CHAMPIONS ARRIVE HERE, WE MUST--"
ARRIVE? THEY AREN'T OF HIGHMOUNTAIN?
NO. THEY WILL COME FROM AFAR.

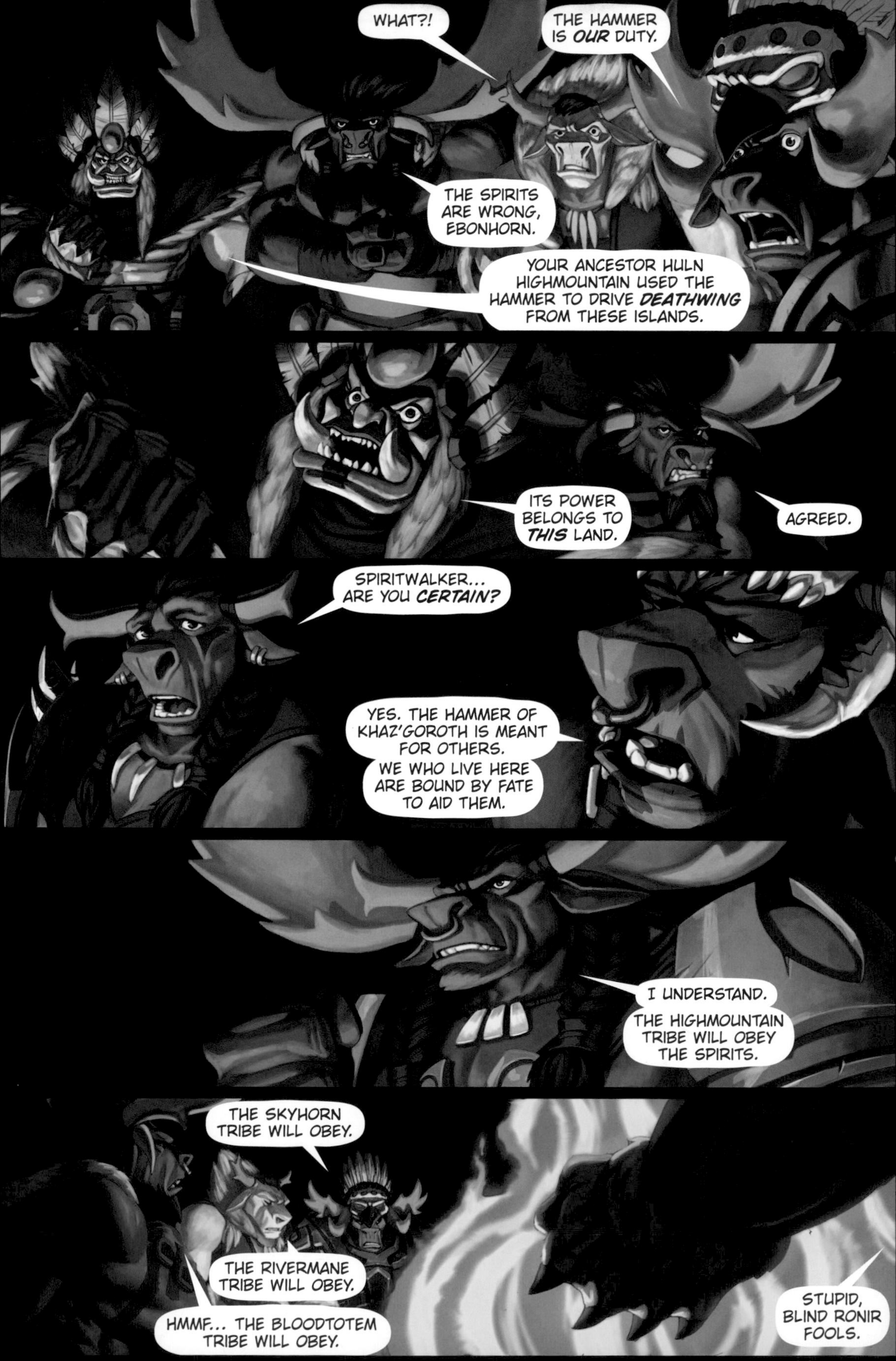
WHAT?!
THE HAMMER IS *OUR* DUTY.
THE SPIRITS ARE WRONG, EBONHORN.
YOUR ANCESTOR HULN HIGHMOUNTAIN USED THE HAMMER TO DRIVE *DEATHWING* FROM THESE ISLANDS.
ITS POWER BELONGS TO *THIS* LAND.
AGREED.
SPIRITWALKER... ARE YOU *CERTAIN?*
YES. THE HAMMER OF KHAZ'GOROTH IS MEANT FOR OTHERS.
WE WHO LIVE HERE ARE BOUND BY FATE TO AID THEM.
I UNDERSTAND.
THE HIGHMOUNTAIN TRIBE WILL OBEY THE SPIRITS.
THE SKYHORN TRIBE WILL OBEY.
THE RIVERMANE TRIBE WILL OBEY.
HMMF... THE BLOODTOTEM TRIBE WILL OBEY.
STUPID, BLIND RONIR FOOLS.

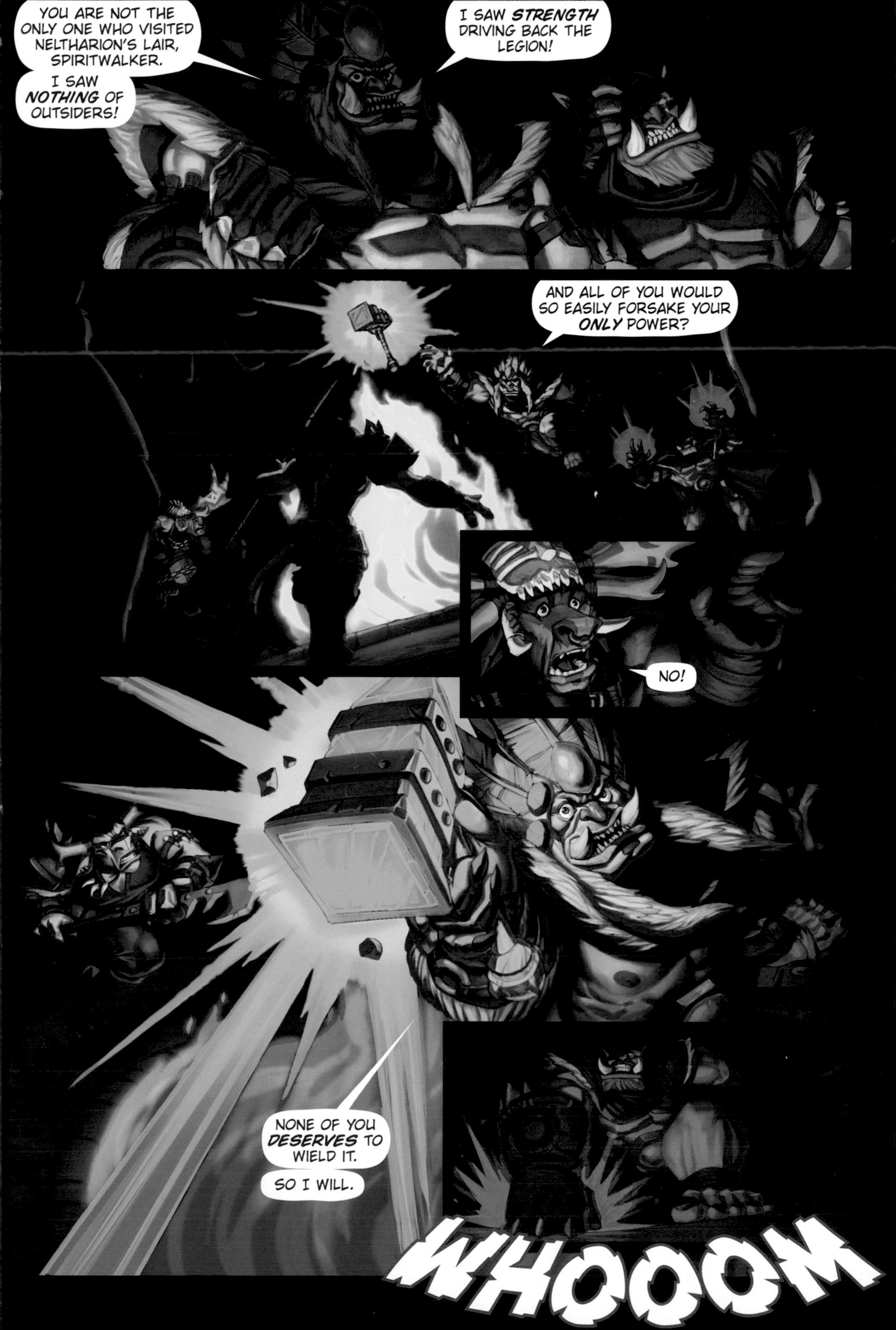
YOU ARE NOT THE ONLY ONE WHO VISITED NELTHARION'S LAIR, SPIRITWALKER.
I SAW *NOTHING* OF OUTSIDERS!
I SAW *STRENGTH* DRIVING BACK THE LEGION!
AND ALL OF YOU WOULD SO EASILY FORSAKE YOUR *ONLY* POWER?
NO!
NONE OF YOU *DESERVES* TO WIELD IT.
SO I WILL.
WHOOOM

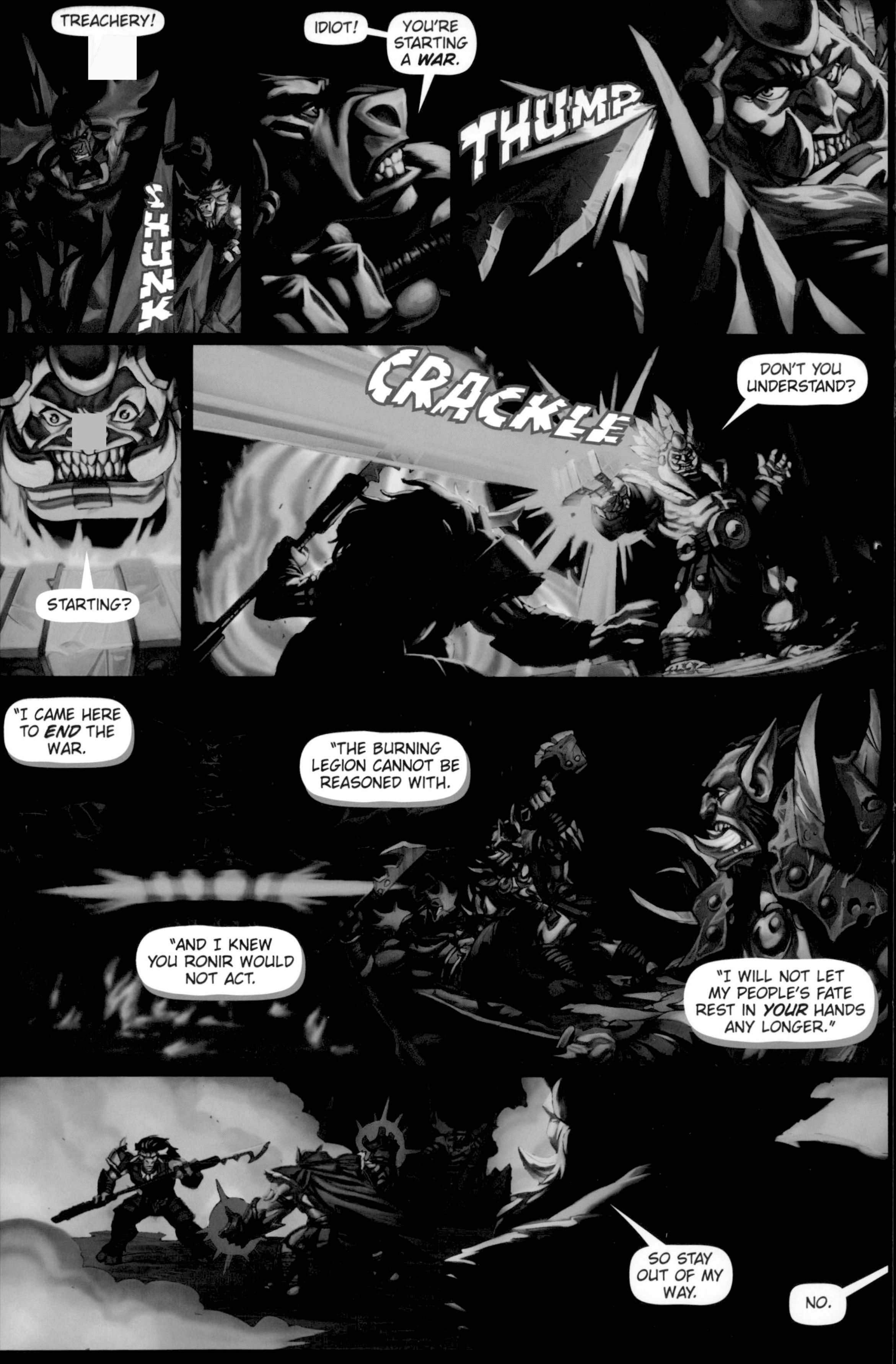
TREACHERY!
SHUNK
IDIOT!
YOU'RE STARTING A WAR.
THUMP
STARTING?
CRACKLE
DON'T YOU UNDERSTAND?
"I CAME HERE TO END THE WAR.
"THE BURNING LEGION CANNOT BE REASONED WITH.
"AND I KNEW YOU RONIR WOULD NOT ACT.
"I WILL NOT LET MY PEOPLE'S FATE REST IN YOUR HANDS ANY LONGER."
SO STAY OUT OF MY WAY.
NO.

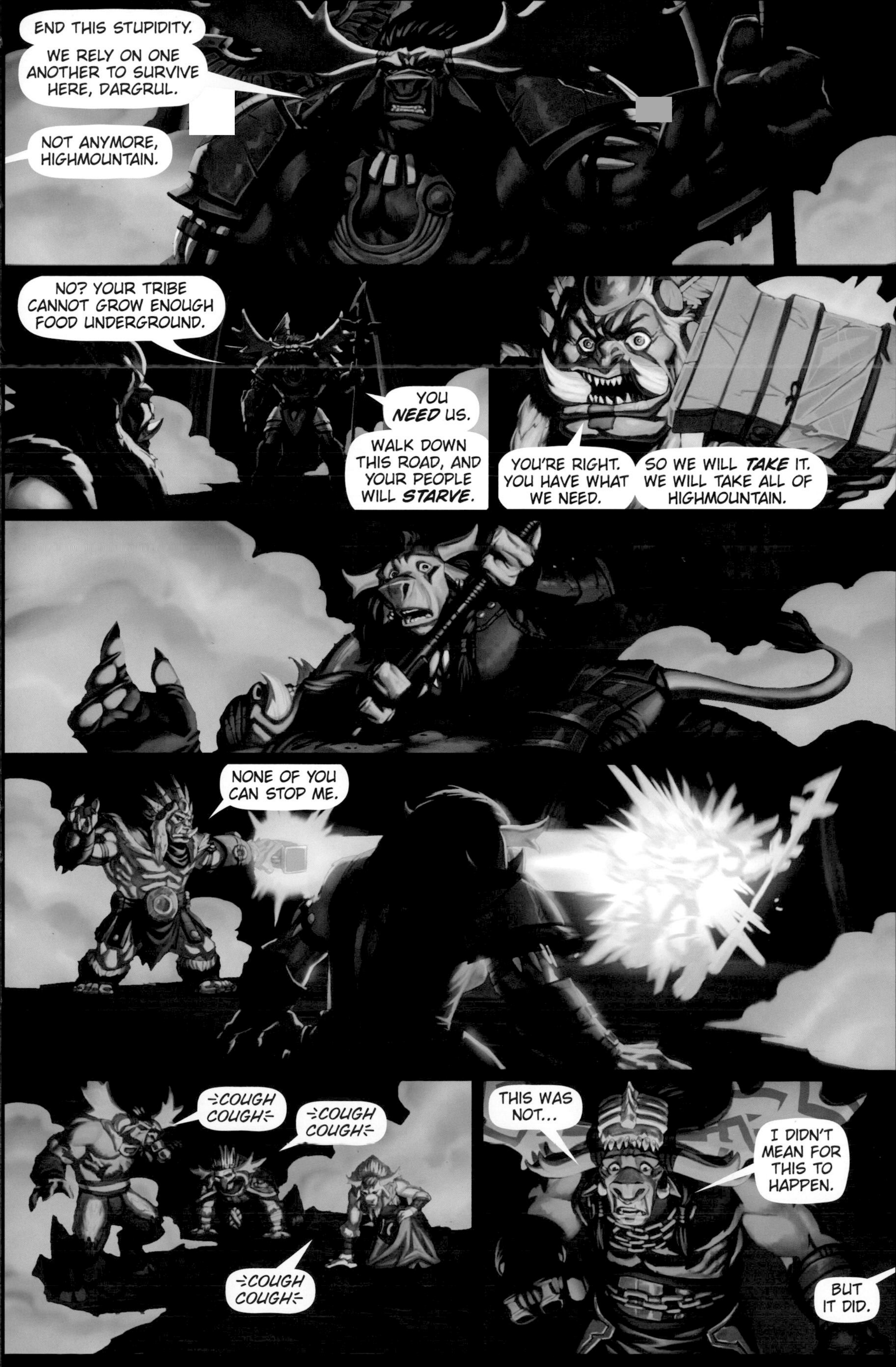

END THIS STUPIDITY.
WE RELY ON ONE ANOTHER TO SURVIVE HERE, DARGRUL.
NOT ANYMORE, HIGHMOUNTAIN.
NO? YOUR TRIBE CANNOT GROW ENOUGH FOOD UNDERGROUND.
YOU NEED US.
WALK DOWN THIS ROAD, AND YOUR PEOPLE WILL STARVE.
YOU'RE RIGHT. YOU HAVE WHAT WE NEED.
SO WE WILL TAKE IT. WE WILL TAKE ALL OF HIGHMOUNTAIN.
NONE OF YOU CAN STOP ME.
=COUGH COUGH=
=COUGH COUGH=
=COUGH COUGH=
THIS WAS NOT...
I DIDN'T MEAN FOR THIS TO HAPPEN.
BUT IT DID.

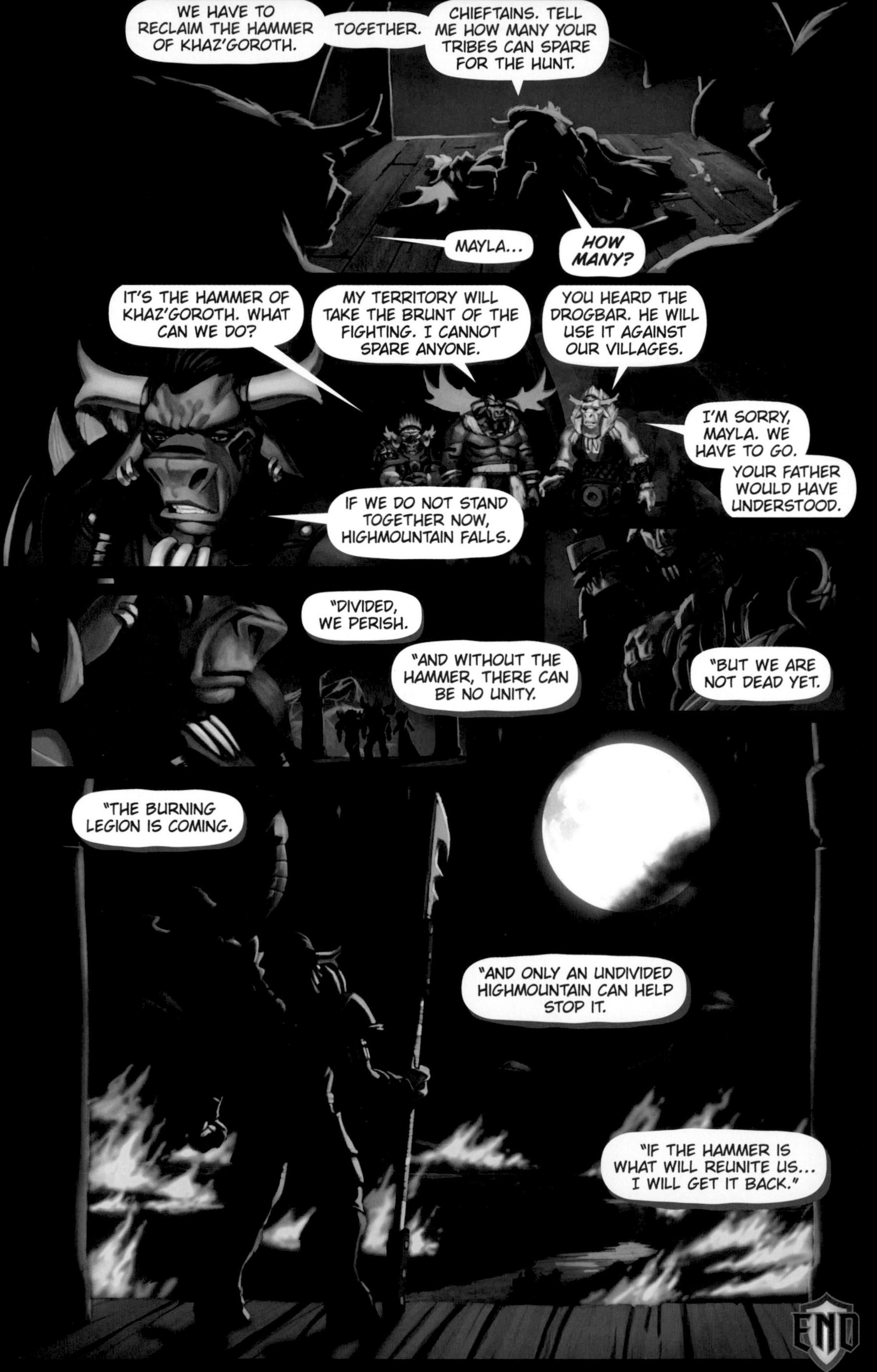
WE HAVE TO RECLAIM THE HAMMER OF KHAZ'GOROTH.
TOGETHER.
CHIEFTAINS. TELL ME HOW MANY YOUR TRIBES CAN SPARE FOR THE HUNT.
MAYLA...
HOW MANY?
IT'S THE HAMMER OF KHAZ'GOROTH. WHAT CAN WE DO?
MY TERRITORY WILL TAKE THE BRUNT OF THE FIGHTING. I CANNOT SPARE ANYONE.
YOU HEARD THE DROGBAR. HE WILL USE IT AGAINST OUR VILLAGES.
I'M SORRY, MAYLA. WE HAVE TO GO.
YOUR FATHER WOULD HAVE UNDERSTOOD.
IF WE DO NOT STAND TOGETHER NOW, HIGHMOUNTAIN FALLS.
"DIVIDED, WE PERISH.
"AND WITHOUT THE HAMMER, THERE CAN BE NO UNITY.
"BUT WE ARE NOT DEAD YET.
"THE BURNING LEGION IS COMING.
"AND ONLY AN UNDIVIDED HIGHMOUNTAIN CAN HELP STOP IT.
"IF THE HAMMER IS WHAT WILL REUNITE US... I WILL GET IT BACK."
END

WORLD OF WARCRAFT
LEGION

ANDUIN

SON OF THE WOLF

SCRIPT BY **ROBERT BROOKS** | ART BY **NESSKAIN** |
LETTERING BY **COMICRAFT**

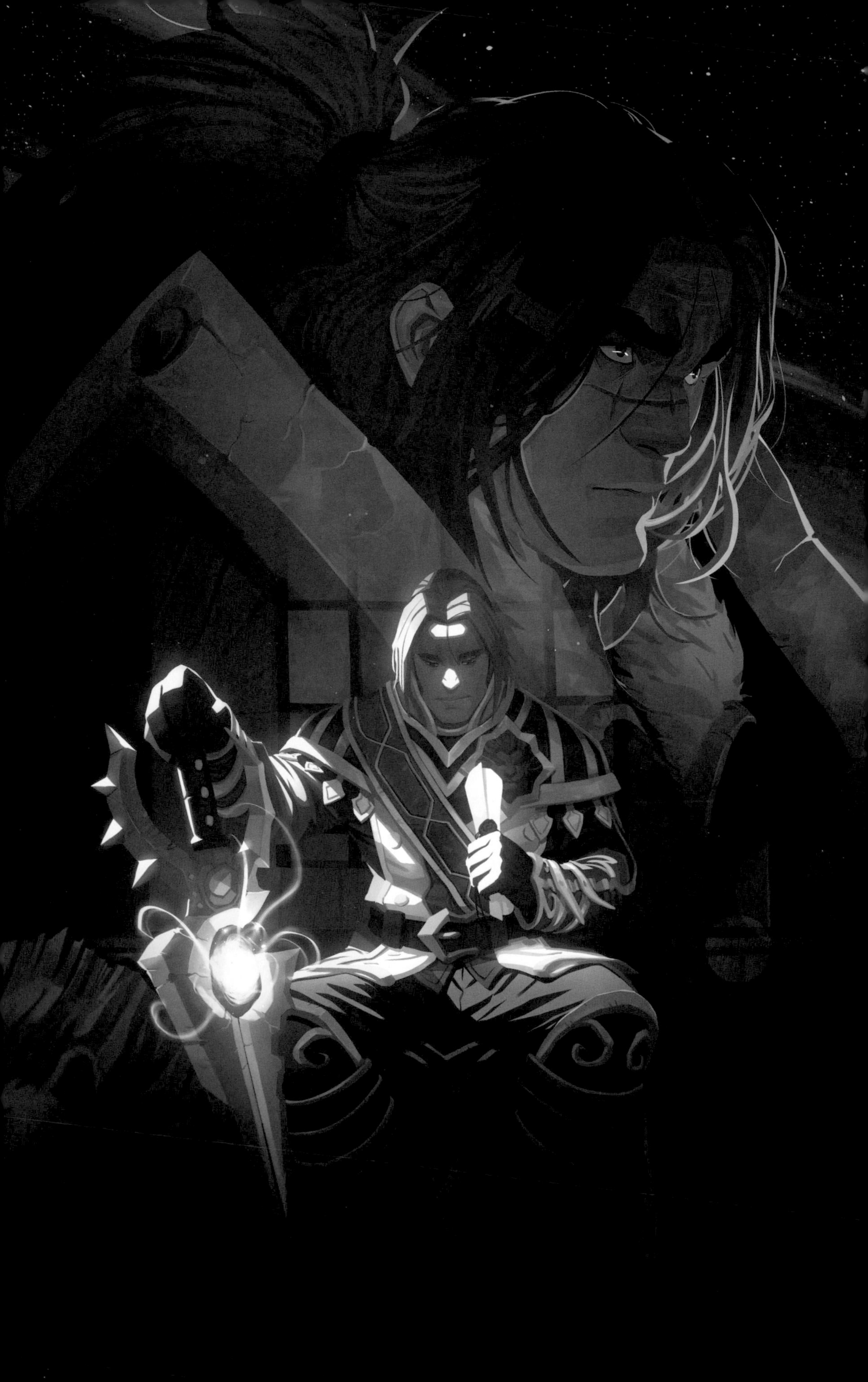

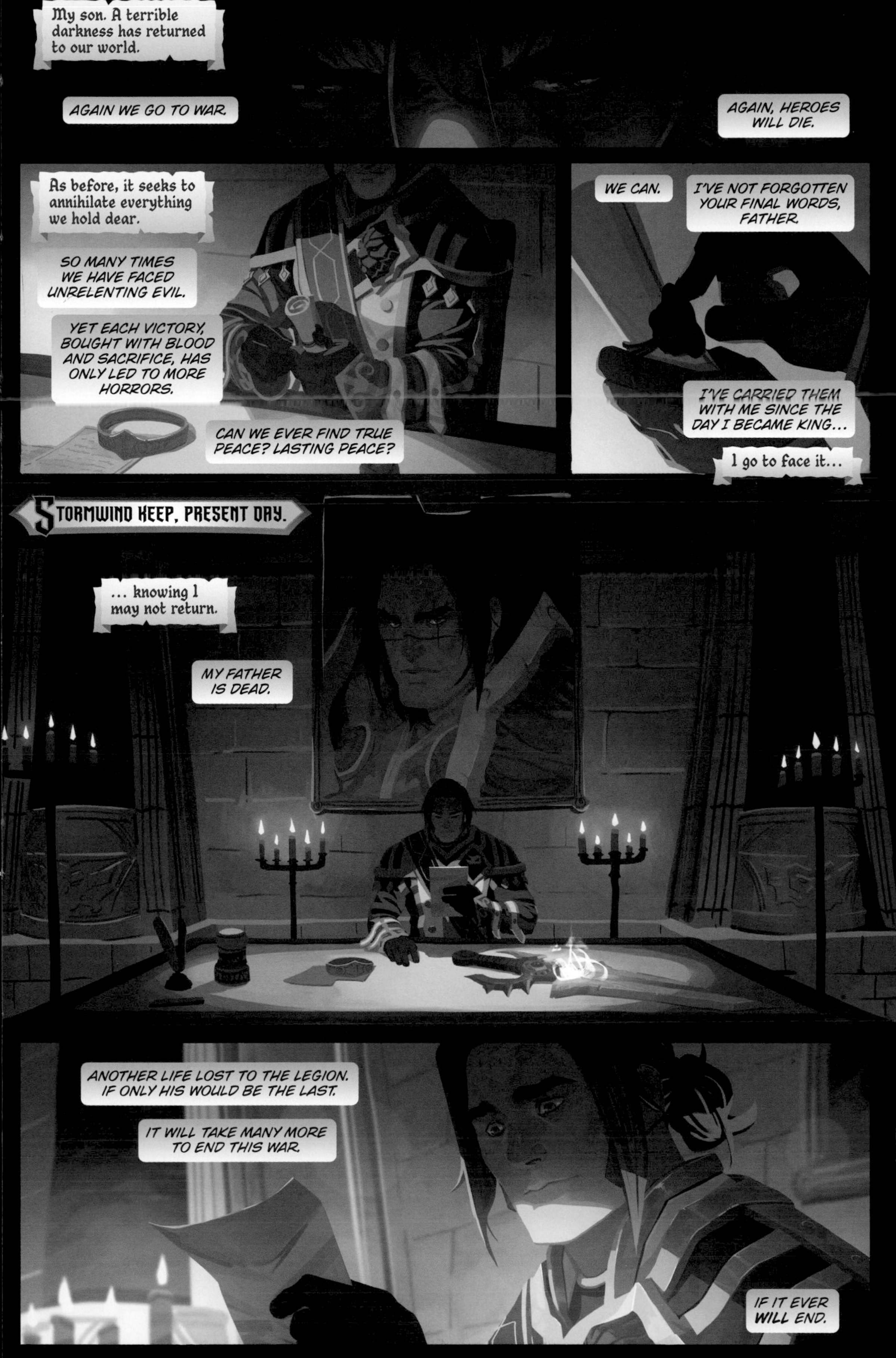
My son. A terrible darkness has returned to our world.
AGAIN WE GO TO WAR.
AGAIN, HEROES WILL DIE.
As before, it seeks to annihilate everything we hold dear.
SO MANY TIMES WE HAVE FACED UNRELENTING EVIL.
YET EACH VICTORY, BOUGHT WITH BLOOD AND SACRIFICE, HAS ONLY LED TO MORE HORRORS.
CAN WE EVER FIND TRUE PEACE? LASTING PEACE?
WE CAN.
I'VE NOT FORGOTTEN YOUR FINAL WORDS, FATHER.
I'VE CARRIED THEM WITH ME SINCE THE DAY I BECAME KING...
I go to face it...
STORMWIND KEEP, PRESENT DAY.
... knowing I may not return.
MY FATHER IS DEAD.
ANOTHER LIFE LOST TO THE LEGION. IF ONLY HIS WOULD BE THE LAST.
IT WILL TAKE MANY MORE TO END THIS WAR.
IF IT EVER WILL END.

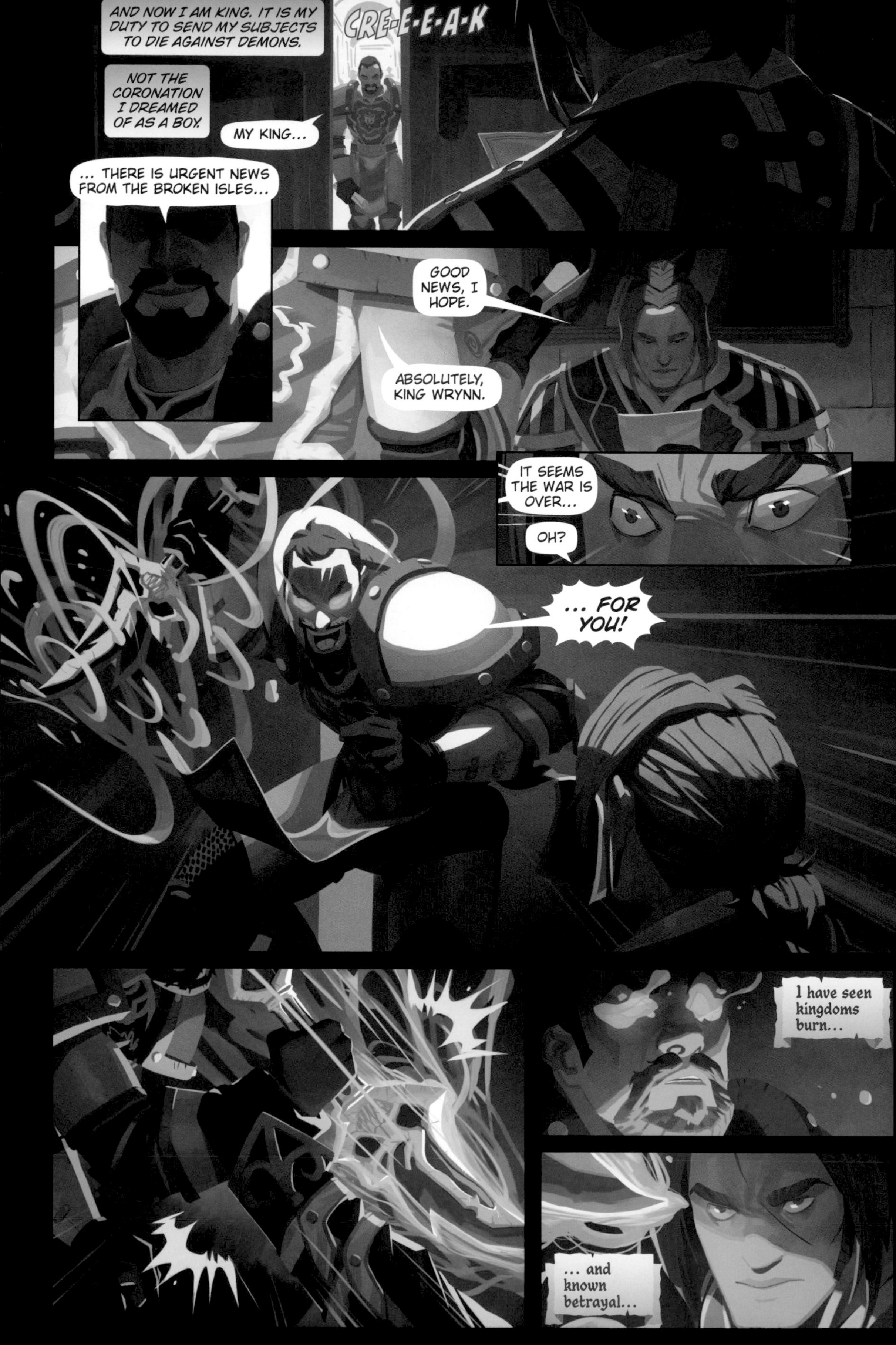
AND NOW I AM KING. IT IS MY DUTY TO SEND MY SUBJECTS TO DIE AGAINST DEMONS.
CRE-E-E-A-K
NOT THE CORONATION I DREAMED OF AS A BOY.
MY KING...
... THERE IS URGENT NEWS FROM THE BROKEN ISLES...
GOOD NEWS, I HOPE.
ABSOLUTELY, KING WRYNN.
IT SEEMS THE WAR IS OVER...
OH?
... FOR YOU!
I have seen kingdoms burn...
... and known betrayal...

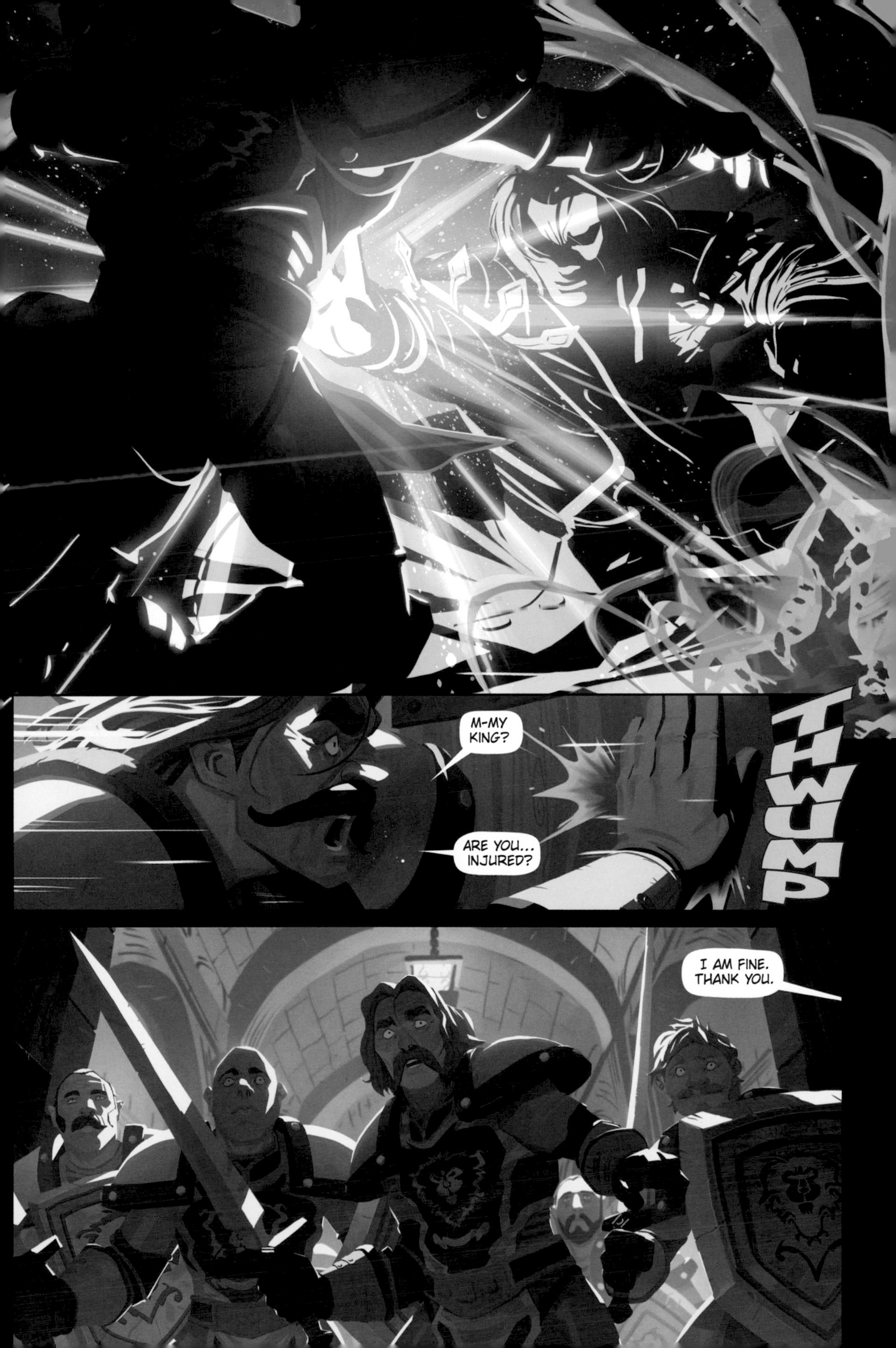
M-MY KING?
ARE YOU... INJURED?
THWUMP
I AM FINE. THANK YOU.

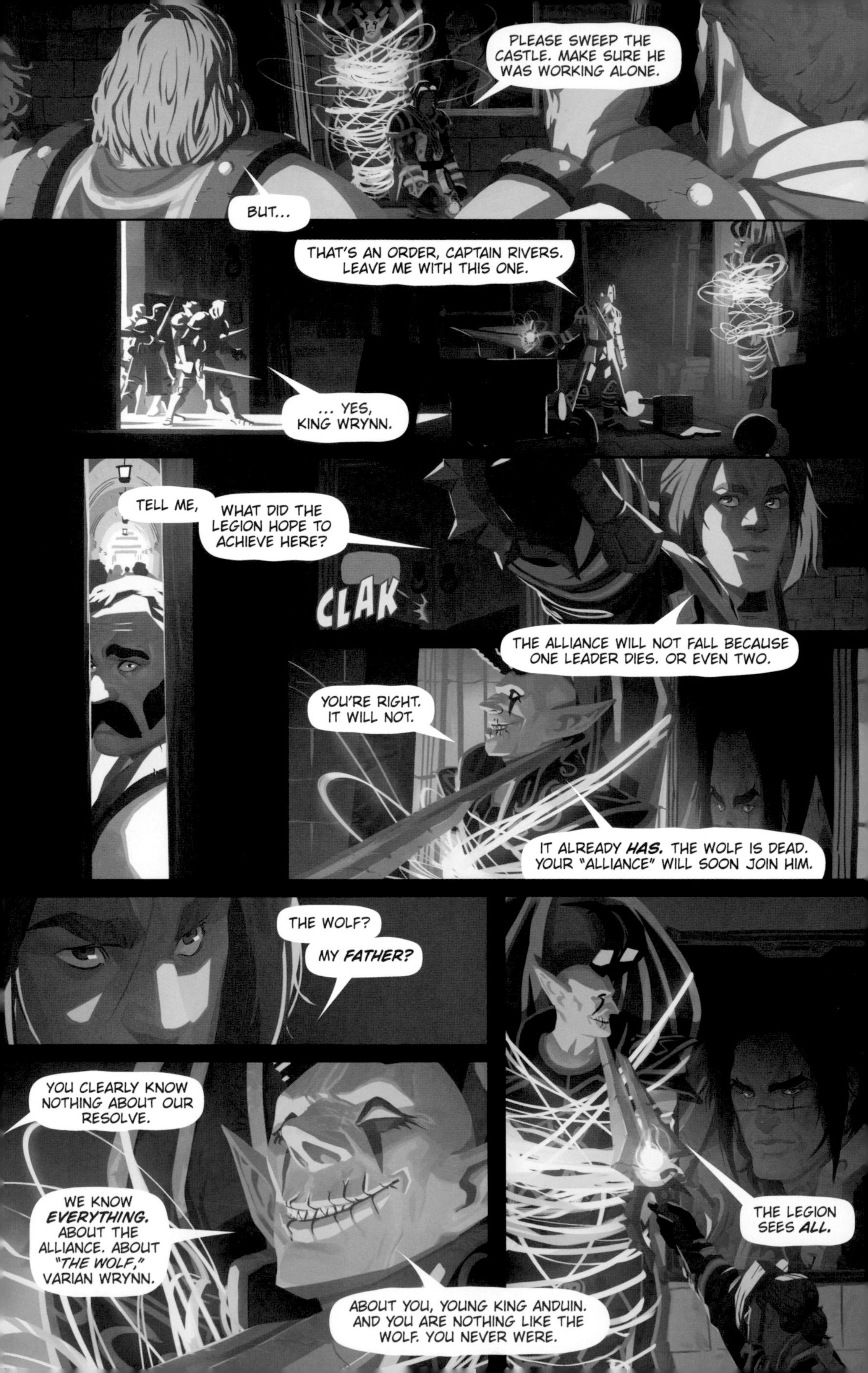
PLEASE SWEEP THE CASTLE. MAKE SURE HE WAS WORKING ALONE.
BUT...
THAT'S AN ORDER, CAPTAIN RIVERS. LEAVE ME WITH THIS ONE.
... YES, KING WRYNN.
TELL ME,
WHAT DID THE LEGION HOPE TO ACHIEVE HERE?
CLAK
THE ALLIANCE WILL NOT FALL BECAUSE ONE LEADER DIES. OR EVEN TWO.
YOU'RE RIGHT. IT WILL NOT.
IT ALREADY ***HAS.*** THE WOLF IS DEAD. YOUR "ALLIANCE" WILL SOON JOIN HIM.
THE WOLF?
MY ***FATHER?***
YOU CLEARLY KNOW NOTHING ABOUT OUR RESOLVE.
WE KNOW ***EVERYTHING.*** ABOUT THE ALLIANCE. ABOUT *"THE WOLF,"* VARIAN WRYNN.
ABOUT YOU, YOUNG KING ANDUIN. AND YOU ARE NOTHING LIKE THE WOLF. YOU NEVER WERE.
THE LEGION SEES ***ALL.***

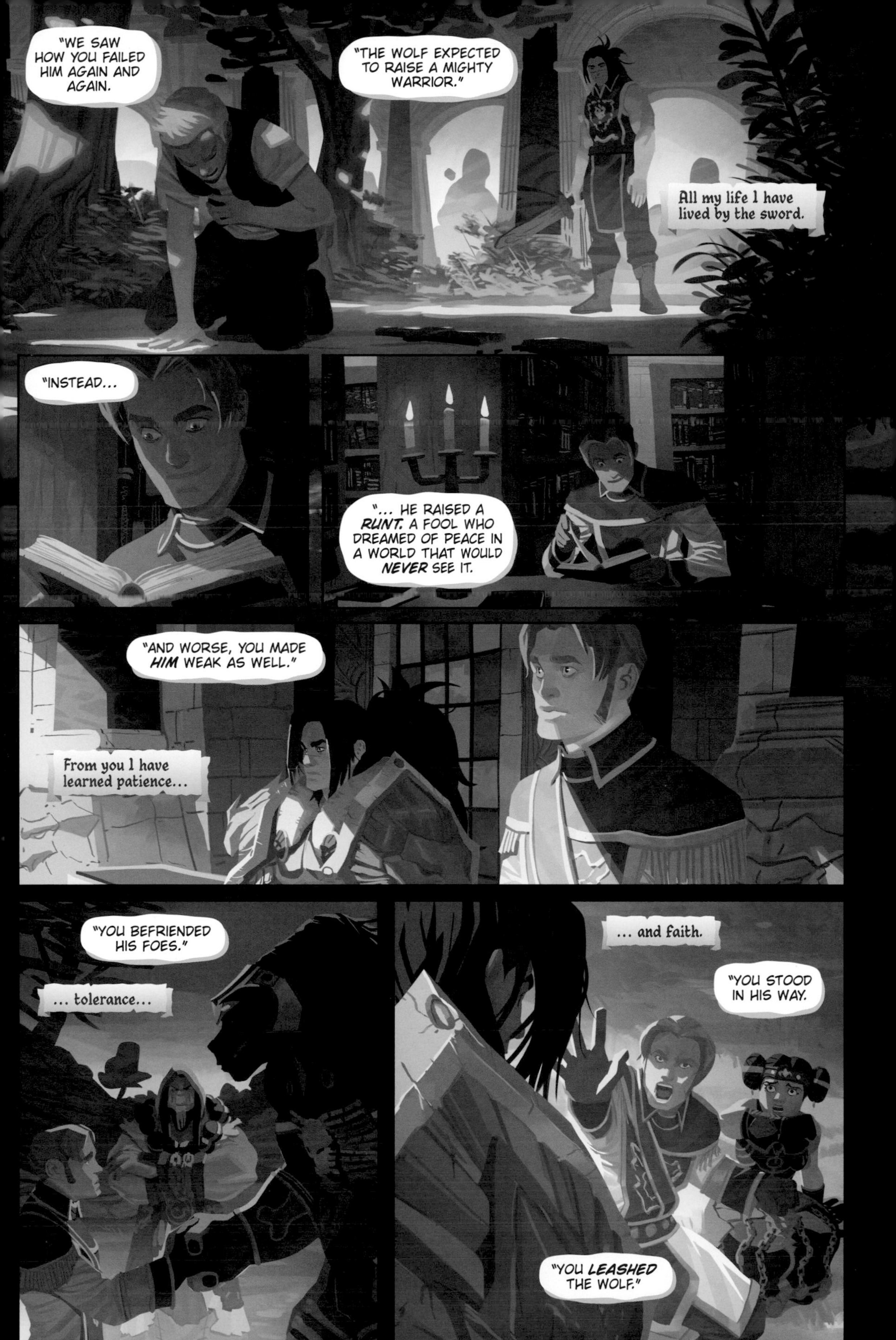
"WE SAW HOW YOU FAILED HIM AGAIN AND AGAIN.
"THE WOLF EXPECTED TO RAISE A MIGHTY WARRIOR."
All my life I have lived by the sword.
"INSTEAD...
"... HE RAISED A RUNT. A FOOL WHO DREAMED OF PEACE IN A WORLD THAT WOULD NEVER SEE IT.
"AND WORSE, YOU MADE HIM WEAK AS WELL."
From you I have learned patience...
"YOU BEFRIENDED HIS FOES."
... tolerance...
... and faith.
"YOU STOOD IN HIS WAY.
"YOU LEASHED THE WOLF."

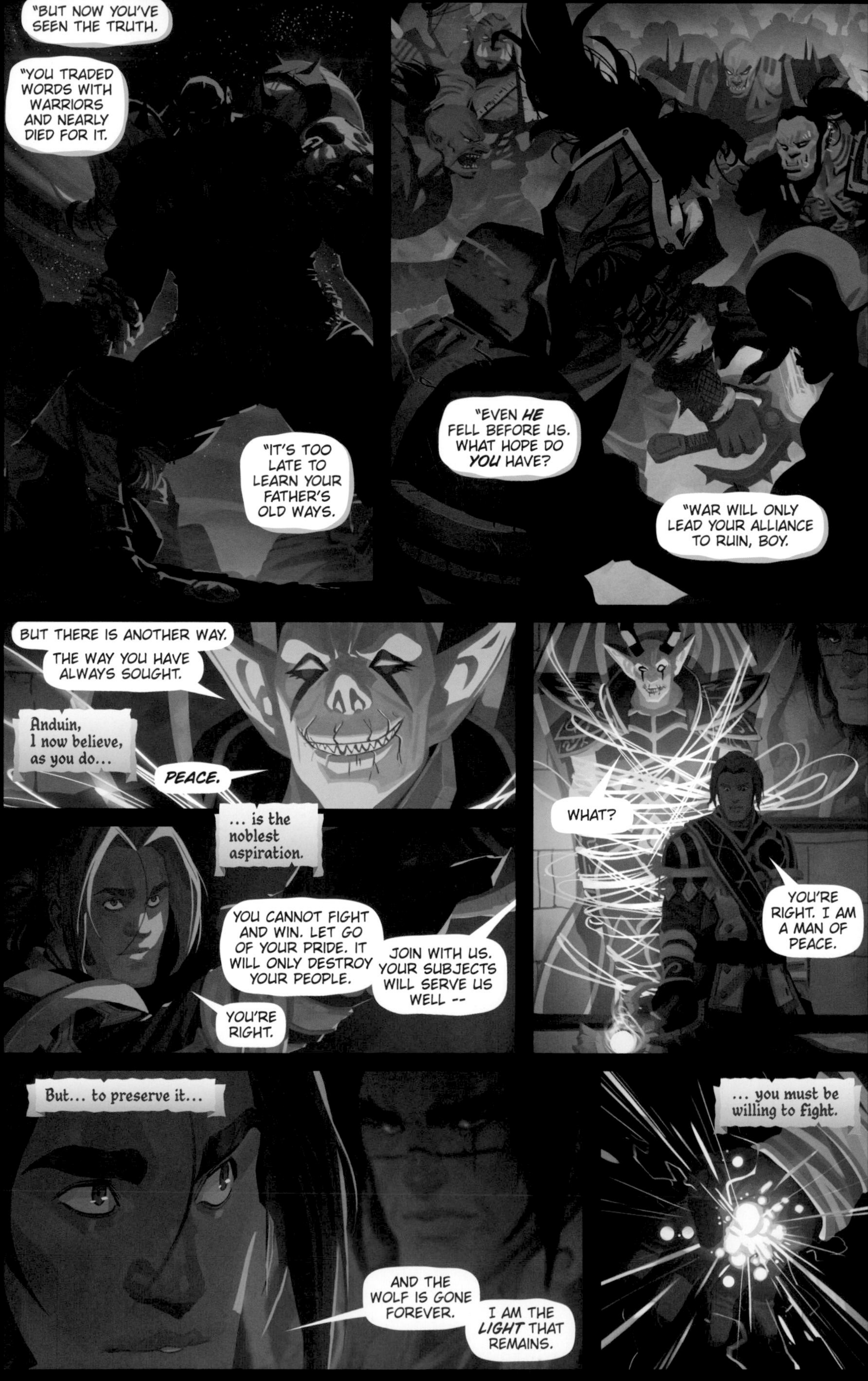

"BUT NOW YOU'VE SEEN THE TRUTH.
"YOU TRADED WORDS WITH WARRIORS AND NEARLY DIED FOR IT.
"IT'S TOO LATE TO LEARN YOUR FATHER'S OLD WAYS.
"EVEN *HE* FELL BEFORE US. WHAT HOPE DO *YOU* HAVE?
"WAR WILL ONLY LEAD YOUR ALLIANCE TO RUIN, BOY.
BUT THERE IS ANOTHER WAY.
THE WAY YOU HAVE ALWAYS SOUGHT.
Anduin, I now believe, as you do...
PEACE.
... is the noblest aspiration.
YOU CANNOT FIGHT AND WIN. LET GO OF YOUR PRIDE. IT WILL ONLY DESTROY YOUR PEOPLE.
JOIN WITH US. YOUR SUBJECTS WILL SERVE US WELL --
YOU'RE RIGHT.
WHAT?
YOU'RE RIGHT. I AM A MAN OF PEACE.
But... to preserve it...
AND THE WOLF IS GONE FOREVER.
I AM THE *LIGHT* THAT REMAINS.
... you must be willing to fight.

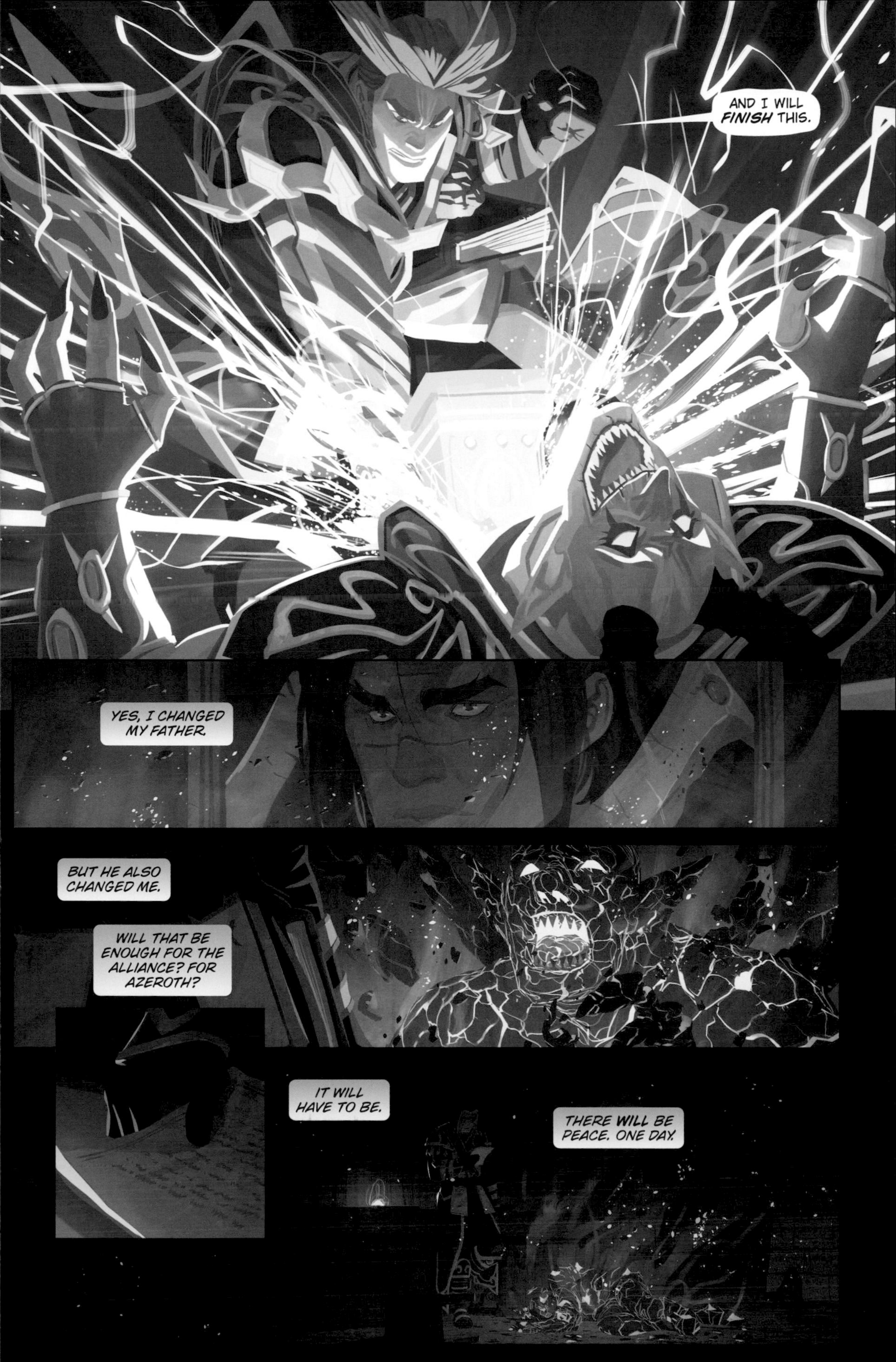
AND I WILL FINISH THIS.
YES, I CHANGED MY FATHER.
BUT HE ALSO CHANGED ME.
WILL THAT BE ENOUGH FOR THE ALLIANCE? FOR AZEROTH?
IT WILL HAVE TO BE.
THERE WILL BE PEACE. ONE DAY.

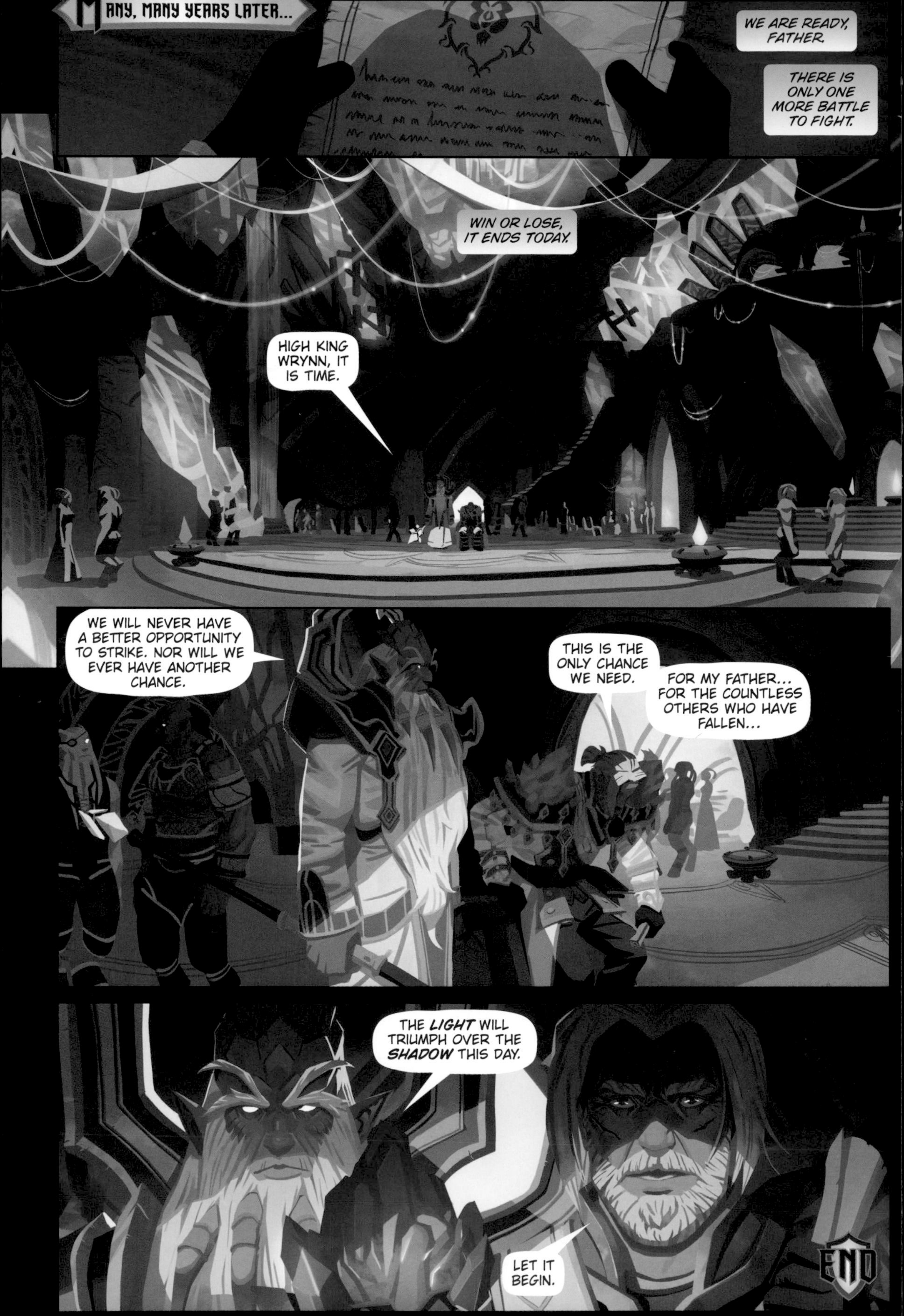
MANY, MANY YEARS LATER...
WE ARE READY, FATHER.
THERE IS ONLY ONE MORE BATTLE TO FIGHT.
WIN OR LOSE, IT ENDS TODAY.
HIGH KING WRYNN, IT IS TIME.
WE WILL NEVER HAVE A BETTER OPPORTUNITY TO STRIKE. NOR WILL WE EVER HAVE ANOTHER CHANCE.
THIS IS THE ONLY CHANCE WE NEED.
FOR MY FATHER... FOR THE COUNTLESS OTHERS WHO HAVE FALLEN...
THE *LIGHT* WILL TRIUMPH OVER THE *SHADOW* THIS DAY.
LET IT BEGIN.
END

JAINA
REUNION

SCRIPT BY **ANDREW ROBINSON** | ART BY **LINDA CAVALLINI** &
EMANUELE TENDERINI | LETTERING BY **COMICCRAFT**

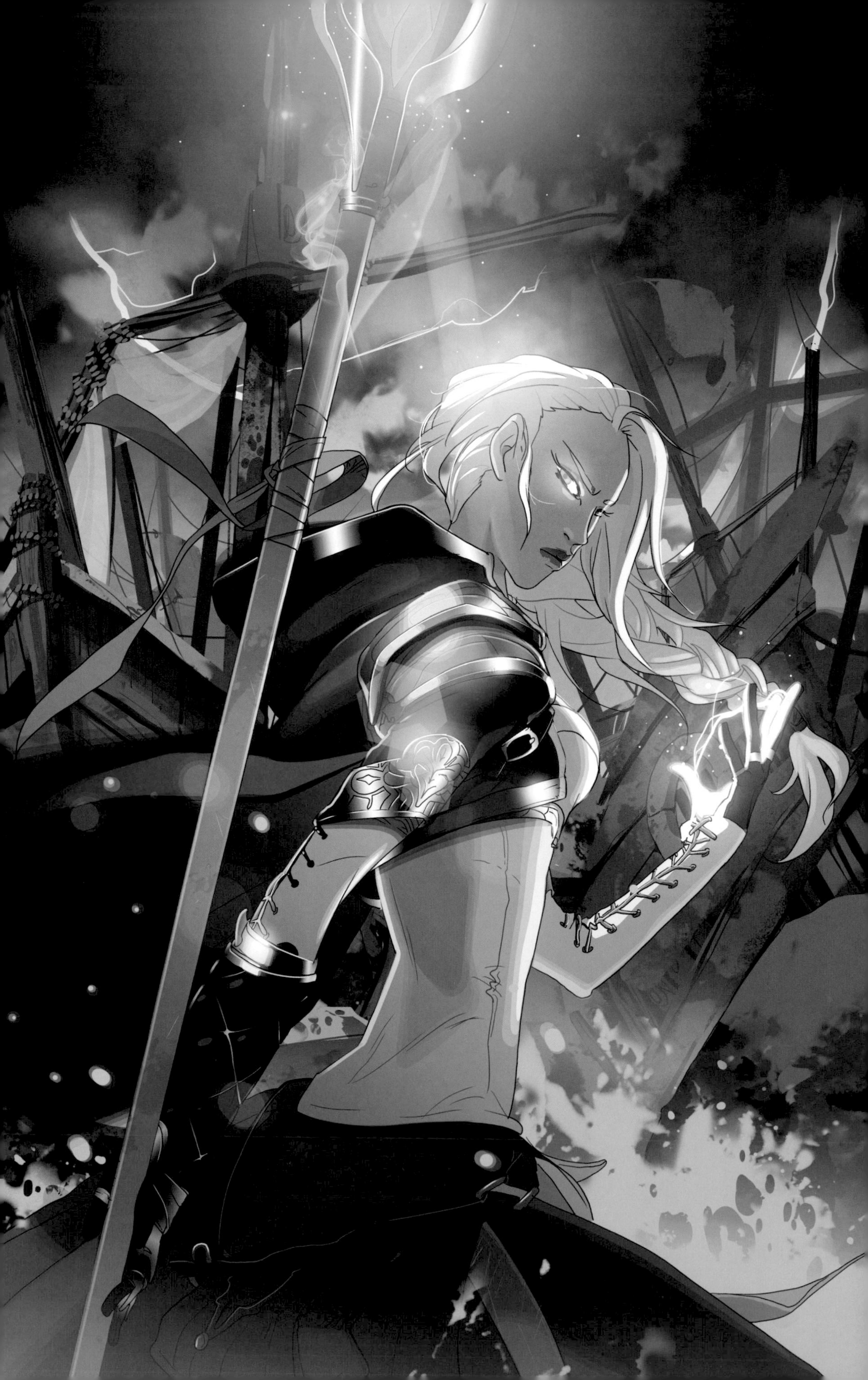

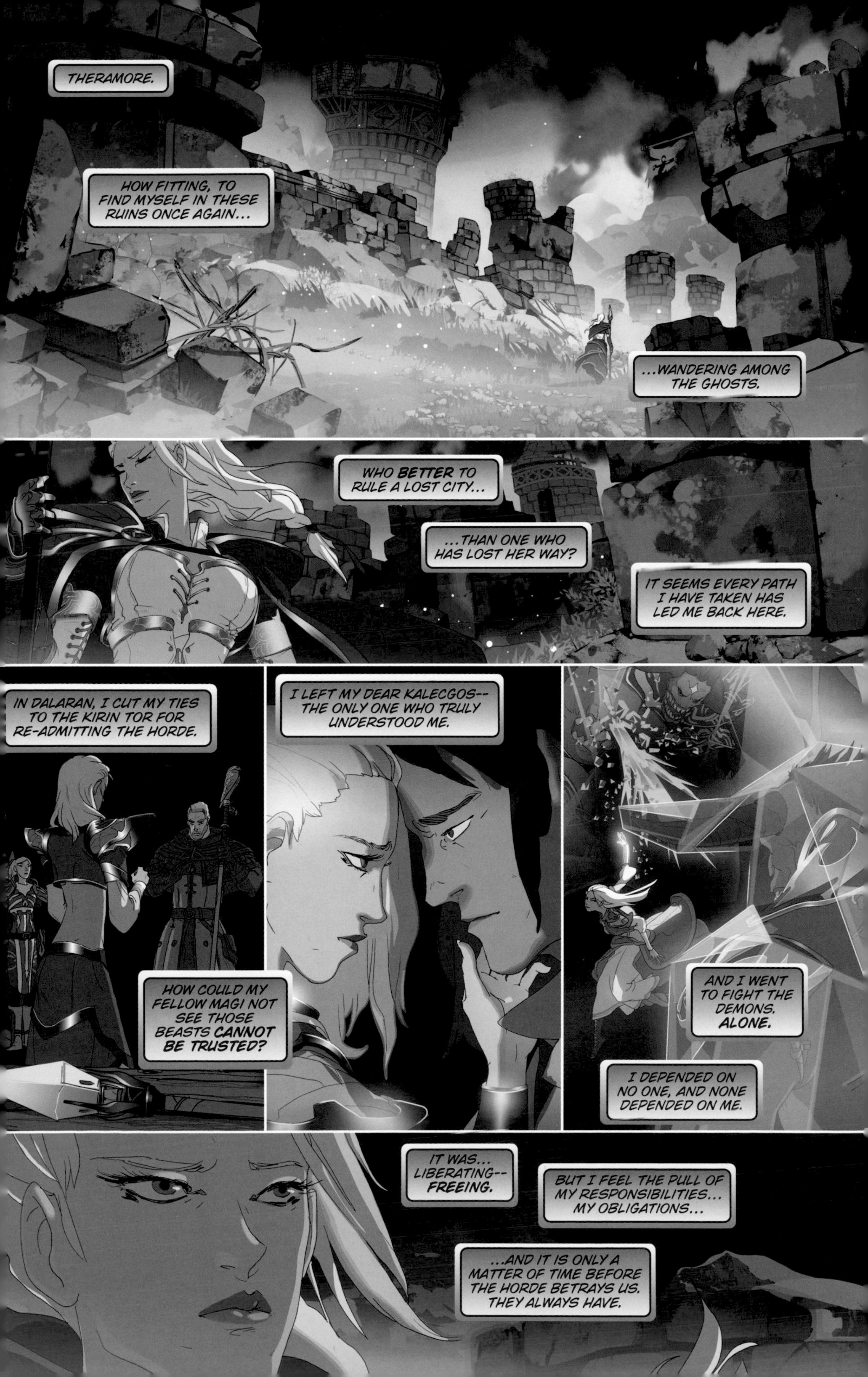
THERAMORE.
HOW FITTING, TO FIND MYSELF IN THESE RUINS ONCE AGAIN...
...WANDERING AMONG THE GHOSTS.
WHO **BETTER** TO RULE A LOST CITY...
...THAN ONE WHO HAS LOST HER WAY?
IT SEEMS EVERY PATH I HAVE TAKEN HAS LED ME BACK HERE.
IN DALARAN, I CUT MY TIES TO THE KIRIN TOR FOR RE-ADMITTING THE HORDE.
HOW COULD MY FELLOW MAGI NOT SEE THOSE BEASTS **CANNOT BE TRUSTED?**
I LEFT MY DEAR KALECGOS-- THE ONLY ONE WHO TRULY UNDERSTOOD ME.
AND I WENT TO FIGHT THE DEMONS. **ALONE.**
I DEPENDED ON NO ONE, AND NONE DEPENDED ON ME.
IT WAS... LIBERATING-- **FREEING.**
BUT I FEEL THE PULL OF MY RESPONSIBILITIES... MY OBLIGATIONS...
...AND IT IS ONLY A MATTER OF TIME BEFORE THE HORDE BETRAYS US. THEY ALWAYS HAVE.

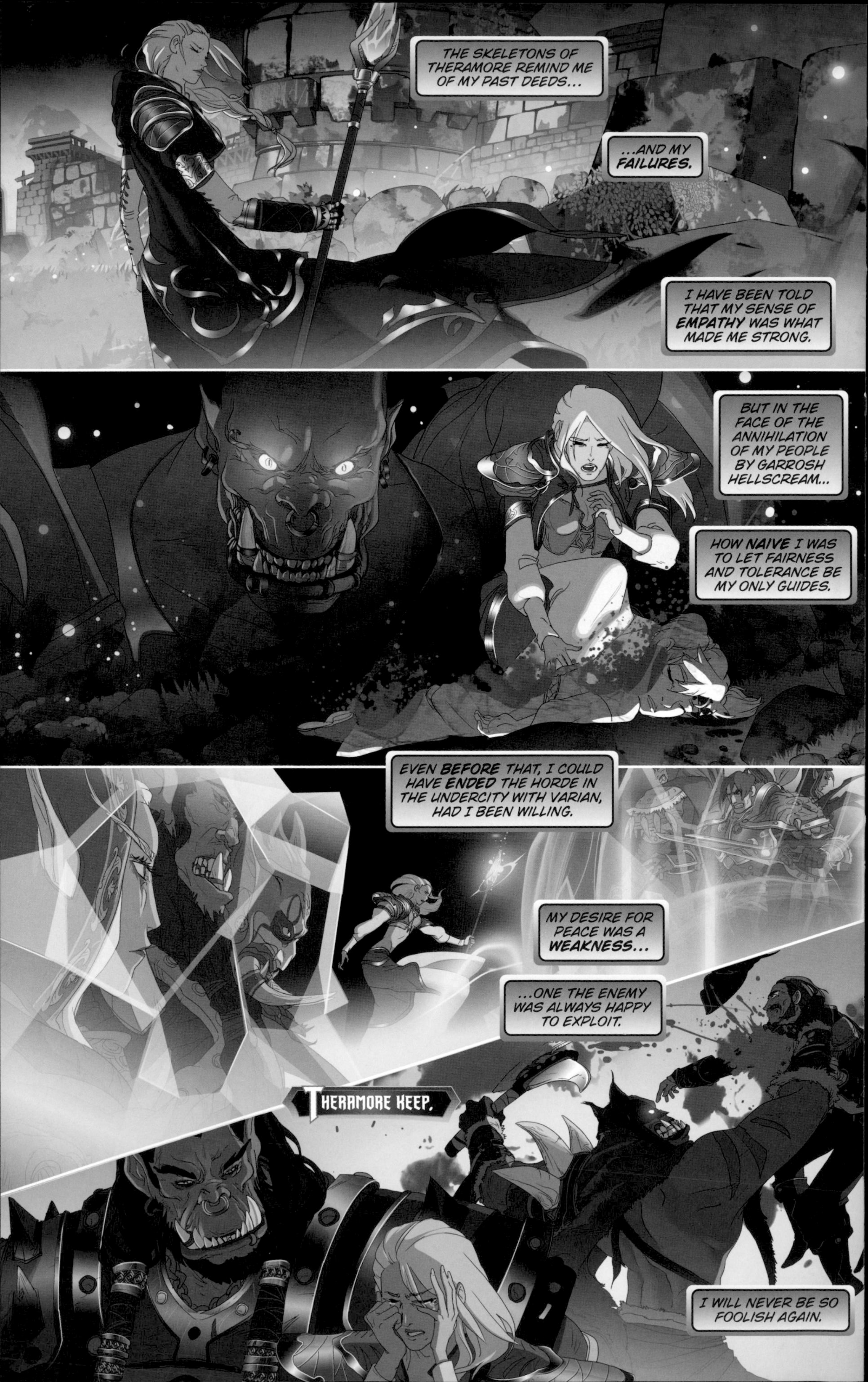
THE SKELETONS OF THERAMORE REMIND ME OF MY PAST DEEDS...
...AND MY FAILURES.
I HAVE BEEN TOLD THAT MY SENSE OF EMPATHY WAS WHAT MADE ME STRONG.
BUT IN THE FACE OF THE ANNIHILATION OF MY PEOPLE BY GARROSH HELLSCREAM...
HOW NAIVE I WAS TO LET FAIRNESS AND TOLERANCE BE MY ONLY GUIDES.
EVEN BEFORE THAT, I COULD HAVE ENDED THE HORDE IN THE UNDERCITY WITH VARIAN, HAD I BEEN WILLING.
MY DESIRE FOR PEACE WAS A WEAKNESS...
...ONE THE ENEMY WAS ALWAYS HAPPY TO EXPLOIT.
THERAMORE KEEP.
I WILL NEVER BE SO FOOLISH AGAIN.

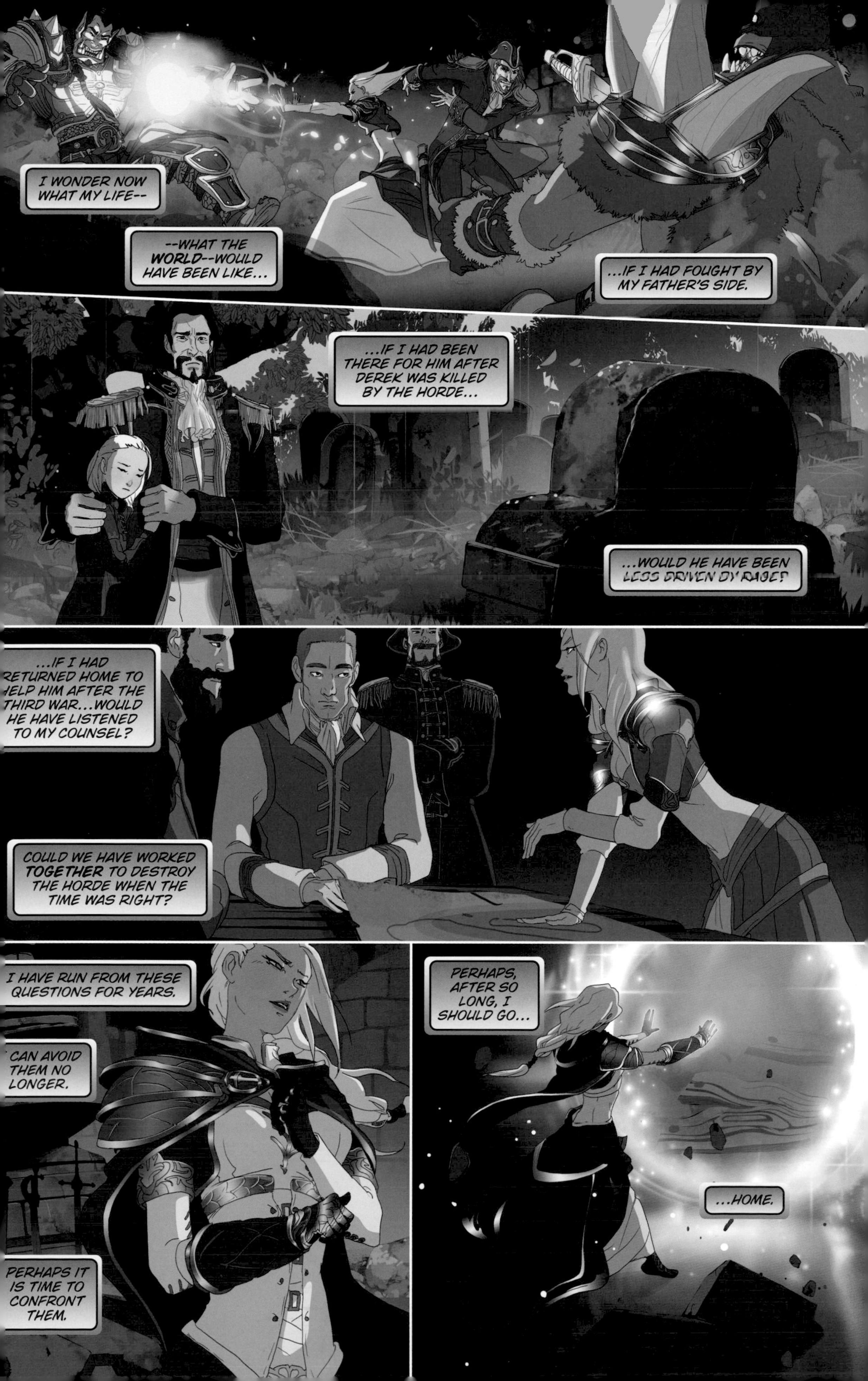
I WONDER NOW WHAT MY LIFE--
--WHAT THE WORLD--WOULD HAVE BEEN LIKE...
...IF I HAD FOUGHT BY MY FATHER'S SIDE.
...IF I HAD BEEN THERE FOR HIM AFTER DEREK WAS KILLED BY THE HORDE...
...WOULD HE HAVE BEEN LESS DRIVEN BY RAGE?
...IF I HAD RETURNED HOME TO IELP HIM AFTER THE THIRD WAR...WOULD HE HAVE LISTENED TO MY COUNSEL?
COULD WE HAVE WORKED TOGETHER TO DESTROY THE HORDE WHEN THE TIME WAS RIGHT?
I HAVE RUN FROM THESE QUESTIONS FOR YEARS.
CAN AVOID THEM NO LONGER.
PERHAPS IT IS TIME TO CONFRONT THEM.
PERHAPS, AFTER SO LONG, I SHOULD GO...
...HOME.

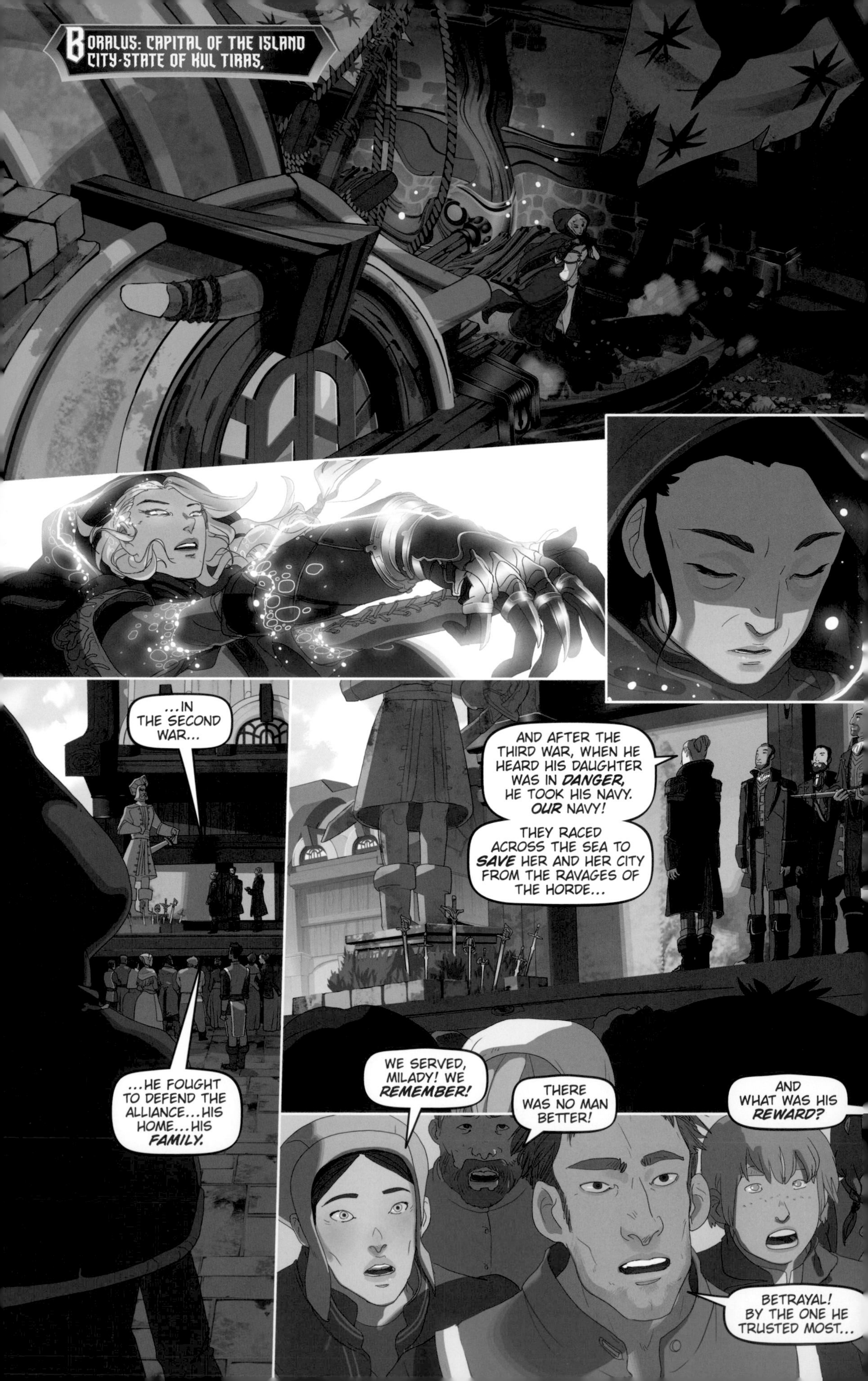
BORALUS: CAPITAL OF THE ISLAND CITY-STATE OF KUL TIRAS,
...IN THE SECOND WAR...
...HE FOUGHT TO DEFEND THE ALLIANCE...HIS HOME...HIS *FAMILY.*
AND AFTER THE THIRD WAR, WHEN HE HEARD HIS DAUGHTER WAS IN *DANGER,* HE TOOK HIS NAVY. *OUR* NAVY!
THEY RACED ACROSS THE SEA TO *SAVE* HER AND HER CITY FROM THE RAVAGES OF THE HORDE...
WE SERVED, MILADY! WE *REMEMBER!*
THERE WAS NO MAN BETTER!
AND WHAT WAS HIS *REWARD?*
BETRAYAL! BY THE ONE HE TRUSTED MOST...

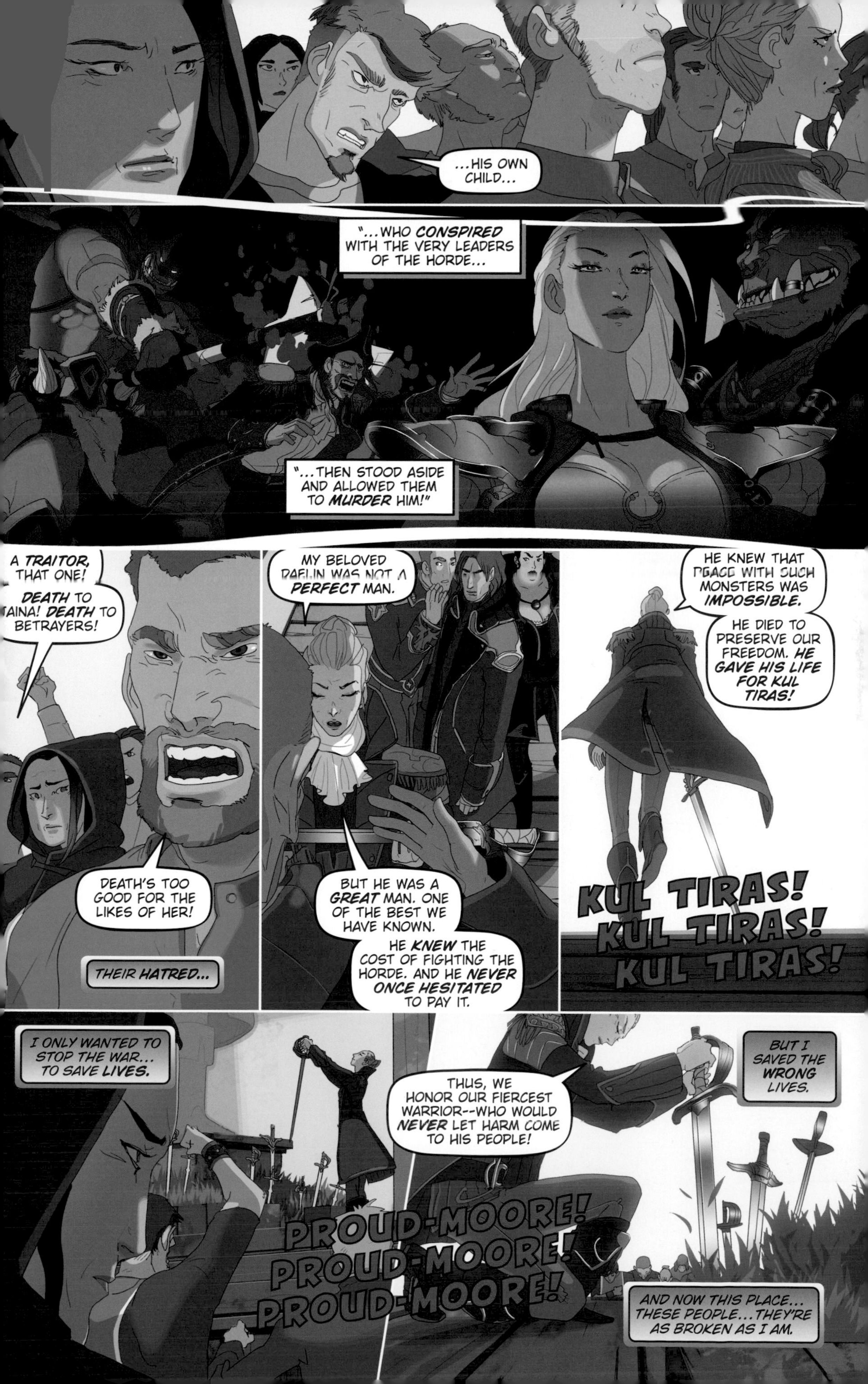
...HIS OWN CHILD...
"...WHO CONSPIRED WITH THE VERY LEADERS OF THE HORDE...
"...THEN STOOD ASIDE AND ALLOWED THEM TO MURDER HIM!"
A TRAITOR, THAT ONE!
DEATH TO JAINA! DEATH TO BETRAYERS!
DEATH'S TOO GOOD FOR THE LIKES OF HER!
THEIR HATRED...
MY BELOVED DAELIN WAS NOT A PERFECT MAN.
BUT HE WAS A GREAT MAN. ONE OF THE BEST WE HAVE KNOWN.
HE KNEW THE COST OF FIGHTING THE HORDE. AND HE NEVER ONCE HESITATED TO PAY IT.
HE KNEW THAT PEACE WITH SUCH MONSTERS WAS IMPOSSIBLE.
HE DIED TO PRESERVE OUR FREEDOM. HE GAVE HIS LIFE FOR KUL TIRAS!
KUL TIRAS! KUL TIRAS! KUL TIRAS!
I ONLY WANTED TO STOP THE WAR... TO SAVE LIVES.
THUS, WE HONOR OUR FIERCEST WARRIOR--WHO WOULD NEVER LET HARM COME TO HIS PEOPLE!
PROUD-MOORE! PROUD-MOORE! PROUD-MOORE!
BUT I SAVED THE WRONG LIVES.
AND NOW THIS PLACE... THESE PEOPLE...THEY'RE AS BROKEN AS I AM.

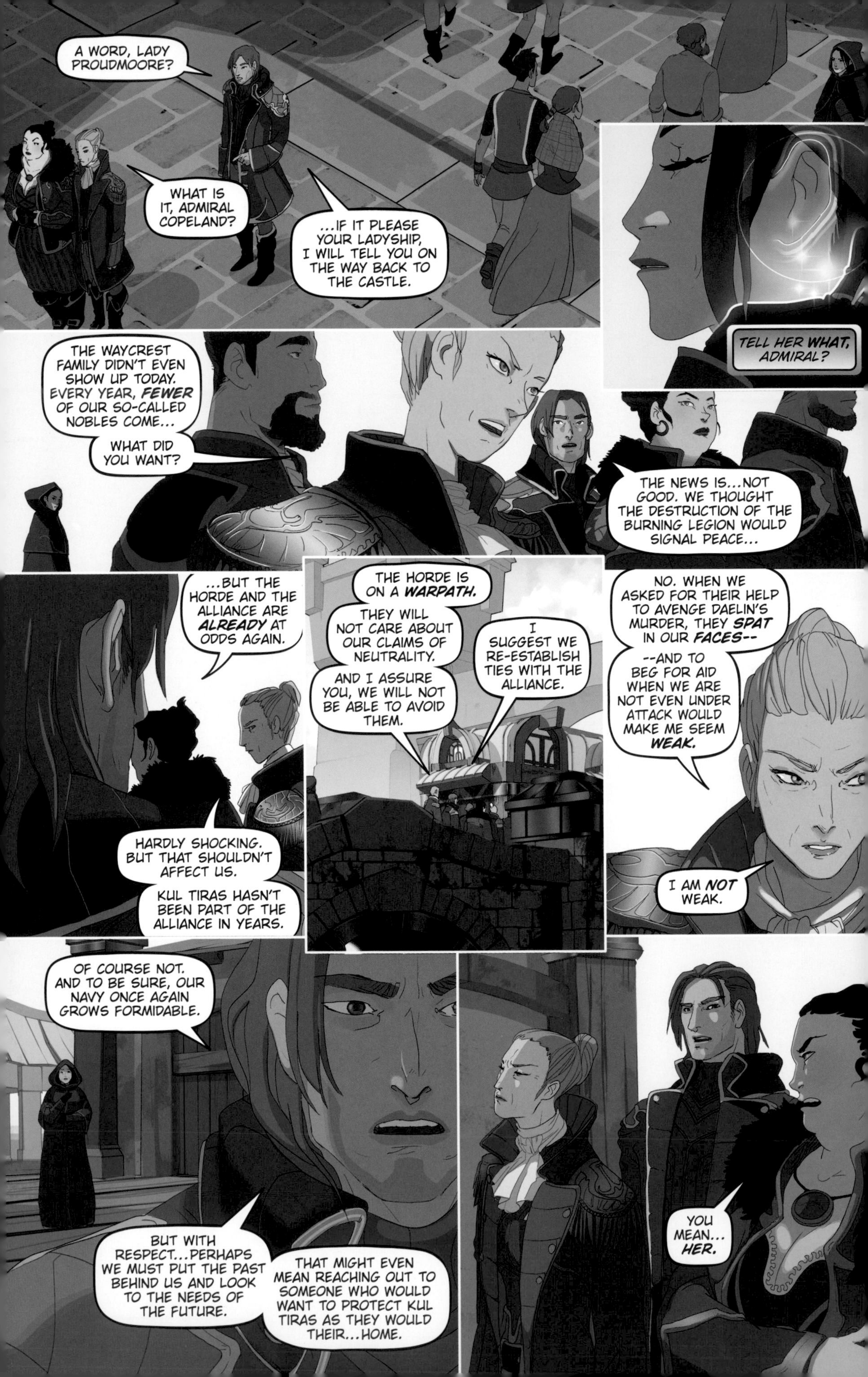
A WORD, LADY PROUDMOORE?
WHAT IS IT, ADMIRAL COPELAND?
...IF IT PLEASE YOUR LADYSHIP, I WILL TELL YOU ON THE WAY BACK TO THE CASTLE.
TELL HER WHAT, ADMIRAL?
THE WAYCREST FAMILY DIDN'T EVEN SHOW UP TODAY. EVERY YEAR, FEWER OF OUR SO-CALLED NOBLES COME...
WHAT DID YOU WANT?
THE NEWS IS...NOT GOOD. WE THOUGHT THE DESTRUCTION OF THE BURNING LEGION WOULD SIGNAL PEACE...
...BUT THE HORDE AND THE ALLIANCE ARE ALREADY AT ODDS AGAIN.
HARDLY SHOCKING. BUT THAT SHOULDN'T AFFECT US.
KUL TIRAS HASN'T BEEN PART OF THE ALLIANCE IN YEARS.
THE HORDE IS ON A WARPATH.
THEY WILL NOT CARE ABOUT OUR CLAIMS OF NEUTRALITY.
AND I ASSURE YOU, WE WILL NOT BE ABLE TO AVOID THEM.
I SUGGEST WE RE-ESTABLISH TIES WITH THE ALLIANCE.
NO. WHEN WE ASKED FOR THEIR HELP TO AVENGE DAELIN'S MURDER, THEY SPAT IN OUR FACES--
--AND TO BEG FOR AID WHEN WE ARE NOT EVEN UNDER ATTACK WOULD MAKE ME SEEM WEAK.
I AM NOT WEAK.
OF COURSE NOT. AND TO BE SURE, OUR NAVY ONCE AGAIN GROWS FORMIDABLE.
BUT WITH RESPECT...PERHAPS WE MUST PUT THE PAST BEHIND US AND LOOK TO THE NEEDS OF THE FUTURE.
THAT MIGHT EVEN MEAN REACHING OUT TO SOMEONE WHO WOULD WANT TO PROTECT KUL TIRAS AS THEY WOULD THEIR...HOME.
YOU MEAN... HER.

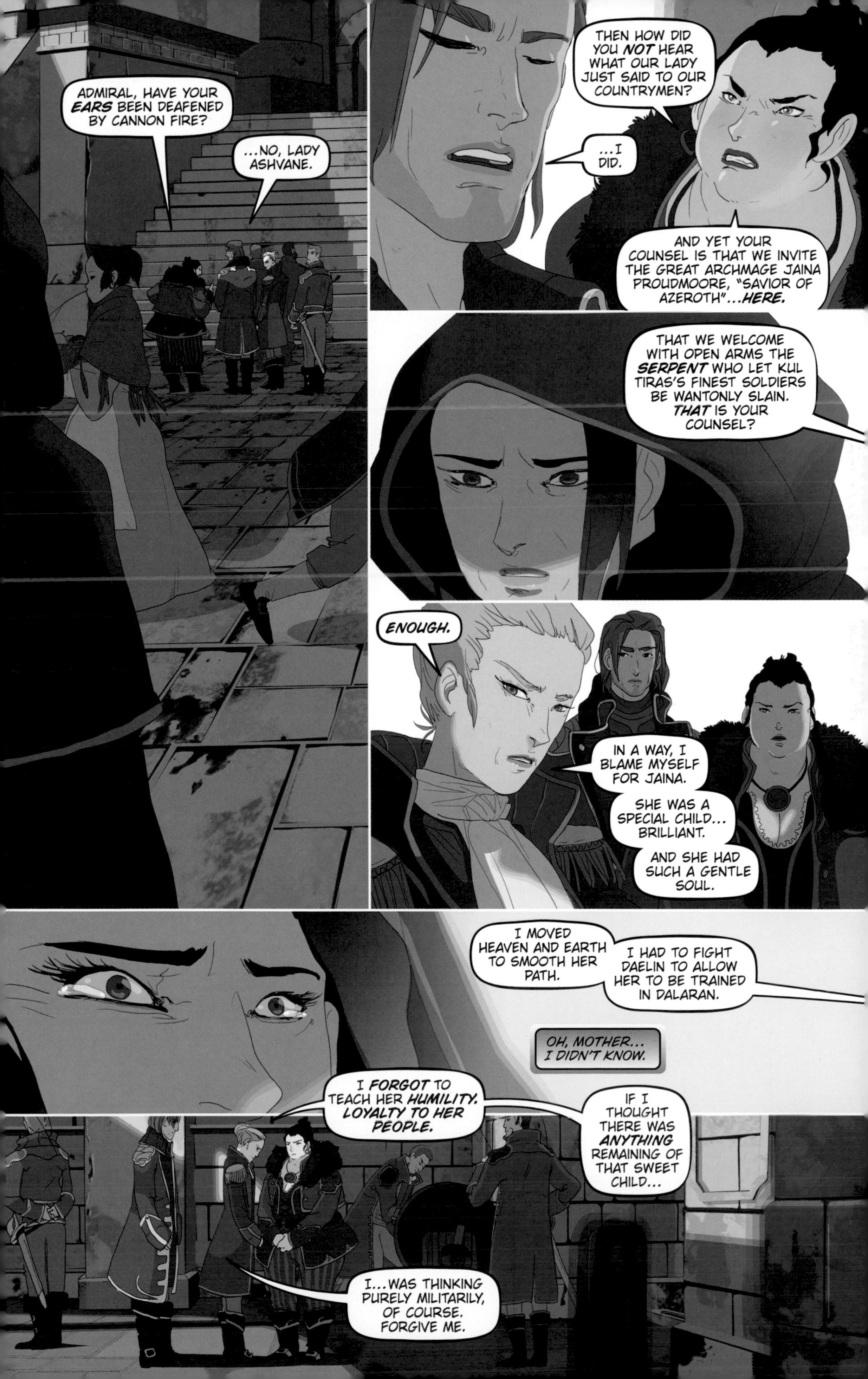
ADMIRAL, HAVE YOUR EARS BEEN DEAFENED BY CANNON FIRE?
...NO, LADY ASHVANE.
THEN HOW DID YOU NOT HEAR WHAT OUR LADY JUST SAID TO OUR COUNTRYMEN?
...I DID.
AND YET YOUR COUNSEL IS THAT WE INVITE THE GREAT ARCHMAGE JAINA PROUDMOORE, "SAVIOR OF AZEROTH"...HERE.
THAT WE WELCOME WITH OPEN ARMS THE SERPENT WHO LET KUL TIRAS'S FINEST SOLDIERS BE WANTONLY SLAIN. THAT IS YOUR COUNSEL?
ENOUGH.
IN A WAY, I BLAME MYSELF FOR JAINA.
SHE WAS A SPECIAL CHILD... BRILLIANT.
AND SHE HAD SUCH A GENTLE SOUL.
I MOVED HEAVEN AND EARTH TO SMOOTH HER PATH.
I HAD TO FIGHT DAELIN TO ALLOW HER TO BE TRAINED IN DALARAN.
OH, MOTHER... I DIDN'T KNOW.
I FORGOT TO TEACH HER HUMILITY. LOYALTY TO HER PEOPLE.
IF I THOUGHT THERE WAS ANYTHING REMAINING OF THAT SWEET CHILD...
I...WAS THINKING PURELY MILITARILY, OF COURSE. FORGIVE ME.

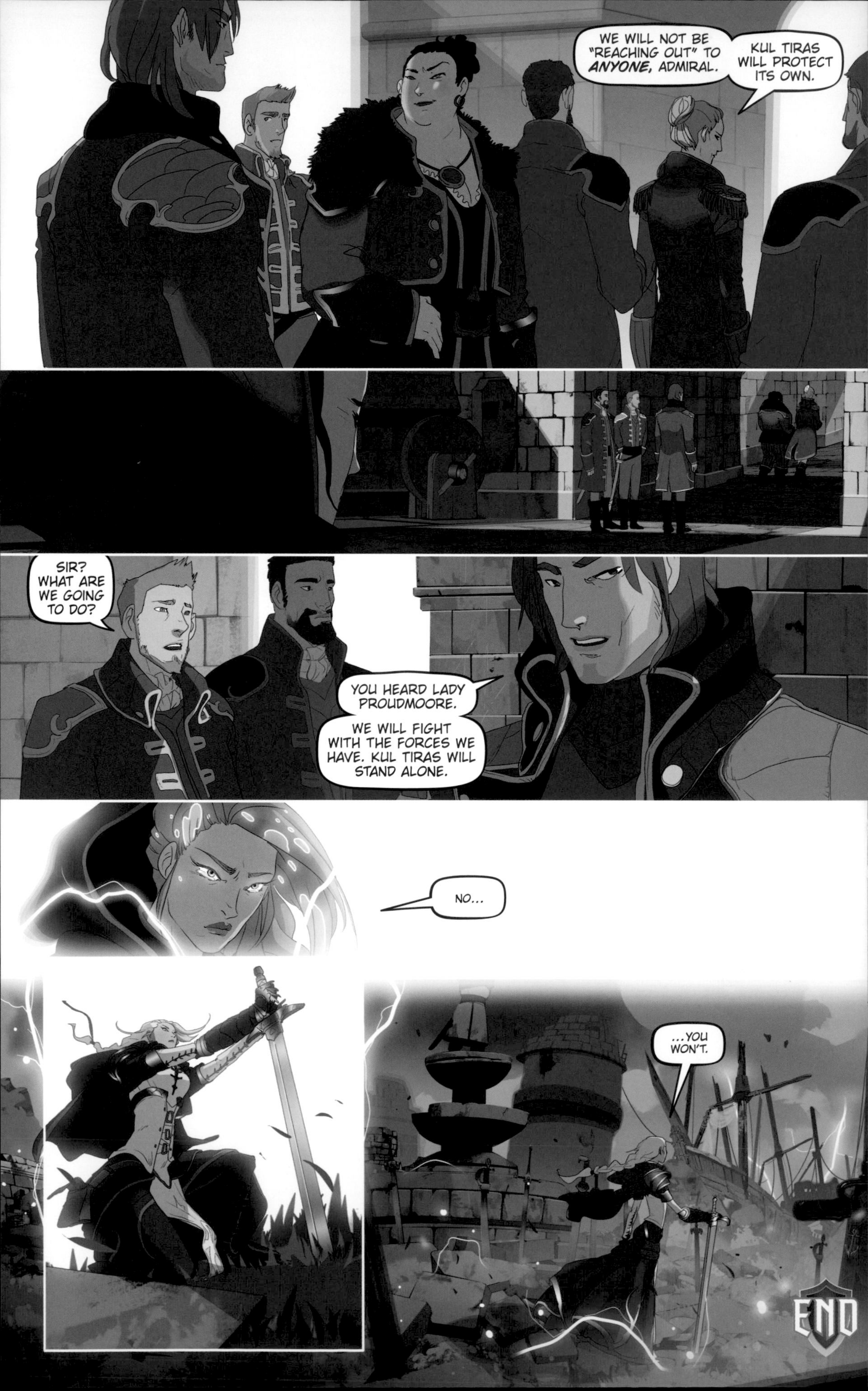
WE WILL NOT BE "REACHING OUT" TO ANYONE, ADMIRAL.
KUL TIRAS WILL PROTECT ITS OWN.
SIR? WHAT ARE WE GOING TO DO?
YOU HEARD LADY PROUDMOORE.
WE WILL FIGHT WITH THE FORCES WE HAVE. KUL TIRAS WILL STAND ALONE.
NO...
...YOU WON'T.
END

WORLD OF WARCRAFT
BATTLE FOR AZEROTH

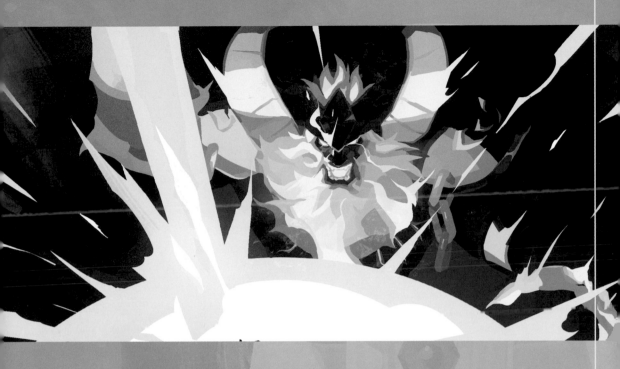

MAGNI

THE SPEAKER

SCRIPT BY **MATT BURNS** | ART BY **SUQLING** |
LETTERING BY **COMICRAFT**

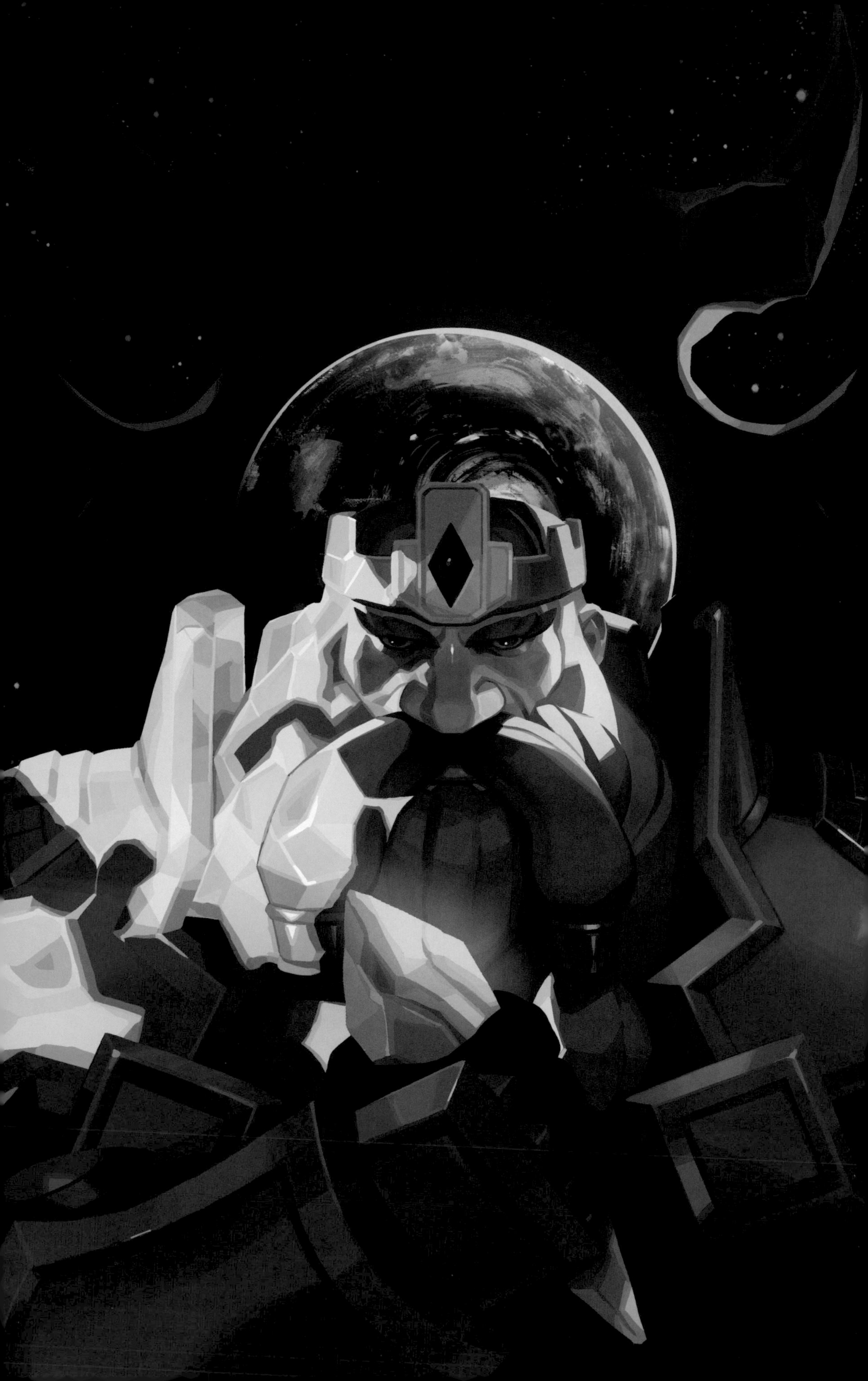

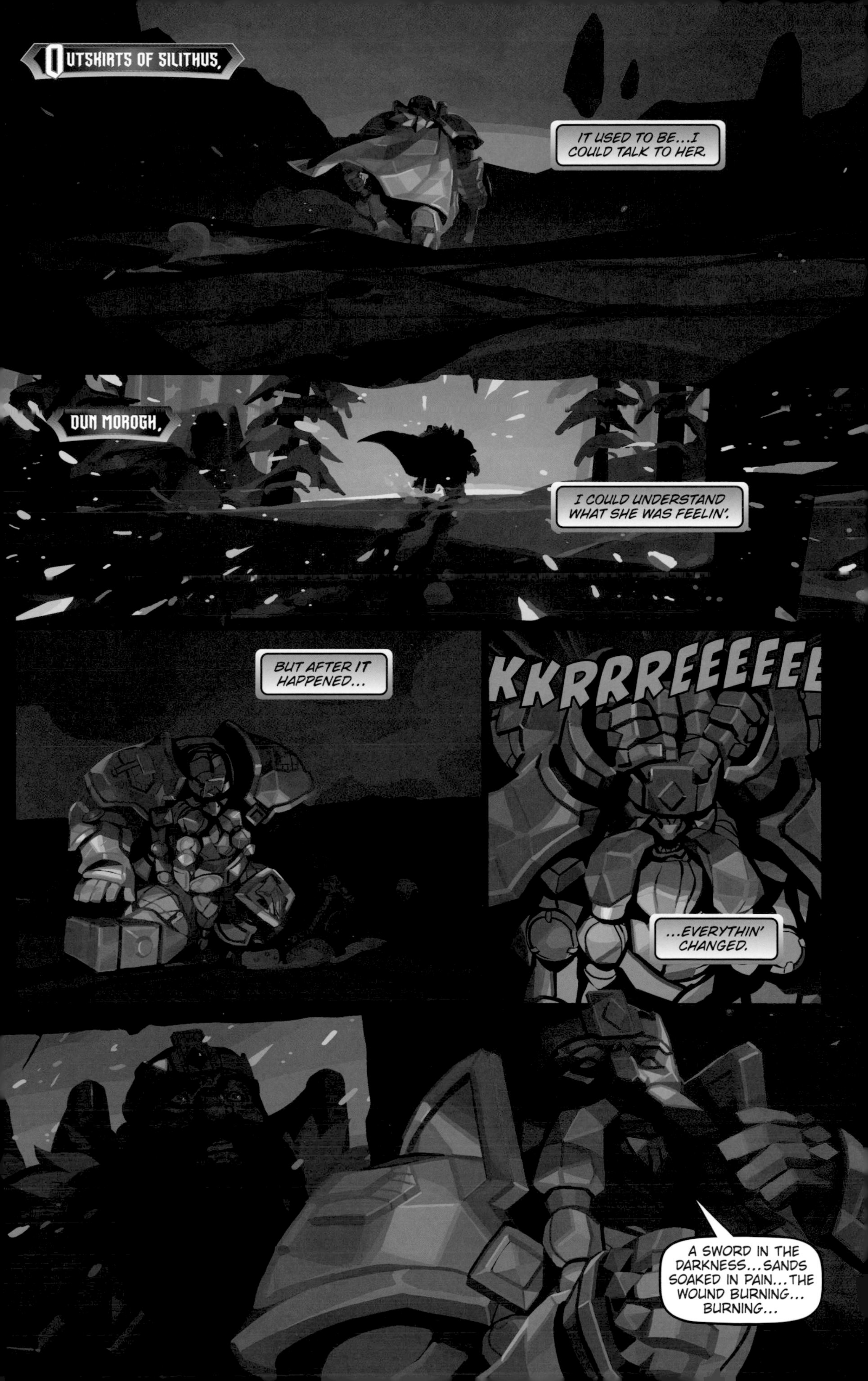
OUTSKIRTS OF SILITHUS,
IT USED TO BE...I COULD TALK TO HER.
DUN MOROGH,
I COULD UNDERSTAND WHAT SHE WAS FEELIN'.
BUT AFTER IT HAPPENED...
KKRRREEEEEEE
...EVERYTHIN' CHANGED.
A SWORD IN THE DARKNESS...SANDS SOAKED IN PAIN...THE WOUND BURNING... BURNING...

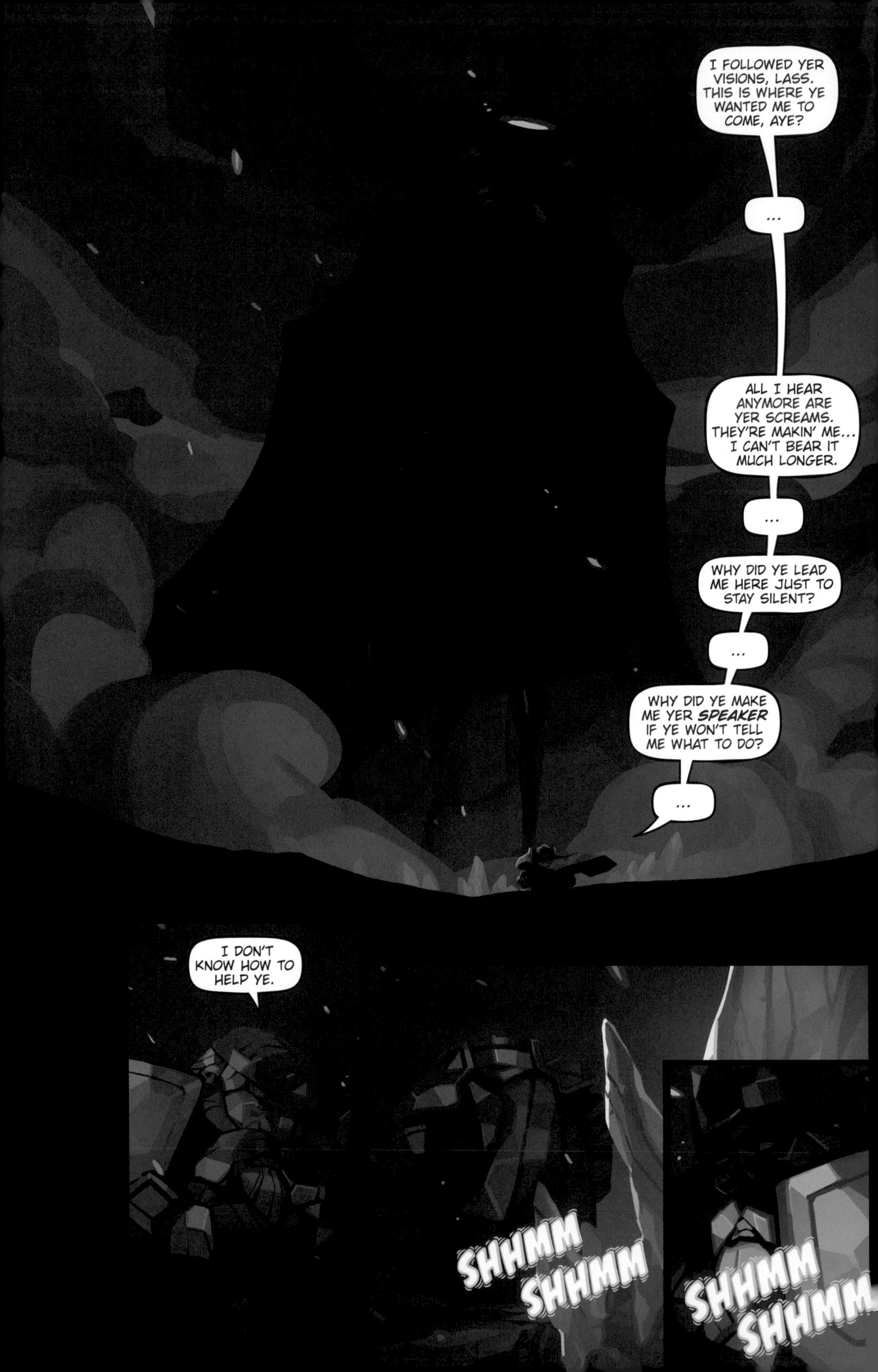

I FOLLOWED YER VISIONS, LASS. THIS IS WHERE YE WANTED ME TO COME, AYE?
...
ALL I HEAR ANYMORE ARE YER SCREAMS. THEY'RE MAKIN' ME... I CAN'T BEAR IT MUCH LONGER.
...
WHY DID YE LEAD ME HERE JUST TO STAY SILENT?
...
WHY DID YE MAKE ME YER *SPEAKER* IF YE WON'T TELL ME WHAT TO DO?
...
I DON'T KNOW HOW TO HELP YE.
SHHMM SHHMM
SHHMM SHHMM

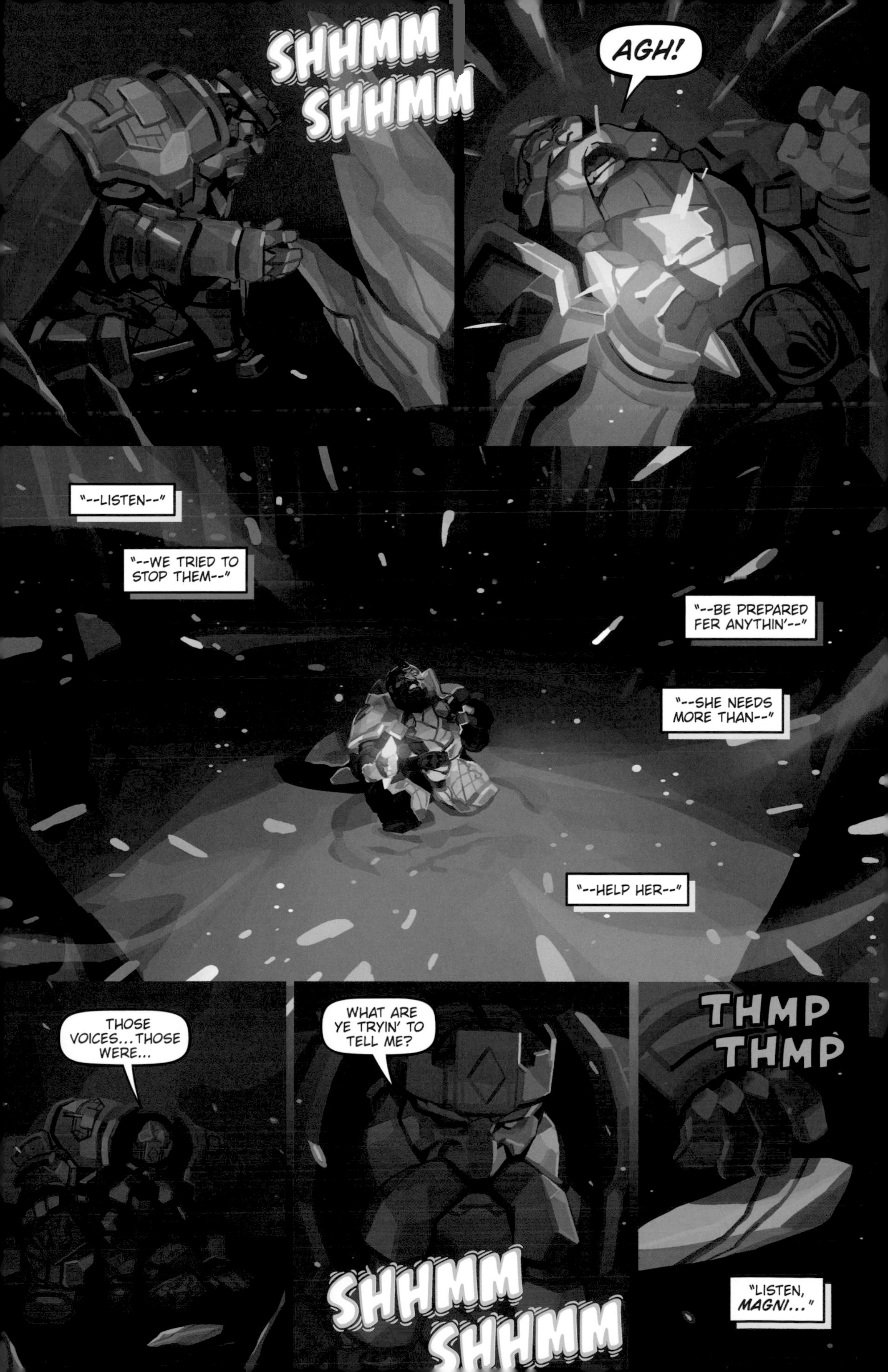
SHHMM SHHMM
AGH!
"--LISTEN--"
"--WE TRIED TO STOP THEM--"
"--BE PREPARED FER ANYTHIN'--"
"--SHE NEEDS MORE THAN--"
"--HELP HER--"
THOSE VOICES...THOSE WERE...
WHAT ARE YE TRYIN' TO TELL ME?
THMP THMP
SHHMM SHHMM
"LISTEN, *MAGNI*..."

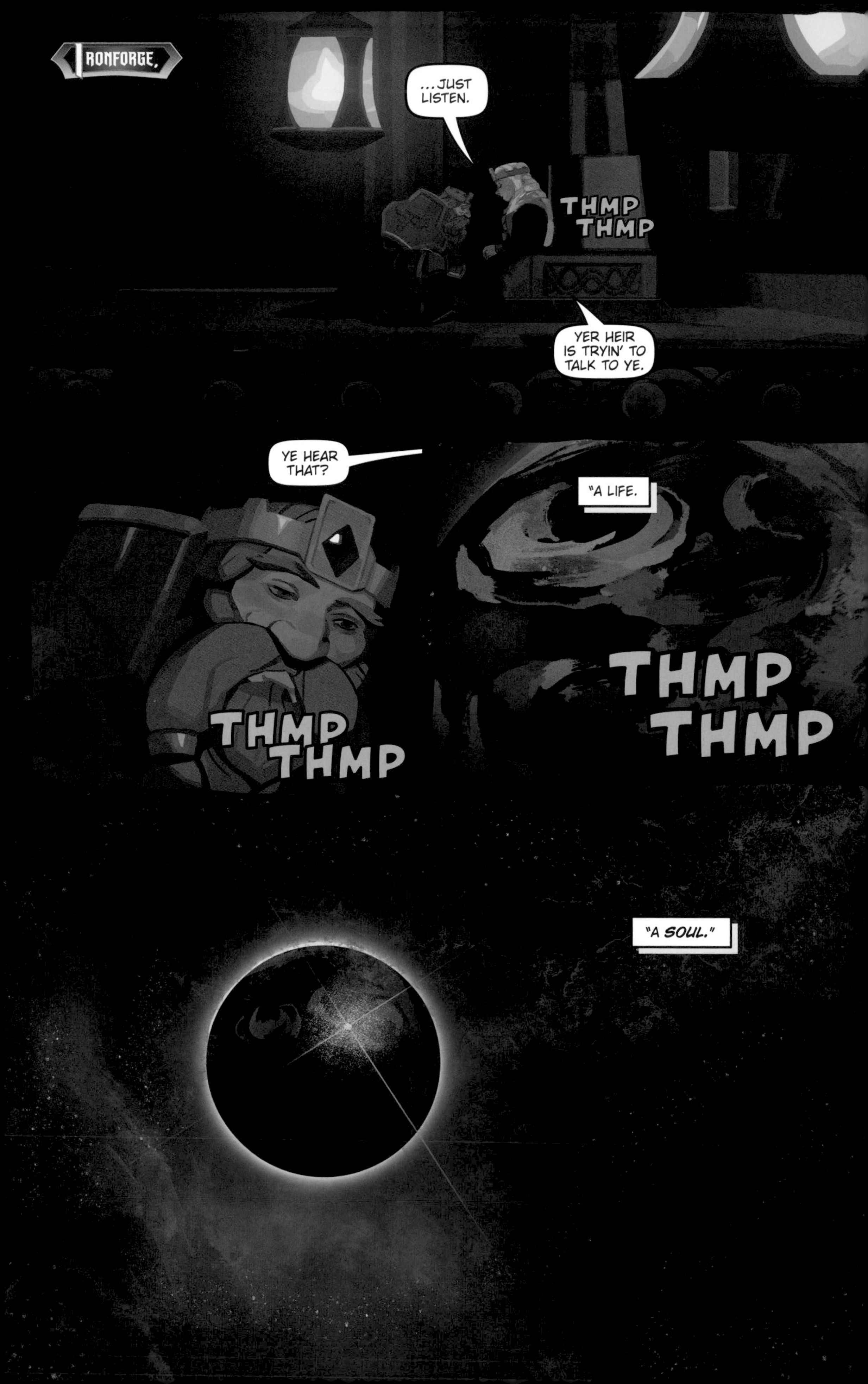
IRONFORGE,
...JUST LISTEN.
THMP THMP
YER HEIR IS TRYIN' TO TALK TO YE.
YE HEAR THAT?
THMP THMP
"A LIFE.
THMP THMP
"A SOUL."

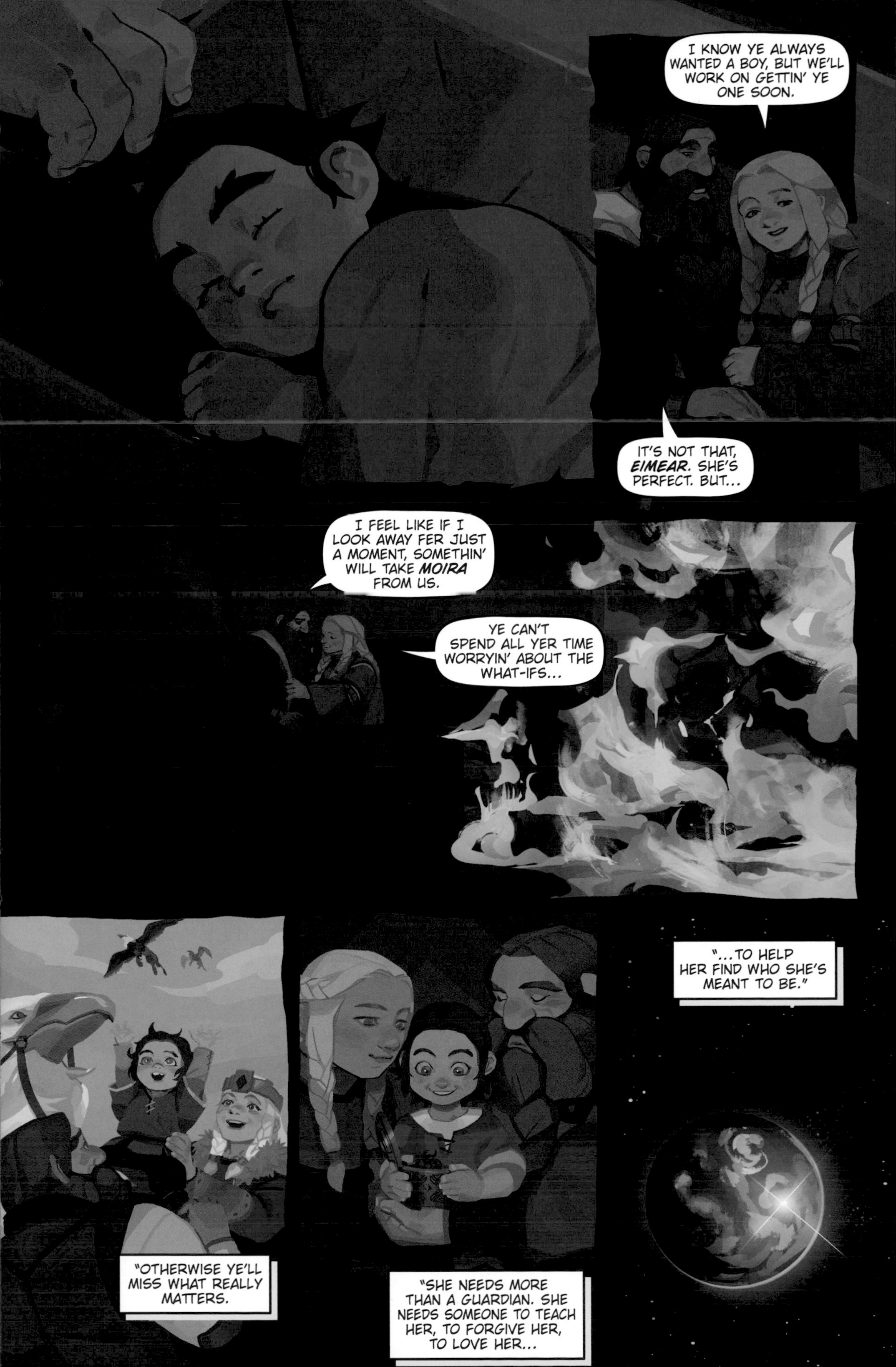
I KNOW YE ALWAYS WANTED A BOY, BUT WE'LL WORK ON GETTIN' YE ONE SOON.
IT'S NOT THAT, EIMEAR. SHE'S PERFECT. BUT...
I FEEL LIKE IF I LOOK AWAY FER JUST A MOMENT, SOMETHIN' WILL TAKE MOIRA FROM US.
YE CAN'T SPEND ALL YER TIME WORRYIN' ABOUT THE WHAT-IFS...
"OTHERWISE YE'LL MISS WHAT REALLY MATTERS.
"SHE NEEDS MORE THAN A GUARDIAN. SHE NEEDS SOMEONE TO TEACH HER, TO FORGIVE HER, TO LOVE HER...
"...TO HELP HER FIND WHO SHE'S MEANT TO BE."

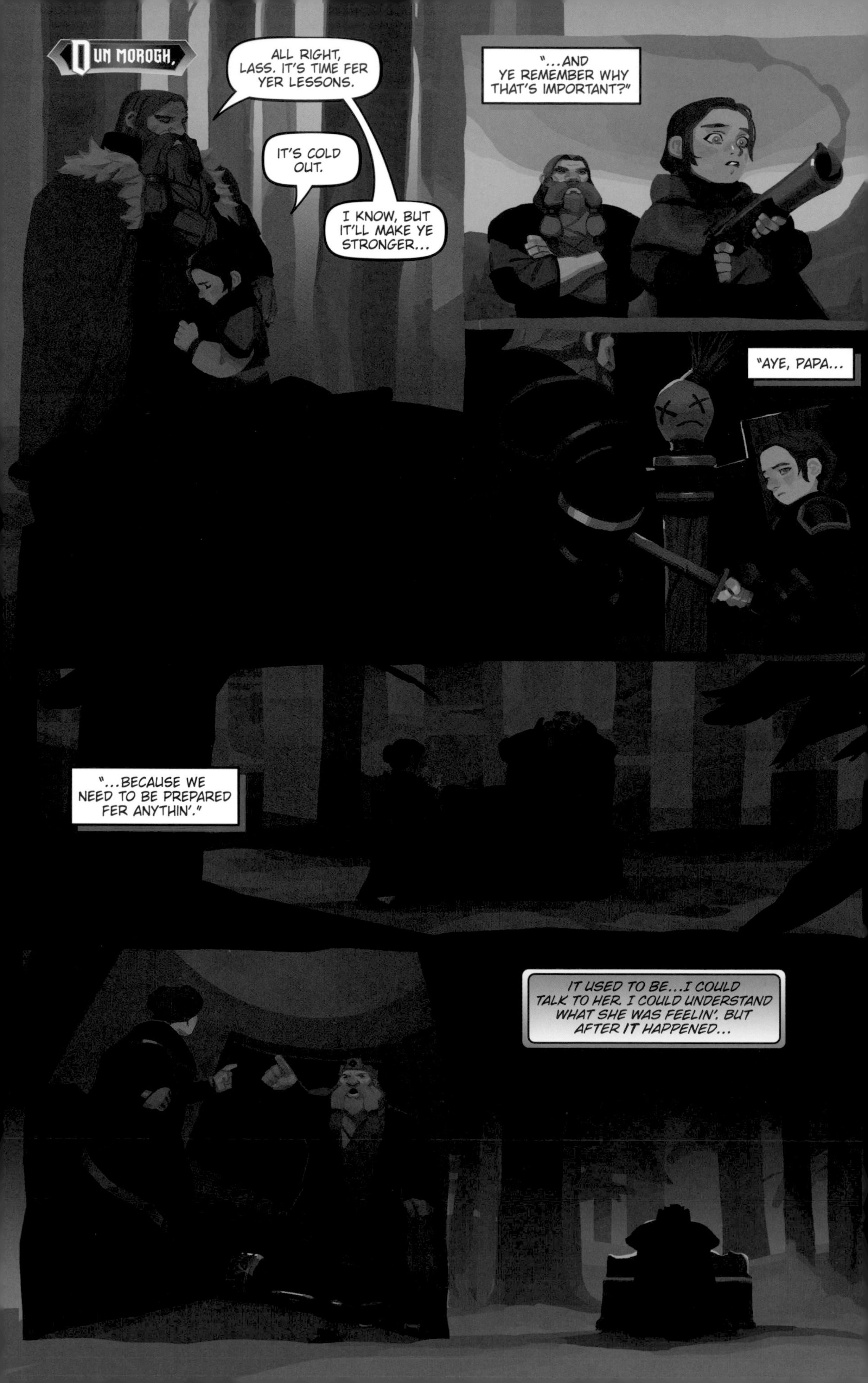
DUN MOROGH,
ALL RIGHT, LASS. IT'S TIME FER YER LESSONS.
IT'S COLD OUT.
I KNOW, BUT IT'LL MAKE YE STRONGER...
"...AND YE REMEMBER WHY THAT'S IMPORTANT?"
"AYE, PAPA...
"...BECAUSE WE NEED TO BE PREPARED FER ANYTHIN'."
IT USED TO BE...I COULD TALK TO HER. I COULD UNDERSTAND WHAT SHE WAS FEELIN'. BUT AFTER IT HAPPENED...

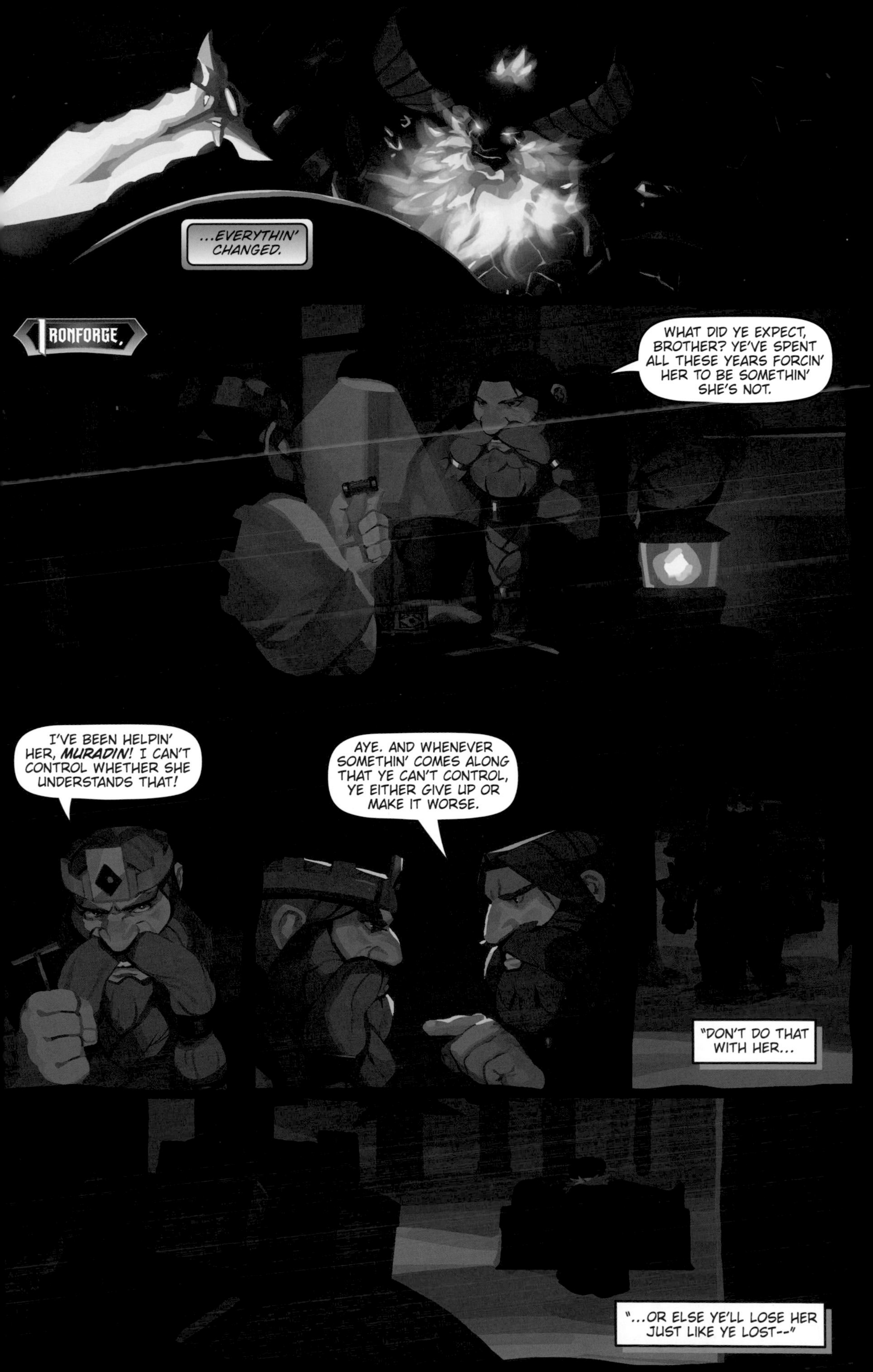
...EVERYTHIN' CHANGED.
IRONFORGE.
WHAT DID YE EXPECT, BROTHER? YE'VE SPENT ALL THESE YEARS FORCIN' HER TO BE SOMETHIN' SHE'S NOT.
I'VE BEEN HELPIN' HER, MURADIN! I CAN'T CONTROL WHETHER SHE UNDERSTANDS THAT!
AYE. AND WHENEVER SOMETHIN' COMES ALONG THAT YE CAN'T CONTROL, YE EITHER GIVE UP OR MAKE IT WORSE.
"DON'T DO THAT WITH HER...
"...OR ELSE YE'LL LOSE HER JUST LIKE YE LOST--"

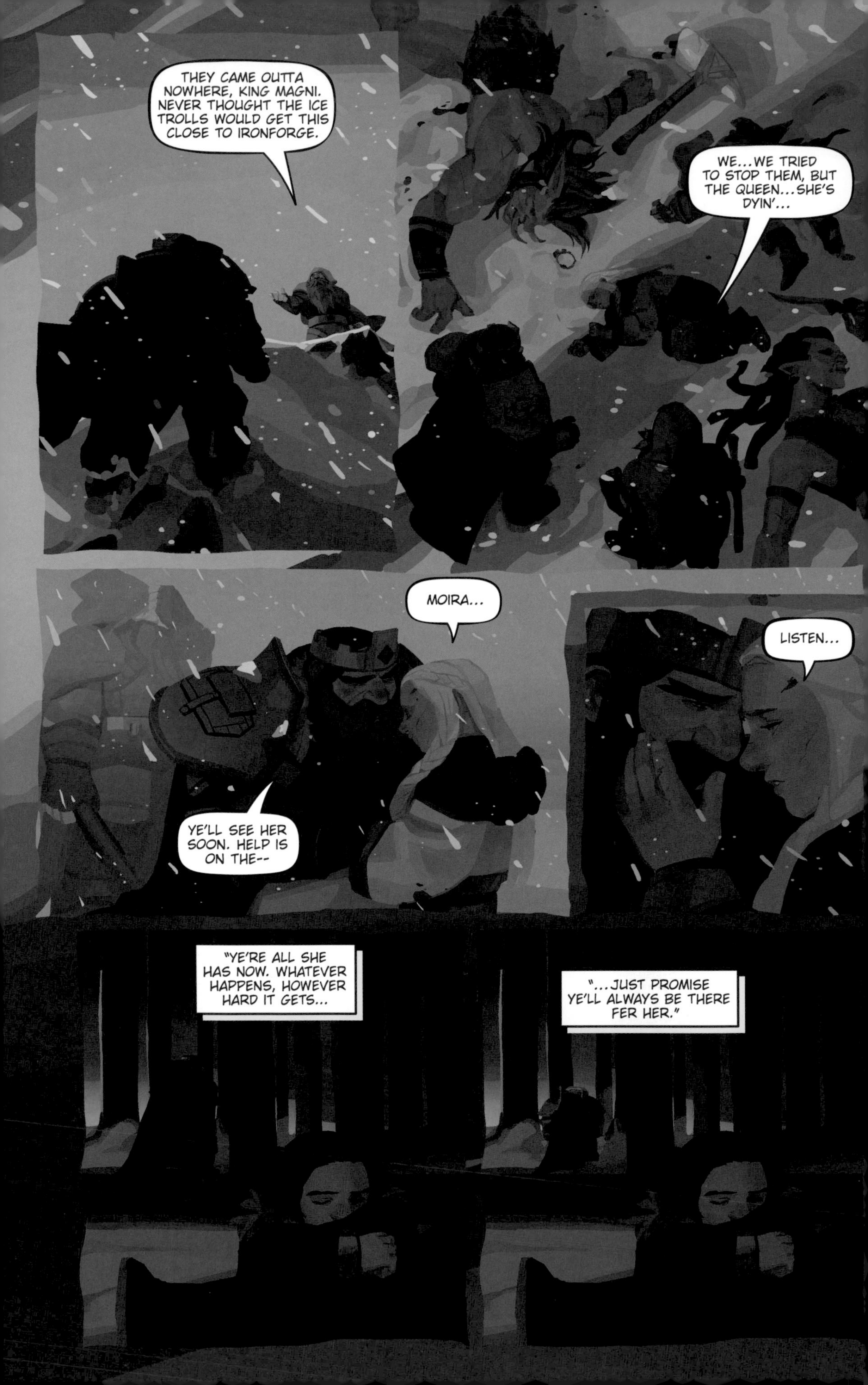
THEY CAME OUTTA NOWHERE, KING MAGNI. NEVER THOUGHT THE ICE TROLLS WOULD GET THIS CLOSE TO IRONFORGE.
WE...WE TRIED TO STOP THEM, BUT THE QUEEN...SHE'S DYIN'...
MOIRA...
YE'LL SEE HER SOON. HELP IS ON THE--
LISTEN...
"YE'RE ALL SHE HAS NOW. WHATEVER HAPPENS, HOWEVER HARD IT GETS...
"...JUST PROMISE YE'LL ALWAYS BE THERE FER HER."

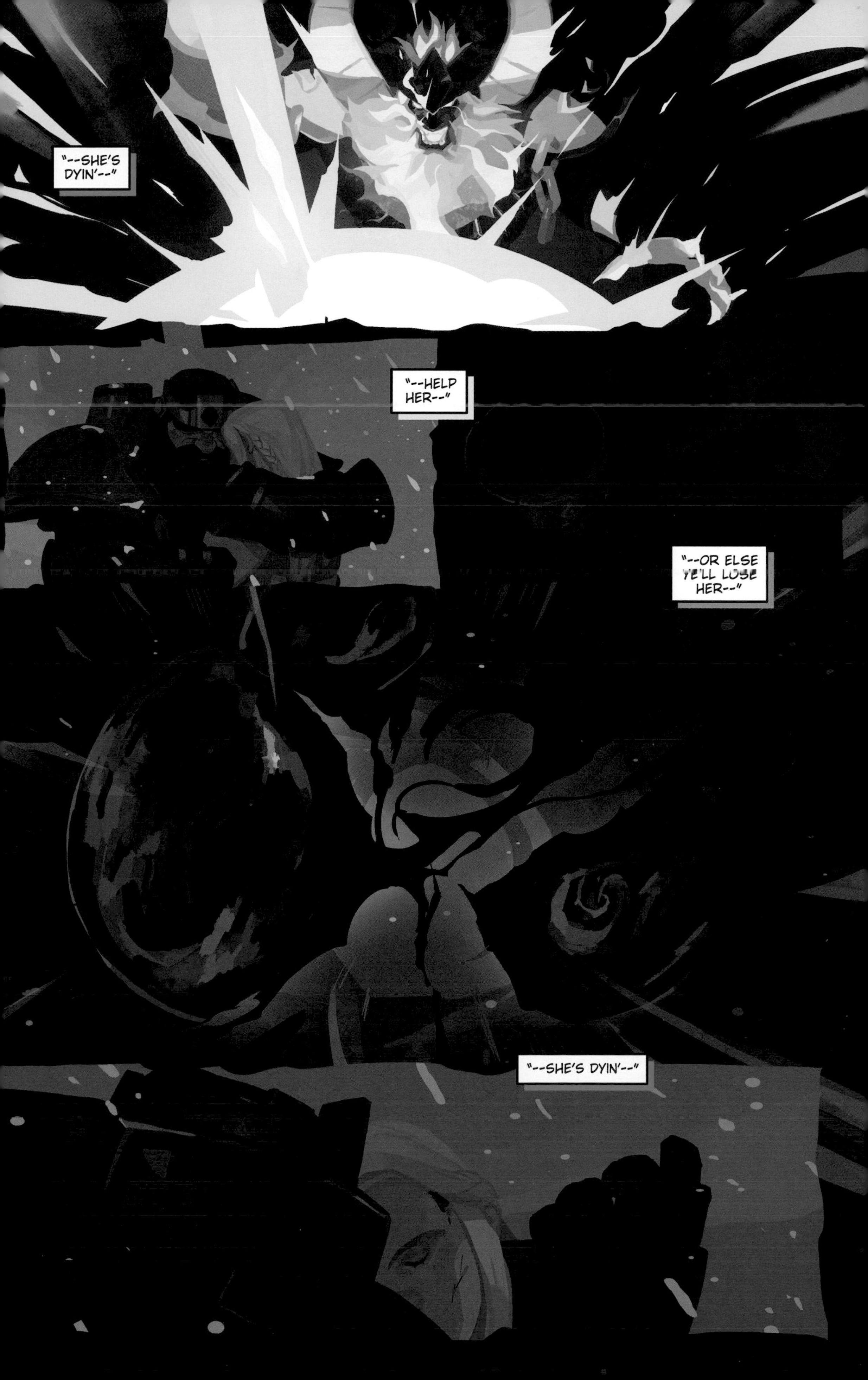
"--SHE'S DYIN'--"
"--HELP HER--"
"--OR ELSE YE'LL LOSE HER--"
"--SHE'S DYIN'--"

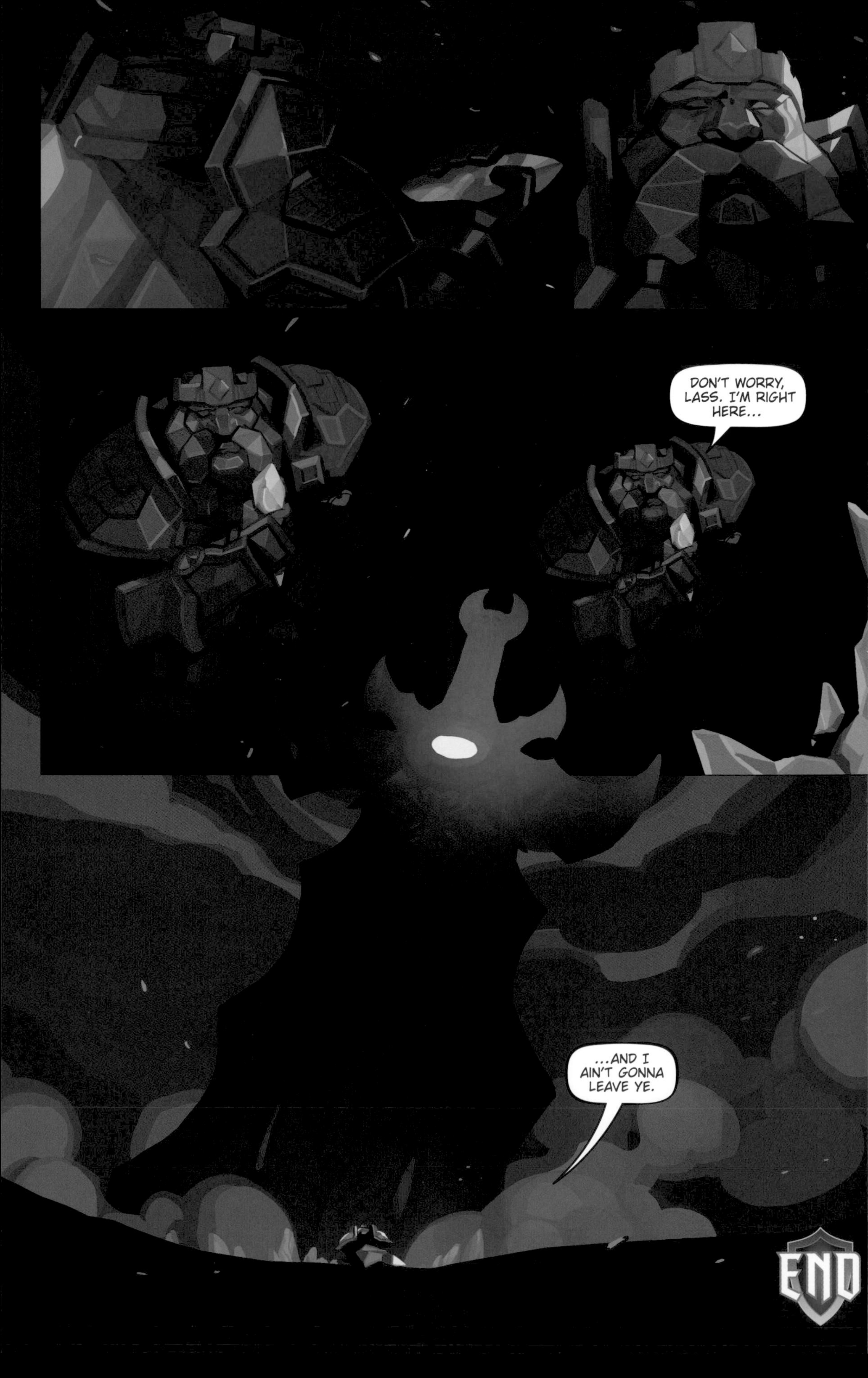
DON'T WORRY, LASS. I'M RIGHT HERE...
...AND I AIN'T GONNA LEAVE YE.
END

World of Warcraft: Battle for Azeroth

WINDRUNNER

THREE SISTERS

PLOT BY **STEVE DANUSER** | SCRIPT BY **CHRISTIE GOLDEN & ANDREW ROBINSON** | ART BY **ANTONIO BIFULCO** | COLORS BY **SEBASTIAN CHENG** | LETTERING BY **COMICRAFT**

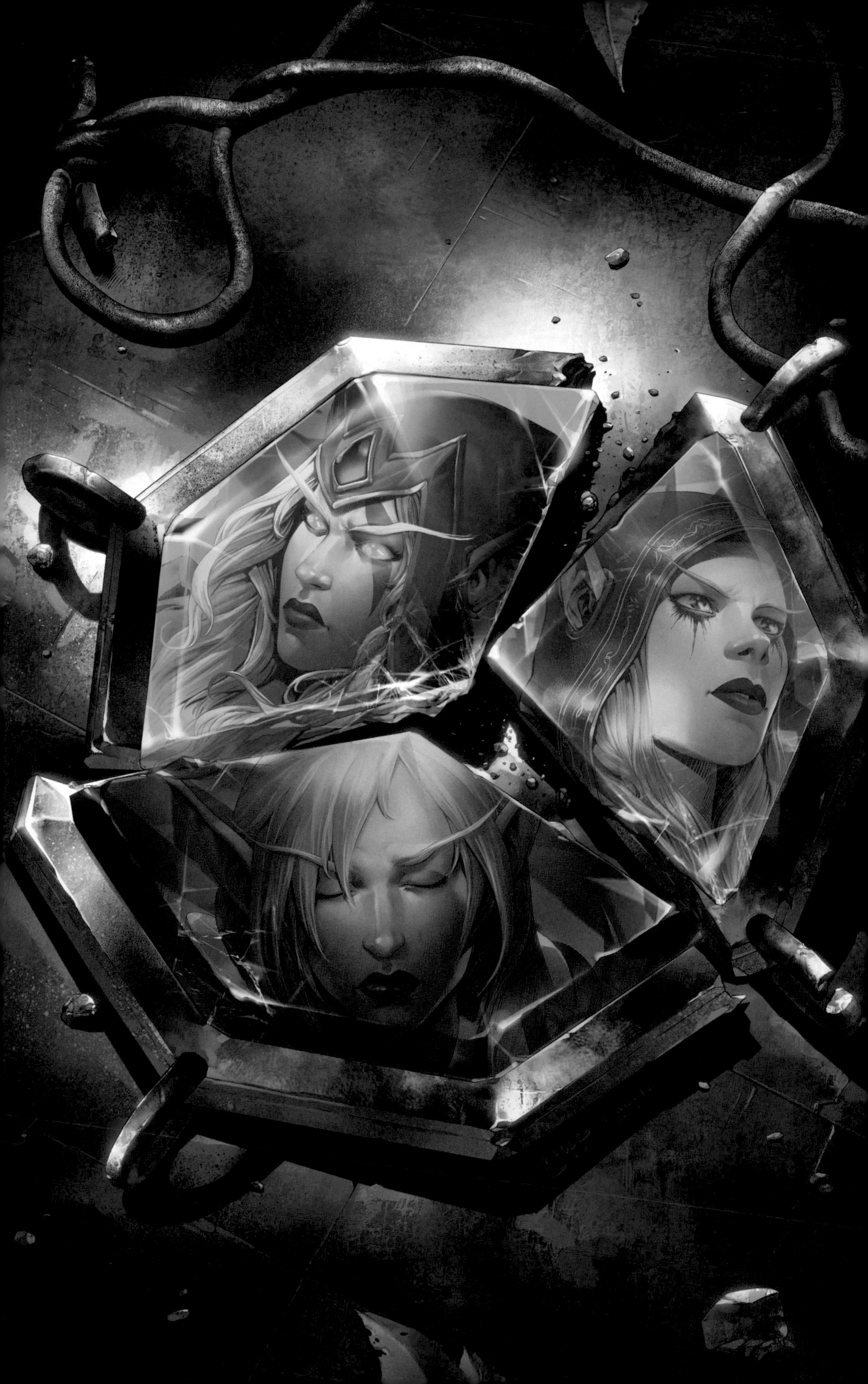

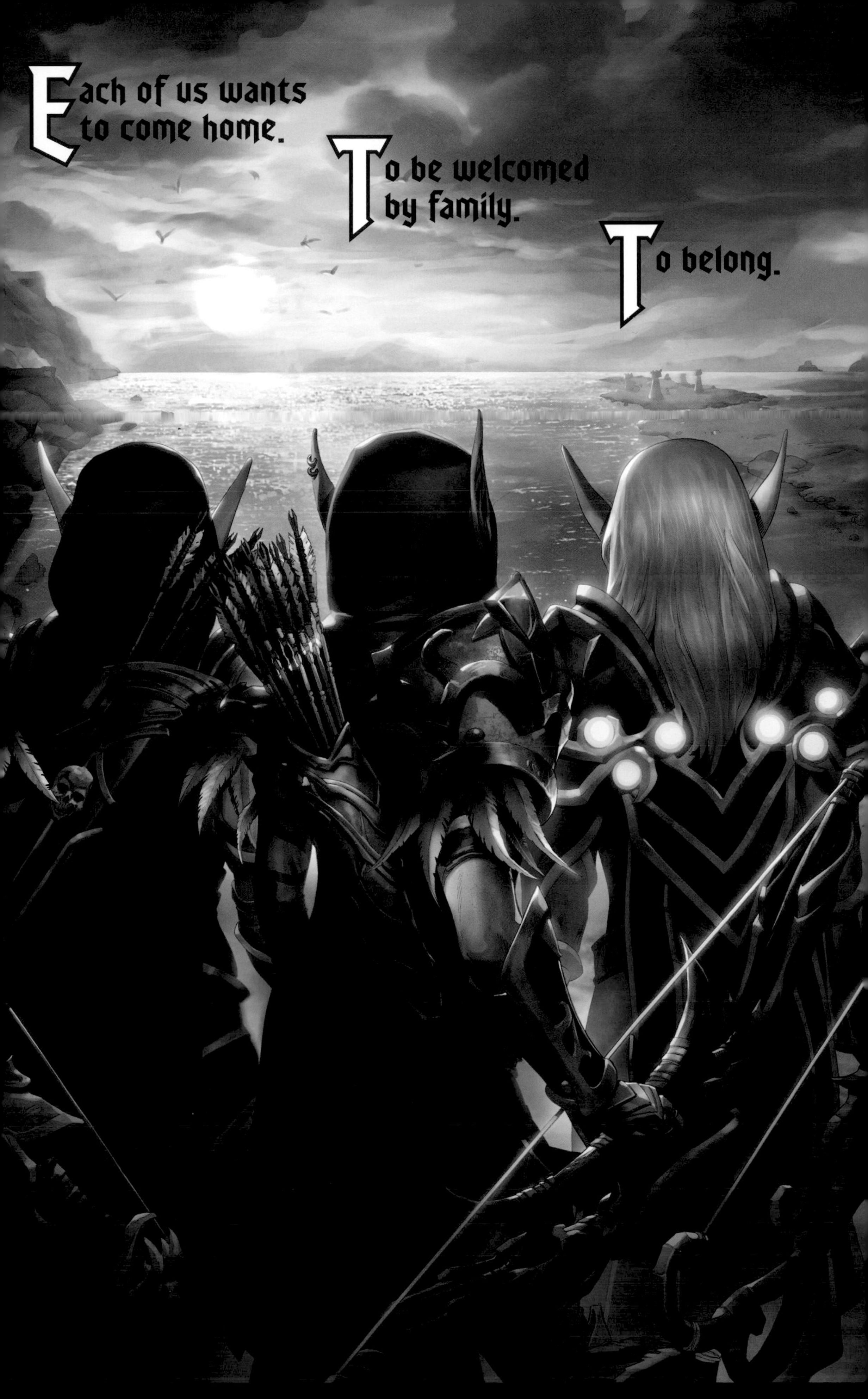
Each of us wants to come home.
To be welcomed by family.
To belong.

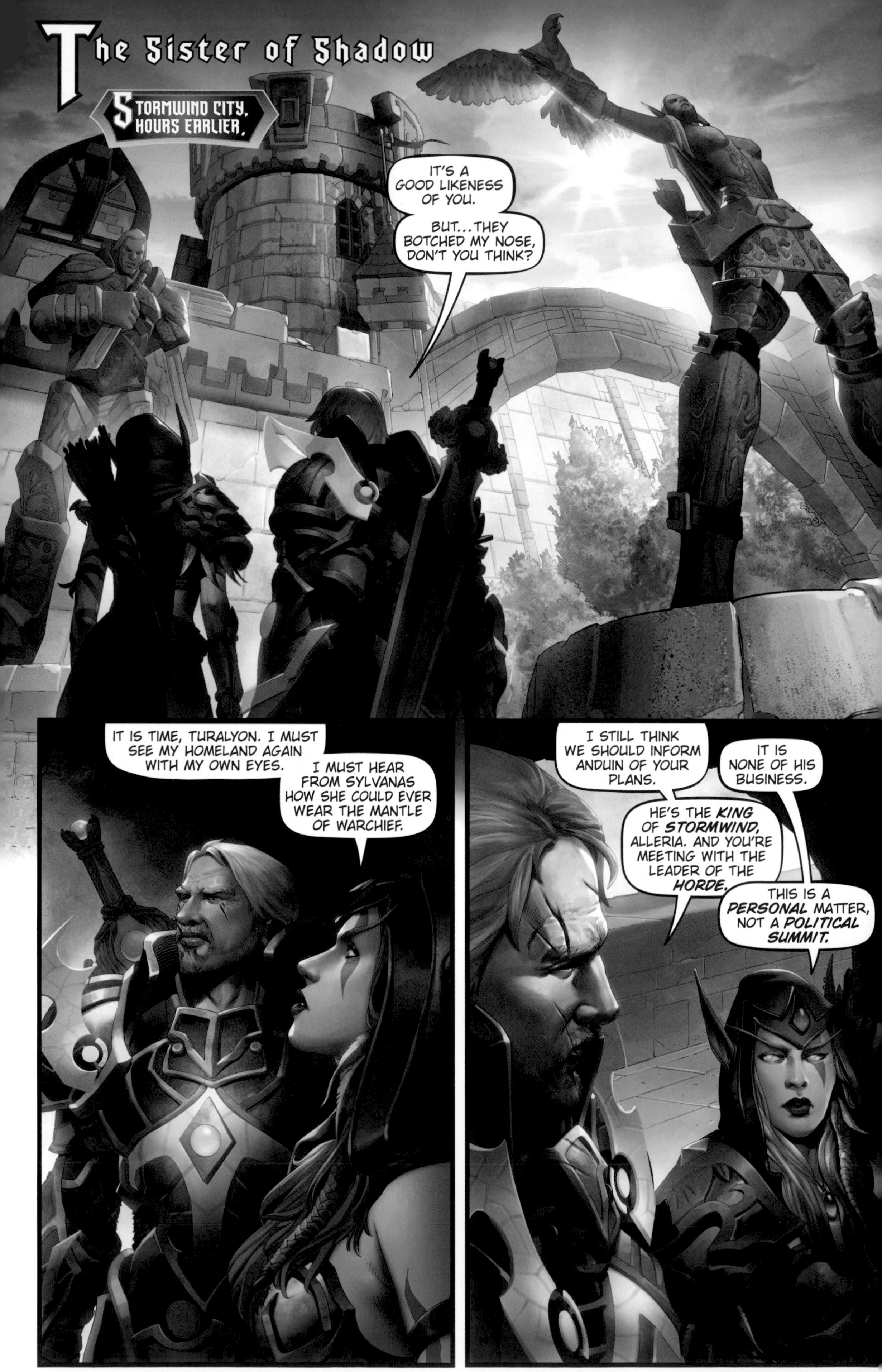
The Sister of Shadow
Stormwind City, hours earlier.
It's a good likeness of you.
But...they botched my nose, don't you think?
It is time, Turalyon. I must see my homeland again with my own eyes.
I must hear from Sylvanas how she could ever wear the mantle of warchief.
I still think we should inform Anduin of your plans.
It is none of his business.
He's the king of Stormwind, Alleria. And you're meeting with the leader of the Horde.
This is a personal matter, not a political summit.

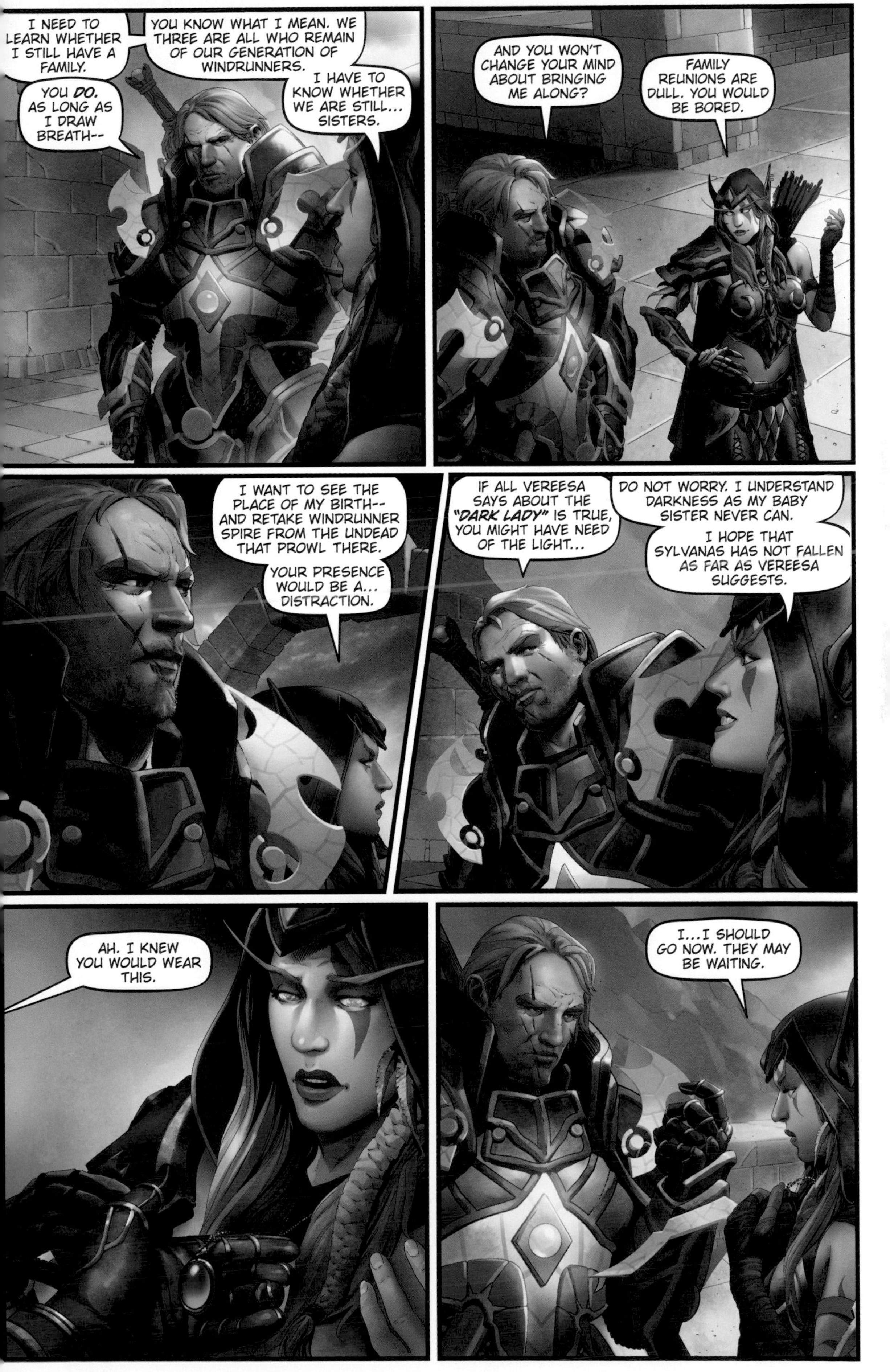
I NEED TO LEARN WHETHER I STILL HAVE A FAMILY.
YOU KNOW WHAT I MEAN. WE THREE ARE ALL WHO REMAIN OF OUR GENERATION OF WINDRUNNERS.
YOU *DO.* AS LONG AS I DRAW BREATH--
I HAVE TO KNOW WHETHER WE ARE STILL... SISTERS.
AND YOU WON'T CHANGE YOUR MIND ABOUT BRINGING ME ALONG?
FAMILY REUNIONS ARE DULL. YOU WOULD BE BORED.
I WANT TO SEE THE PLACE OF MY BIRTH--AND RETAKE WINDRUNNER SPIRE FROM THE UNDEAD THAT PROWL THERE.
YOUR PRESENCE WOULD BE A... DISTRACTION.
IF ALL VEREESA SAYS ABOUT THE *"DARK LADY"* IS TRUE, YOU MIGHT HAVE NEED OF THE LIGHT...
DO NOT WORRY. I UNDERSTAND DARKNESS AS MY BABY SISTER NEVER CAN.
I HOPE THAT SYLVANAS HAS NOT FALLEN AS FAR AS VEREESA SUGGESTS.
AH. I KNEW YOU WOULD WEAR THIS.
I...I SHOULD GO NOW. THEY MAY BE WAITING.

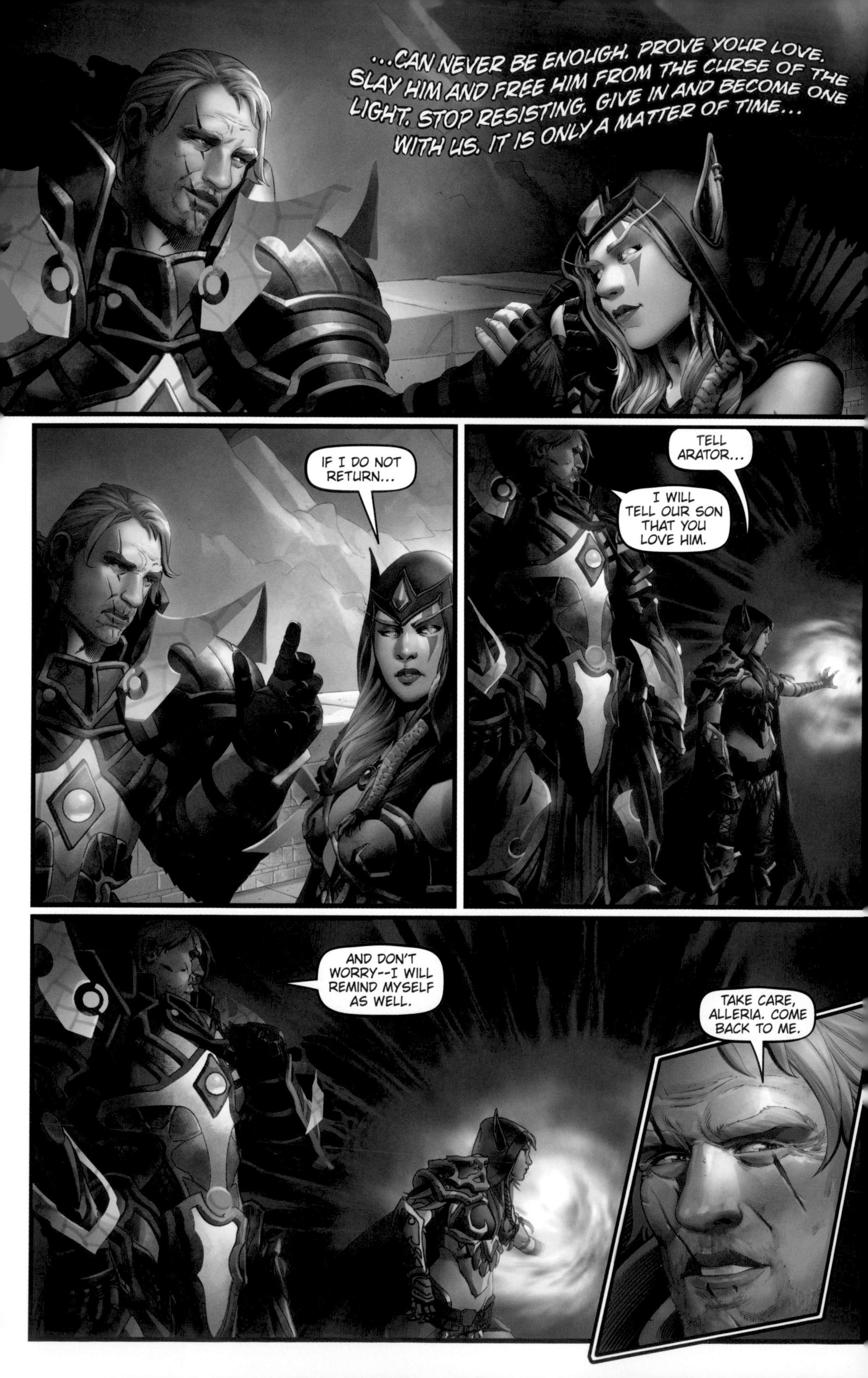
...CAN NEVER BE ENOUGH. PROVE YOUR LOVE. SLAY HIM AND FREE HIM FROM THE CURSE OF THE LIGHT. STOP RESISTING, GIVE IN AND BECOME ONE WITH US. IT IS ONLY A MATTER OF TIME...
IF I DO NOT RETURN...
TELL ARATOR...
I WILL TELL OUR SON THAT YOU LOVE HIM.
AND DON'T WORRY--I WILL REMIND MYSELF AS WELL.
TAKE CARE, ALLERIA. COME BACK TO ME.

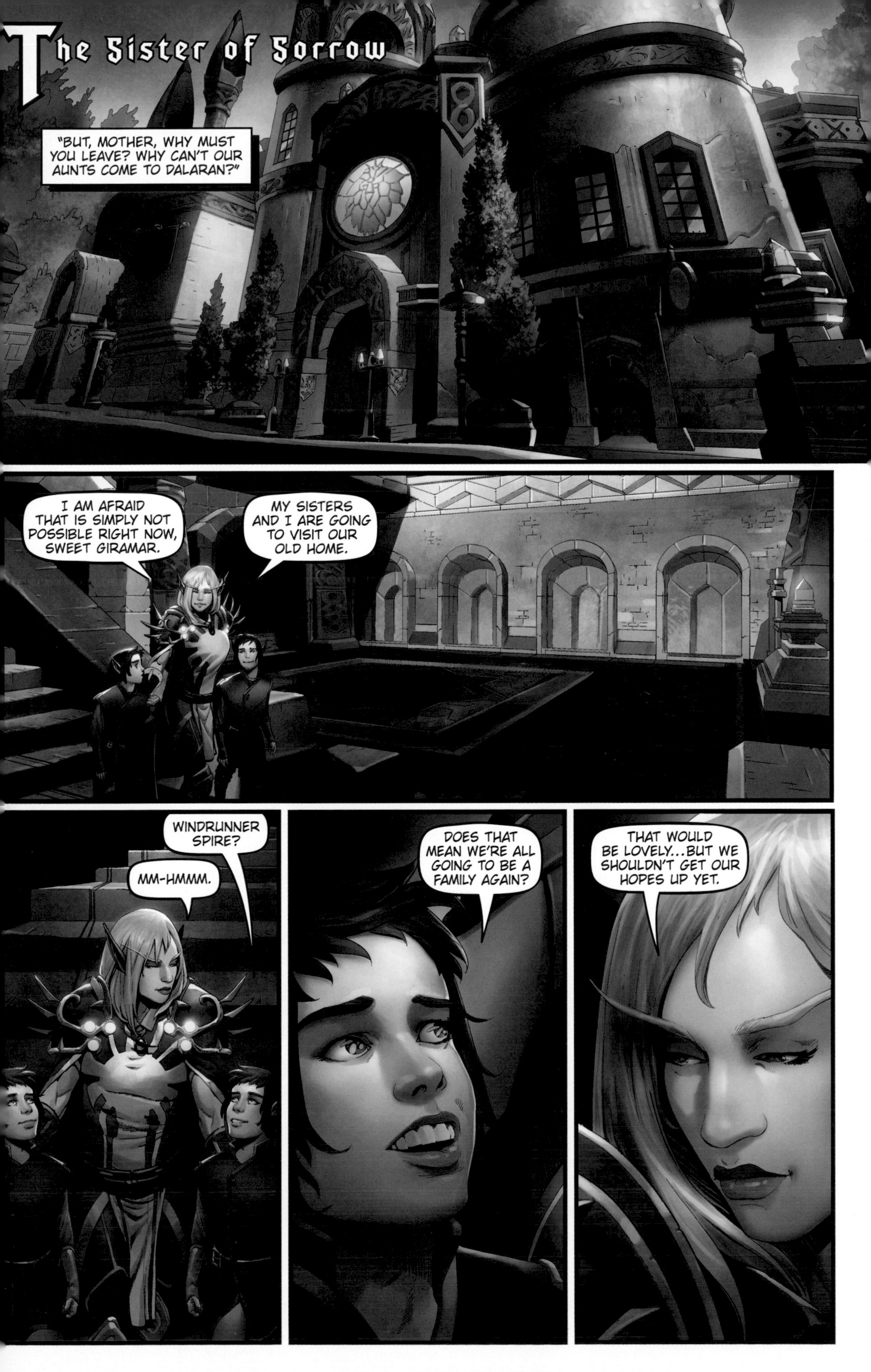
The Sister of Sorrow
"BUT, MOTHER, WHY MUST YOU LEAVE? WHY CAN'T OUR AUNTS COME TO DALARAN?"
I AM AFRAID THAT IS SIMPLY NOT POSSIBLE RIGHT NOW, SWEET GIRAMAR.
MY SISTERS AND I ARE GOING TO VISIT OUR OLD HOME.
WINDRUNNER SPIRE?
MM-HMMM.
DOES THAT MEAN WE'RE ALL GOING TO BE A FAMILY AGAIN?
THAT WOULD BE LOVELY...BUT WE SHOULDN'T GET OUR HOPES UP YET.

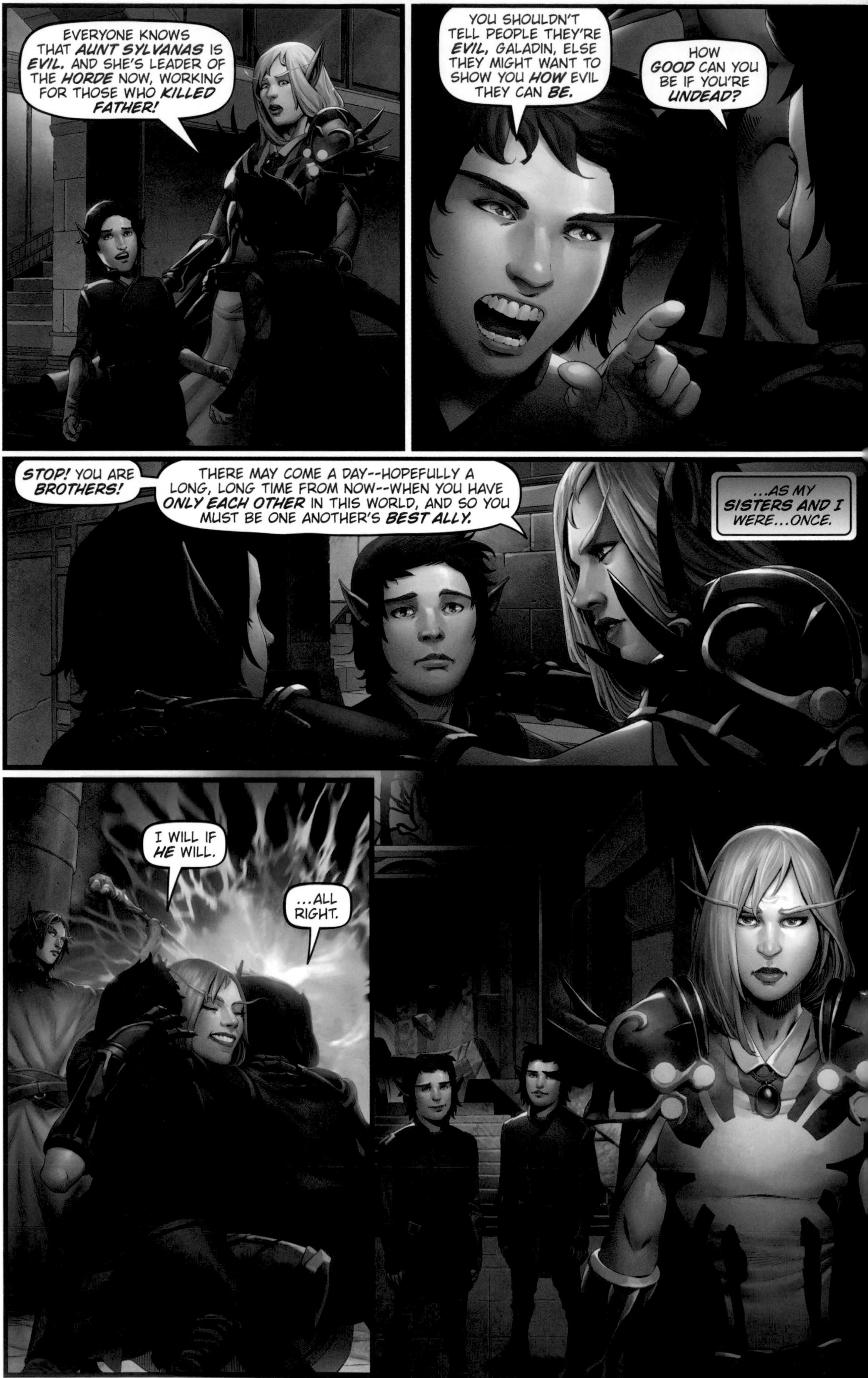
EVERYONE KNOWS THAT AUNT SYLVANAS IS EVIL. AND SHE'S LEADER OF THE HORDE NOW, WORKING FOR THOSE WHO KILLED FATHER!
YOU SHOULDN'T TELL PEOPLE THEY'RE EVIL, GALADIN, ELSE THEY MIGHT WANT TO SHOW YOU HOW EVIL THEY CAN BE.
HOW GOOD CAN YOU BE IF YOU'RE UNDEAD?
STOP! YOU ARE BROTHERS!
THERE MAY COME A DAY--HOPEFULLY A LONG, LONG TIME FROM NOW--WHEN YOU HAVE ONLY EACH OTHER IN THIS WORLD, AND SO YOU MUST BE ONE ANOTHER'S BEST ALLY.
...AS MY SISTERS AND I WERE...ONCE.
I WILL IF HE WILL.
...ALL RIGHT.

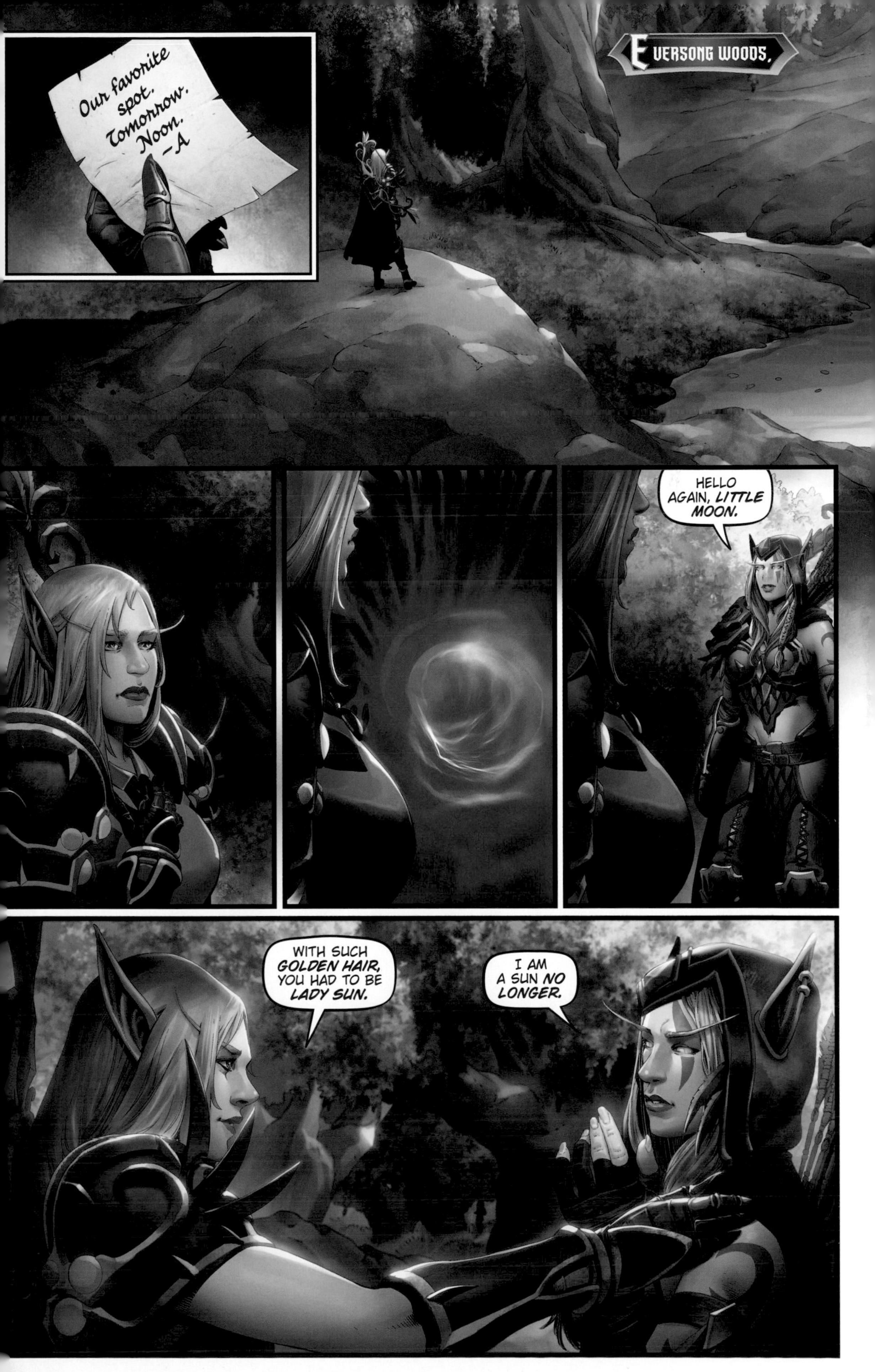

Our favorite spot. Tomorrow. Noon. -A
EVERSONG WOODS,
HELLO AGAIN, LITTLE MOON.
WITH SUCH GOLDEN HAIR, YOU HAD TO BE LADY SUN.
I AM A SUN NO LONGER.

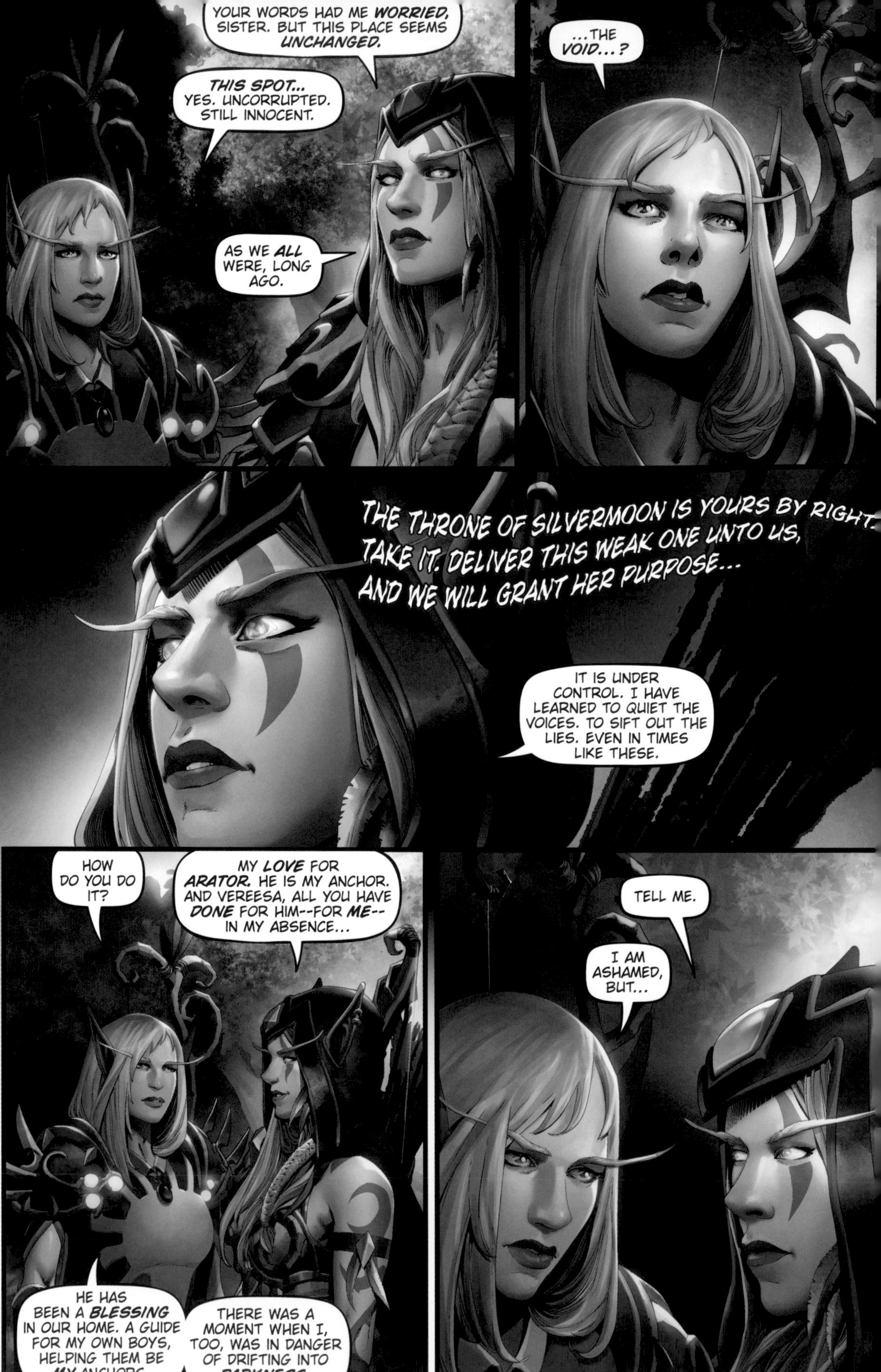
YOUR WORDS HAD ME WORRIED, SISTER. BUT THIS PLACE SEEMS UNCHANGED.
THIS SPOT... YES. UNCORRUPTED. STILL INNOCENT.
AS WE ALL WERE, LONG AGO.
...THE VOID...?
THE THRONE OF SILVERMOON IS YOURS BY RIGHT. TAKE IT. DELIVER THIS WEAK ONE UNTO US, AND WE WILL GRANT HER PURPOSE...
IT IS UNDER CONTROL. I HAVE LEARNED TO QUIET THE VOICES. TO SIFT OUT THE LIES. EVEN IN TIMES LIKE THESE.
HOW DO YOU DO IT?
MY LOVE FOR ARATOR. HE IS MY ANCHOR. AND VEREESA, ALL YOU HAVE DONE FOR HIM--FOR ME--IN MY ABSENCE...
HE HAS BEEN A BLESSING IN OUR HOME. A GUIDE FOR MY OWN BOYS, HELPING THEM BE MY ANCHORS.
THERE WAS A MOMENT WHEN I, TOO, WAS IN DANGER OF DRIFTING INTO DARKNESS.
TELL ME.
I AM ASHAMED, BUT...

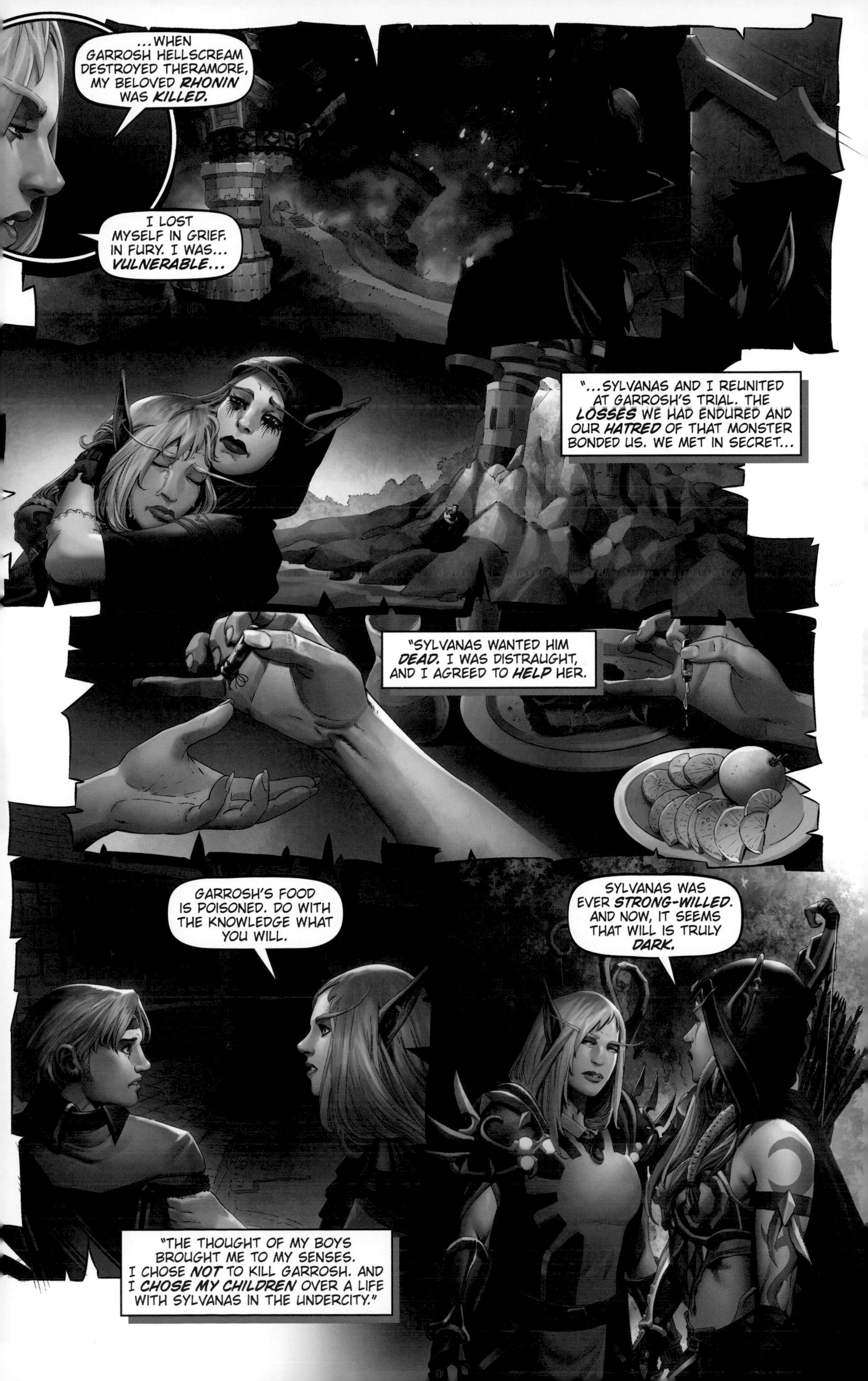
...WHEN GARROSH HELLSCREAM DESTROYED THERAMORE, MY BELOVED RHONIN WAS KILLED.
I LOST MYSELF IN GRIEF. IN FURY. I WAS... VULNERABLE...
"...SYLVANAS AND I REUNITED AT GARROSH'S TRIAL. THE LOSSES WE HAD ENDURED AND OUR HATRED OF THAT MONSTER BONDED US. WE MET IN SECRET...
"SYLVANAS WANTED HIM DEAD. I WAS DISTRAUGHT, AND I AGREED TO HELP HER.
GARROSH'S FOOD IS POISONED. DO WITH THE KNOWLEDGE WHAT YOU WILL.
SYLVANAS WAS EVER STRONG-WILLED. AND NOW, IT SEEMS THAT WILL IS TRULY DARK.
"THE THOUGHT OF MY BOYS BROUGHT ME TO MY SENSES. I CHOSE NOT TO KILL GARROSH. AND I CHOSE MY CHILDREN OVER A LIFE WITH SYLVANAS IN THE UNDERCITY."

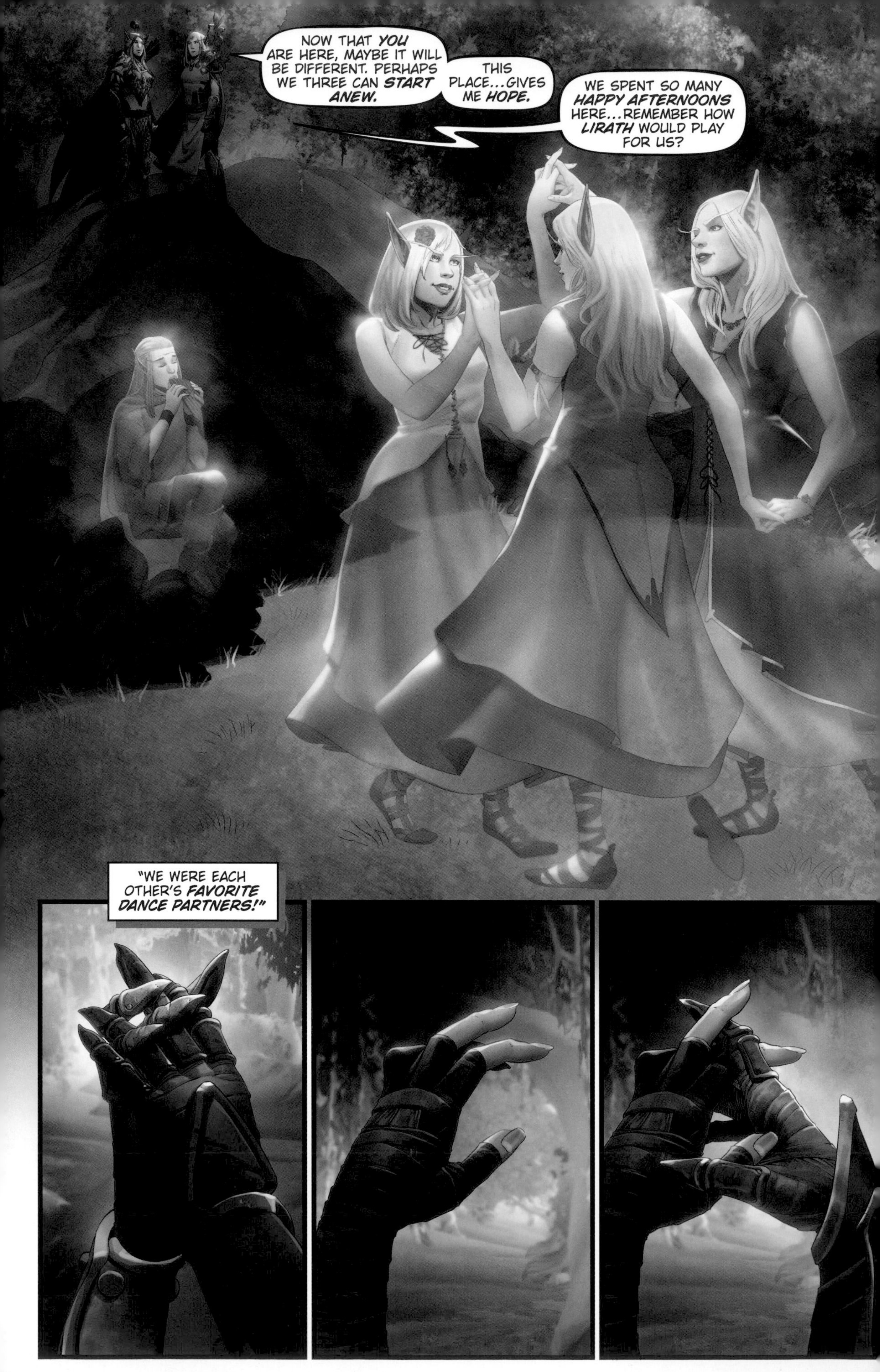
NOW THAT YOU ARE HERE, MAYBE IT WILL BE DIFFERENT. PERHAPS WE THREE CAN START ANEW.
THIS PLACE...GIVES ME HOPE.
WE SPENT SO MANY HAPPY AFTERNOONS HERE...REMEMBER HOW LIRATH WOULD PLAY FOR US?
"WE WERE EACH OTHER'S FAVORITE DANCE PARTNERS!"

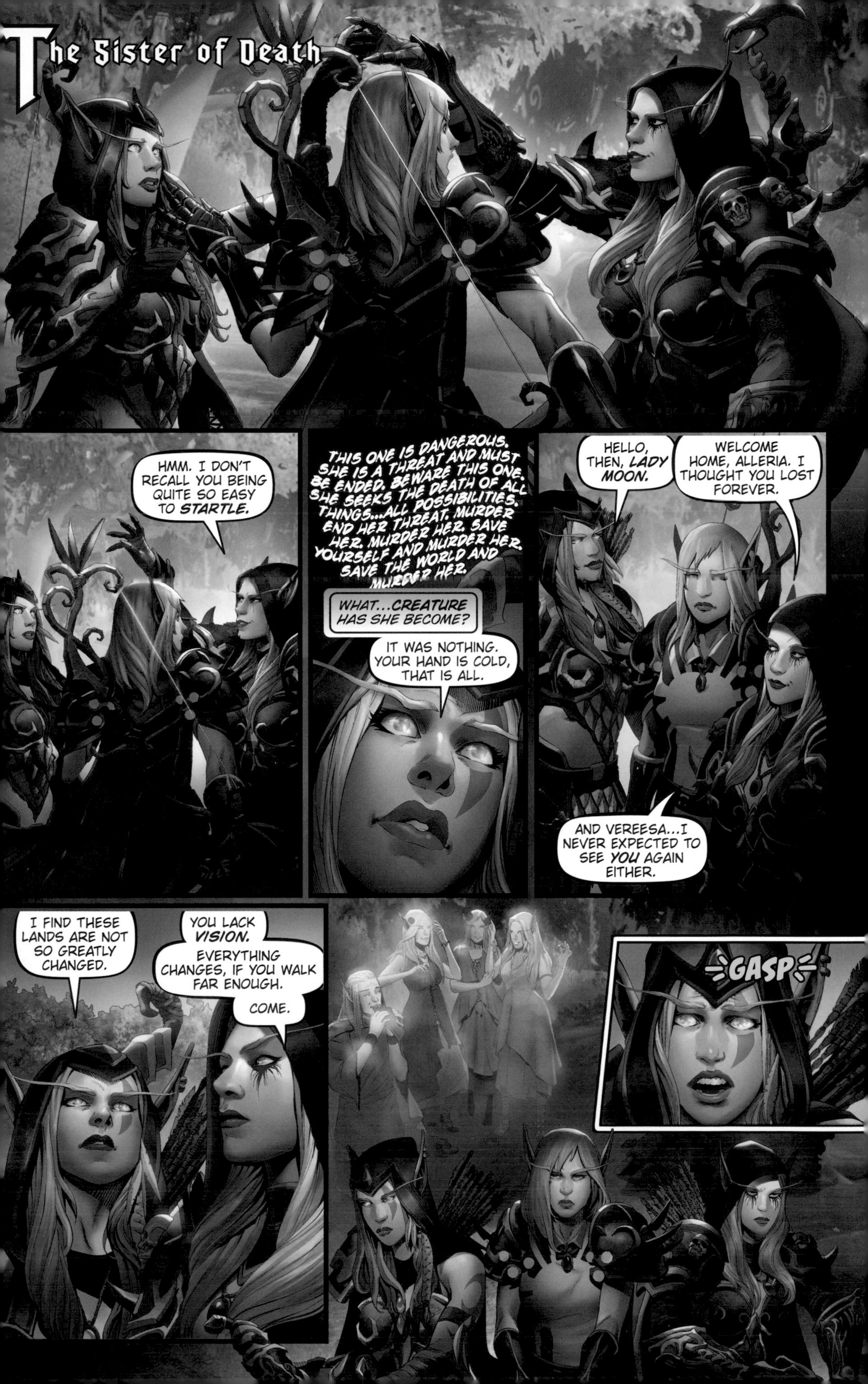
The Sister of Death
HMM. I DON'T RECALL YOU BEING QUITE SO EASY TO STARTLE.
THIS ONE IS DANGEROUS. SHE IS A THREAT AND MUST BE ENDED. BEWARE THIS ONE. SHE SEEKS THE DEATH OF ALL THINGS...ALL POSSIBILITIES. END HER THREAT. MURDER HER. MURDER HER. SAVE YOURSELF AND MURDER HER. SAVE THE WORLD AND MURDER HER.
WHAT...CREATURE HAS SHE BECOME?
IT WAS NOTHING. YOUR HAND IS COLD, THAT IS ALL.
HELLO, THEN, LADY MOON.
WELCOME HOME, ALLERIA. I THOUGHT YOU LOST FOREVER.
AND VEREESA...I NEVER EXPECTED TO SEE YOU AGAIN EITHER.
I FIND THESE LANDS ARE NOT SO GREATLY CHANGED.
YOU LACK VISION.
EVERYTHING CHANGES, IF YOU WALK FAR ENOUGH.
COME.
GASP

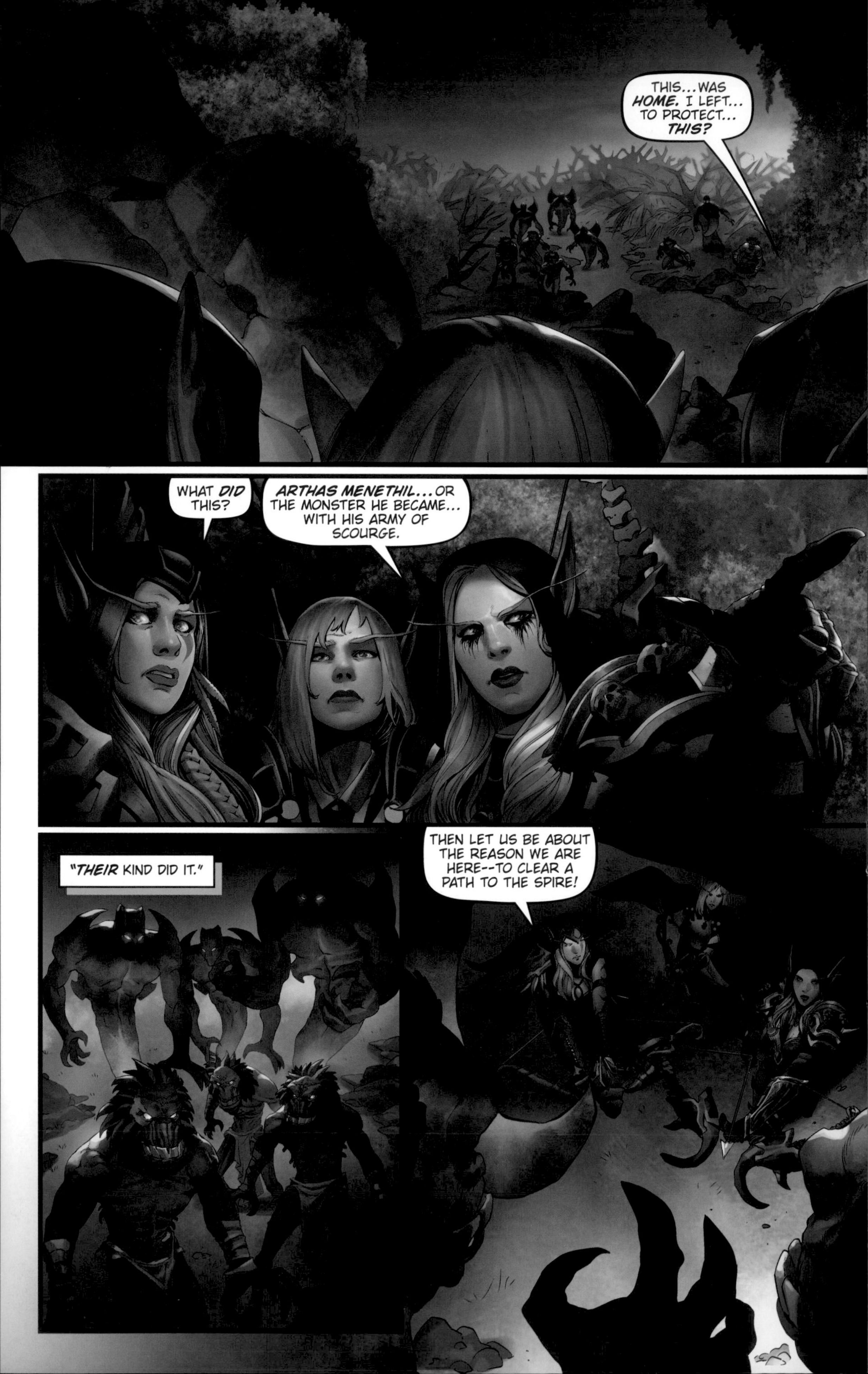
THIS...WAS HOME. I LEFT... TO PROTECT... THIS?
WHAT DID THIS?
ARTHAS MENETHIL...OR THE MONSTER HE BECAME... WITH HIS ARMY OF SCOURGE.
"THEIR KIND DID IT."
THEN LET US BE ABOUT THE REASON WE ARE HERE--TO CLEAR A PATH TO THE SPIRE!

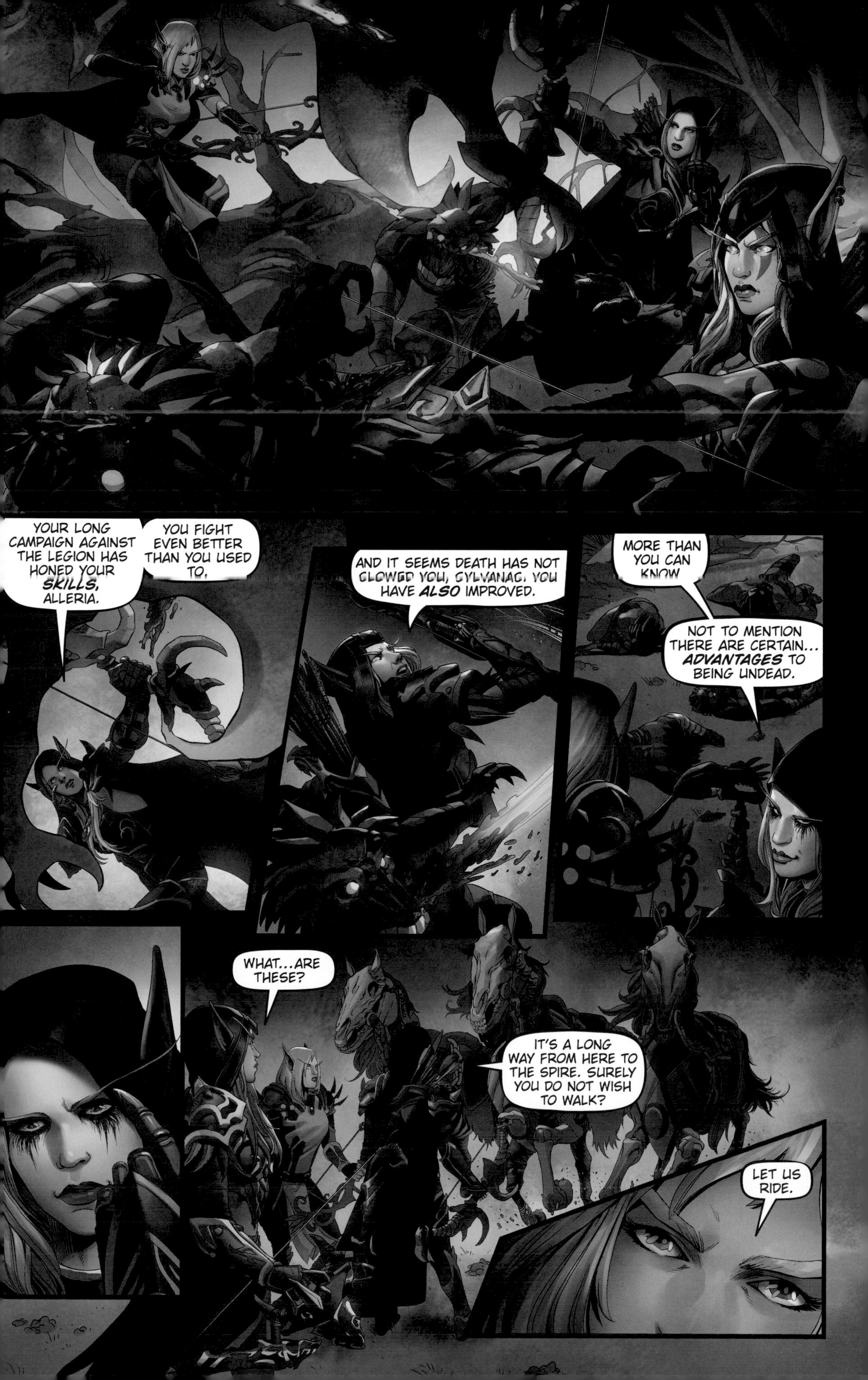
YOUR LONG CAMPAIGN AGAINST THE LEGION HAS HONED YOUR SKILLS, ALLERIA.
YOU FIGHT EVEN BETTER THAN YOU USED TO.
AND IT SEEMS DEATH HAS NOT SLOWED YOU, SYLVANAS. YOU HAVE ALSO IMPROVED.
MORE THAN YOU CAN KNOW.
NOT TO MENTION THERE ARE CERTAIN... ADVANTAGES TO BEING UNDEAD.
WHAT...ARE THESE?
IT'S A LONG WAY FROM HERE TO THE SPIRE. SURELY YOU DO NOT WISH TO WALK?
LET US RIDE.

WE SHOULD PLAY A GAME ON OUR JOURNEY, SISTERS.

DO YOU RECALL "ONE IS A LIE"?

EACH OF US WILL MAKE *THREE* STATEMENTS--

--AND *TWO* WILL BE TRUE. WE REMEMBER.

BUT WITH A *NEW* RULE.

WE WILL NOT REVEAL WHICH IS THE LIE UNTIL *AFTER* WE RETAKE WINDRUNNER SPIRE.

YOU FIRST, ALLERIA. AFTER ALL, YOU'RE ELDEST.

VERY WELL. FIRST...

...I HAVE MISSED YOU BOTH TERRIBLY.

SECOND: THE POWERS OF THE VOID ARE A TREMENDOUS GIFT.

AREN'T THE TREANTS OUR FRIENDS?

THEY ONCE WERE. BUT NOW, THEY ARE FRIENDS TO NO ONE.

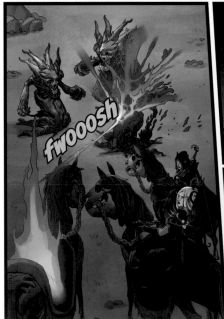

fwooosh

HAH!

WHAT OF YOUR LAST STATEMENT, ALLERIA?

...MY LAST? I HAVE NO REGRETS ABOUT STEPPING THROUGH THE DARK PORTAL SO MANY YEARS AGO.

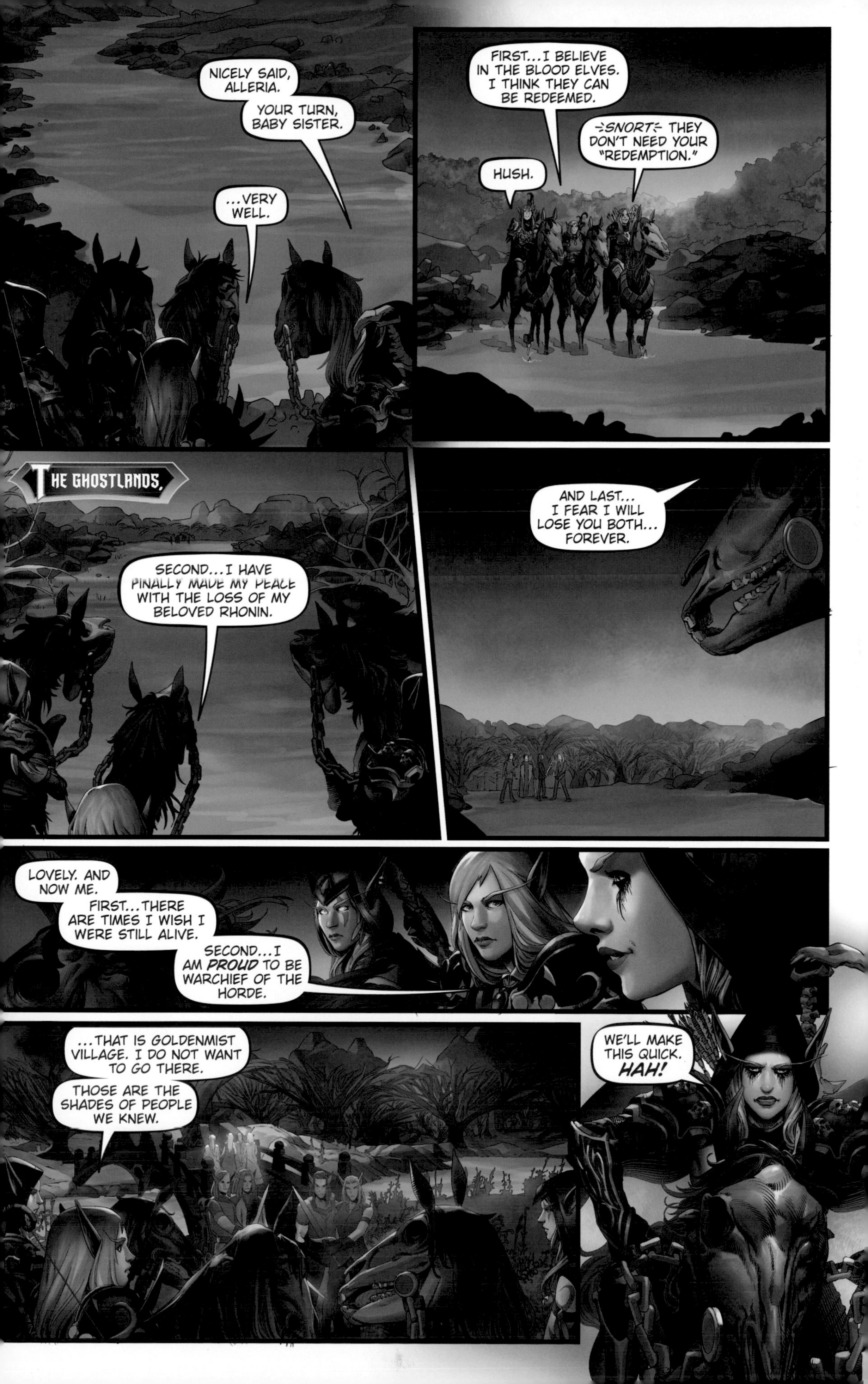
NICELY SAID, ALLERIA.
YOUR TURN, BABY SISTER.
...VERY WELL.
FIRST...I BELIEVE IN THE BLOOD ELVES. I THINK THEY CAN BE REDEEMED.
HUSH.
=SNORT= THEY DON'T NEED YOUR "REDEMPTION."
THE GHOSTLANDS.
SECOND...I HAVE FINALLY MADE MY PEACE WITH THE LOSS OF MY BELOVED RHONIN.
AND LAST... I FEAR I WILL LOSE YOU BOTH... FOREVER.
LOVELY. AND NOW ME.
FIRST...THERE ARE TIMES I WISH I WERE STILL ALIVE.
SECOND...I AM PROUD TO BE WARCHIEF OF THE HORDE.
...THAT IS GOLDENMIST VILLAGE. I DO NOT WANT TO GO THERE.
THOSE ARE THE SHADES OF PEOPLE WE KNEW.
WE'LL MAKE THIS QUICK. HAH!

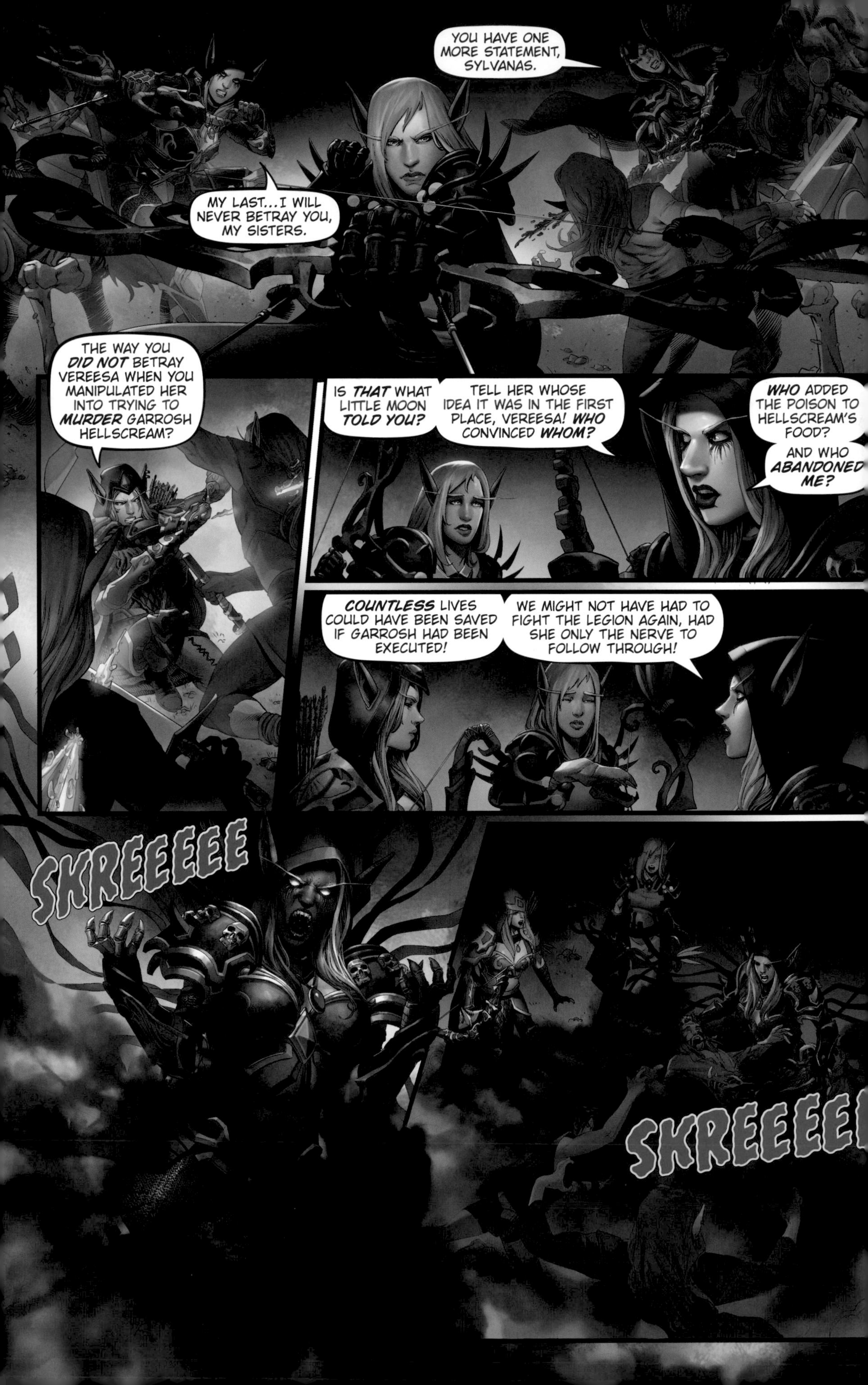
YOU HAVE ONE MORE STATEMENT, SYLVANAS.
MY LAST...I WILL NEVER BETRAY YOU, MY SISTERS.
THE WAY YOU DID NOT BETRAY VEREESA WHEN YOU MANIPULATED HER INTO TRYING TO MURDER GARROSH HELLSCREAM?
IS THAT WHAT LITTLE MOON TOLD YOU?
TELL HER WHOSE IDEA IT WAS IN THE FIRST PLACE, VEREESA! WHO CONVINCED WHOM?
WHO ADDED THE POISON TO HELLSCREAM'S FOOD?
AND WHO ABANDONED ME?
COUNTLESS LIVES COULD HAVE BEEN SAVED IF GARROSH HAD BEEN EXECUTED!
WE MIGHT NOT HAVE HAD TO FIGHT THE LEGION AGAIN, HAD SHE ONLY THE NERVE TO FOLLOW THROUGH!
SKREEEEEE
SKREEEEE

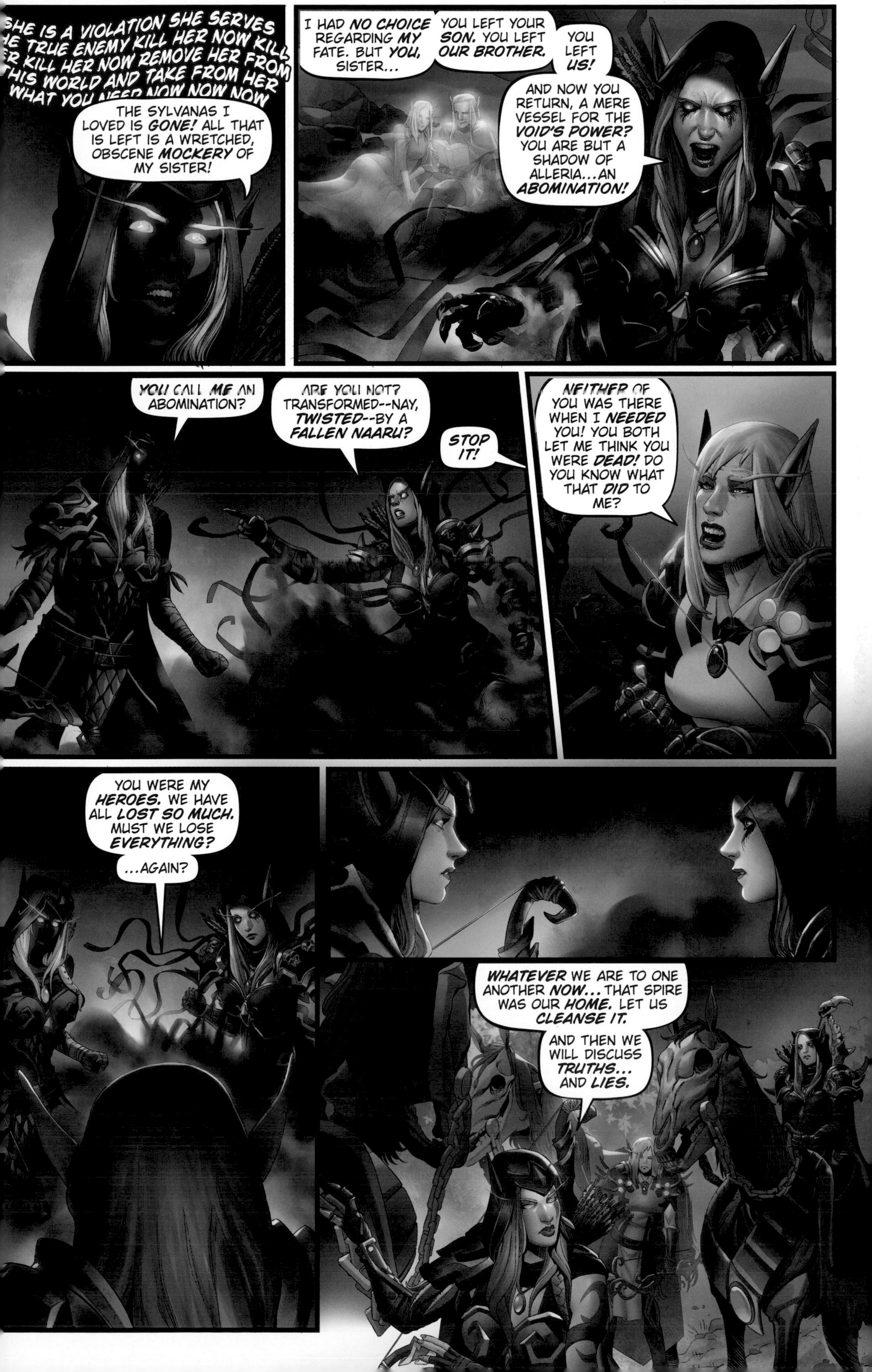
SHE IS A VIOLATION SHE SERVES
TRUE ENEMY KILL HER NOW KILL
KILL HER NOW REMOVE HER FROM
THIS WORLD AND TAKE FROM HER
WHAT YOU NOW NOW
THE SYLVANAS I LOVED IS GONE! ALL THAT IS LEFT IS A WRETCHED, OBSCENE MOCKERY OF MY SISTER!
I HAD NO CHOICE REGARDING MY FATE. BUT YOU, SISTER...
YOU LEFT YOUR SON. YOU LEFT OUR BROTHER.
YOU LEFT US!
AND NOW YOU RETURN, A MERE VESSEL FOR THE VOID'S POWER? YOU ARE BUT A SHADOW OF ALLERIA...AN ABOMINATION!
YOU CALL ME AN ABOMINATION?
ARE YOU NOT? TRANSFORMED--NAY, TWISTED--BY A FALLEN NAARU?
STOP IT!
NEITHER OF YOU WAS THERE WHEN I NEEDED YOU! YOU BOTH LET ME THINK YOU WERE DEAD! DO YOU KNOW WHAT THAT DID TO ME?
YOU WERE MY HEROES. WE HAVE ALL LOST SO MUCH. MUST WE LOSE EVERYTHING?
...AGAIN?
WHATEVER WE ARE TO ONE ANOTHER NOW...THAT SPIRE WAS OUR HOME. LET US CLEANSE IT.
AND THEN WE WILL DISCUSS TRUTHS... AND LIES.

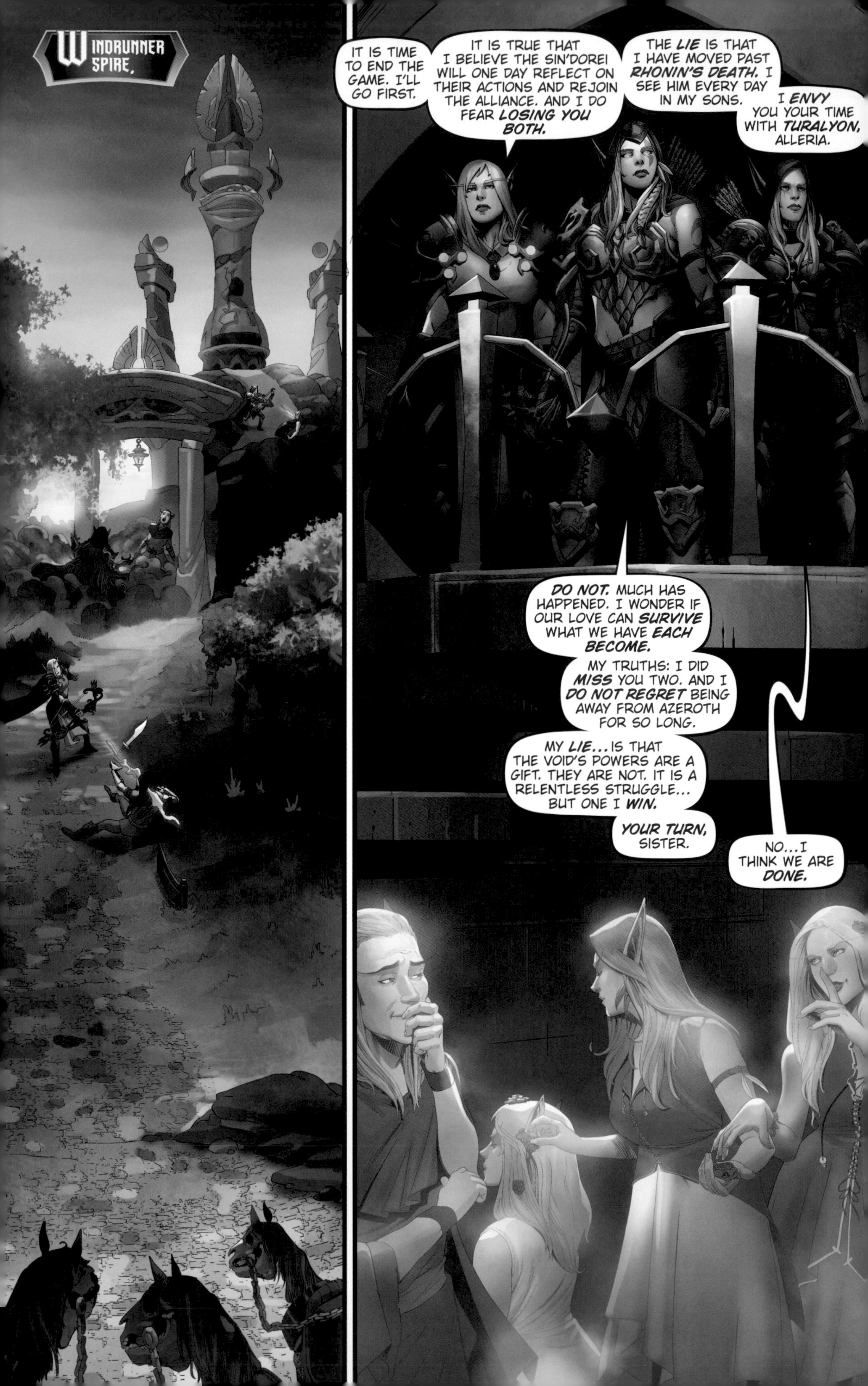
WINDRUNNER SPIRE,
IT IS TIME TO END THE GAME. I'LL GO FIRST.
IT IS TRUE THAT I BELIEVE THE SIN'DOREI WILL ONE DAY REFLECT ON THEIR ACTIONS AND REJOIN THE ALLIANCE. AND I DO FEAR LOSING YOU BOTH.
THE LIE IS THAT I HAVE MOVED PAST RHONIN'S DEATH. I SEE HIM EVERY DAY IN MY SONS.
I ENVY YOU YOUR TIME WITH TURALYON, ALLERIA.
DO NOT. MUCH HAS HAPPENED. I WONDER IF OUR LOVE CAN SURVIVE WHAT WE HAVE EACH BECOME.
MY TRUTHS: I DID MISS YOU TWO. AND I DO NOT REGRET BEING AWAY FROM AZEROTH FOR SO LONG.
MY LIE... IS THAT THE VOID'S POWERS ARE A GIFT. THEY ARE NOT. IT IS A RELENTLESS STRUGGLE... BUT ONE I WIN.
YOUR TURN, SISTER.
NO... I THINK WE ARE DONE.

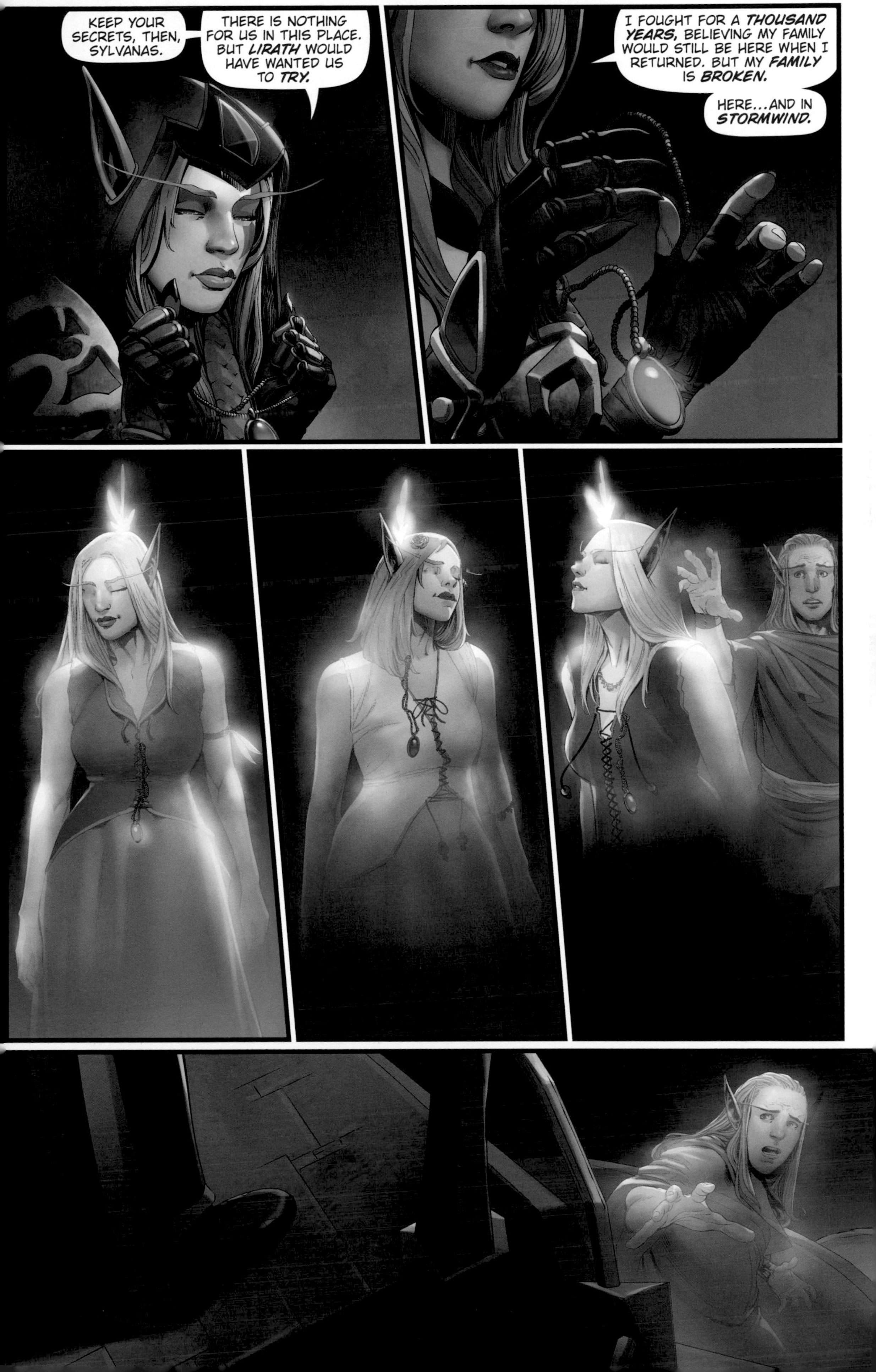
KEEP YOUR SECRETS, THEN, SYLVANAS.
THERE IS NOTHING FOR US IN THIS PLACE. BUT *LIRATH* WOULD HAVE WANTED US TO *TRY.*
I FOUGHT FOR A *THOUSAND YEARS,* BELIEVING MY FAMILY WOULD STILL BE HERE WHEN I RETURNED. BUT MY *FAMILY* IS *BROKEN.*
HERE...AND IN *STORMWIND.*

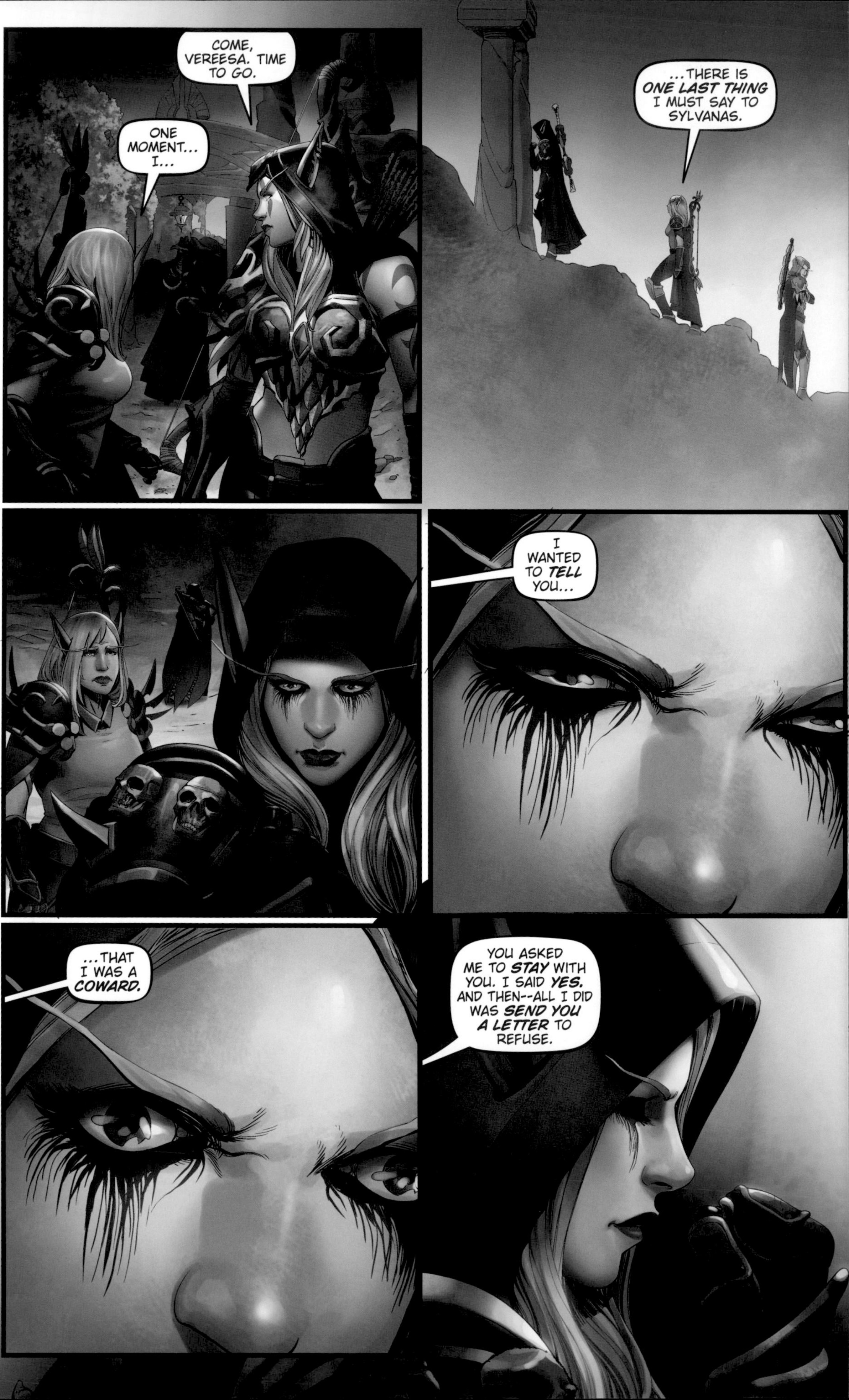
COME, VEREESA. TIME TO GO.
ONE MOMENT... I...
...THERE IS ONE LAST THING I MUST SAY TO SYLVANAS.
I WANTED TO TELL YOU...
...THAT I WAS A COWARD.
YOU ASKED ME TO STAY WITH YOU. I SAID YES. AND THEN--ALL I DID WAS SEND YOU A LETTER TO REFUSE.

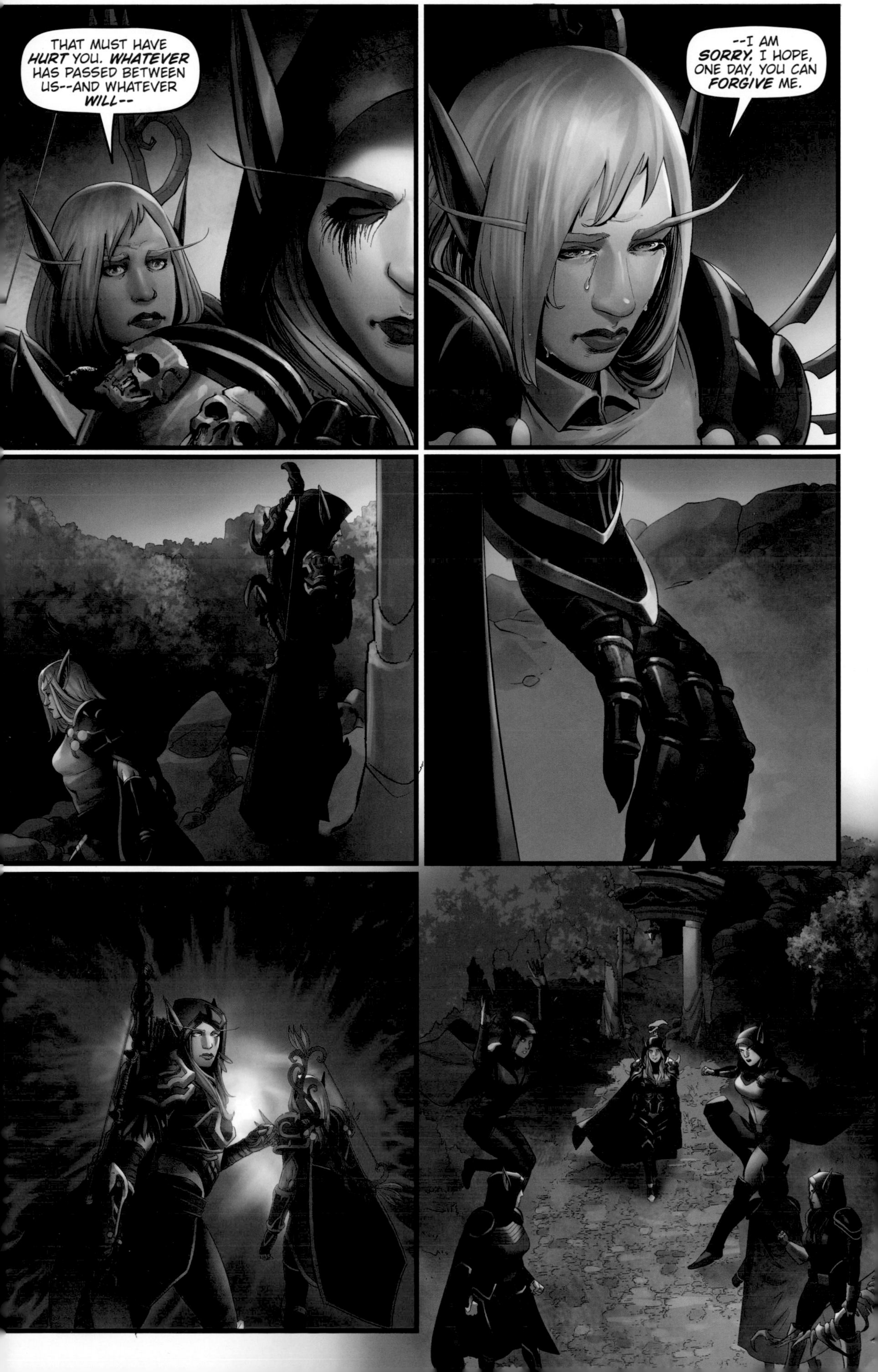
THAT MUST HAVE HURT YOU. WHATEVER HAS PASSED BETWEEN US--AND WHATEVER WILL--
--I AM SORRY. I HOPE, ONE DAY, YOU CAN FORGIVE ME.

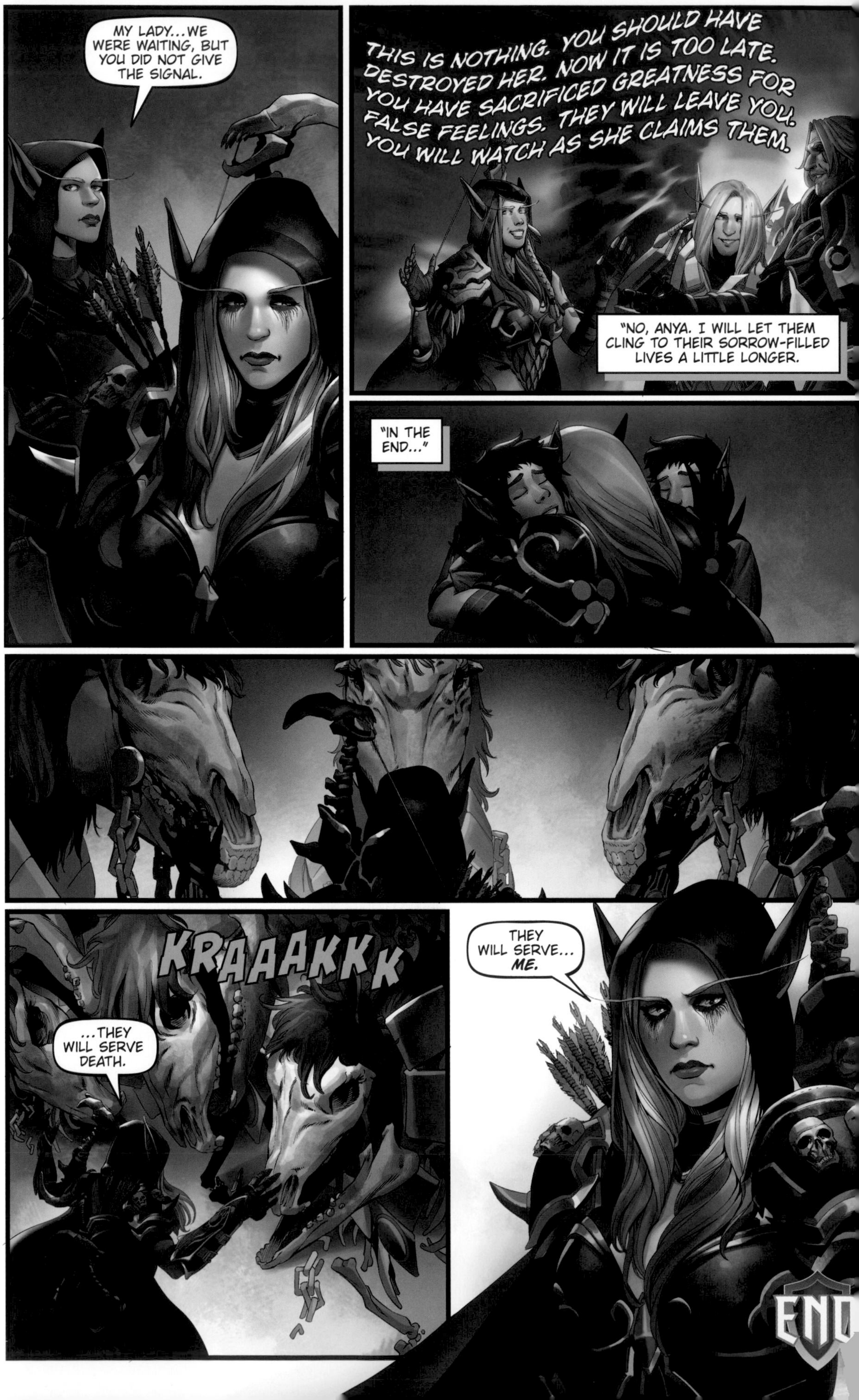
MY LADY...WE WERE WAITING, BUT YOU DID NOT GIVE THE SIGNAL.
THIS IS NOTHING. YOU SHOULD HAVE DESTROYED HER. NOW IT IS TOO LATE. YOU HAVE SACRIFICED GREATNESS FOR FALSE FEELINGS. THEY WILL LEAVE YOU. YOU WILL WATCH AS SHE CLAIMS THEM.
"NO, ANYA. I WILL LET THEM CLING TO THEIR SORROW-FILLED LIVES A LITTLE LONGER.
"IN THE END..."
KRAAAKKK
...THEY WILL SERVE DEATH.
THEY WILL SERVE... ME.
END

WORLD OF WARCRAFT
BATTLE FOR AZEROTH

MECHAGON

SCRIPT BY **MATT BURNS** | ART BY **MIKI MONTLLÓ** |
LETTERING BY **COMICCRAFT**

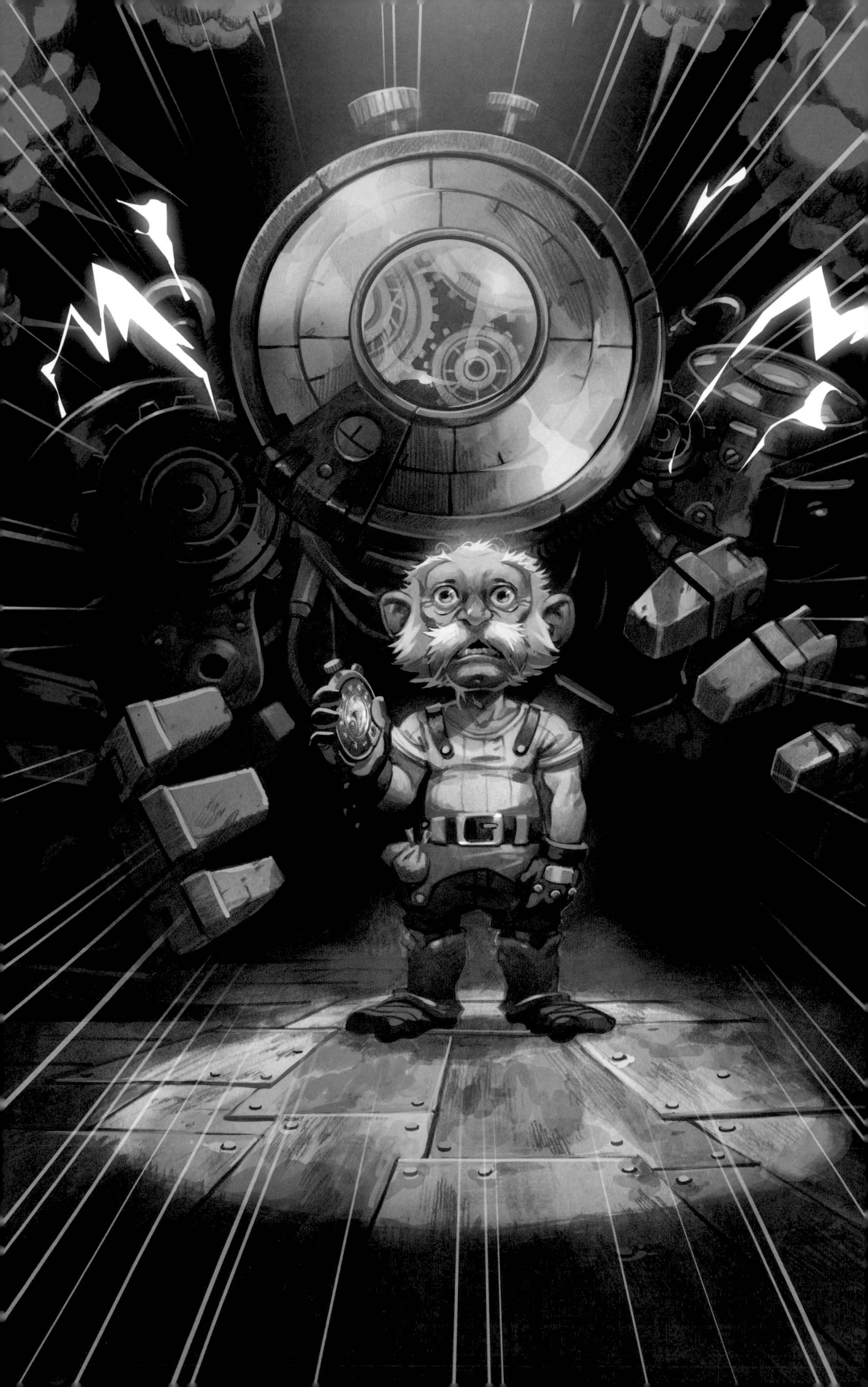

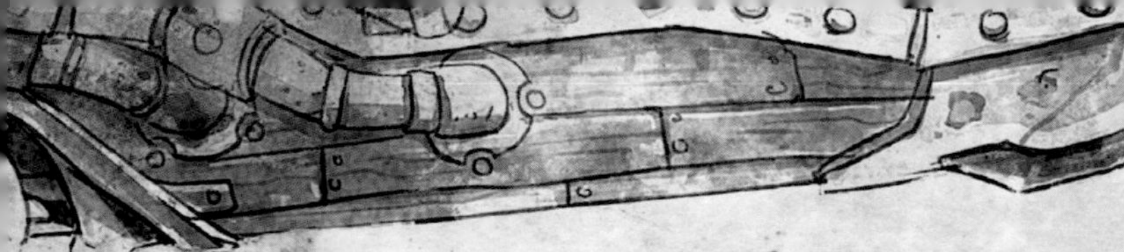

DAY 37

FUEL LOW. INSTRUMENTS BREAKING DOWN.
TWO, MAYBE THREE DAYS LEFT OF RATIONS.

~~I SHOULD TURN BACK.~~

IT'D BE CRAZY TO KEEP GOING, BUT EVEN CRAZIER TO TURN BACK WHEN I'M THIS CLOSE.

MECHAGON IS NEAR.

~~OR MAYBE IT'S NOT REAL. MAYBE I'M JUST DESPERATE.~~

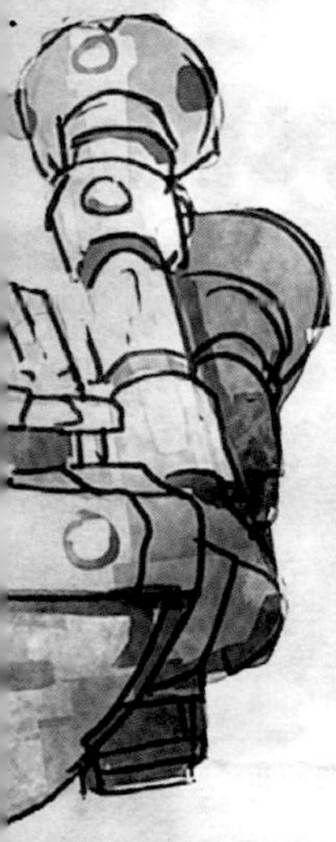

THE NAYSAYERS BACK HOME CALLED ME A
FOOL FOR CHASING AFTER THE LOST CITY. SAID
MY THEORIES ABOUT IT HOLDING THE KEY TO
IMMORTALITY WERE JUST THE DREAMS OF AN
OLD GNOME.

~~SOMETIMES I THINK THEY'RE RIGHT.~~

I KNOW I'M RIGHT. MECHAGON IS OUT THERE, AND IT'S MY DISCOVERY TO MAKE.

I'LL FIND ITS SECRETS AND OUTLIVE EVERYONE WHO DOUBTED ME.

~~I DON'T HAVE WHAT IT TAKES ANYMORE.~~

JUST NEED TO PUSH ON A LITTLE FARTHER.
I CAN DO THIS.

EVERYTHING HURTS. NOTHING IS GOING AS PLANNED. BUT THAT'S HOW I KNOW I'M CLOSE...

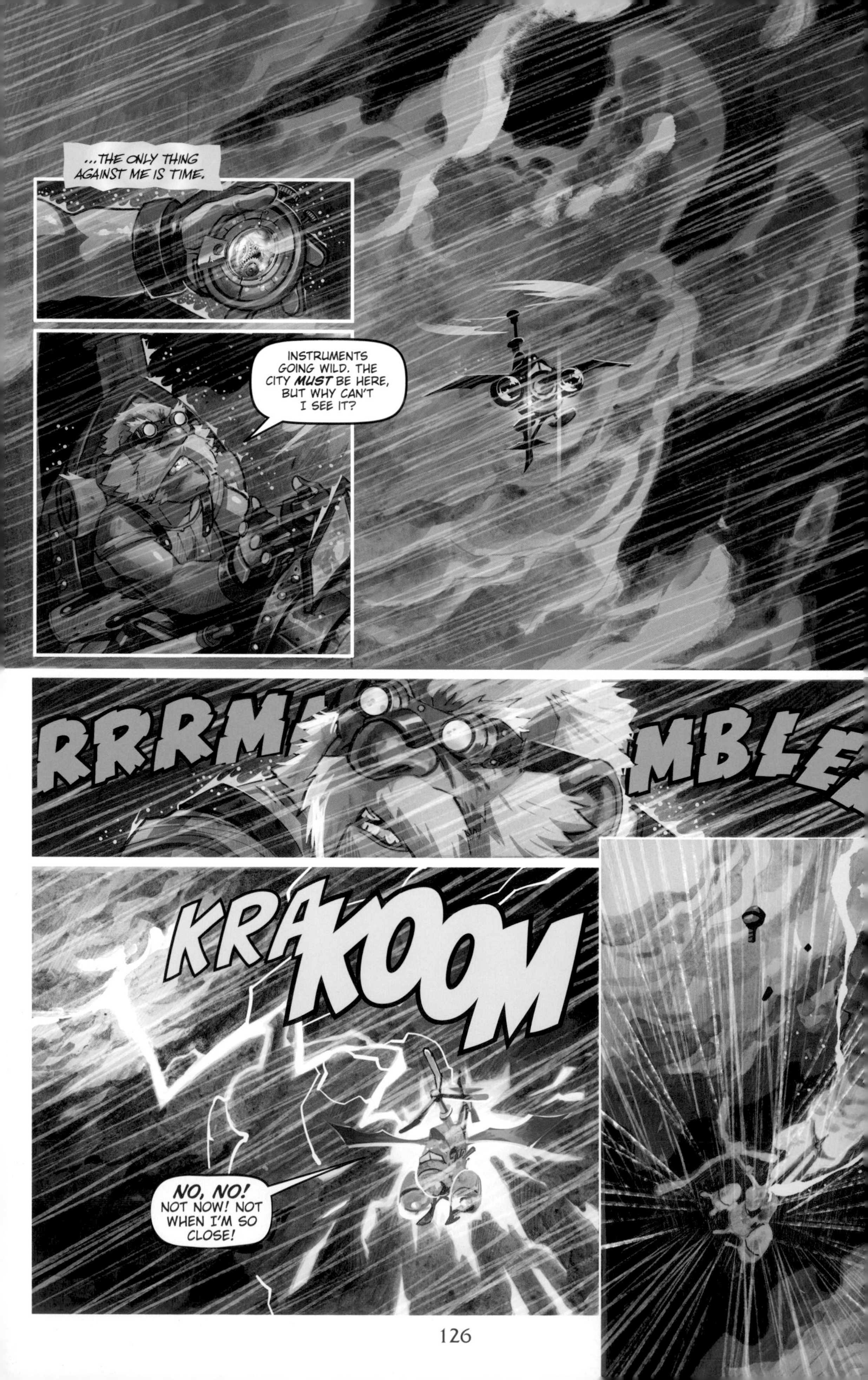
...THE ONLY THING AGAINST ME IS TIME.
INSTRUMENTS GOING WILD. THE CITY MUST BE HERE, BUT WHY CAN'T I SEE IT?
RRRM
MBLE
KRAKOOM
NO, NO! NOT NOW! NOT WHEN I'M SO CLOSE!

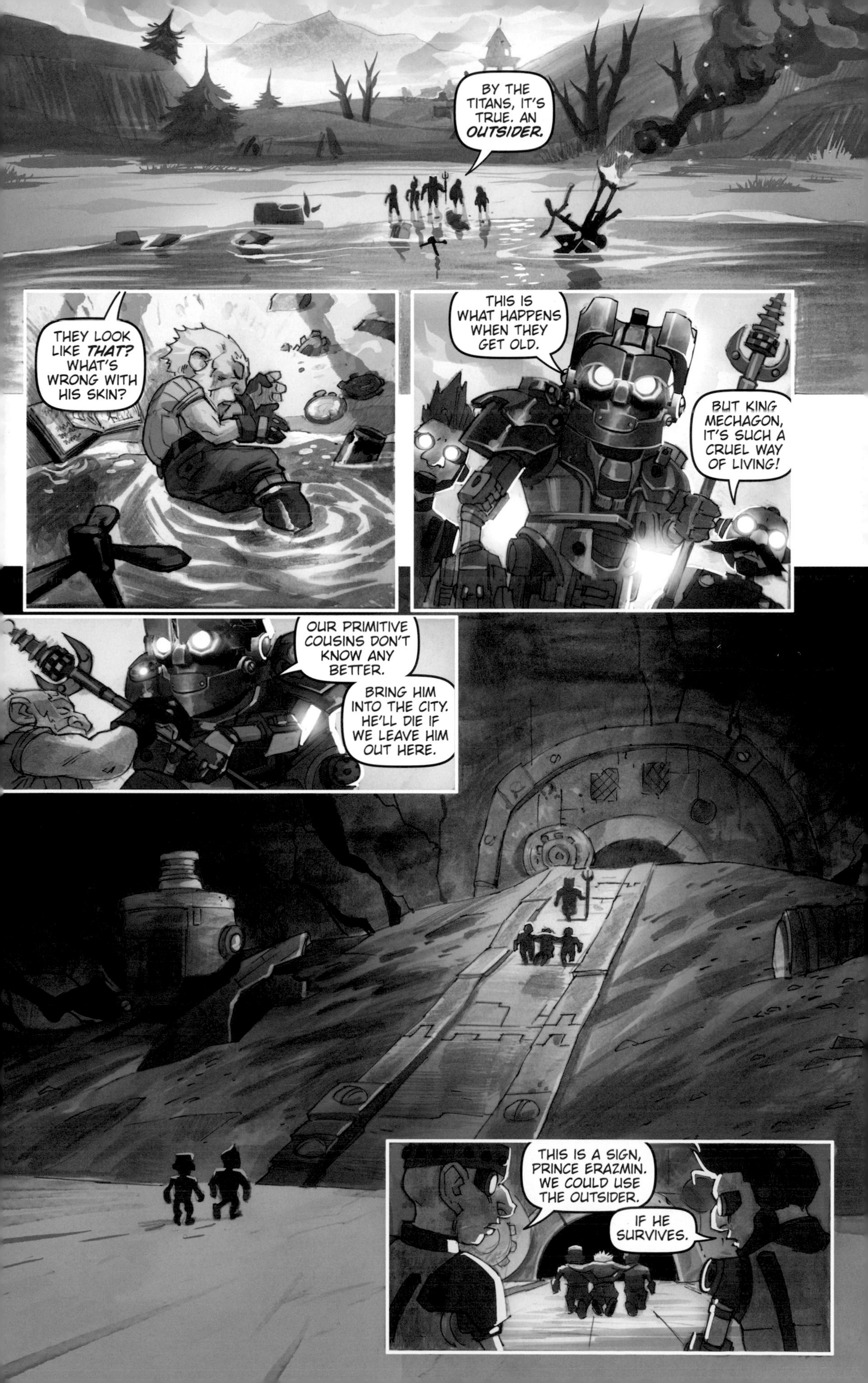
BY THE TITANS, IT'S TRUE. AN *OUTSIDER.*
THEY LOOK LIKE *THAT?* WHAT'S WRONG WITH HIS SKIN?
THIS IS WHAT HAPPENS WHEN THEY GET OLD.
BUT KING MECHAGON, IT'S SUCH A CRUEL WAY OF LIVING!
OUR PRIMITIVE COUSINS DON'T KNOW ANY BETTER.
BRING HIM INTO THE CITY. HE'LL DIE IF WE LEAVE HIM OUT HERE.
THIS IS A SIGN, PRINCE ERAZMIN. WE COULD USE THE OUTSIDER.
IF HE SURVIVES.

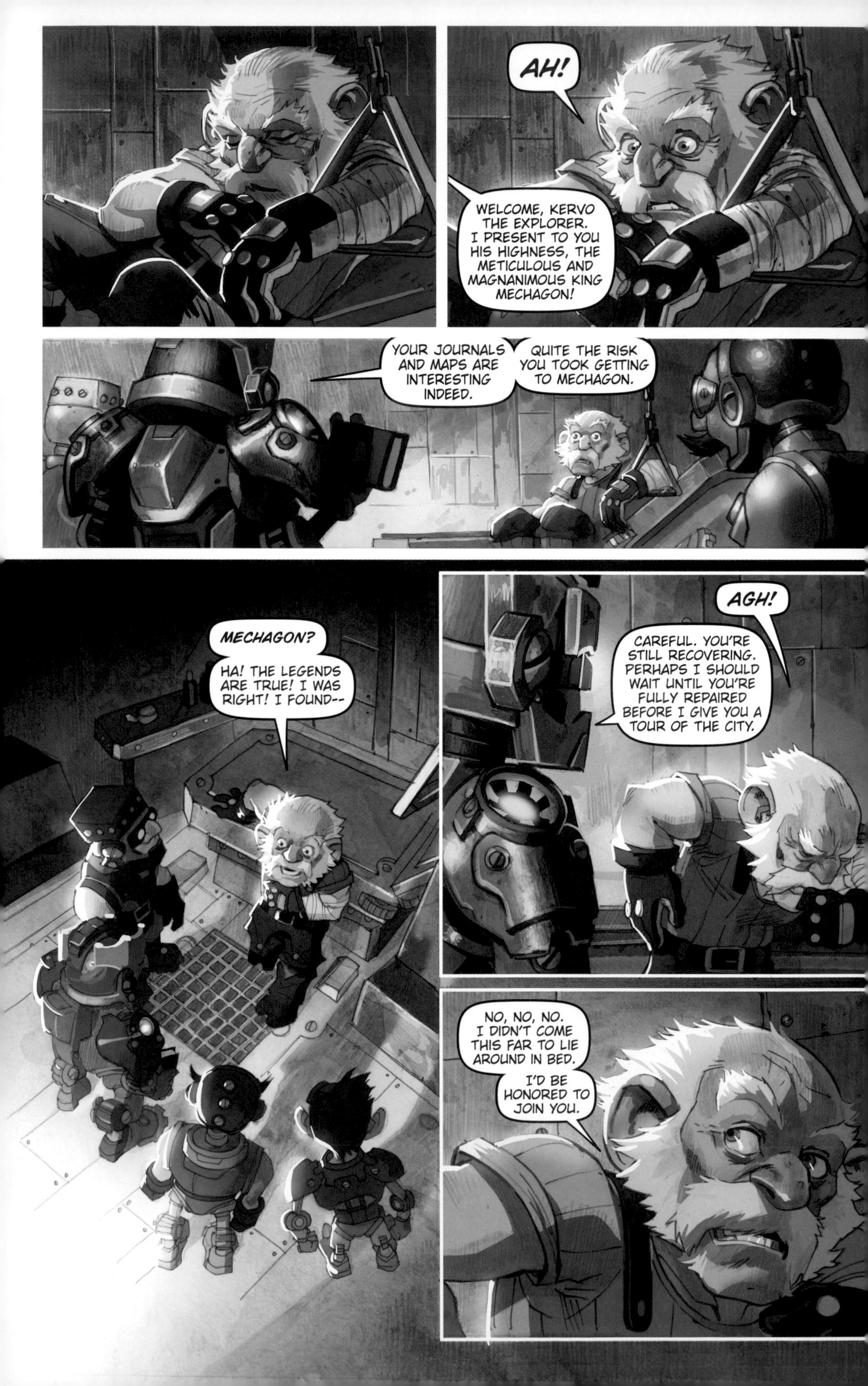
AH!
WELCOME, KERVO THE EXPLORER. I PRESENT TO YOU HIS HIGHNESS, THE METICULOUS AND MAGNANIMOUS KING MECHAGON!
YOUR JOURNALS AND MAPS ARE INTERESTING INDEED.
QUITE THE RISK YOU TOOK GETTING TO MECHAGON.
MECHAGON?
HA! THE LEGENDS ARE TRUE! I WAS RIGHT! I FOUND--
AGH!
CAREFUL. YOU'RE STILL RECOVERING. PERHAPS I SHOULD WAIT UNTIL YOU'RE FULLY REPAIRED BEFORE I GIVE YOU A TOUR OF THE CITY.
NO, NO, NO. I DIDN'T COME THIS FAR TO LIE AROUND IN BED.
I'D BE HONORED TO JOIN YOU.

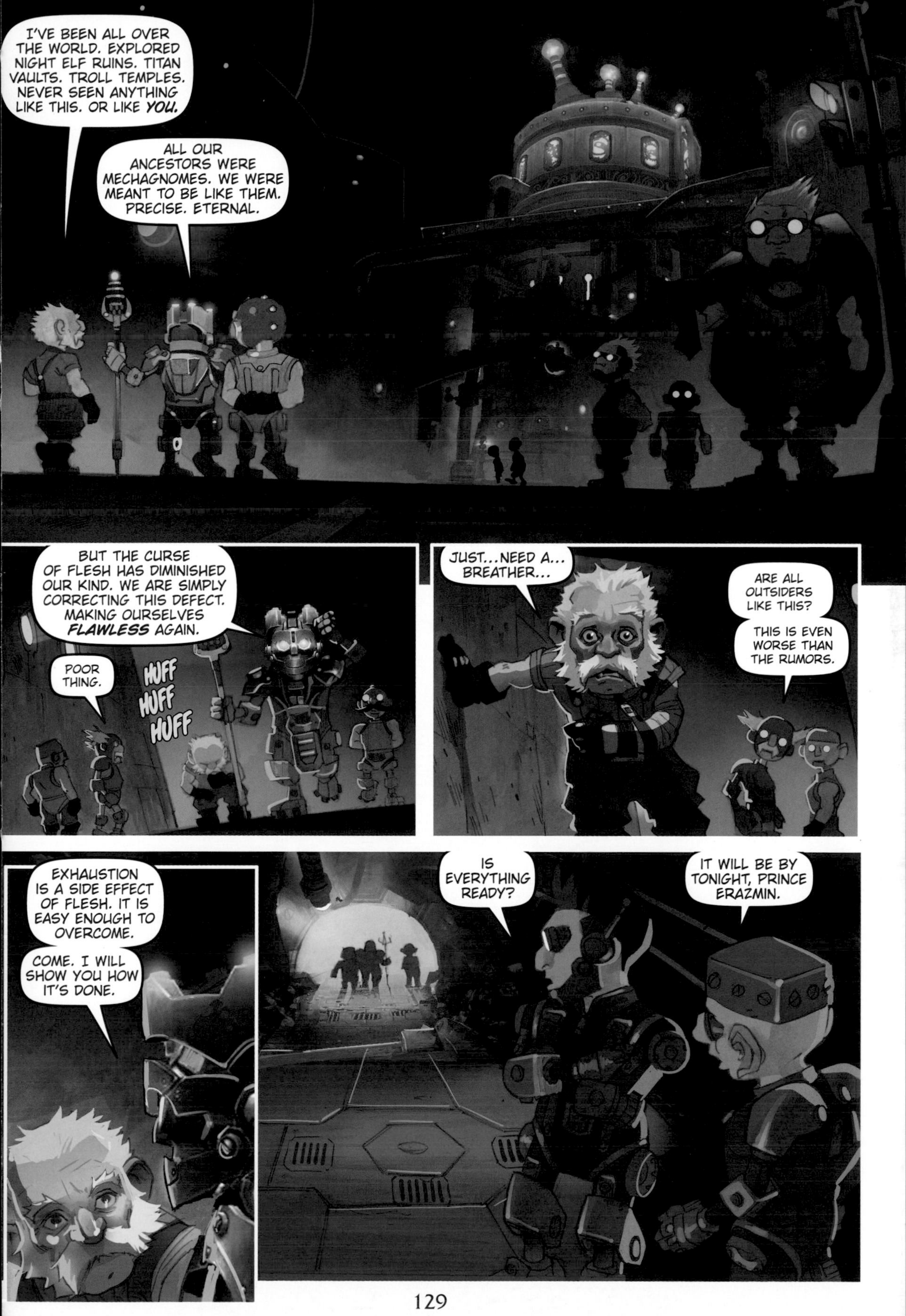
I'VE BEEN ALL OVER THE WORLD. EXPLORED NIGHT ELF RUINS. TITAN VAULTS. TROLL TEMPLES. NEVER SEEN ANYTHING LIKE THIS. OR LIKE YOU.
ALL OUR ANCESTORS WERE MECHAGNOMES. WE WERE MEANT TO BE LIKE THEM. PRECISE. ETERNAL.
BUT THE CURSE OF FLESH HAS DIMINISHED OUR KIND. WE ARE SIMPLY CORRECTING THIS DEFECT. MAKING OURSELVES FLAWLESS AGAIN.
POOR THING.
HUFF HUFF HUFF
JUST...NEED A... BREATHER...
ARE ALL OUTSIDERS LIKE THIS?
THIS IS EVEN WORSE THAN THE RUMORS.
EXHAUSTION IS A SIDE EFFECT OF FLESH. IT IS EASY ENOUGH TO OVERCOME.
COME. I WILL SHOW YOU HOW IT'S DONE.
IS EVERYTHING READY?
IT WILL BE BY TONIGHT, PRINCE ERAZMIN.

MY PEOPLE MUST EARN THEIR TRANSFORMATION, PIECE BY PIECE. IT IS A SIGN OF STATUS.

NO OFFENSE, BUT IT LOOKS LIKE TORTURE.

BZZZZZZZZ SQUISHH

THE PAIN IS ONLY TEMPORARY. YOURS IS CONSTANT. A SLOW, INESCAPABLE DETERIORATION UNTO DEATH.

BZZZZZ

MORTALITY IS A DARK FATE THAT WILL NEVER TROUBLE THE PEOPLE OF MECHAGON!

WOULD IT NOT BE MERCIFUL TO HELP THE OUTSIDERS TRANSCEND THE CURSE OF FLESH AS WE HAVE? TO SHARE OUR TECHNOLOGY WITH THOSE WHO PROVE WORTHY?

YES!

WE SHOULDN'T KEEP IT ALL TO OURSELVES!

HELP THEM!

YOU'VE ALREADY ACCOMPLISHED SO MUCH, KERVO THE EXPLORER...

...IMAGINE WHAT YOU COULD DISCOVER IF YOU WEREN'T TRAPPED IN THAT ROTTING HUSK.

YOU LOOK TIRED. MY ASSISTANT WILL TAKE YOU BACK TO YOUR CHAMBERS.

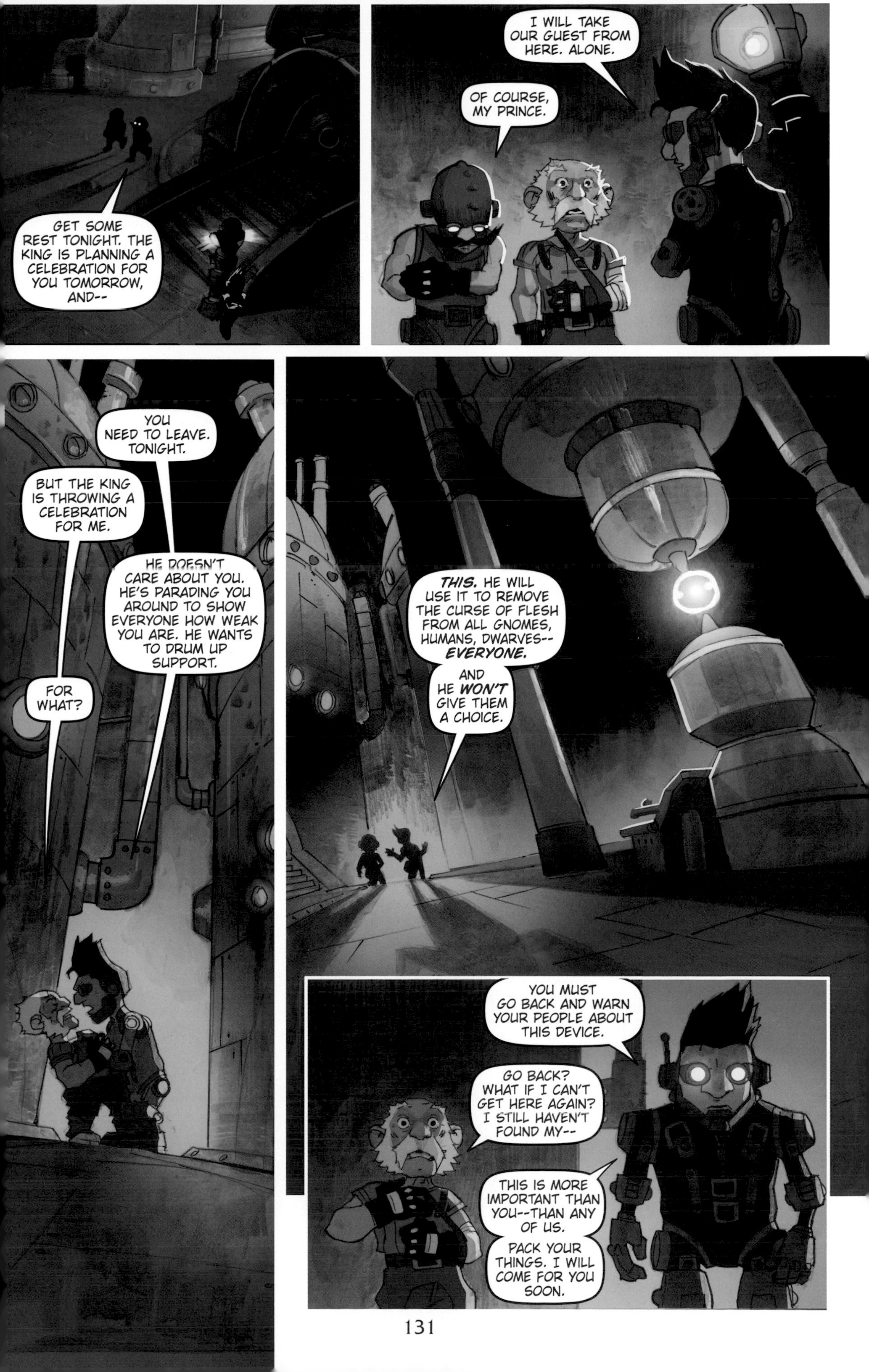
GET SOME REST TONIGHT. THE KING IS PLANNING A CELEBRATION FOR YOU TOMORROW, AND--
I WILL TAKE OUR GUEST FROM HERE. ALONE.
OF COURSE, MY PRINCE.
YOU NEED TO LEAVE. TONIGHT.
BUT THE KING IS THROWING A CELEBRATION FOR ME.
HE DOESN'T CARE ABOUT YOU. HE'S PARADING YOU AROUND TO SHOW EVERYONE HOW WEAK YOU ARE. HE WANTS TO DRUM UP SUPPORT.
FOR WHAT?
THIS. HE WILL USE IT TO REMOVE THE CURSE OF FLESH FROM ALL GNOMES, HUMANS, DWARVES--EVERYONE.
AND HE WON'T GIVE THEM A CHOICE.
YOU MUST GO BACK AND WARN YOUR PEOPLE ABOUT THIS DEVICE.
GO BACK? WHAT IF I CAN'T GET HERE AGAIN? I STILL HAVEN'T FOUND MY--
THIS IS MORE IMPORTANT THAN YOU--THAN ANY OF US.
PACK YOUR THINGS. I WILL COME FOR YOU SOON.

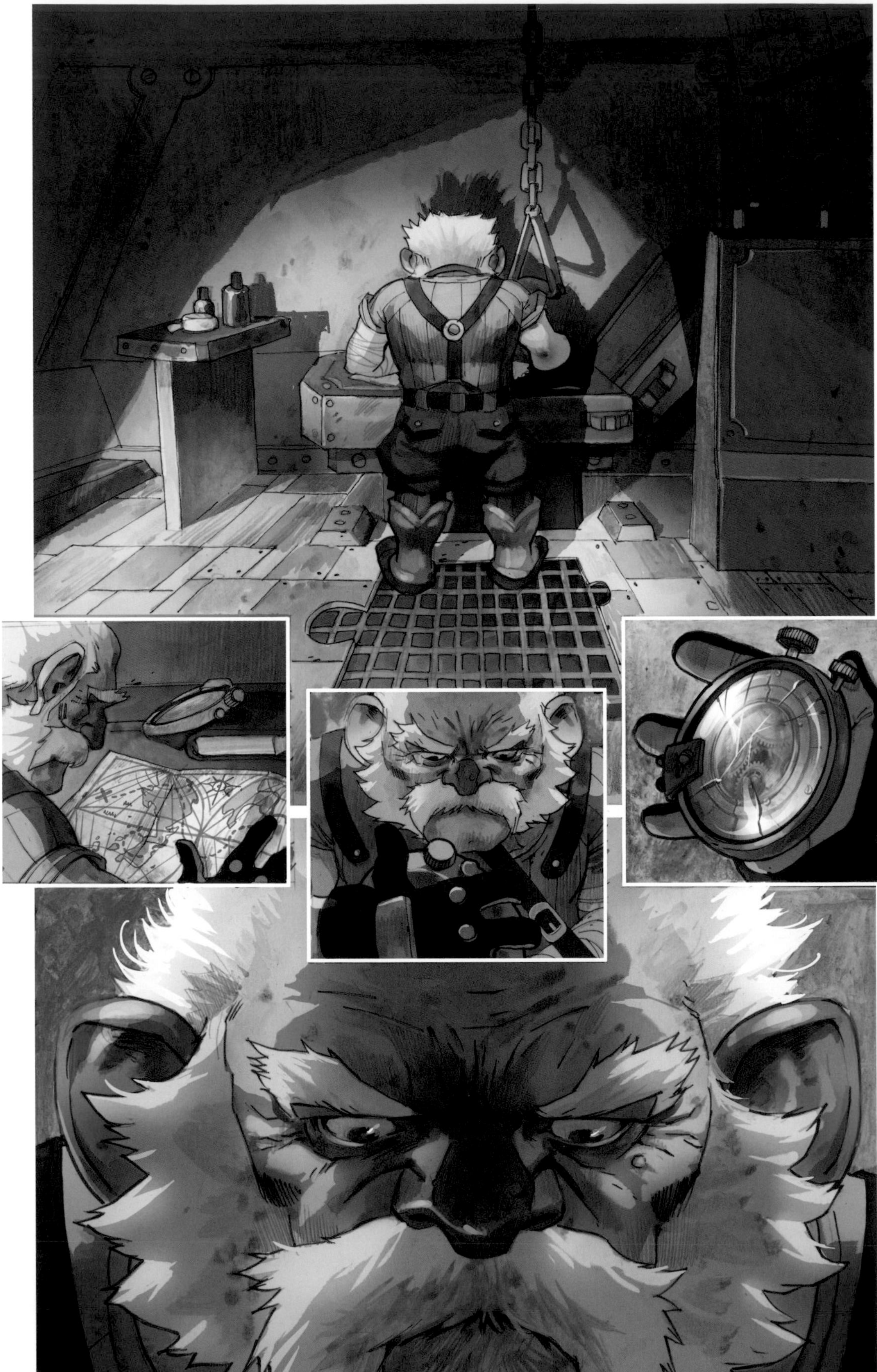

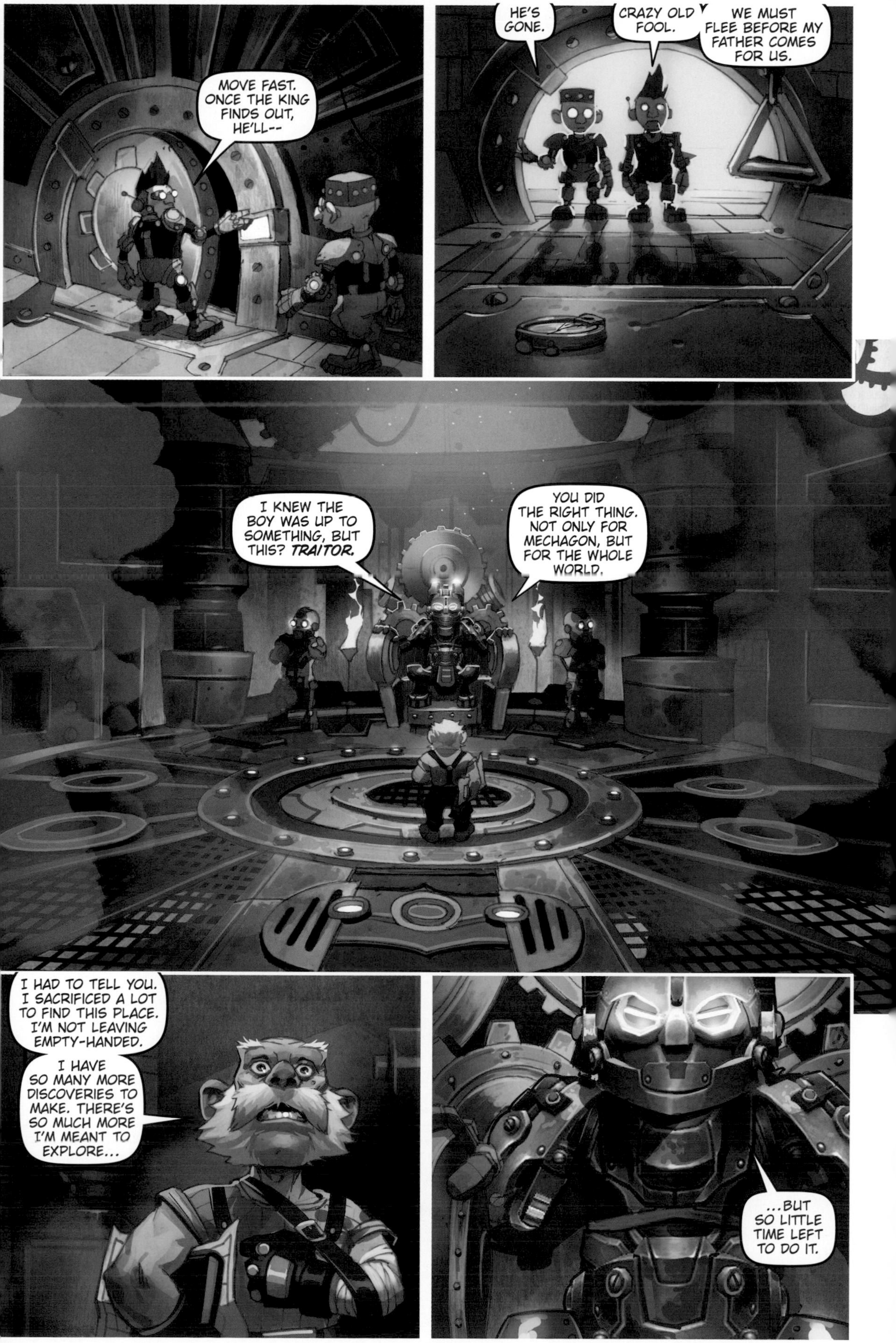
MOVE FAST. ONCE THE KING FINDS OUT, HE'LL--
HE'S GONE.
CRAZY OLD FOOL.
WE MUST FLEE BEFORE MY FATHER COMES FOR US.
I KNEW THE BOY WAS UP TO SOMETHING, BUT THIS? TRAITOR.
YOU DID THE RIGHT THING. NOT ONLY FOR MECHAGON, BUT FOR THE WHOLE WORLD.
I HAD TO TELL YOU. I SACRIFICED A LOT TO FIND THIS PLACE. I'M NOT LEAVING EMPTY-HANDED.
I HAVE SO MANY MORE DISCOVERIES TO MAKE. THERE'S SO MUCH MORE I'M MEANT TO EXPLORE...
...BUT SO LITTLE TIME LEFT TO DO IT.

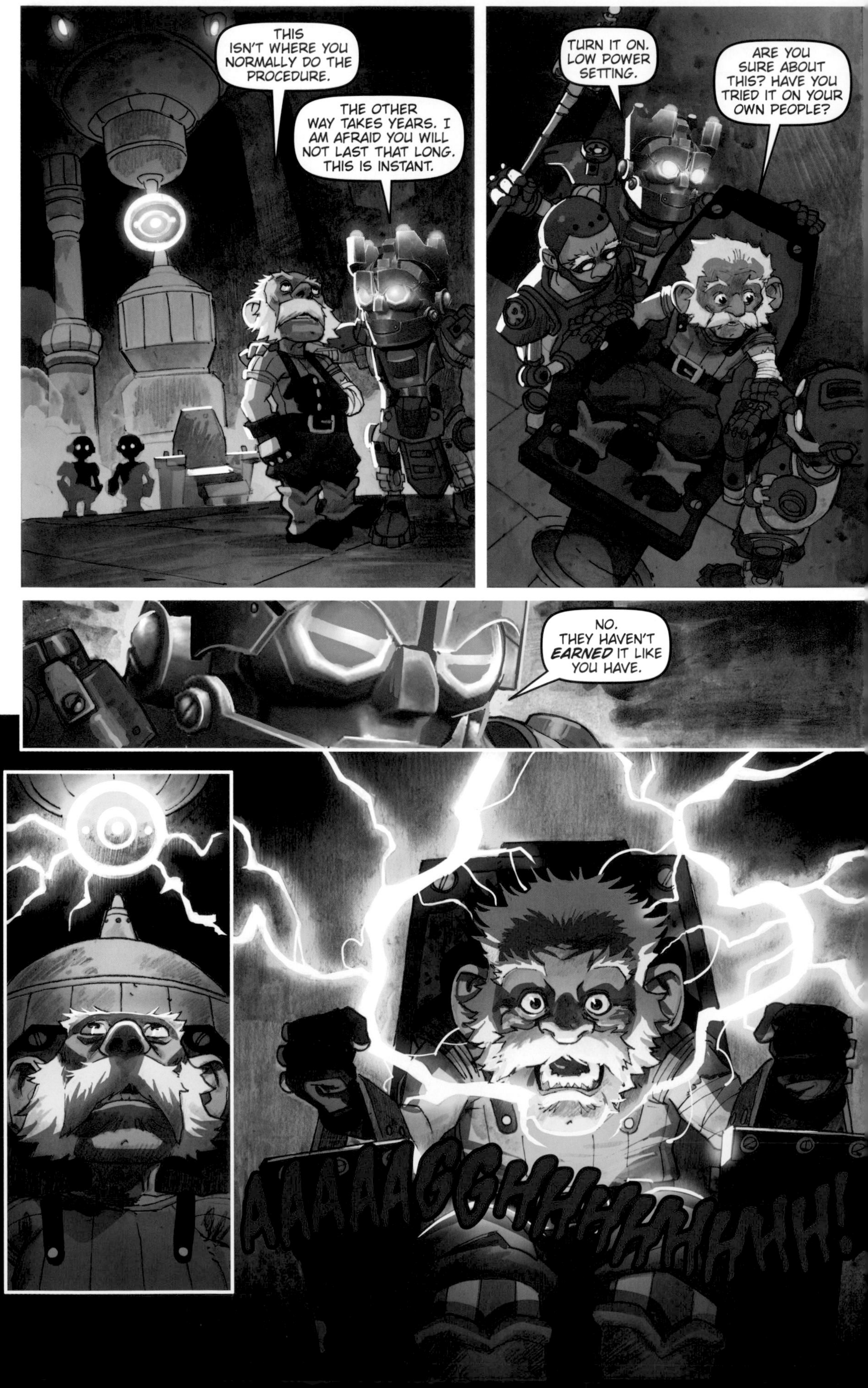

THIS ISN'T WHERE YOU NORMALLY DO THE PROCEDURE.
THE OTHER WAY TAKES YEARS. I AM AFRAID YOU WILL NOT LAST THAT LONG. THIS IS INSTANT.
TURN IT ON. LOW POWER SETTING.
ARE YOU SURE ABOUT THIS? HAVE YOU TRIED IT ON YOUR OWN PEOPLE?
NO. THEY HAVEN'T *EARNED* IT LIKE YOU HAVE.
AAAAAGGHHHHHHHHHH!

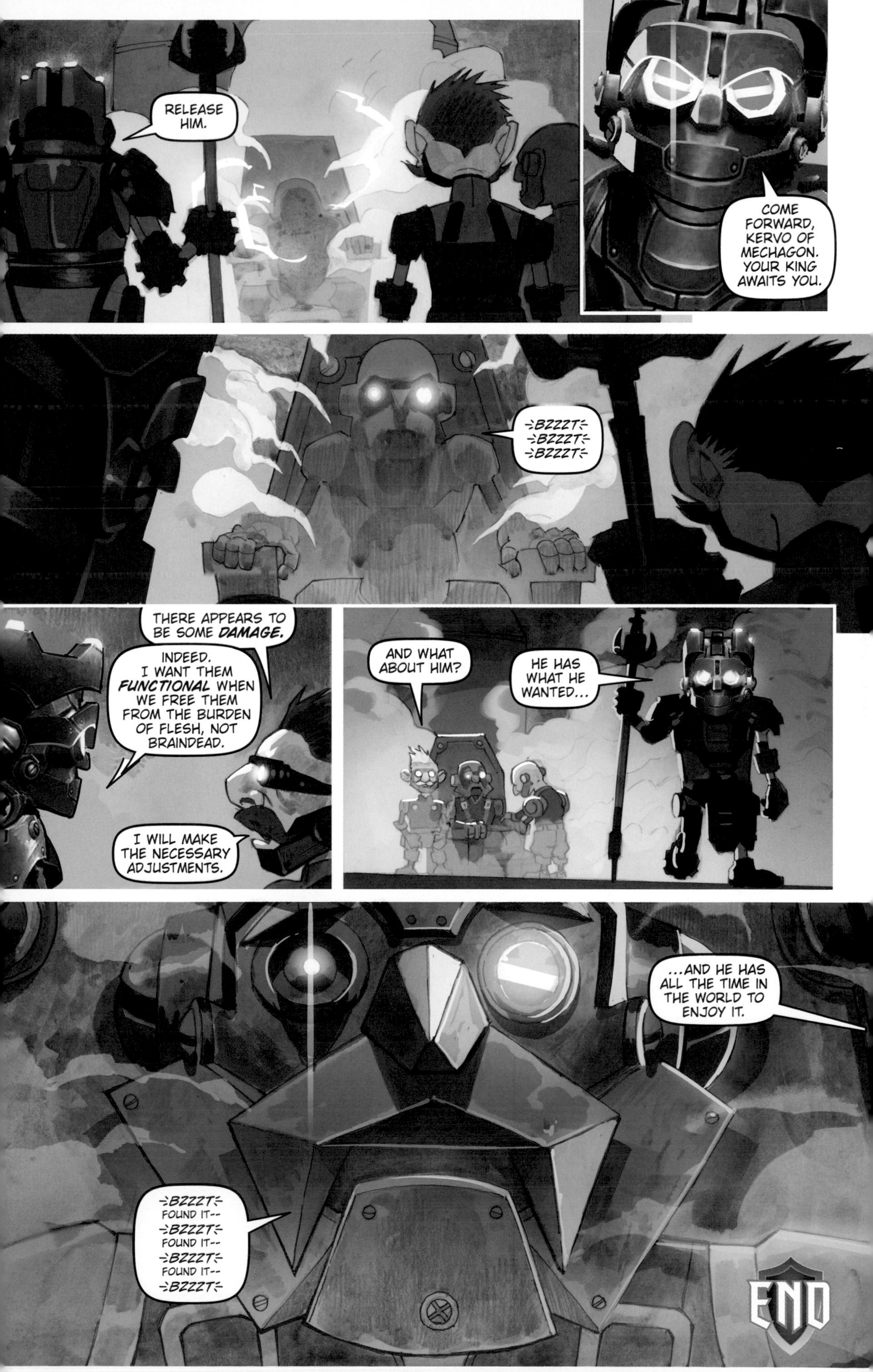
RELEASE HIM.
COME FORWARD, KERVO OF MECHAGON. YOUR KING AWAITS YOU.
-BZZZT- -BZZZT- -BZZZT-
THERE APPEARS TO BE SOME DAMAGE.
INDEED. I WANT THEM FUNCTIONAL WHEN WE FREE THEM FROM THE BURDEN OF FLESH, NOT BRAINDEAD.
I WILL MAKE THE NECESSARY ADJUSTMENTS.
AND WHAT ABOUT HIM?
HE HAS WHAT HE WANTED...
...AND HE HAS ALL THE TIME IN THE WORLD TO ENJOY IT.
-BZZZT- FOUND IT-- -BZZZT- FOUND IT-- -BZZZT- FOUND IT-- -BZZZT-
END

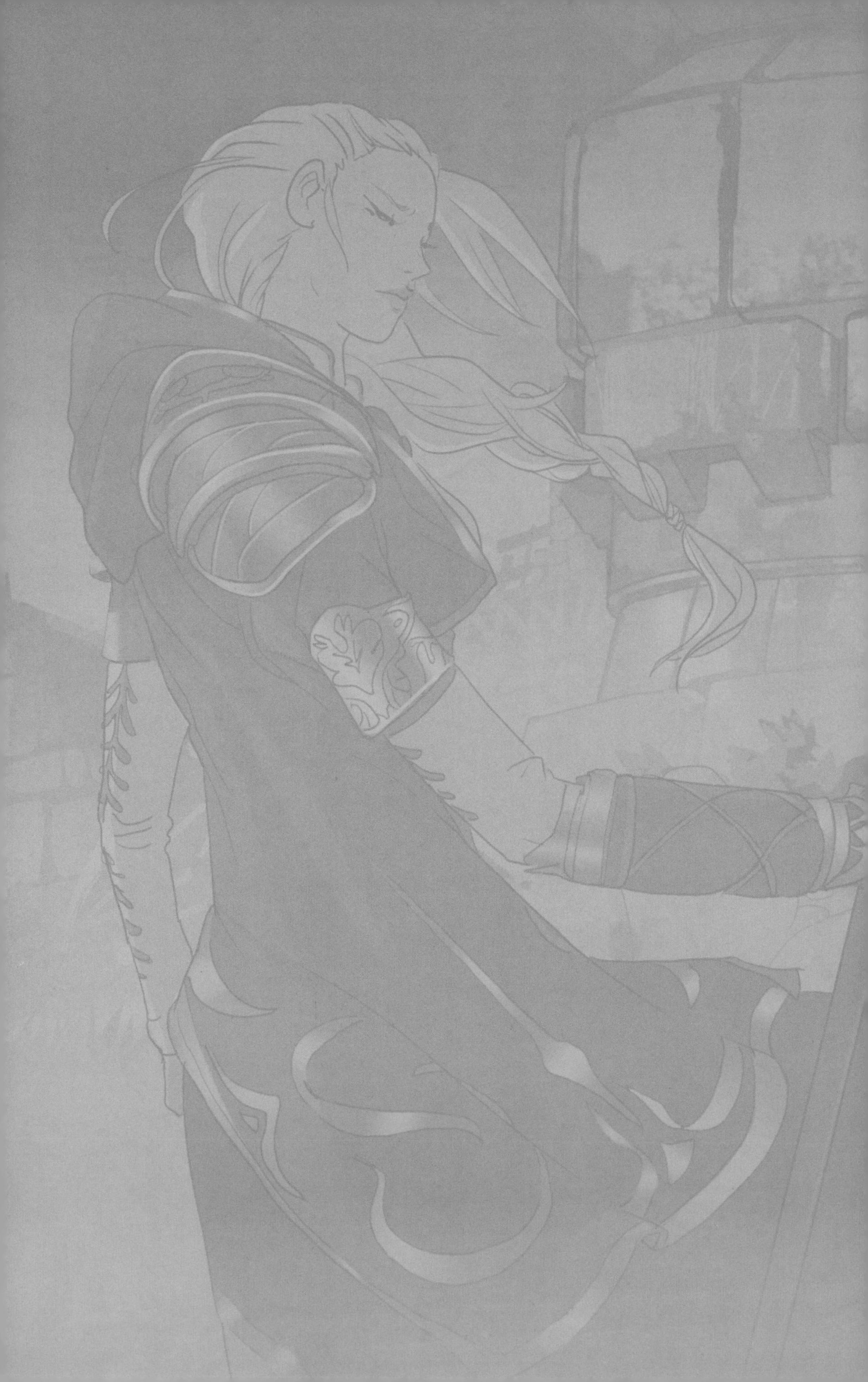

COMIC COLLECTION

- VOLUME ONE -

SKETCHBOOK

GUL'DAN AND THE STRANGER

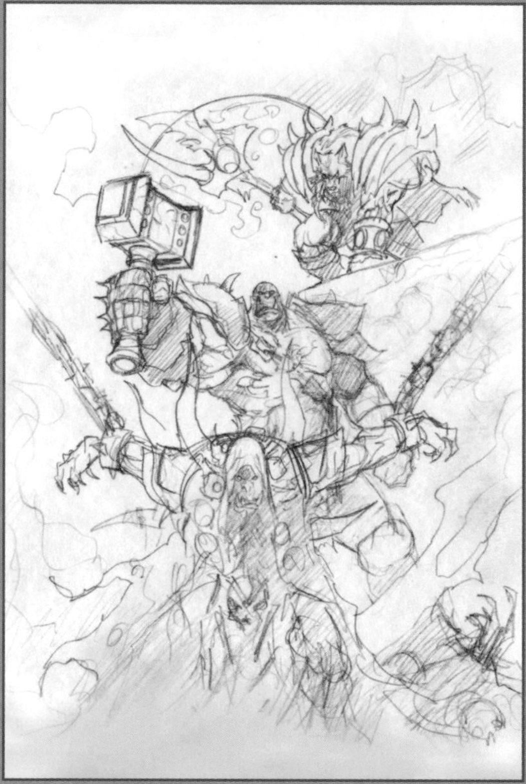

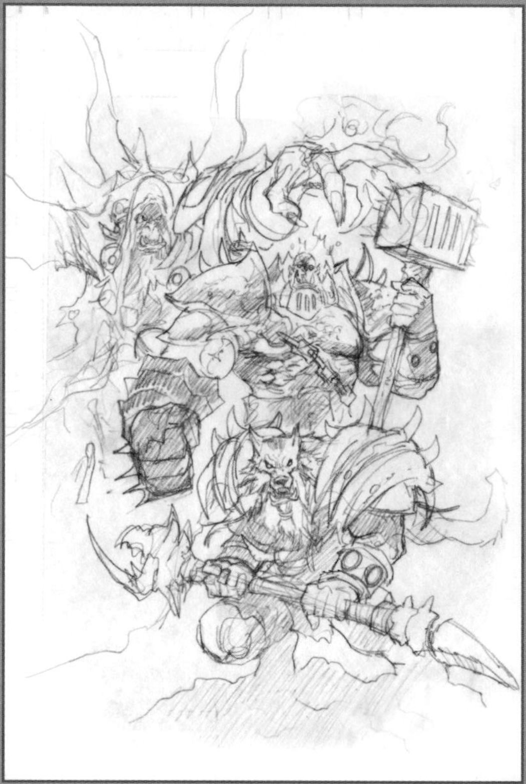

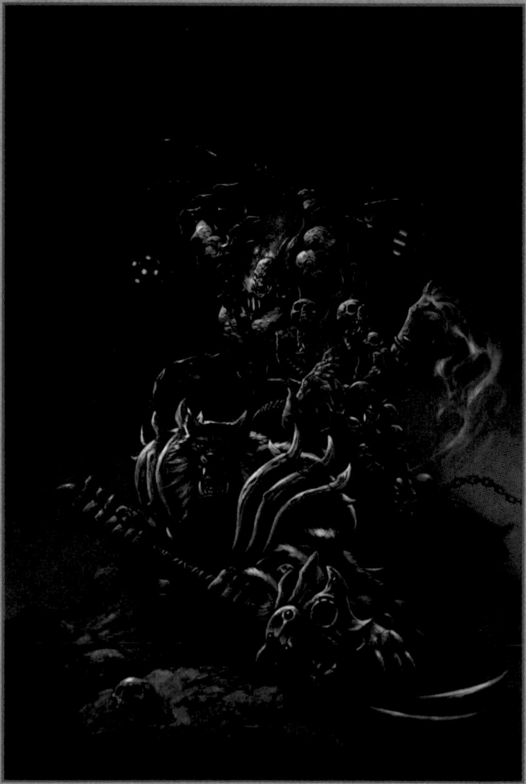

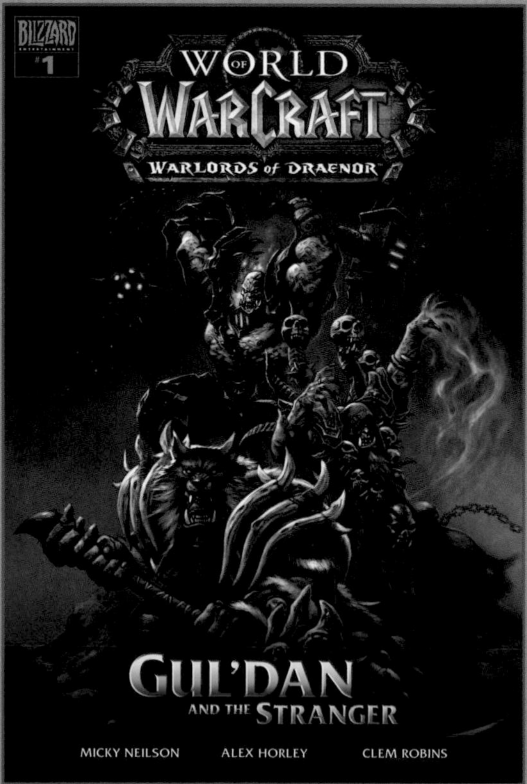
BLIZZARD ENTERTAINMENT
#1
WORLD OF WARCRAFT
WARLORDS of DRAENOR
GUL'DAN
AND THE STRANGER
MICKY NEILSON
ALEX HORLEY
CLEM ROBINS

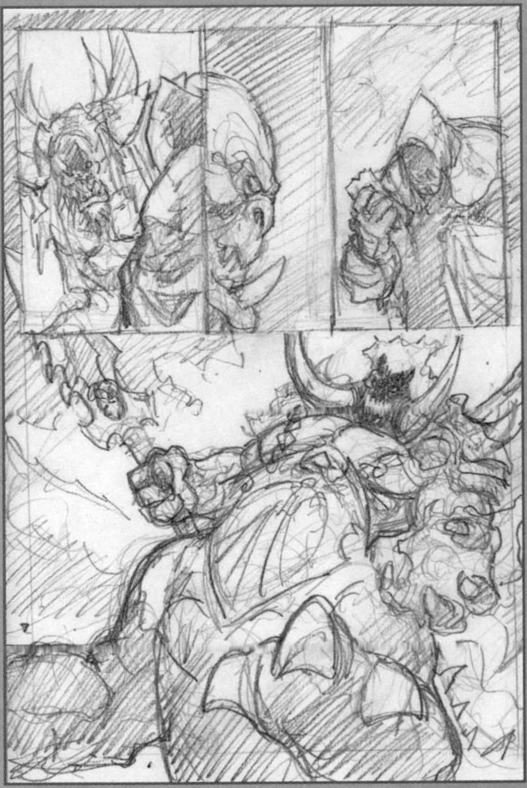

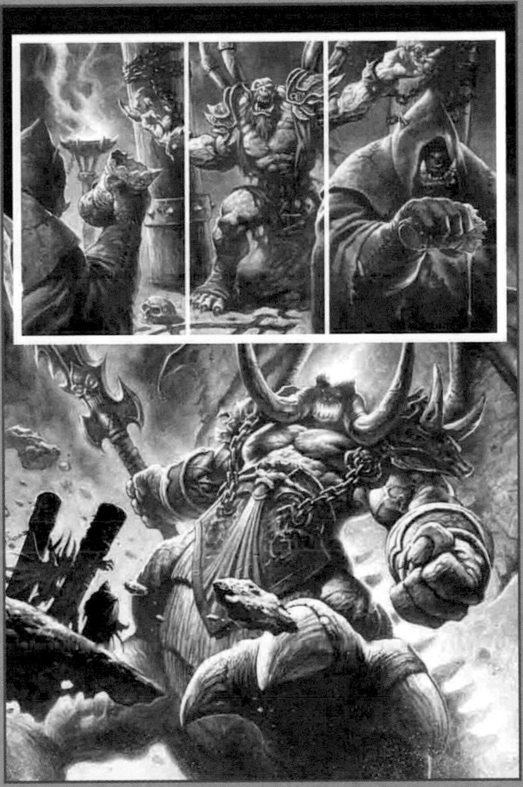

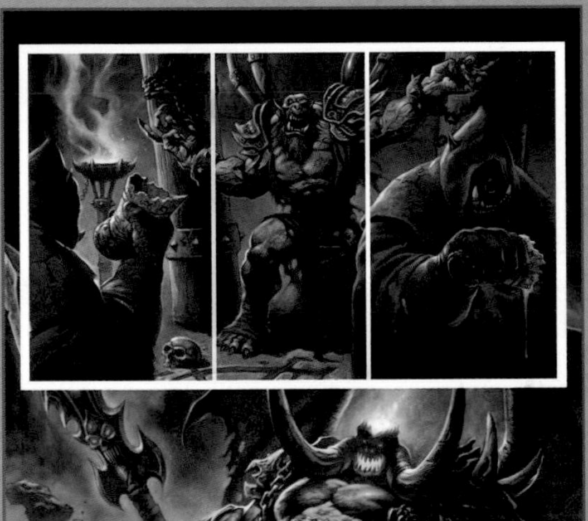

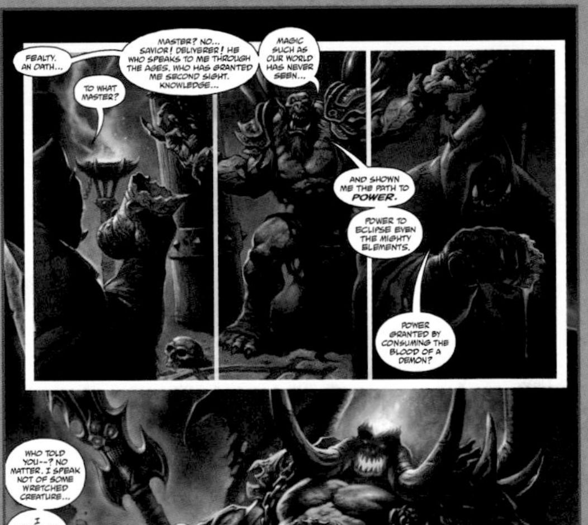
FEALTY. AN OATH...
TO WHAT MASTER?
MASTER? NO... SAVIOR! DELIVERER! HE WHO SPEAKS TO ME THROUGH THE AGES. WHO HAS GRANTED ME SECOND SIGHT. KNOWLEDGE...
MAGIC SUCH AS OUR WORLD HAS NEVER SEEN...
AND SHOWN ME THE PATH TO POWER.
POWER TO ECLIPSE EVEN THE MIGHTY ELEMENTS.
POWER GRANTED BY CONSUMING THE BLOOD OF A DEMON?
WHO TOLD YOU--? NO MATTER. I SPEAK NOT OF SOME WRETCHED CREATURE...
I SPEAK OF MANNOROTH, THE EXALTED ONE!
TO BEHOLD HIM IS TO KNOW UNBOUND STRENGTH...

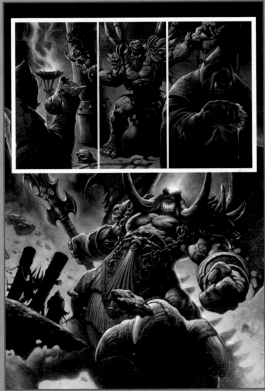

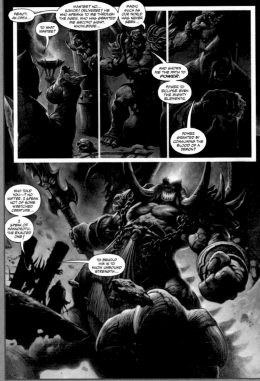

BLACKHAND

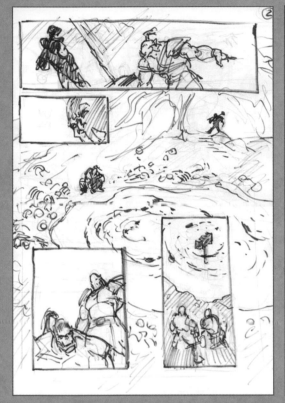

BLOOD AND THUNDER

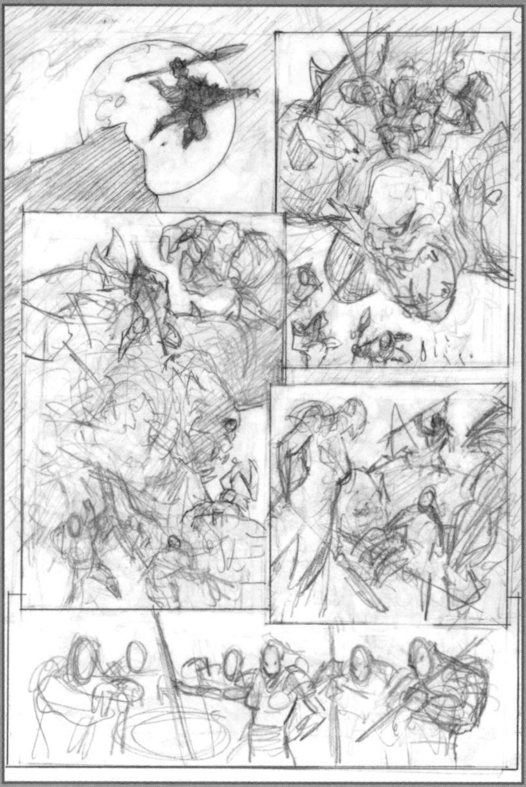

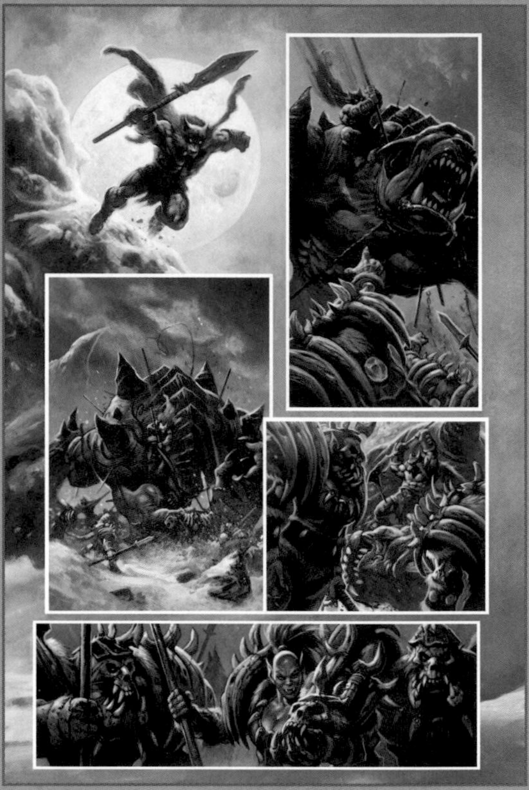

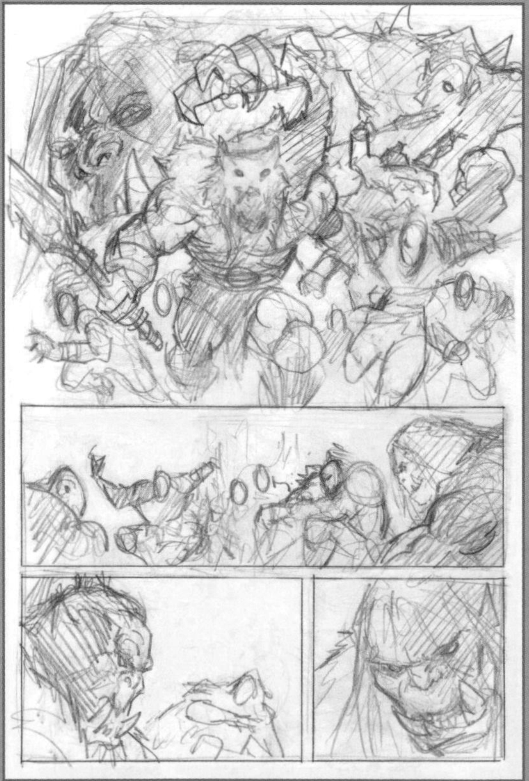

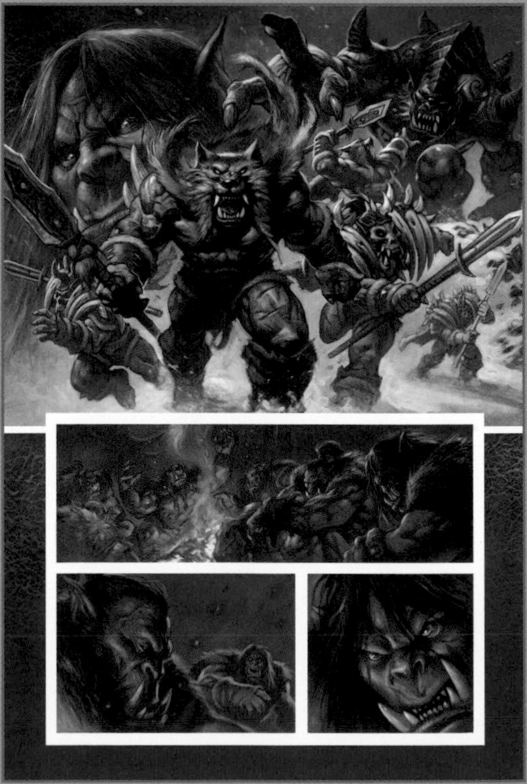

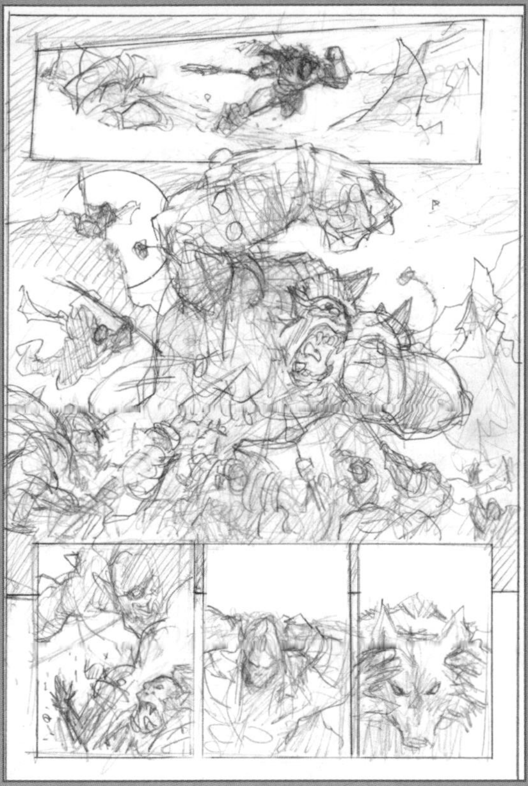
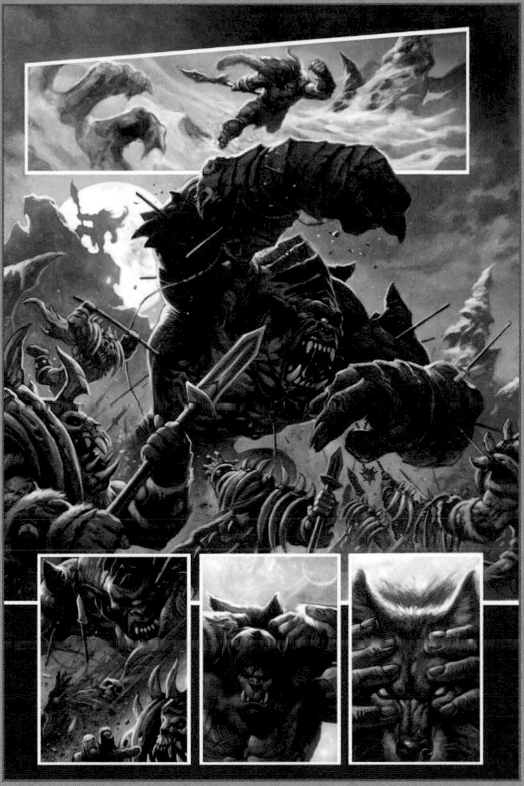
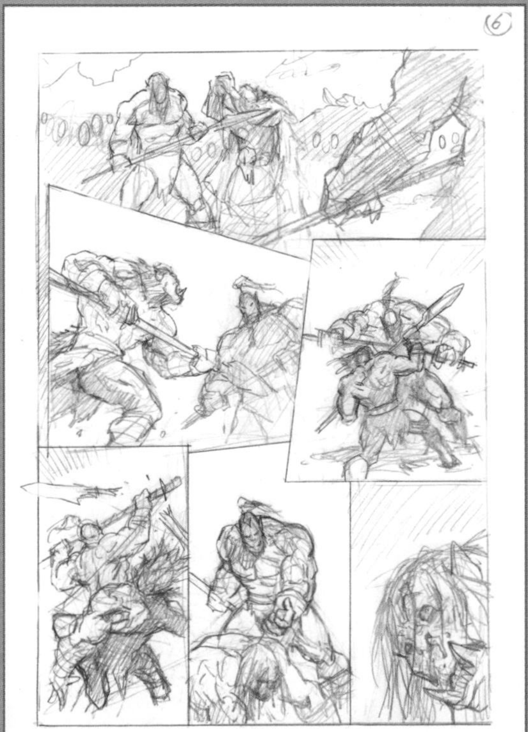
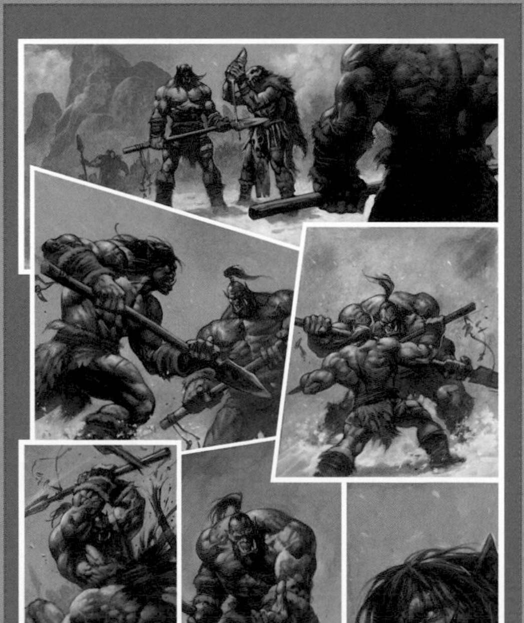

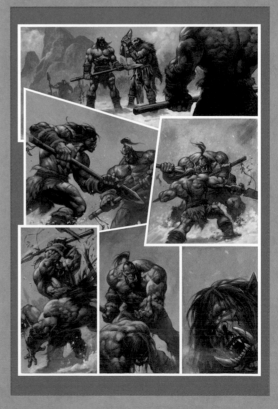

MAGNI: FAULT LINES

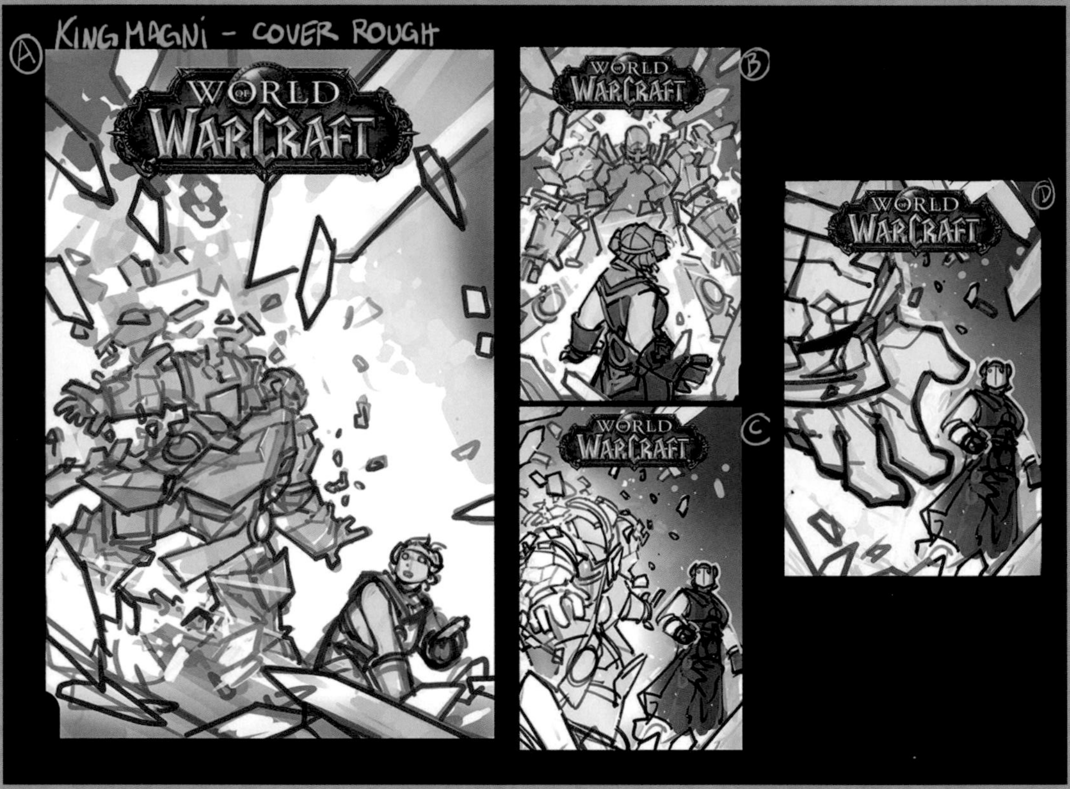
KING MAGNI - COVER ROUGH
A
WORLD WARCRAFT
B
WORLD WARCRAFT
C
WORLD WARCRAFT
D
WORLD WARCRAFT

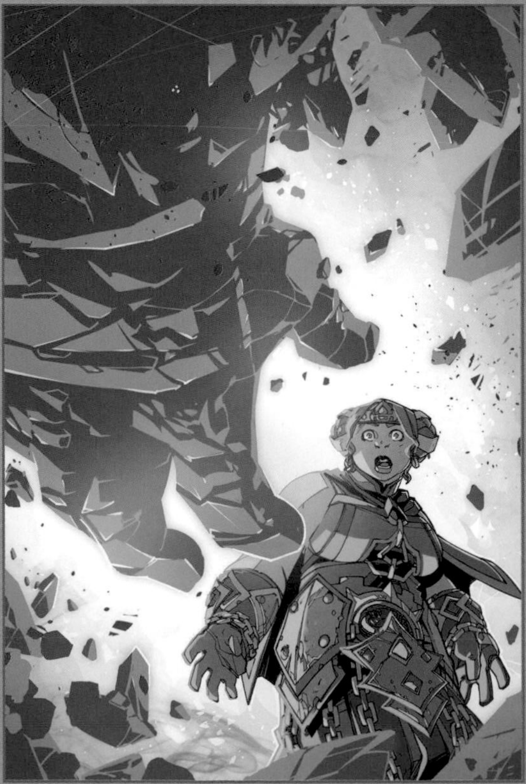

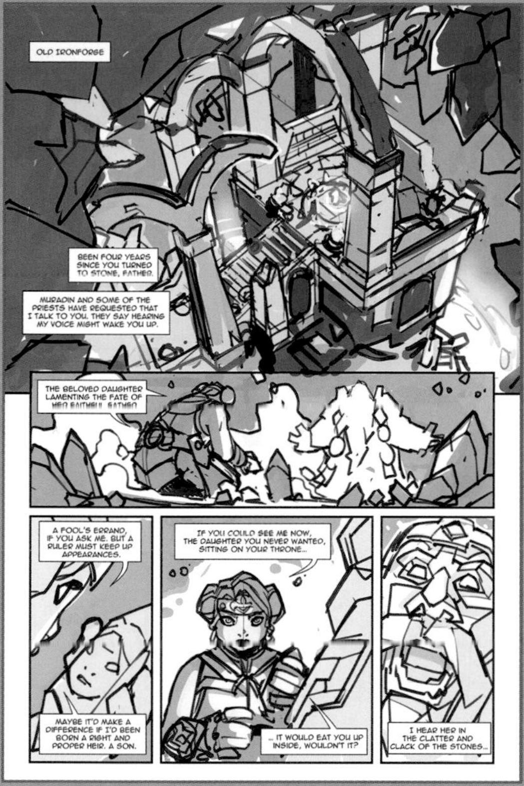
OLD IRONFORGE
BEEN FOUR YEARS SINCE YOU TURNED TO STONE, FATHER.
MURADIN AND SOME OF THE PRIESTS HAVE REQUESTED THAT I TALK TO YOU. THEY SAY HEARING MY VOICE MIGHT WAKE YOU UP.
THE BELOVED DAUGHTER LAMENTING THE FATE OF
A FOOL'S ERRAND, IF YOU ASK ME. BUT A RULER MUST KEEP UP APPEARANCES.
MAYBE IT'D MAKE A DIFFERENCE IF I'D BEEN BORN A RIGHT AND PROPER HEIR. A SON.
IF YOU COULD SEE ME NOW, THE DAUGHTER YOU NEVER WANTED, SITTING ON YOUR THRONE...
... IT WOULD EAT YOU UP INSIDE, WOULDN'T IT?
I HEAR HER IN THE CLATTER AND CLACK OF THE STONES...

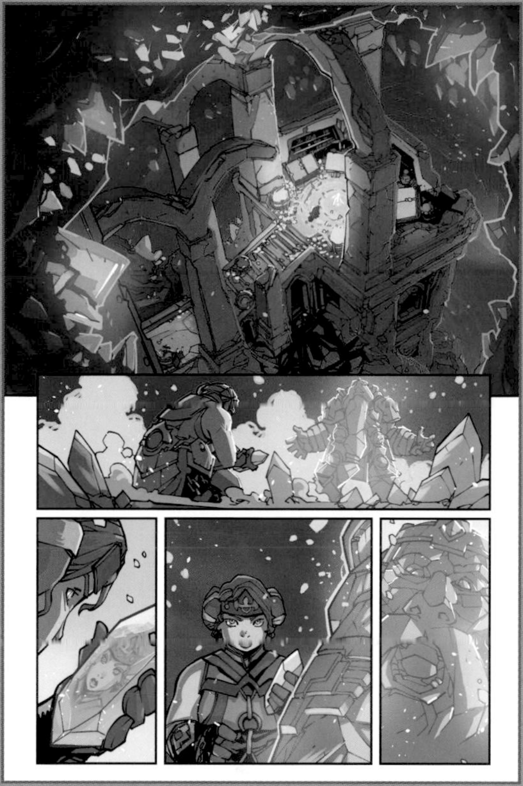

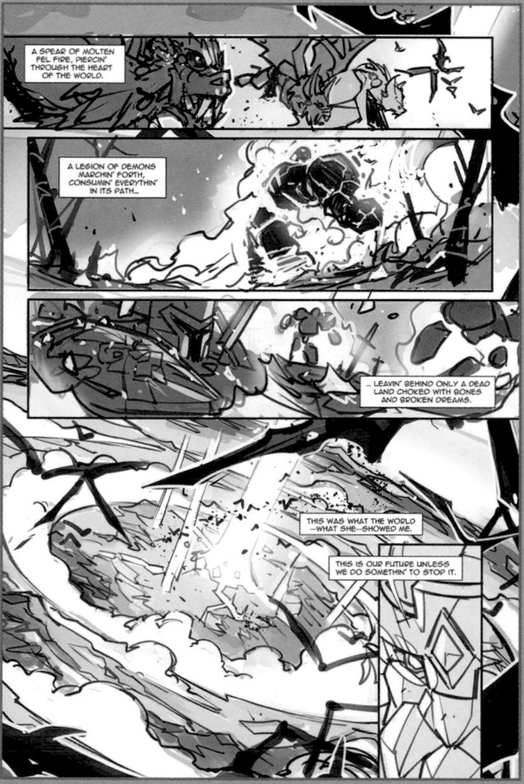
A SPEAR OF MOLTEN FEL FIRE, PIERCIN' THROUGH THE HEART OF THE WORLD.
A LEGION OF DEMONS MARCHIN' FORTH, CONSUMIN' EVERYTHIN' IN ITS PATH...
... LEAVIN' BEHIND ONLY A DEAD LAND CHOKED WITH BONES AND BROKEN DREAMS.
THIS WAS WHAT THE WORLD —WHAT SHE—SHOWED ME.
THIS IS OUR FUTURE UNLESS WE DO SOMETHIN' TO STOP IT.

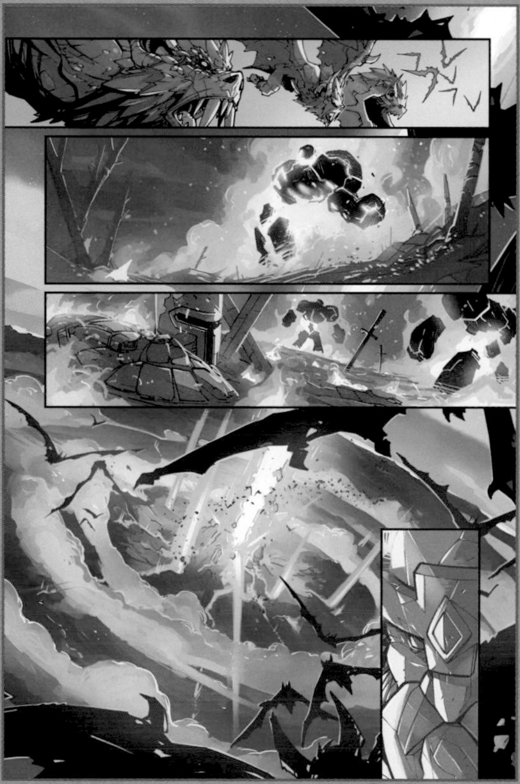

NIGHTBORNE: TWILIGHT OF SURAMAR

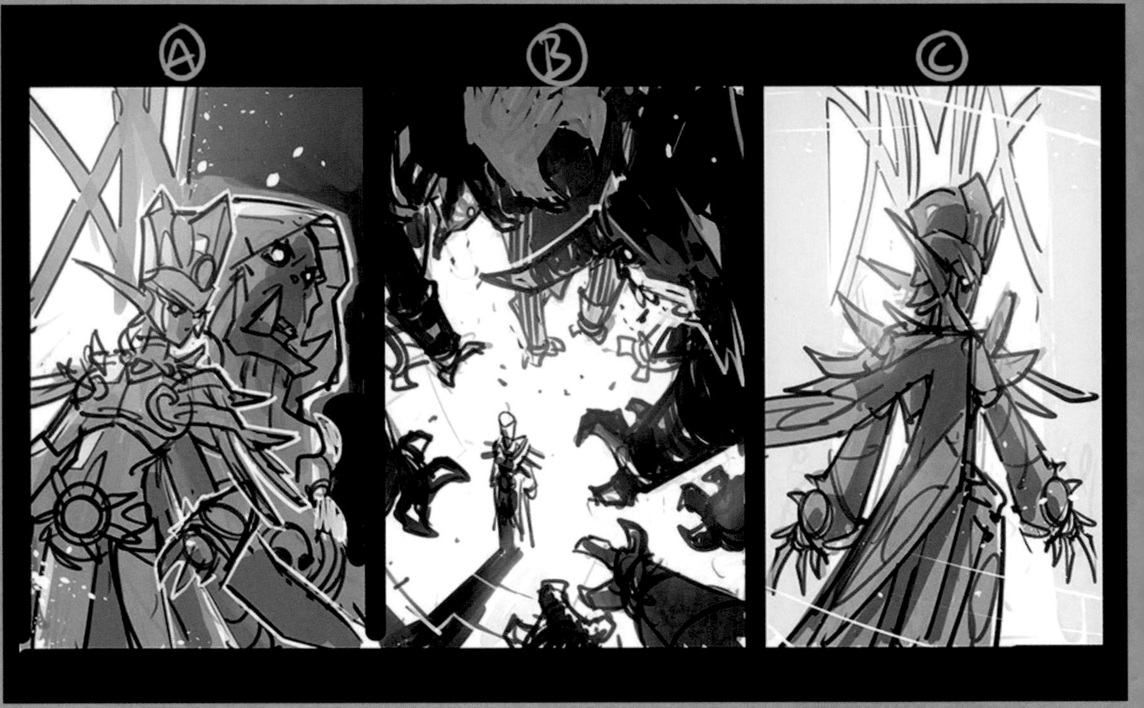
A
B
C

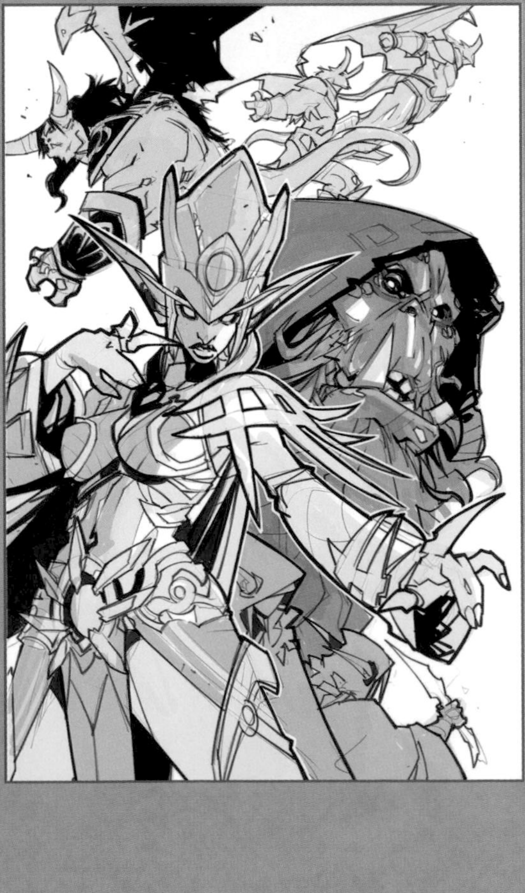

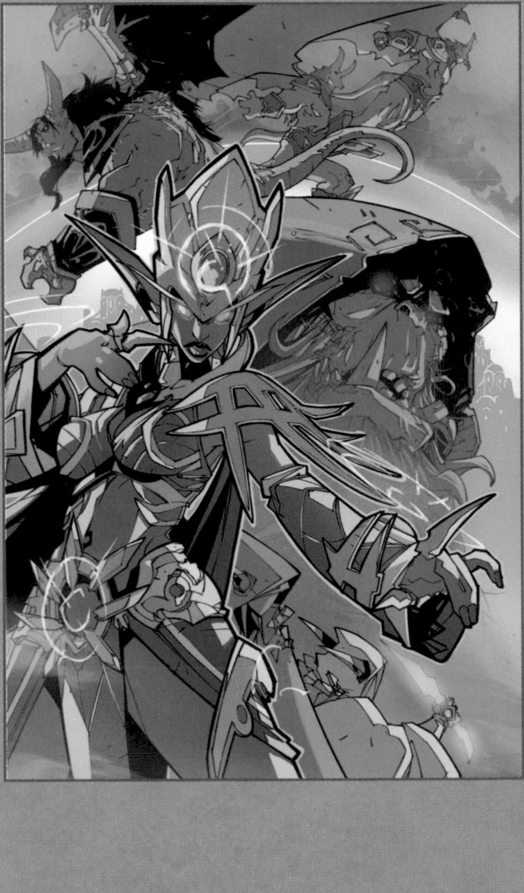

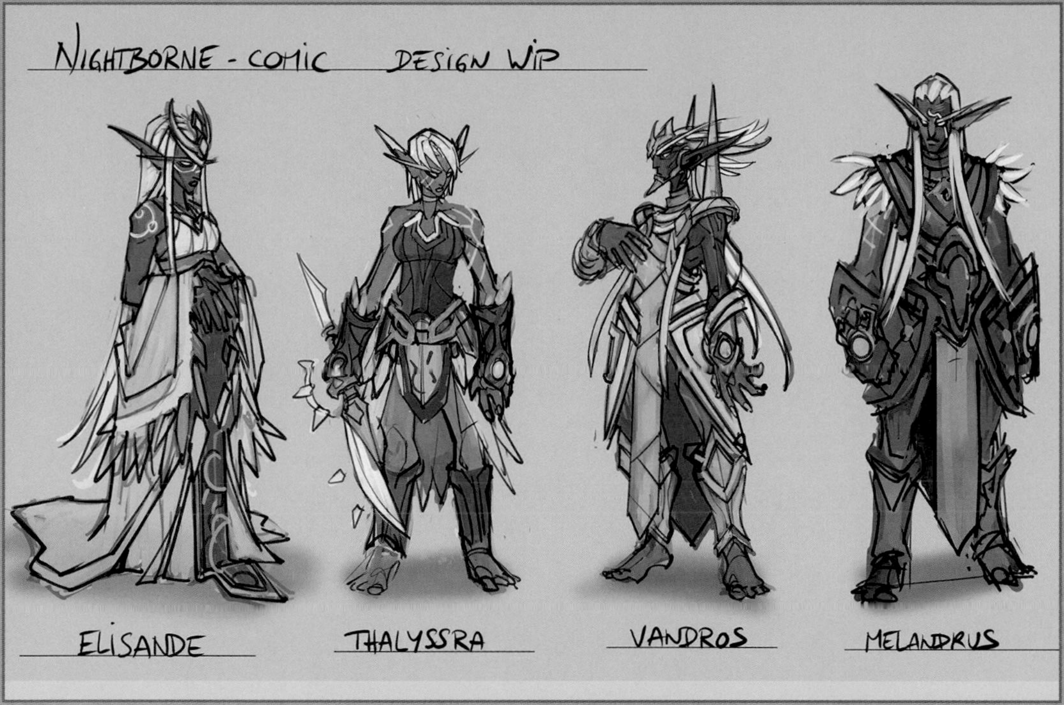

NIGHTBORNE - COMIC DESIGN WIP
ELISANDE
THALYSSRA
VANDROS
MELANDRUS

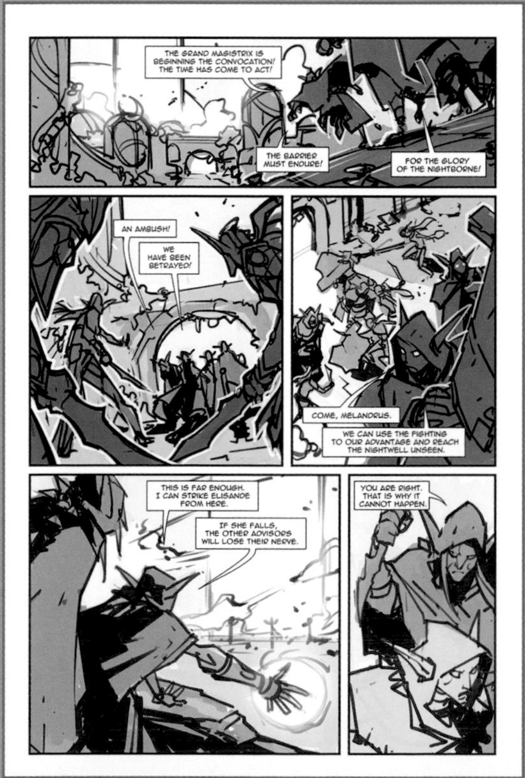

THE GRAND MAGISTRIX IS BEGINNING THE CONVOCATION! THE TIME HAS COME TO ACT!
THE BARRIER MUST ENDURE!
FOR THE GLORY OF THE NIGHTBORNE!
AN AMBUSH!
WE HAVE BEEN BETRAYED!
COME, MELANDRUS.
WE CAN USE THE FIGHTING TO OUR ADVANTAGE AND REACH THE NIGHTWELL UNSEEN.
THIS IS FAR ENOUGH. I CAN STRIKE ELISANDE FROM HERE.
IF SHE FALLS, THE OTHER ADVISORS WILL LOSE THEIR NERVE.
YOU ARE RIGHT. THAT IS WHY IT CANNOT HAPPEN.

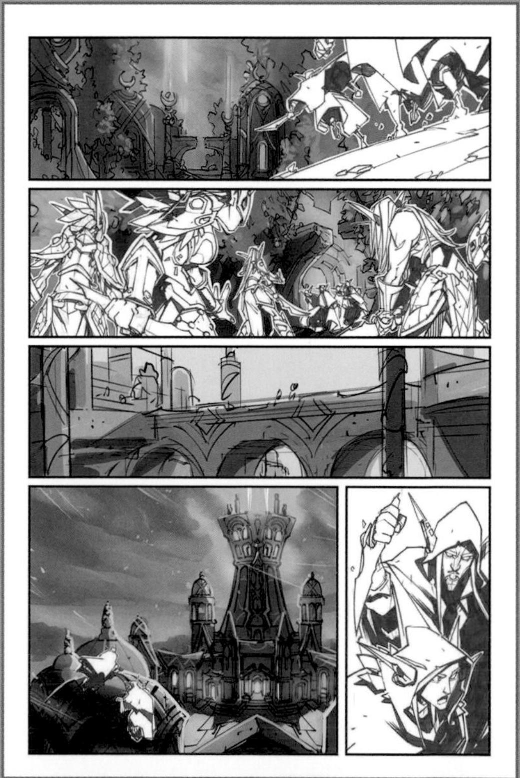

HIGHMOUNTAIN: A MOUNTAIN DIVIDED

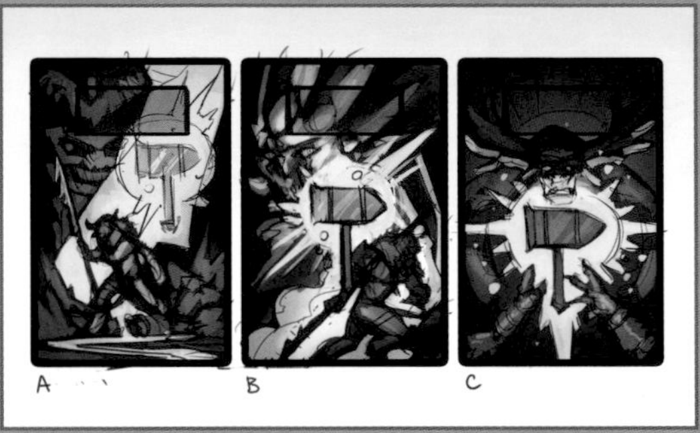
A
B
C

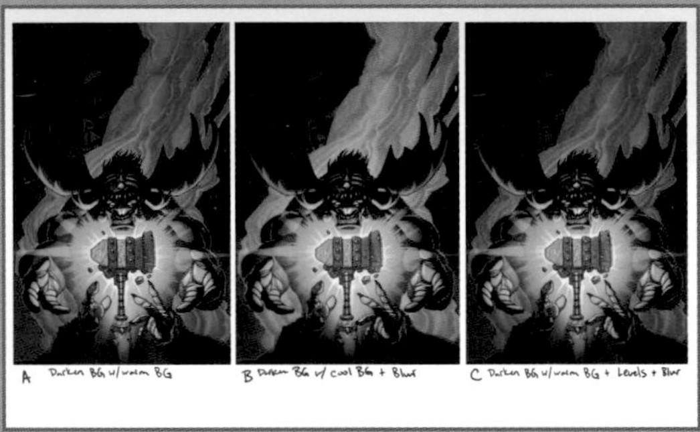
A Darken BG w/ warm BG
B Darken BG w/ cool BG + Blur
C Darken BG w/ warm BG + Levels + Blur

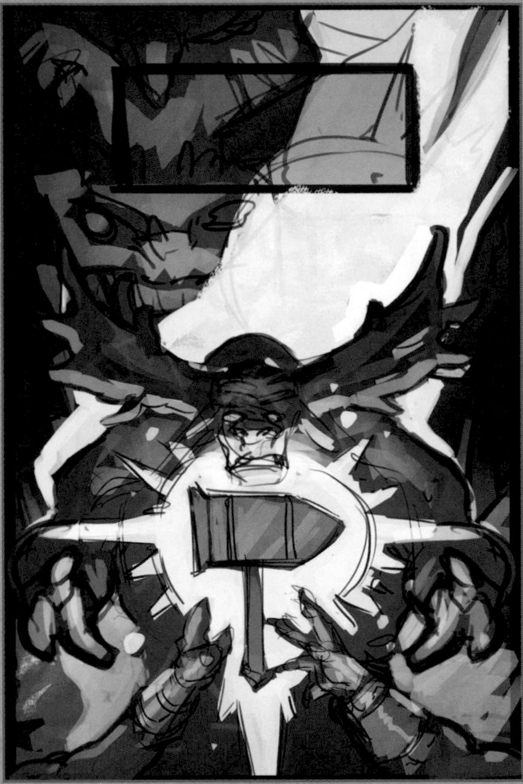

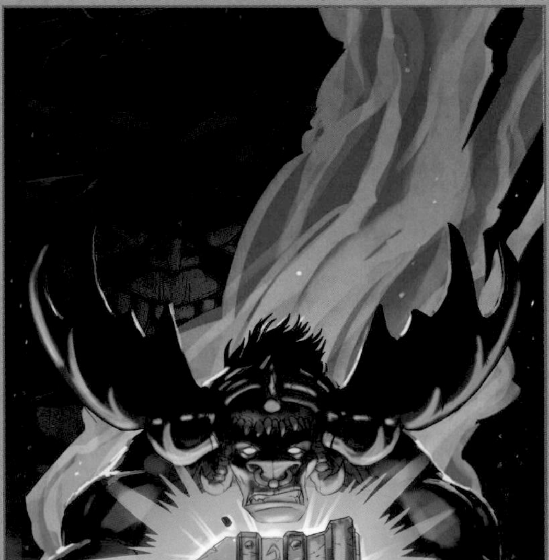

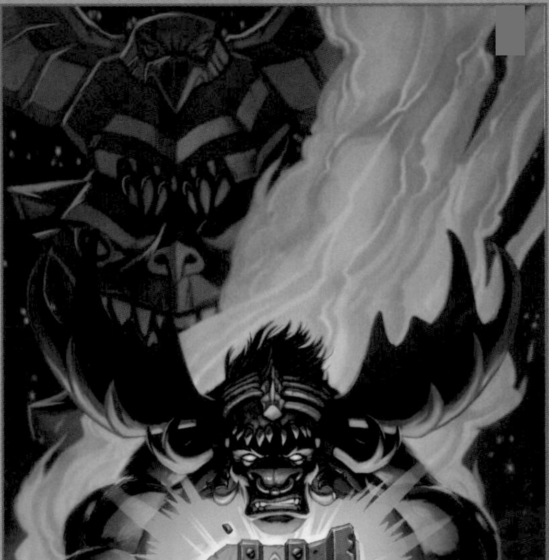

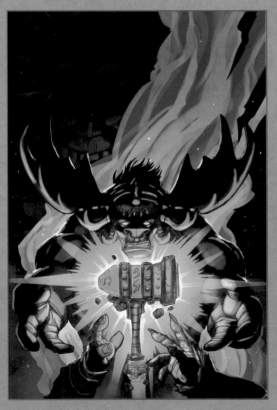

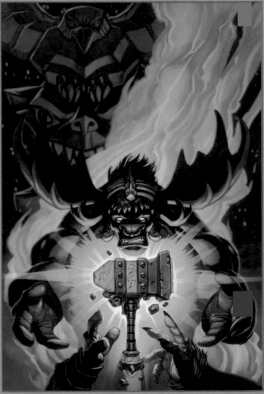

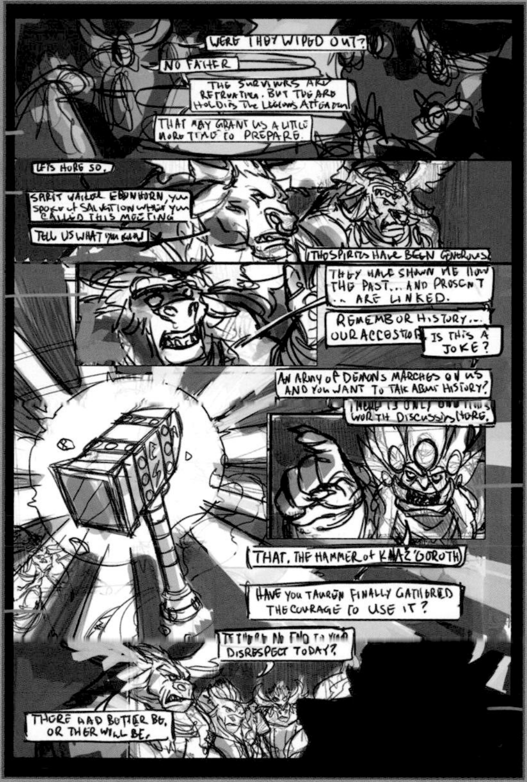
WERE THEY WIPED OUT?
NO FATHER
THE SURVIVORS ARE RETREATING. BUT THEY ARE HOLDING THE LEGIONS ATTENTION
THAT MAY GRANT US A LITTLE MORE TIME TO PREPARE.
LETS HOPE SO.
SPIRIT WALKER EBONHORN, YOU SPOKE OF SALVATION WHEN YOU CALLED THIS MEETING
TELL US WHAT YOU
THE SPIRITS HAVE BEEN GENEROUS.
THEY HAVE SHOWN ME HOW THE PAST... AND PRESENT .. ARE LINKED.
REMEMBER HISTORY... OUR ACCESTOR
IS THIS A JOKE?
AN ARMY OF DEMONS MARCHES ON US AND YOU WANT TO TALK ABOUT HISTORY?
WORTH DISCUSSING HERE.
THAT. THE HAMMER OF KHAZ'GOROTH
HAVE YOU TAUREN FINALLY GATHERED THE COURAGE TO USE IT?
DISRESPECT TODAY?
THERE HAD BETTER BE, OR THERE WILL BE.

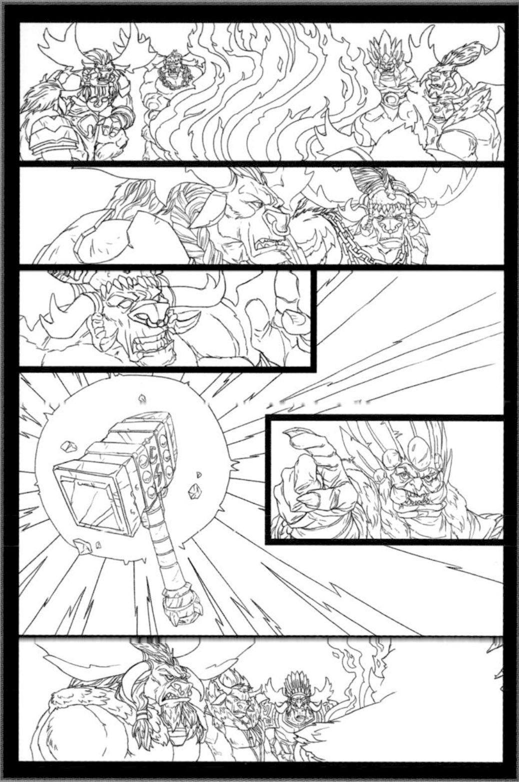

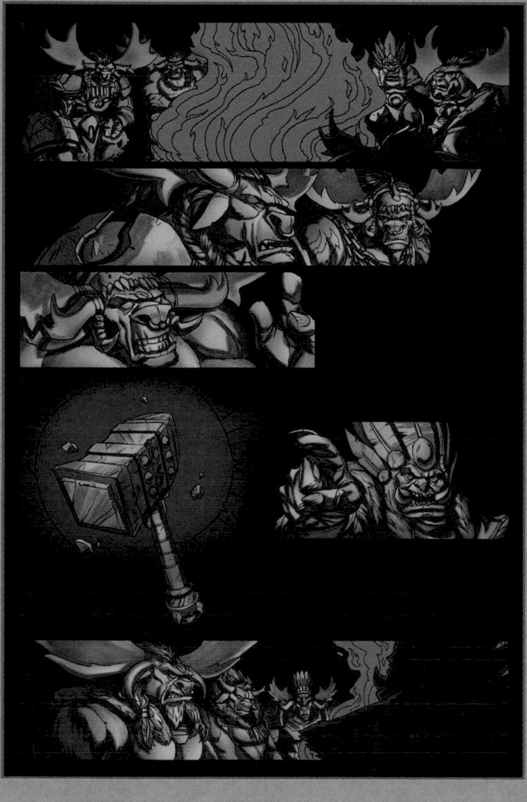

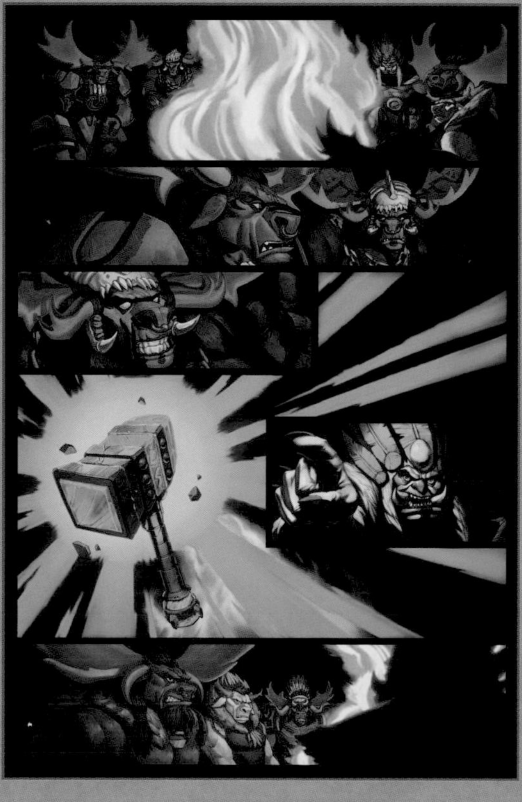

ANDUIN: SON OF THE WOLF

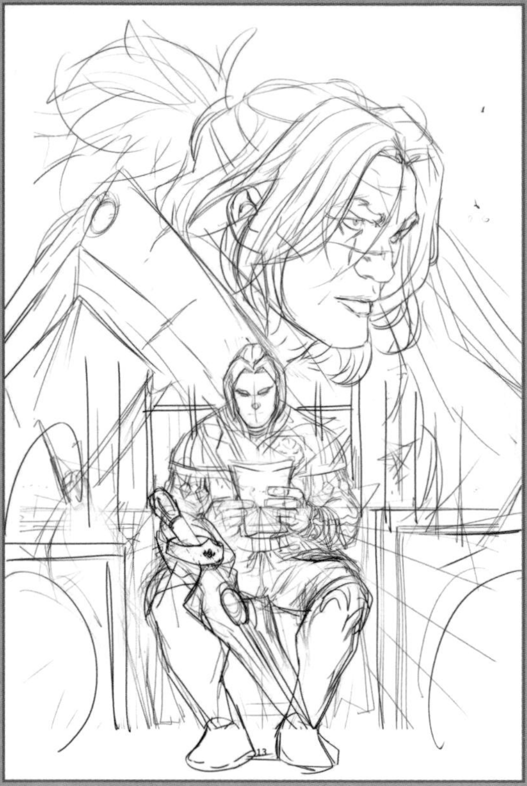

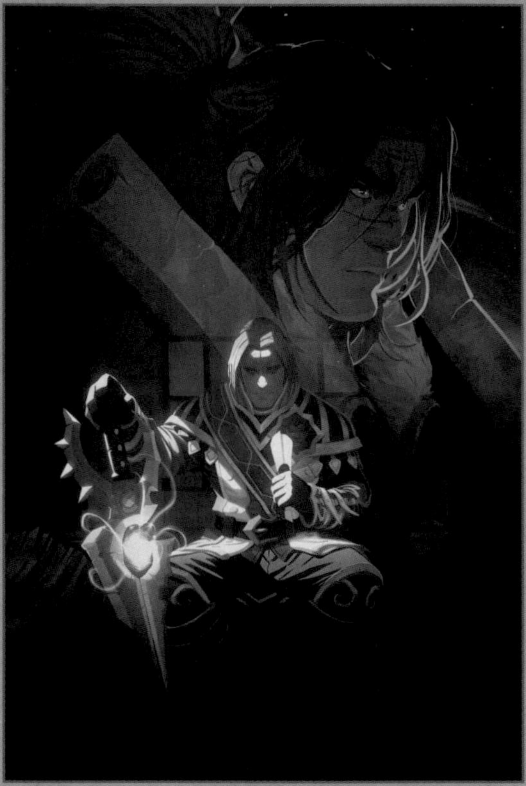

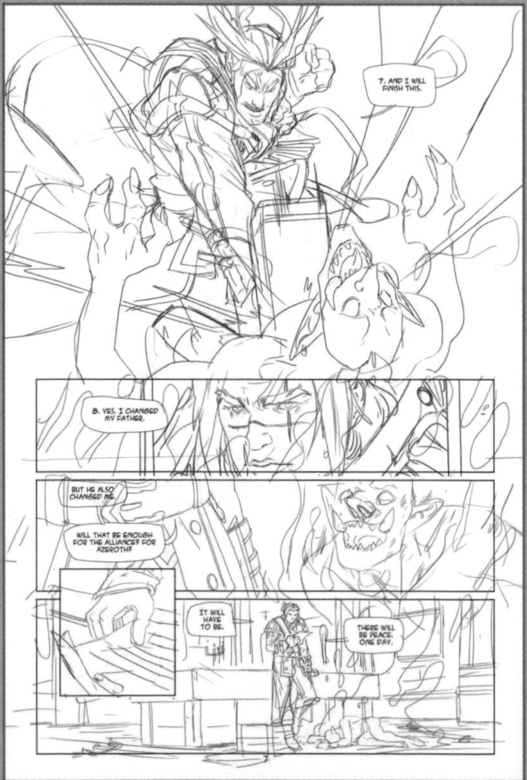
7. AND I WILL FINISH THIS.
8. YES. I CHANGED MY FATHER.
BUT HE ALSO CHANGED ME.
WILL THAT BE ENOUGH FOR THE ALLIANCE? FOR AZEROTH?
IT WILL HAVE TO BE.
THERE WILL BE PEACE. ONE DAY.

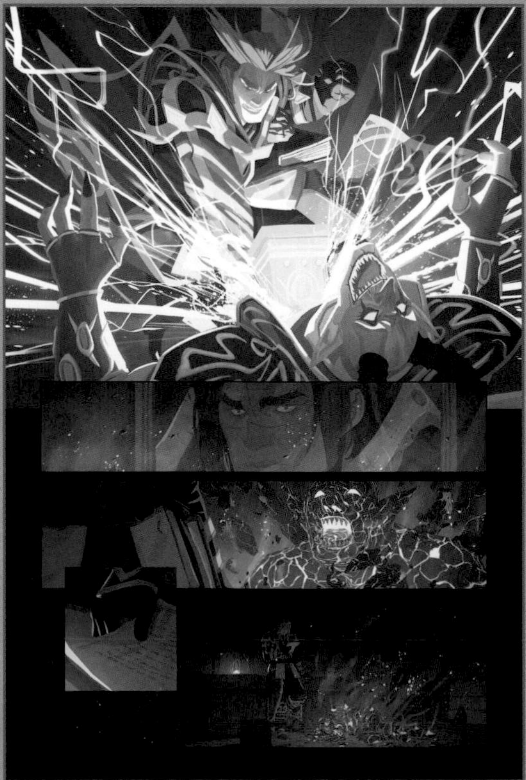

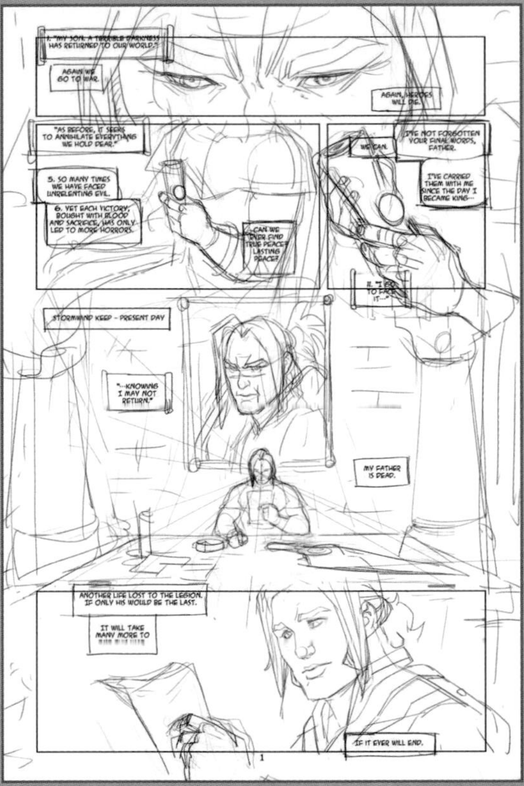
1. "MY SON. A TERRIBLE DARKNESS HAS RETURNED TO OUR WORLD."
AGAIN WE GO TO WAR.
AGAIN, HEROES WILL DIE.
"AS BEFORE, IT SEEKS TO ANNIHILATE EVERYTHING WE HOLD DEAR."
5. SO MANY TIMES WE HAVE FACED UNRELENTING EVIL.
6. YET EACH VICTORY, BOUGHT WITH BLOOD AND SACRIFICE, HAS ONLY LED TO MORE HORRORS.
CAN WE EVER FIND TRUE PEACE? LASTING PEACE?
WE CAN.
I'VE NOT FORGOTTEN YOUR FINAL WORDS, FATHER.
I'VE CARRIED THEM WITH ME SINCE THE DAY I BECAME KING--
11. "I GO TO FACE IT--"
STORMWIND KEEP - PRESENT DAY
"--KNOWING I MAY NOT RETURN."
MY FATHER IS DEAD.
ANOTHER LIFE LOST TO THE LEGION. IF ONLY HIS WOULD BE THE LAST.
IT WILL TAKE MANY MORE TO
IF IT EVER WILL END.
1

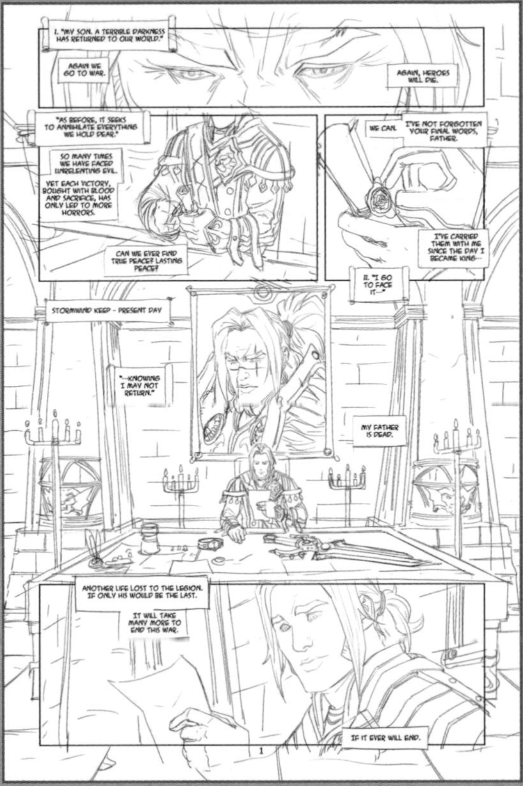
1. "MY SON. A TERRIBLE DARKNESS HAS RETURNED TO OUR WORLD."
AGAIN WE GO TO WAR.
AGAIN, HEROES WILL DIE.
"AS BEFORE, IT SEEKS TO ANNIHILATE EVERYTHING WE HOLD DEAR."
SO MANY TIMES WE HAVE FACED UNRELENTING EVIL.
YET EACH VICTORY, BOUGHT WITH BLOOD AND SACRIFICE, HAS ONLY LED TO MORE HORRORS.
CAN WE EVER FIND TRUE PEACE? LASTING PEACE?
WE CAN.
I'VE NOT FORGOTTEN YOUR FINAL WORDS, FATHER.
I'VE CARRIED THEM WITH ME SINCE THE DAY I BECAME KING--
11. "I GO TO FACE IT--"
STORMWIND KEEP - PRESENT DAY
"--KNOWING I MAY NOT RETURN."
MY FATHER IS DEAD.
ANOTHER LIFE LOST TO THE LEGION. IF ONLY HIS WOULD BE THE LAST.
IT WILL TAKE MANY MORE TO END THIS WAR.
IF IT EVER WILL END.
1

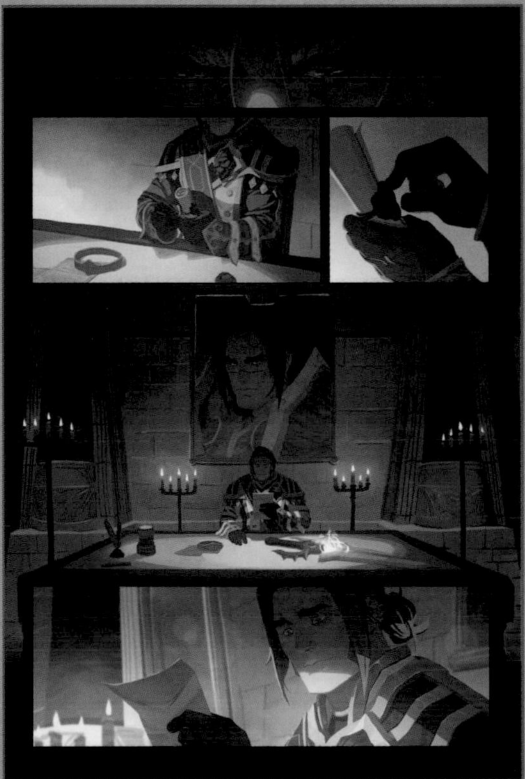

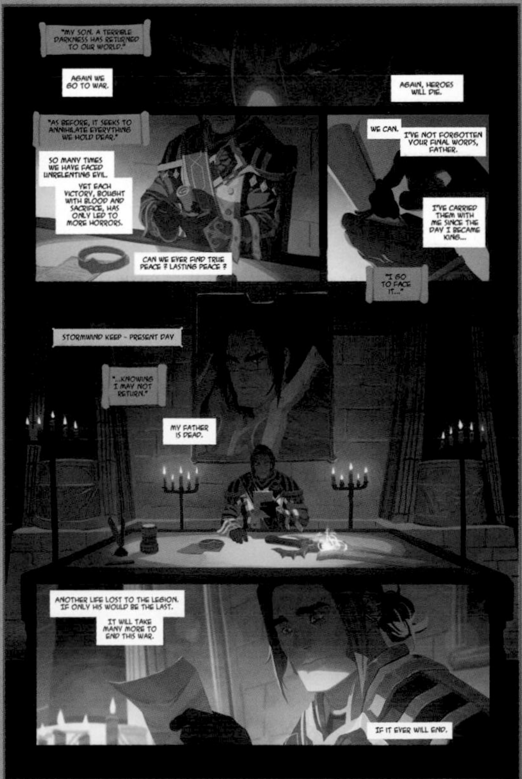
"MY SON. A TERRIBLE DARKNESS HAS RETURNED TO OUR WORLD."
AGAIN WE GO TO WAR.
AGAIN, HEROES WILL DIE.
"AS BEFORE, IT SEEKS TO ANNIHILATE EVERYTHING WE HOLD DEAR."
SO MANY TIMES WE HAVE FACED UNRELENTING EVIL.
YET EACH VICTORY, BOUGHT WITH BLOOD AND SACRIFICE, HAS ONLY LED TO MORE HORRORS.
CAN WE EVER FIND TRUE PEACE ? LASTING PEACE ?
WE CAN.
I'VE NOT FORGOTTEN YOUR FINAL WORDS, FATHER.
I'VE CARRIED THEM WITH ME SINCE THE DAY I BECAME KING...
"I GO TO FACE IT..."
STORMWIND KEEP - PRESENT DAY
"...KNOWING I MAY NOT RETURN."
MY FATHER IS DEAD.
ANOTHER LIFE LOST TO THE LEGION. IF ONLY HIS WOULD BE THE LAST.
IT WILL TAKE MANY MORE TO END THIS WAR.
IF IT EVER WILL END.

JAINA: REUNION

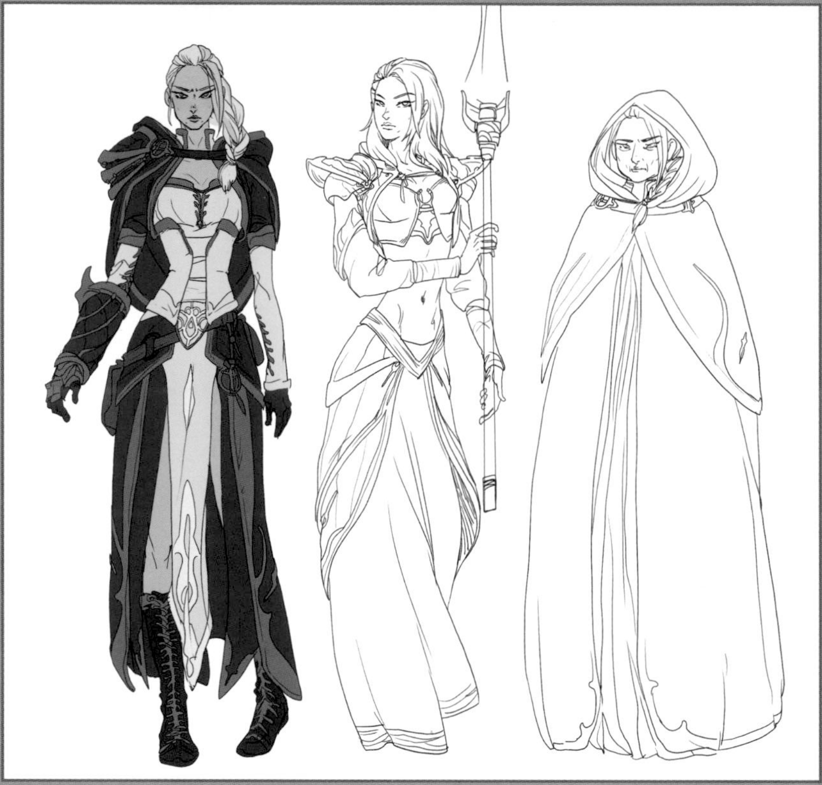

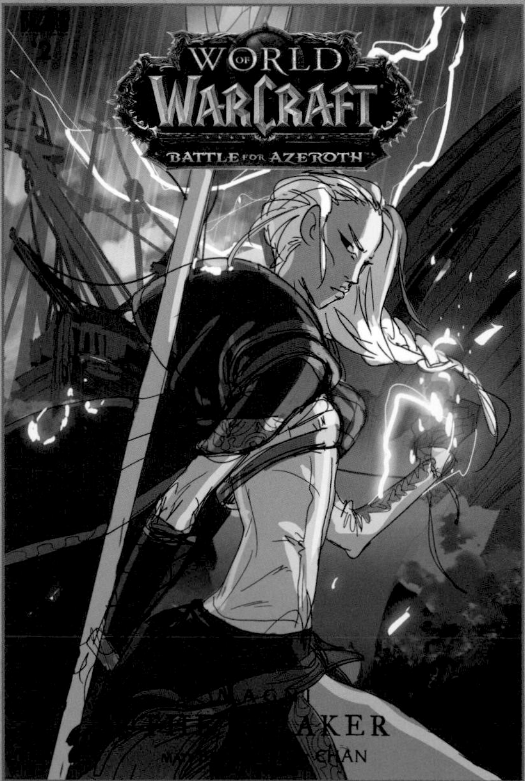
WORLD OF
WARCRAFT
BATTLE FOR AZEROTH

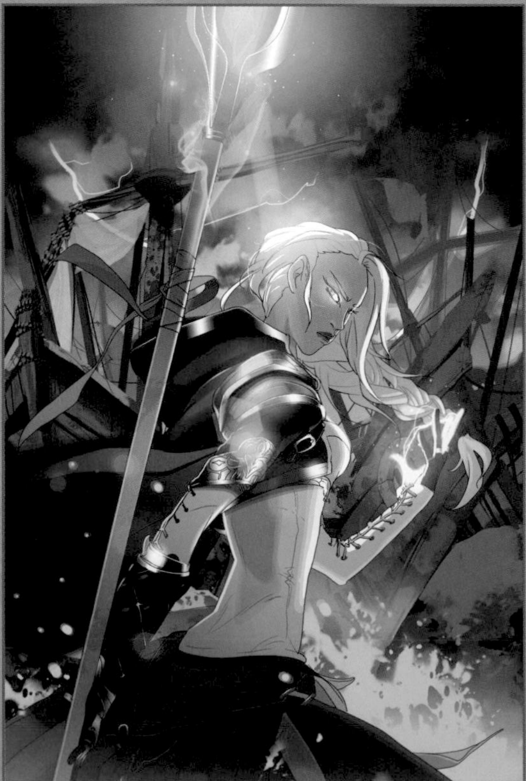

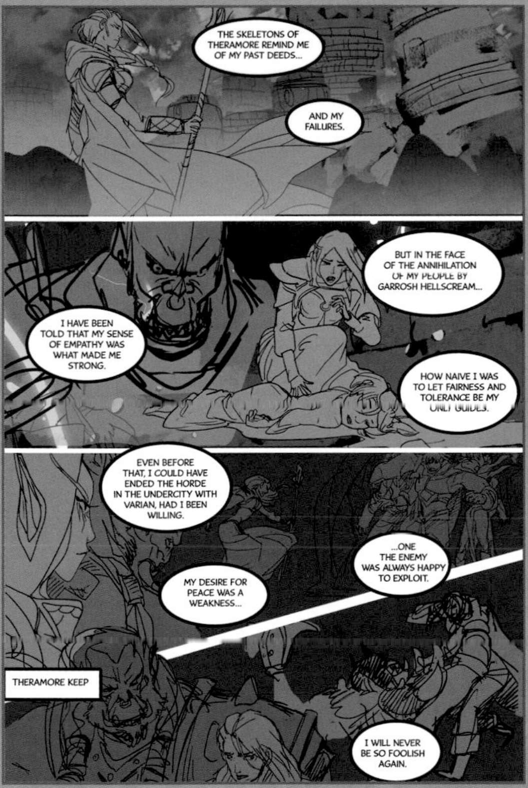
THE SKELETONS OF THERAMORE REMIND ME OF MY PAST DEEDS...
AND MY FAILURES.
BUT IN THE FACE OF THE ANNIHILATION OF MY PEOPLE BY GARROSH HELLSCREAM...
I HAVE BEEN TOLD THAT MY SENSE OF EMPATHY WAS WHAT MADE ME STRONG.
HOW NAIVE I WAS TO LET FAIRNESS AND TOLERANCE BE MY ONLY GUIDES.
EVEN BEFORE THAT, I COULD HAVE ENDED THE HORDE IN THE UNDERCITY WITH VARIAN, HAD I BEEN WILLING.
...ONE THE ENEMY WAS ALWAYS HAPPY TO EXPLOIT.
MY DESIRE FOR PEACE WAS A WEAKNESS...
THERAMORE KEEP
I WILL NEVER BE SO FOOLISH AGAIN.

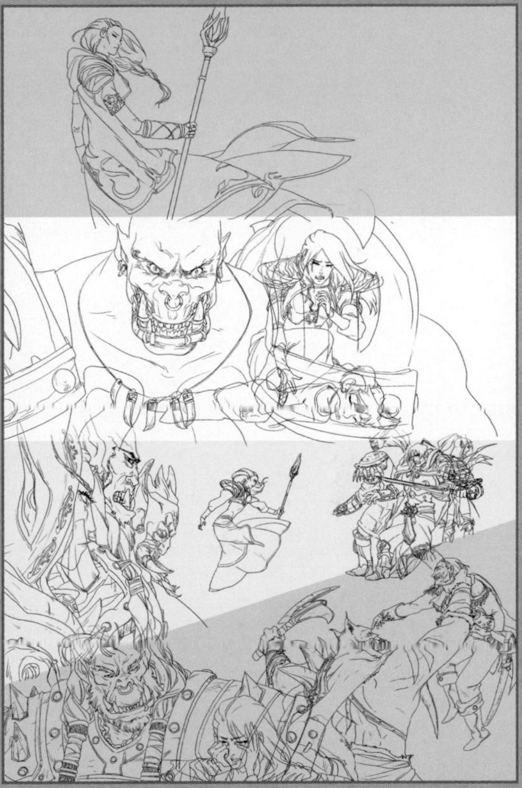

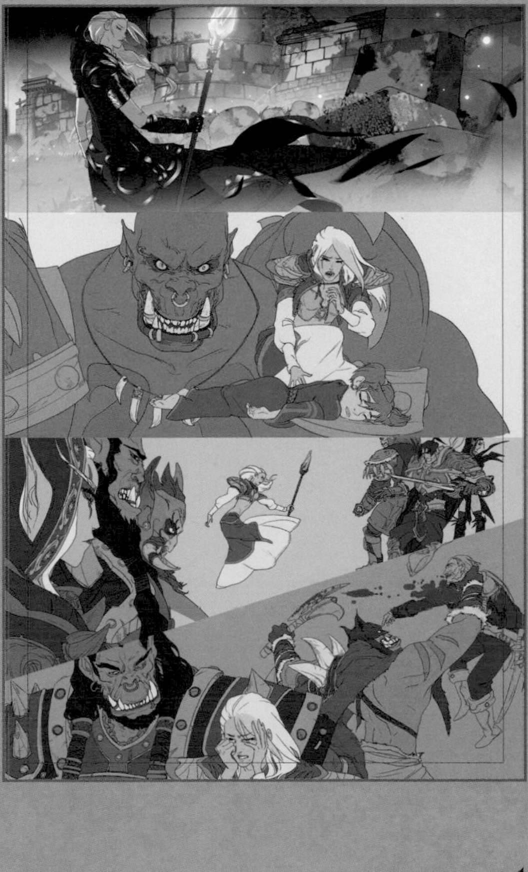

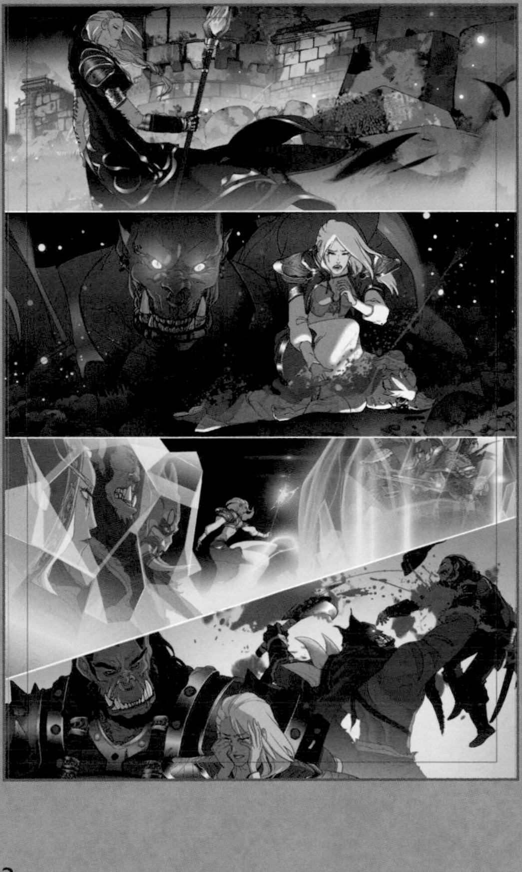

MAGNI: THE SPEAKER

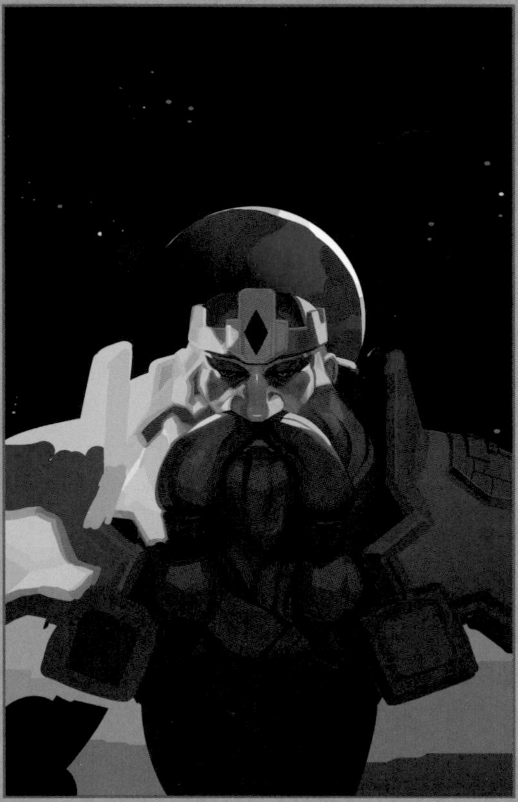

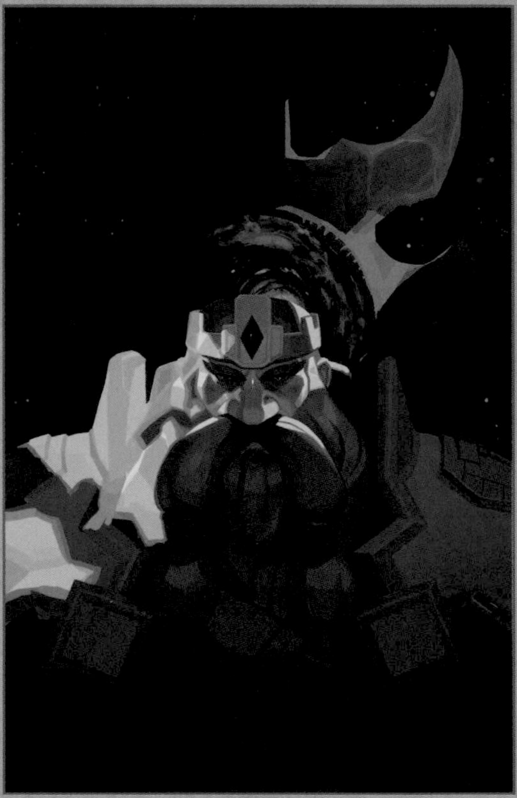

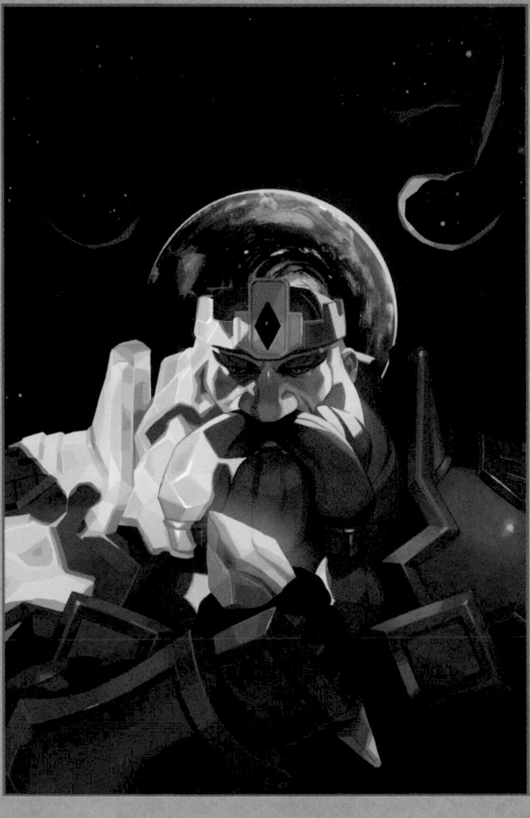

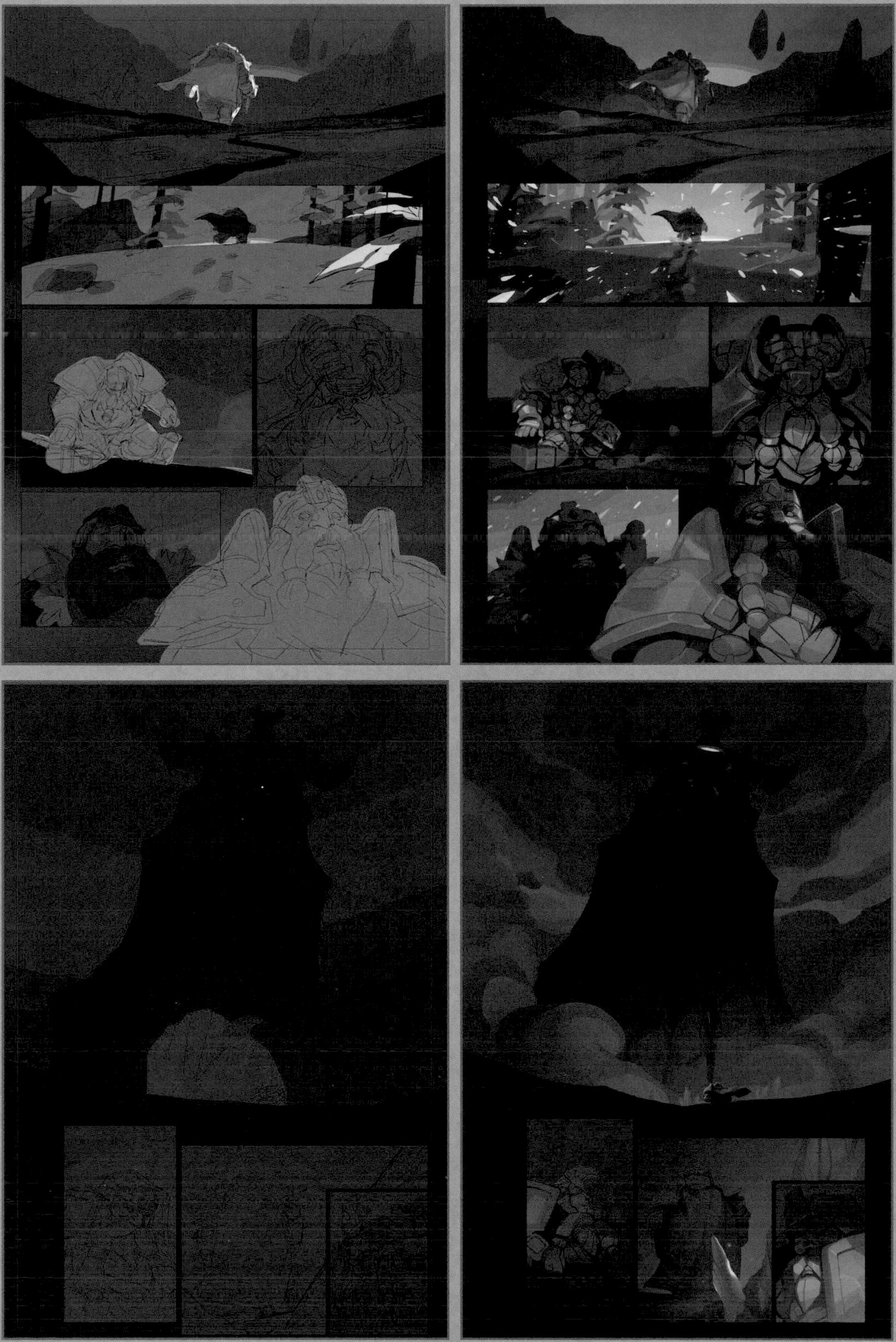

WINDRUNNER: THREE SISTERS

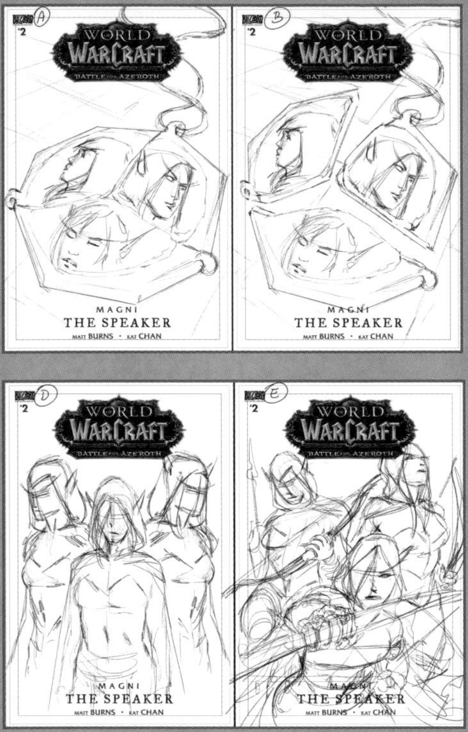

WORLD
WARCRAFT
BATTLE FOR AZEROTH
MAGNI
THE SPEAKER
MATT BURNS • KAT CHAN

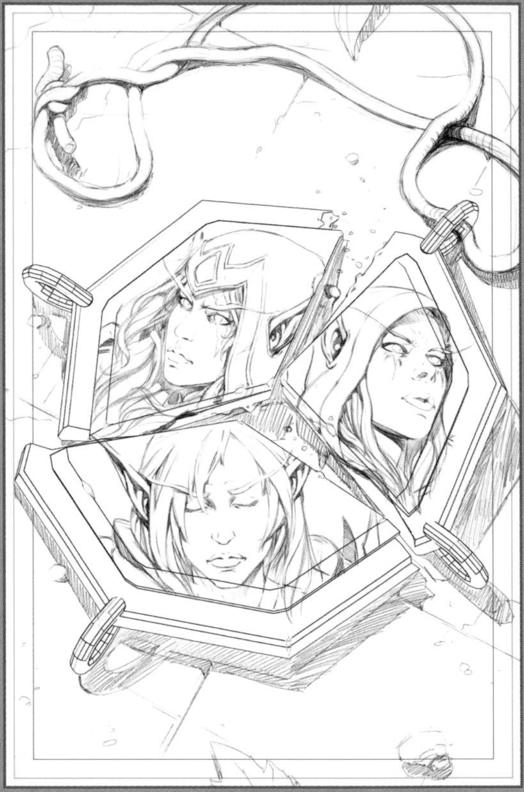

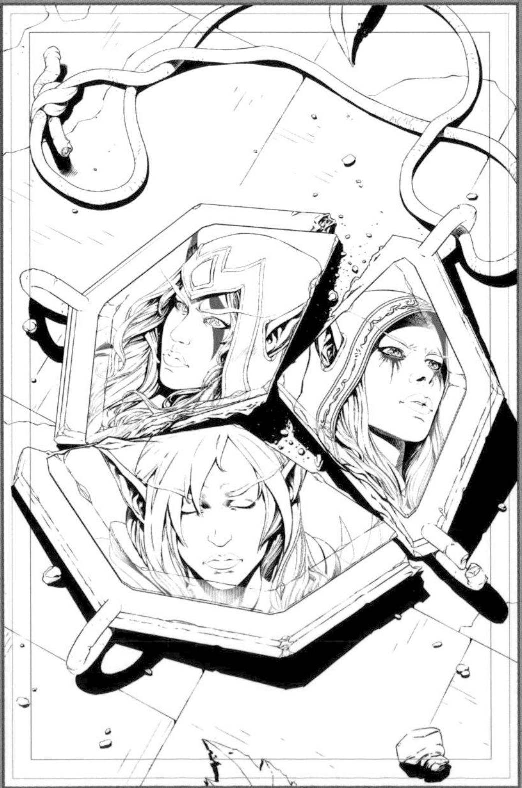

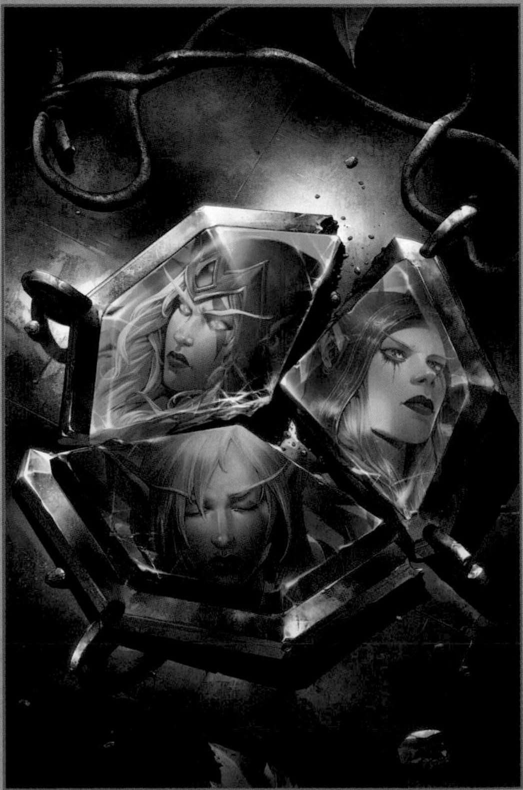

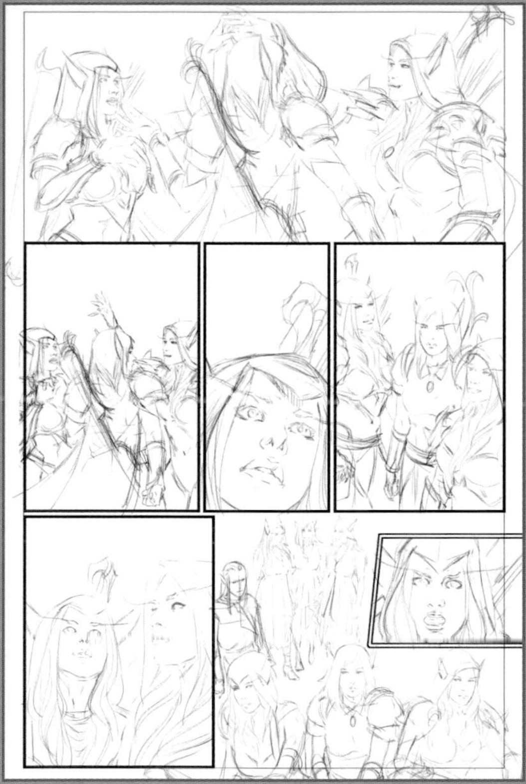
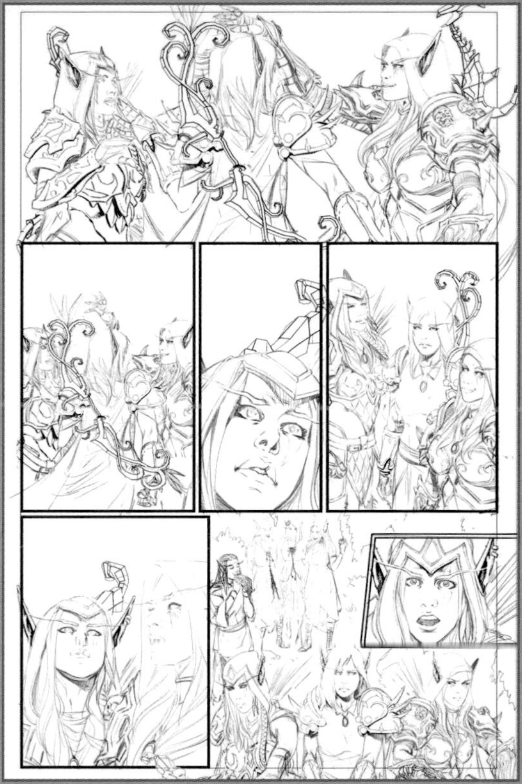
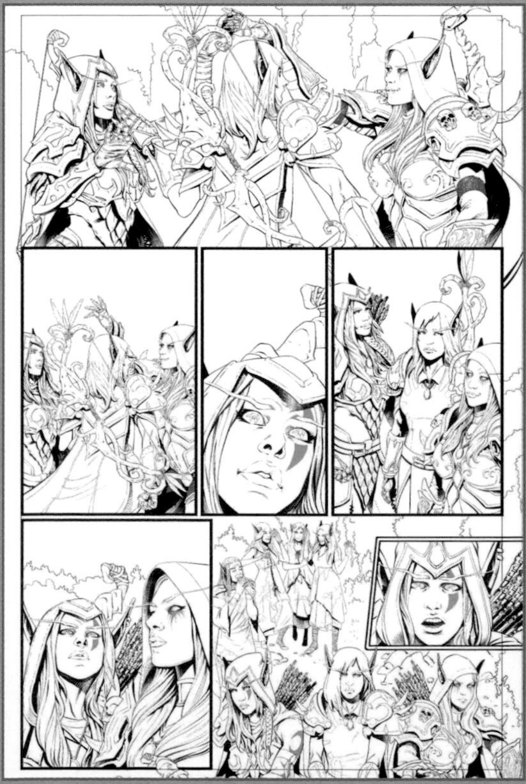
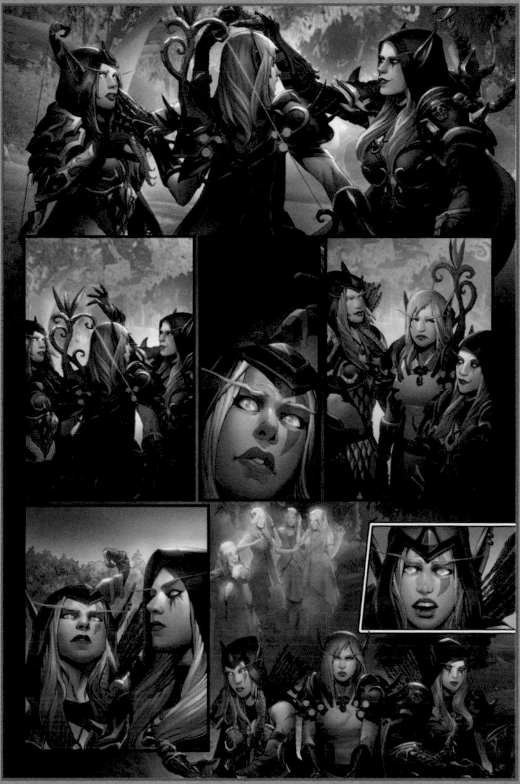

MECHAGON

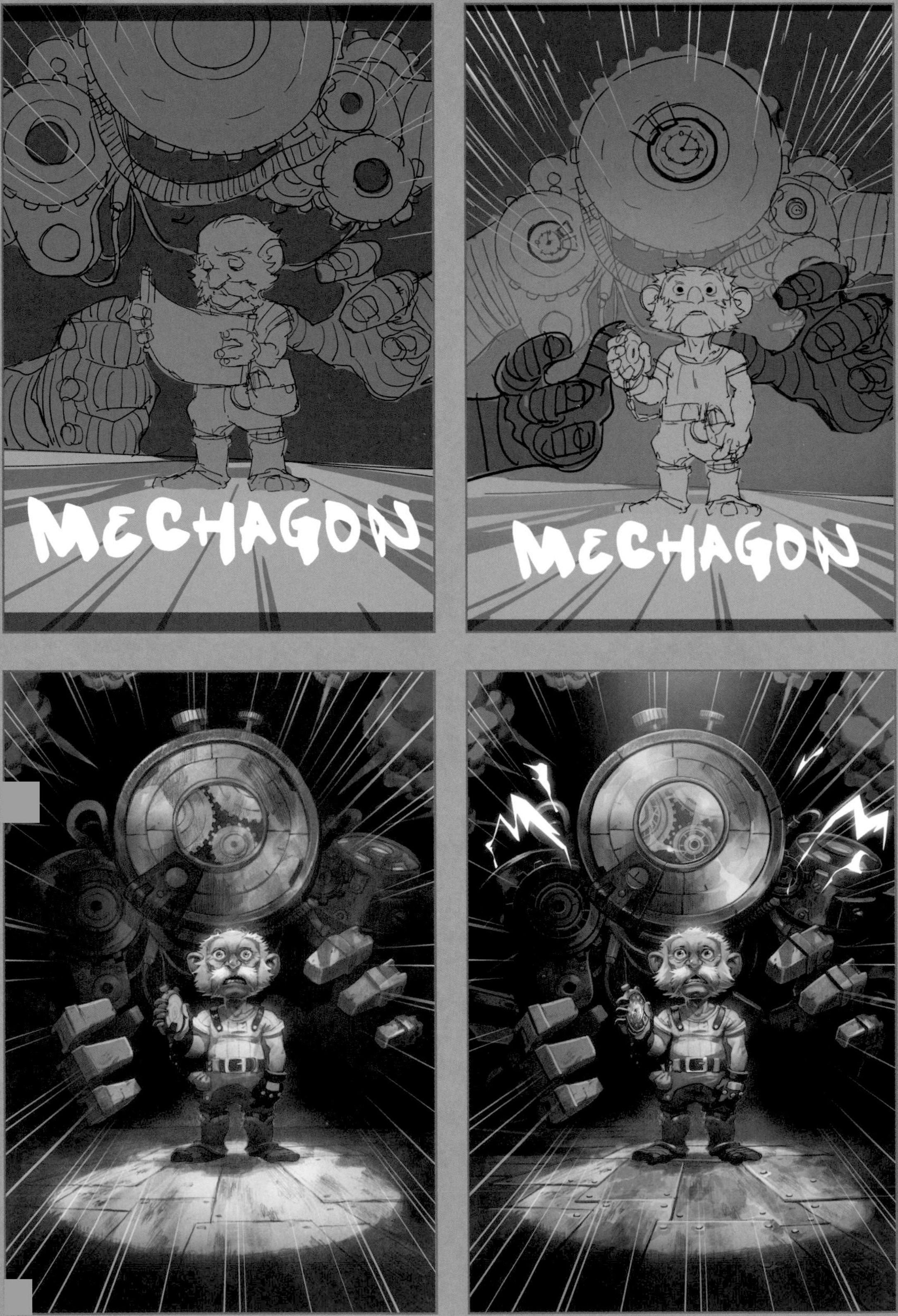
MECHAGON
MECHAGON

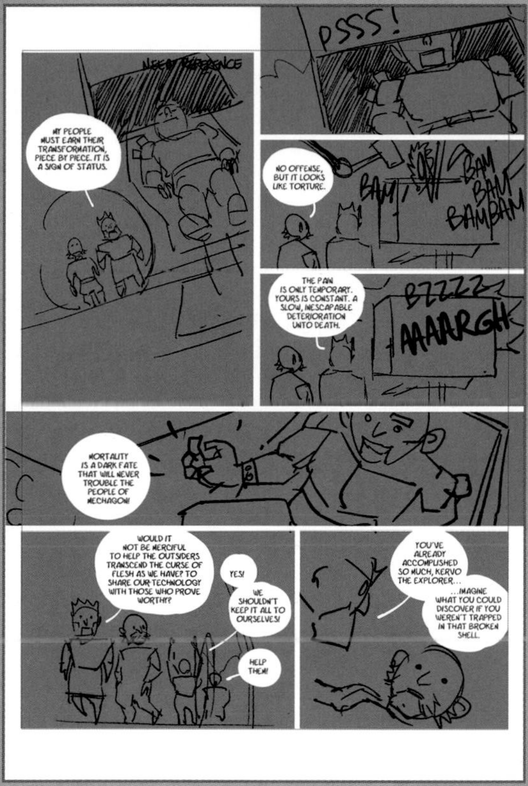
PSSS!
MY PEOPLE MUST EARN THEIR TRANSFORMATION, PIECE BY PIECE. IT IS A SIGN OF STATUS.
NO OFFENSE, BUT IT LOOKS LIKE TORTURE.
THE PAIN IS ONLY TEMPORARY. YOURS IS CONSTANT. A SLOW, INESCAPABLE DETERIORATION UNTO DEATH.
BZZZZ
AAARRGH
MORTALITY IS A DARK FATE THAT WILL NEVER TROUBLE THE PEOPLE OF MECHAGON!
WOULD IT NOT BE MERCIFUL TO HELP THE OUTSIDERS TRANSCEND THE CURSE OF FLESH AS WE HAVE? TO SHARE OUR TECHNOLOGY WITH THOSE WHO PROVE WORTHY?
YES!
WE SHOULDN'T KEEP IT ALL TO OURSELVES!
HELP THEM!
YOU'VE ALREADY ACCOMPLISHED SO MUCH, KERVO THE EXPLORER...
...IMAGINE WHAT YOU COULD DISCOVER IF YOU WEREN'T TRAPPED IN THAT BROKEN SHELL.

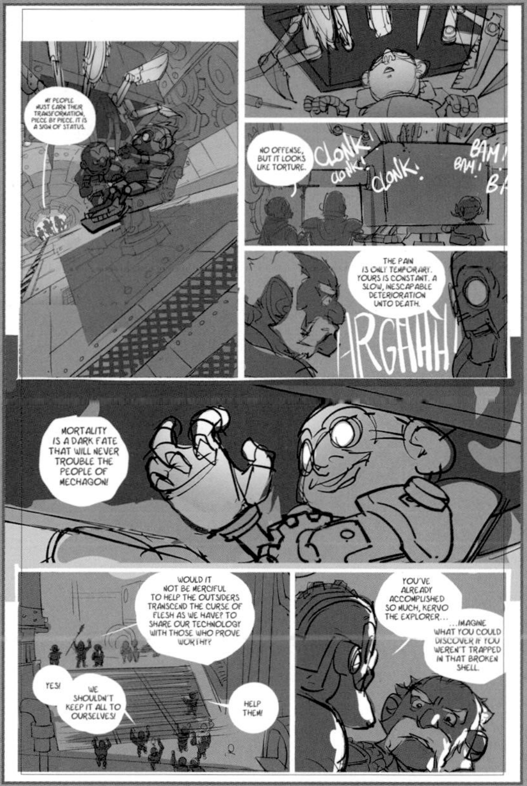
MY PEOPLE MUST EARN THEIR TRANSFORMATION, PIECE BY PIECE. IT IS A SIGN OF STATUS.
NO OFFENSE, BUT IT LOOKS LIKE TORTURE.
CLONK!
CLONK!
THE PAIN IS ONLY TEMPORARY. YOURS IS CONSTANT. A SLOW, INESCAPABLE DETERIORATION UNTO DEATH.
MORTALITY IS A DARK FATE THAT WILL NEVER TROUBLE THE PEOPLE OF MECHAGON!
WOULD IT NOT BE MERCIFUL TO HELP THE OUTSIDERS TRANSCEND THE CURSE OF FLESH AS WE HAVE? TO SHARE OUR TECHNOLOGY WITH THOSE WHO PROVE WORTHY?
YES!
WE SHOULDN'T KEEP IT ALL TO OURSELVES!
HELP THEM!
YOU'VE ALREADY ACCOMPLISHED SO MUCH, KERVO THE EXPLORER...
...IMAGINE WHAT YOU COULD DISCOVER IF YOU WEREN'T TRAPPED IN THAT BROKEN SHELL.

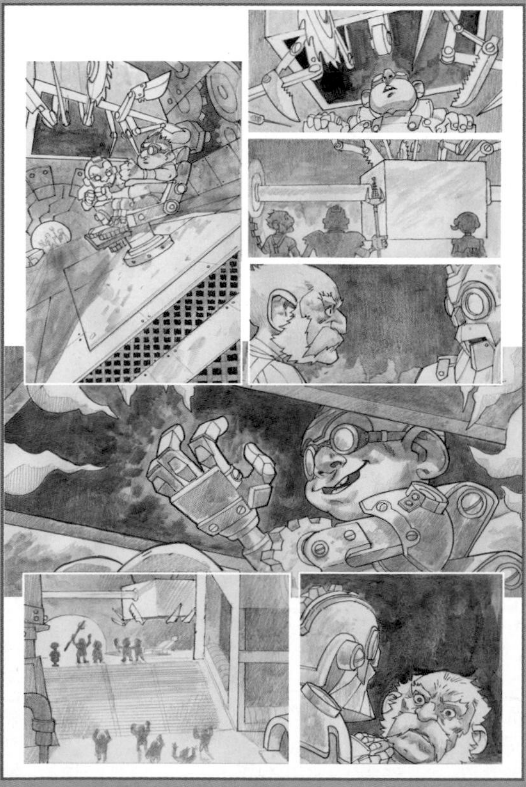

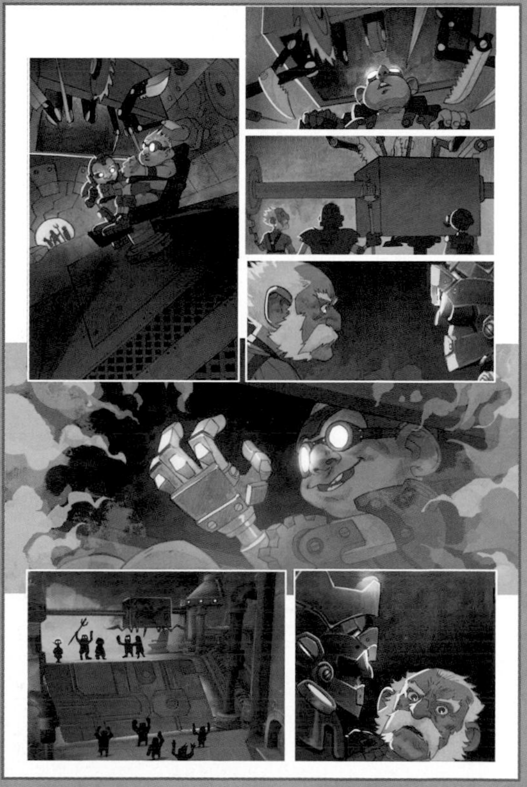

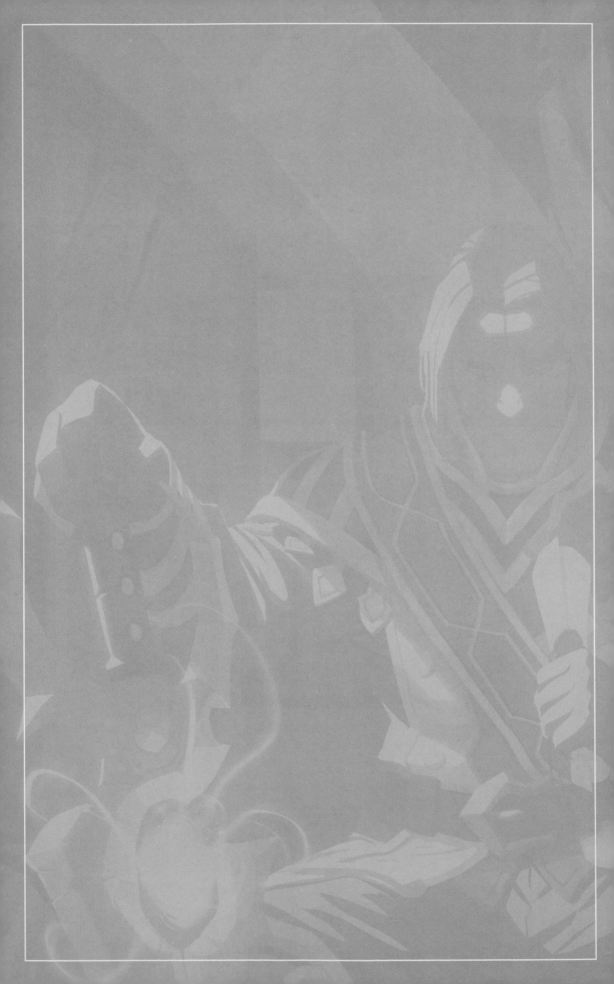